THE
ICE

JOHN KÅRE RAAKE is Norway's most successful screen-writer. His films *The Wave*, *The Quake* and *Ragnarok* have been exported to 120 countries and sold millions of movie tickets. *The Ice* is his debut novel, and is the first thriller in a series starring Anna Aune. It is being translated into 7 languages and is in development for a television series.

ADAM KING learned Norwegian by reading bedtime stories to his son. Originally from York, he is now based in Fredrikstad, eastern Norway, where he translates from a shed in his garden.

THE
ICE

JOHN
KÅRE RAAKE

TRANSLATED FROM THE NORWEGIAN
BY ADAM KING

PUSHKIN
VERTIGO

Pushkin Vertigo
71–75 Shelton Street
London, WC2H 9JQ

The Ice was first published as *Isen* by Gyldendal
Norsk Forlag in Oslo, 2019

First published by Pushkin Press in 2021

This translation has been published with the financial support of NORLA

1 3 5 7 9 8 6 4 2

ISBN 13: 978-1-78227-692-0

Designed and typeset by Tetragon, London

Printed and bound by CPI Group (UK) Ltd, Croydon, CR0 4YY

www.pushkinpress.com

The North Pole and the regions surrounding it do not belong to any nation, but are a resource that belongs to all the people of the world. China has a population of over one billion inhabitants, one-fifth of the global total, and will use its strengths to participate actively in the development of the Arctic. The battle that certain countries are now conducting in order to gain sovereignty over the Arctic is tantamount to a violation of the interests of every nation on Earth. In light of this new reality, it is difficult to predict the future of "the war for the Arctic", but the voice of every country must be heard, including China's.

Rear Admiral Yin Zhuo in an interview with
China News, Beijing, 5 March 2010

You never really know your friends from your enemies until the ice breaks.

Inuit proverb

THE NORTH POLE

November 2018

1

Each step brought the man from Xian closer to death. It was minus twenty degrees Celsius, not so cold for the Pole, but the northerly wind had increased in strength in the last hour, sending the relative temperature plummeting to almost minus forty.

North Pole explorers have survived temperatures of minus fifty and colder wearing a double layer of wool underwear, windproof outer clothing, and trousers and jackets stuffed with down.

Gai Zhanhai might as well have been naked.

Over his meagre upper body he was wearing only a checked lumberjack shirt, with thin long johns torn above the left knee and green Adidas trainers. The only thing keeping his head and brain warm was his bearskin hat.

Zhanhai knew he was going to freeze to death if he kept running, but also that each step was distancing him from death's clutches.

From the man hunting him down.

Zhanhai had lost all feeling in his legs. In extreme cold, the torso has to come first, the warm blood being withdrawn from the limbs and skin in order to keep the heart pumping. His legs had developed their own intelligence to anticipate the obstacles in the terrain. They jumped over or skirted around the ice blocks forced up to the surface by the movement of the massive floes. They automatically regained their balance as Zhanhai stumbled on the blanket of fresh, grainy snow under his feet.

Green curtains of light billowed in the sky above Zhanhai. The aurora was powerful enough for him to be able to see the contours of the landscape ahead of him. Zhanhai had longed to see the day when the icy landscape would be bathed in sunlight, to experience the North Pole just as his instructors at China's Arctic and Antarctic Administration's training base had shown him in pictures.

More curtains cascaded from space, the Northern Lights becoming so strong that Zhanhai feared that it was only a matter of time before his predator spotted him on the flat landscape.

Inside the warm bearskin, his brain sent a pulse of neurons down towards his numb legs, asking them to change course further towards the west. The only plan Zhanhai had managed to come up with as he ran on autopilot through the polar night was to lure his pursuer out onto the ice far enough, then use his superior speed to circle back around to where he had begun.

To the warmth.

To the weapons.

Zhanhai sensed the salty tang in his nose just in time.

He forced his hurried legs to stop before they carried him right out into the Arctic Ocean. From horizon to horizon, a ten-metre-wide crack in the ice had cut a black channel so fresh that only a fine layer of slush had formed on its surface. Ice fog floated up from the pitch-black sea, smothering the Northern Lights in a damp mist.

In half an hour the fracture's frosty crust would be thick and rigid enough to be crossed on skis. Zhanhai had neither skis nor time.

Except for the clothes on his back, the only thing he had was the flare gun, which, to his amazement, he was still holding in his numbed fingers. He turned his back to the channel and raised an arm so that the gun aimed towards the tracks his Adidas shoes had made in the newly fallen snow. The tracks the hunter would follow to find him.

Before him, Zhanhai saw huge slabs of ice strewn like enormous, grey pieces of candy in the murky landscape. He could see no movement between them.

Zhanhai's arms had begun shivering so much that he barely managed to keep hold of the flare gun. From what his Arctic instructors had taught him, he knew his body would soon lose the tension pulling together the veins that kept the blood in the warmer parts of the body. When this happened, warm blood would run back down to his ice-cold arms and legs. The cold would cool the blood down to a viscous soup. When the chilled blood returned to the heart, its muscles would beat slower, leading to less blood reaching the brain. It would eventually cease to function. Hallucinations would follow. What was left of the blood circulating under his ice-cold skin would begin to feel far too warm. He would be consumed by an urge to start taking off his clothes.

Then he would die.

He decided to retrace his own footsteps in the hope that his pursuer had got lost in the darkness of the ice desert. In the same instant, Zhanhai heard the splash.

If Zhanhai had made that decision a couple of seconds earlier, perhaps the polar bear would not have been able to reach him.

Not that it would have altered the outcome.

An adult polar bear can run at a speed of over thirty kilometres an hour for short distances. Even faster if it is famished and lean. This young female, now bursting out of the water like a live missile, had not eaten for weeks.

Its powerful front claws swung out at one of Zhanhai's calves, flaying his ragged long johns and morsels of frozen skin and sending him spinning to the ground. Zhanhai felt neither the cold from the ice nor the jagged crystals cutting into his face as he was thrust across the snow. His body had long since switched off such unnecessary, energy-sapping senses. The optic nerves in Zhanhai's eyes, however, registered the bear's maw as it gaped before him. Four long canine teeth. A row of small, sharp molars. A blood-red tongue. His pupils barely had time to send these impressions to his brain before the polar bear locked its jaws around his head. Zhanhai's skull split, pieces of his brain spraying out over the ice.

In his death throes, his spinal cord sent billions of unsynchronized nerve signals out along the body's neural pathways. One of these reached through the frozen nerve endings all the way to the fingertip of the hand holding the flare gun.

Zhanhai was already dead when his finger twitched, pulling the trigger. The flare gun's hammer struck the primer of the cartridge loaded in the steel barrel. Its propellant chamber exploded, the pressure from the gases launching the flare skyward.

The flare burned a stripe deep into the bear's fur as it shot past. The carnivore dropped Zhanhai's crushed head and fled back to the channel, diving in and breaking a hole in the crust that had already begun to form on the surface of the sea. The waves beat the thick ice particles towards the edge, where they were immediately stiffened by the cold.

Held aloft by its parachute, the flare burned brightly high up in the sky, casting a red glow on the icy landscape where Zhanhai's battered body lay—a fleeting vision of hell.

2

"Fuck."

Anna Aune sat up in bed. Her left arm was freezing. It had slipped out of the sleeping bag while she slept and had ended up lying against the outer wall of the hovercraft, *Sabvabaa*. The wall was always ice cold due to the draughts that entered through the poorly sealed window above her bed. She should have changed the seal, but the nearest parts dealer was 1,300 kilometres away and the only way to get hold of anything was to have it carried by transport plane all the way from Norway to the North Pole, then thrown out attached to a parachute. So, it was just easier to try sleeping with both arms inside the sleeping bag.

Anna stuck her hand in under her thermal jersey. Under the cold tips of her fingers, her heart was beating. The daily medical check: Anna Aune was still alive. The hands of her watch glowed in the dark: 23:13. She had no idea what had woken her up, and no clue when she had fallen asleep. Without sunlight as a guide, all the days at the North Pole blended into one.

She yawned and glanced out through the frost crystals on the window, just catching a glimpse of the reflection of her rangy body, like a larva, inside the tight sleeping bag. A red star shone in the sky. Fucking huge, she thought. A supernova. Anna blinked and rubbed her eyes. The star was still shining. She pressed her nose against the cold glass to see better, holding her breath so that the damp air from her lungs wouldn't form even more ice on the window. Now Anna could see something above the red star.

White smoke, and a parachute. Then she realized that what she was seeing out of the window wasn't a dying star.

It was a flare. The sight of it got her nervous system pumping adrenalin into her blood. She knew all too well what these things meant.

Danger.

Death.

Everything she was running from.

Anna sat completely still. She could hear the whistling of the wind in the antennae on the hovercraft's roof but clung to the hope that she was still sleeping, that she was in the middle of a hyperrealistic dream and didn't even know it. The serenity of the North Pole and the absence of sights and sounds had got her dreaming again, or, at least, now she could remember what she dreamt.

Anna was far from keen to wake the man sleeping at the other end of the cabin, but since she'd studied the flare long enough to realize that it wasn't an illusion, instinct took over.

"Daniel, wake up!" she heard herself shout.

Professor Daniel Zakariassen, asleep on the other side of the curtain that divided the hovercraft's cabin at night, grunted softly. The bed creaked as he turned over. The old man was a heavy sleeper.

Anna stood up out of bed, pulled the curtain to one side and stepped past the worktable where three laptops hummed quietly, crunching the data streaming up from instruments at the other end of kilometres-long cables beneath the surface.

"Daniel, I see a flare!"

She shook Zakariassen, who startled and sat up. A hint of rosemary hit her. He swore by camphor drops to keep colds at bay, even though on the ice there were no viruses other than those they had brought along with them.

"What is it?" he said, his voice thick with sleep.

"I can see a flare."

"Flare… now?"

His words sounded even more clear-cut than usual. Zakariassen was originally from Tromsø, but his northern lilt had adapted to the dry language that prevails in science's ivory towers.

Anna walked up to the large windows at the front of the cabin. The red flare had dropped in the sky, but was still clearly visible.

"The position, have you been able to fix the position?" shouted Zakariassen.

"No."

Zakariassen tramped past her and wiped away the condensation on the instrument panel's large compass. He mumbled something that at first she didn't hear.

"Distance?" he repeated. "How far away is it?"

Anna tried to estimate the distance. The flare was hanging directly above the short pressure ridge of icy rubble that had been pushed up from the pack ice in crunching, rumbling birth pangs more than two weeks ago. There was a pair of rangefinder binoculars in a bag under her bed, but the flare would probably vanish by the time she pulled them out. Her quick fix was a simple Girl Scout trick.

She closed her right eye and stretched out her arm in front of her with her thumb trained on one of the peaks on the pack ice. When she switched eyes, her thumb shifted in her field of vision two peaks further to the left. She estimated the distance between the first and the second peaks to be around four hundred metres. The trick was to multiply this distance by ten. The frozen peaks were four kilometres away. The flare looked to be even further back.

"At least four, maybe five kilometres," she said.

Even though it was her own voice, Anna felt as if she were having an out-of-body experience. All she wanted was to go back

15

to bed, pull the hood of her sleeping bag over her head, and dream on.

Zakariassen took out a little case. Inside there was something that looked like a clunky, old-fashioned video camera. "I'll see if I can see anyone in the thermal imaging camera." He turned it on, holding it out in front of him. On a little screen at the back, Anna saw the icy dark now depicted in blue shapes. The only thing that wasn't shaded blue was the flare, which glowed bright red on the screen too. The professor swept the camera back and forth, but out on the ice nothing else was radiating heat. He put the camera back in its case and sat down in front of a computer.

As he pushed up his glasses, the lenses magnified the deep wrinkles in his forehead. A map of the North Pole appeared on the screen as he woke the machine from its slumber. The professor set his thin fingers on the keyboard, punching numbers onto the white landscape.

"Five kilometres, 89 degrees… 35 minutes, 7 seconds north… 22 minutes… 9 seconds west. It doesn't make any damn sense, I have no record of anything at that position."

In her previous line of work, Anna's rigorous training had drilled into her the crucial importance of knowing the theatre of war. Understand the terrain. Always be ready to engage the enemy, but keep a back door open in case of the need to beat a hasty retreat. Zakariassen was right: nobody was supposed to be at the position the flare was coming from. That meant that whoever had fired it must have come from the only other inhabited place for hundreds of kilometres in any direction.

She took a deep breath. It had to be the Chinese.

3

"Ice Dragon," said Anna loudly. "The flare must have been fired near the Ice Dragon base. The bearing is right. The Chinese drift station is there—it must be seven or eight kilometres north of us."

She looked out of the window. The flare was about to drop down behind the ice mounds. The horizon was outlined brightly in red, as if streaked in blood. She had seen these signs before, burning above an unknown town. A plateau. A mountain beneath a distant sky. The warnings were always the same.

War comes in many guises.

This one began with an innocuous suggestion over an old seventies kitchen table with a view over Tromsø and the surrounding fjord.

"There must be hundreds of students who would jump at the chance of an expedition to the North Pole, though?" was Anna's first objection when her father, Johannes Aune, suggested that she might be a suitable expedition partner for Professor Zakariassen.

"Of course." Her father hesitated a little. "People are interested and Daniel has spoken to many of them, but there's probably something not quite right with any of them. Daniel is... a little odd. It could be good for you too, Anna."

She hadn't bothered to ask her father what psychological insights convinced him that it would be a good idea for his thirty-six-year-old daughter to spend nine months drifting on an ice floe across the North Pole with a difficult, seventy-three-year-old widower she had barely seen or spoken to in the last fifteen years.

Johannes Aune had grown up on the same street as Daniel Zakariassen in Tromsø. Daniel was bright and gave private tuition to fellow pupils who were dropping behind in their grades. One of these was Anna's father, who sorely needed a pass in Norwegian to get onto a course in mechanics at the technical college. In Johannes, Daniel recognized a natural gift for engines and engineering that, over the years, brought the theoretician and the mechanic together as close friends. The scientist paid Johannes a visit whenever he needed to build a scientific instrument, and the mechanic came to Daniel with a shopping bag full of receipts when it was time to submit his tax return. It was Johannes who had proposed a North Pole expedition as the brilliant finale to an otherwise anonymous career.

"Daniel needs this," her father said, as his nicotine-yellow fingertips fidgeted with the old pack of cards with which he would play solitaire before breakfast TV began. "After Solveig died, you know… he's got nothing."

"Dad, I'm not a therapist."

He stood up, taking two of the fragile cups that Anna's mother had inherited from her Russian babushka out of the cupboard above the sink, and picked up the jug from the worn-out coffee machine.

"There's not much time, you know. Daniel got the last sponsor on board yesterday. Almost three million kroner from a research institution in Switzerland. But they need him to leave for the ice *now*. Daniel's a theorist, a smart guy with numbers and that kind of thing, but he needs someone to look out for him. You've been out in a long, cold winter before," he argued as he poured the coffee.

"I'm not so keen on the cold these days," Anna said, taking a sip of the bitter coffee.

"Yes, but you've been through training in the Special Command… all the military exercises you've been on up here. You know how to survive in Arctic conditions."

For a second Anna thought about snapping back at him with a wisecrack that, above all else, she was best at making sure that others didn't make it home. But she bit her tongue. He was only trying to help. These last two years had been tough on him, too.

A call from the Armed Forces Special Command at its base in Rena had woken Johannes up in the middle of the night. "Your daughter has been seriously wounded in action in Syria," was the brief message. "We don't know whether she is going to survive or not." An hour later, Johannes was sitting in a black car with the Special Command insignia on its door. On the way to the airport in Tromsø, the car picked up Anna's half-sister, Kirsten, from the comfortable neighbourhood on a hill above the city where she lived with her husband and their three children.

They were taken to the airport from where a jet usually reserved for the chief of defence, the prime minister and the king flew them straight to a military airbase in Germany. From there a helicopter from the German Air Force delivered them to the American military hospital in Landstuhl. When her father and sister came in to see her, Anna was lying unconscious in a hospital bed with tubes feeding her oxygen and nutrition. She had been placed in an induced coma to give her body a chance to recover after suffering three heart stoppages over two operations. The doctors explained she had been hit by a powerful projectile that had travelled through her body, from the shoulder down to the hip.

After watching over Anna for a week without her regaining consciousness, Kirsten had to return home. She had a family and a business to take care of. Johannes Aune stayed on at the hospital in Landstuhl for two months. At home in Tromsø, three employees made sure that Aune Motorworks stayed afloat. Two weeks after she was admitted to military hospital, the doctors woke her up.

The first words she said to her father were "Yann's dead". Johannes had cried with joy that his daughter had survived. Anna cried in sorrow for the same reason.

A month later, Johannes pushed his daughter in a wheelchair into reception at Sunnaas Rehabilitation Hospital at Nesodden, outside Oslo. After six months of painful treatment there, she was able to walk again. That same day, she took a taxi down to the quay from where the ferry sailed towards Oslo. When the Nesodden ferry docked at Aker Brygge, she walked a few hundred metres to an anonymous office to meet Victoria Hammer, who, many years ago, had recruited her into E 14, a secret military unit whose existence was known only to a select few. Victoria tried convincing Anna not to quit her job. She failed.

Since then, Anna had been living in her old room at her father's house. In the end, and as an excuse not to make a decision, she agreed to join Daniel Zakariassen's expedition. An excuse to avoid the hassle and the many good suggestions about what she should do with her life. An excuse to postpone her return to the world and a fresh start in life. Zakariassen's hovercraft would drift on an ice floe towards the North Pole, even further away from civilization.

Anna saw her reflection in the hovercraft's window. Her dark hair hung down over her forehead like a tired old mop. Her skin was pale, her eyes mere black hollows. Her cheekbones cast long shadows, like a vampire with a serious case of iron deficiency, she thought.

The loudspeaker on the radio transmitter crackled. "This is ice drift station Fram X calling ice drift station Ice Dragon... over!"

Zakariassen was leaning in towards the microphone, speaking slowly and clearly, following radio protocol. His English was sharp and clipped, but heavily accented.

"This is the hovercraft *Sabvabaa*, the Norwegian Fram X expedition calling Ice Dragon operating base. Are you receiving us? Over."

Anna noticed a green light burning through the reflection of her face. The long, billowing curtains of the Northern Lights glimmered in the cosmic wind blowing in from space. Unusually powerful solar storms had been interfering with their communications all week.

The University of Tromsø had warned them that several satellites were out of action due to the storms. The professor had pointlessly slammed the palm of his hand against the computer's monitor when his weekly sponsors' report bounced back from space. *Server not found.*

Anna had been more annoyed about the new episode of *The Big Bang Theory* that she was missing out on.

"Fram X expedition calling Ice Dragon. Are you receiving us? Over."

Zakariassen listened to the scratching of the loudspeaker. "Fram X expedition calling Ice Dragon. Are you receiving us? Over," he repeated.

"I'm calling Boris," Anna said.

4

"We can't get through to Ice Dragon either," said Boris.

The Russian's deep baritone came and went with the flickering of the Northern Lights. In Anna's mind, the voice evoked a picture of a short, fat man trapped in an even more cramped space than she was.

"Is there a problem?" she asked.

"Not before you rang, Anna," he answered, laughing out loud. "They haven't issued a Mayday…"

Anna was hoping that Boris would offer to take care of it. That this was a matter for the Russian authorities.

Boris was a meteorologist stationed on the Taymyr Peninsula, at the northernmost tip of Siberia. He chatted with Anna daily as he sent out his weather and ice reports. Since she received satellite images and the reports by email, it was not really necessary, but Boris liked to chat.

The Russian became even more eager when he realized that Anna was interested in classical music, a legacy passed down from her mother, who loved film scores and was always playing the piano. She absolutely had to come to his home city of St Petersburg, Boris insisted. He would be her guide and take her to concerts, the opera and the ballet.

Sometimes she wondered how a middle-aged man from St Petersburg with a taste for the finer things in life had ended up in one of the most desolate places in Russia. Had the connoisseur been having an affair with the wife of a university director? Embezzling funds? Fooling around with young boys? She thought about all of this because she, too, had banished herself to a place found on no map; the ice never stood still long enough for one to be drawn.

Daniel reached out his hand, motioning for the satellite phone receiver. Anna held it out for him to speak into.

"Have you spoken to CAAA?" he asked.

Boris wasn't laughing any more.

The Chinese Arctic and Antarctic Administration was far from popular with the Russians. China didn't border the North Pole, but that hadn't prevented them from asserting their claim to the resources beneath the ice. To demonstrate this, they sent the icebreaker *Snow Dragon*, or *Xue Long* as it was called in Chinese, to the North Pole at regular intervals. The Russians took exception to the flame-red steel giant anchoring at the pole, directly above the Russian flag they had planted on the ocean floor.

"The Chinese are struggling with the solar storms too, but the Yellow River base on Svalbard was in contact with the commander of Ice Dragon a couple of hours ago. It was a fucking terrible connection. Give them some time."

Anna looked out of the window. She was surrounded by pitch-darkness. The flare had vanished for ever.

"It might have been an accident. The Chinese might have mixed up the dates and thought it was New Year. Set off some fireworks. Shit happens," said Boris.

It was late and Boris's baritone was husky with vodka. His English sounded like a dissonant Mussorgsky symphony, touched by genius and drunken madness.

"What I saw was no firework. Can you send a helicopter?" Anna yelled, so loud that Boris would hear it through the interference created by the solar storms.

"Yes, when the winds have calmed down tomorrow—if the Chinese ask for help."

"How bad is the wind going to be?"

"*Nooot* good… up to seventy-five kilometres an hour. Gusting to storm force."

Zakariassen grabbed the receiver and pressed it against his ear.

"It's not blowing so much over here yet."

Boris's laughter crackled through. "Well, call me in two to three hours and tell me who's right."

"*Sabvabaa* will get to the Ice Dragon base in two hours, no problem," said Zakariassen firmly as Boris broke off the connection. "We're the only ones who can help the Chinese if they're in trouble."

"How do you know we'll be able to ride out the storm?" asked Anna. The Northern Lights had vanished and outside total blackness reigned. She switched on the searchlight on the roof of the hovercraft, turning the lamp so that the light hit the weather station standing out on the ice. The wind vane was already spinning at a clip.

"*Sabvabaa* has endured the winter before. Her hull can take it," replied Zakariassen.

"The Americans have a base on Thule. With their helicopters they'll get there quicker from Greenland than we can."

The professor had to admit that Anna had a good point, but when Zakariassen finally got through to the duty officer at 821 Air Base Group on Greenland's west coast, he was given the same message. If the Chinese thought there was an emergency situation at their base, they would have to ask for help formally. And the conditions were too bad right now. Even if the American rescue helicopters could fly to the North Pole, they would not be able to land in the storm that was making its way in from the Russian tundra.

Before the final decision to cast off was taken, Zakariassen called *Sabvabaa*'s owners, the Nansen Environmental and Remote Sensing Center in Bergen. The head of the institute shared Anna's concerns for the coming storm, but agreed that they were obliged to offer help. Zakariassen was given permission to go. Anna heard Zakariassen start the hovercraft's engine as she pulled on her clothes behind the curtain, a flowery tablecloth she had borrowed from her father's house. The hovercraft rattled and shook as the engine idled erratically.

As she swiped a stray tangle of hair away from her mouth, it revealed a narrow scar on the side of her face. It cut across the skin straight down towards a larger scar that was just visible over the neck of her thermal vest. Above the scar on her shoulder, the lobe was missing from her right ear. The visible traces of the bullet that had almost killed her in Syria.

She quickly pulled on her thermal underwear and, on top of that, another layer of clothing. As she yanked down the curtain, she saw the professor on his way out of the hatch.

"I'll start clearing things away outside. Come when you're ready," he shouted, opening the hatch all the way. The wind blew straight in and the cabin temperature dropped quicker than a lead weight on its way to the seabed. Zakariassen switched on his headlamp and crawled out into the blizzard.

Anna's head nearly touched the ceiling of the cramped cabin. A single step brought her to her survival suit, which was hanging on a peg above a gas burner and a kettle. Next to the burner was a samovar, a large, beautifully decorated Russian tea kettle, much too big, really, for this little cabin, but a departing gift Anna had not been able to refuse. It had been given to her by Galina, the Russian woman Johannes had employed when he began renting out rooms to tourists in his large, Swiss-style house, beautifully located next to the Tromsø straits.

"My father made tea for tourists with this samovar when he was a conductor on the Trans-Siberian Railway. Nothing like strong, sweet tea when it's cold," Galina said, before giving Anna a kiss on each cheek and waving goodbye at the airport.

After three weeks at the North Pole, Anna agreed. There really was nothing like steaming-hot, sweet tea to get the body moving. But now it would have to wait. She pulled on the fluorescent-yellow survival suit with reflective stripes over the chest and knees and stepped into a pair of blue moon boots. The North Pole was no place for fashion junkies.

She got dressed in silence. Only the slight sound of her breath and the creaking of her shoes on the wooden floorboards could be heard above the engine's hum. As she opened the hatch outwards, the Arctic wind bit in fury.

A warning of the storm that was yet to come.

5

Anna saw Zakariassen standing some distance away. He was disconnecting the cables that lay in coils on the ice from their instruments—the very reason they were at the North Pole. Or, to be more precise, the reason that Daniel Zakariassen was at the North Pole.

Most of the instruments were coupled to long cables hanging thousands of metres down into the ocean. Delicate sensors could capture the sound of seals in the water, or the echoing cries from a school of beluga whales looking for a breathing hole. Other instruments hung right in the middle of the ocean's invisible highway, the currents beneath the surface. When the first measurements came in it didn't take Zakariassen long to conclude that the ocean temperature had risen and the salt concentration was lower than the previous year.

He explained to Anna that the fresh water from the ice melt diluted the ocean's salt content, weakening the currents sending cold water from the north down to the equator, where the seawater would evaporate, cooling down the atmosphere. When this declined, the temperature in the entire atmosphere increased and the air over the North Pole also became warmer—on one random November day in 2016, an incredible twenty degrees warmer than usual. Now the very backbone of the North Pole itself was beginning to melt—the ancient, hard blue ice that had always lasted from one year to the next.

"Your children are most likely going to be the first for three million years to grow up without ice at the North Pole," sighed Zakariassen late one evening after having published the first expedition blog on Fram X's website.

"Lucky that I wasn't planning on having kids, then," was Anna's terse reply.

She closed the hatch behind her, walking into the headwind across the hull of the hovercraft, and jumped down onto the ice. Zakariassen motioned for her to come over to him.

"I just have to fix something." Her words drifted away with the wind, but Zakariassen had heard enough, and waved both arms to stop her.

"No, we have to get moving before the storm hits."

Anna ignored his protests and walked quickly past the large propeller at the rear of *Sabvabaa* and deeper into the dark. She let the light from her headlamp lead her along the poles stuck at regular intervals into the ice. Between them tripwires were strung, almost invisible, that would trigger a flare at the top of each pole if an intruder walked through them. In this corner of the world, that intruder was usually a polar bear.

The light from her headlamp struck a rise in the ice. Anna walked over to it and dropped to her knees. She pulled off her gloves and blew warm air onto her frozen fingers, then brushed away the snow covering the block of ice that she had buried earlier in the day, it being 1st November. The Day of the Dead. All Saints' Day. Beneath the snow a photograph became visible, frozen in time inside the ice block.

It was a picture of a man.

The man was standing under a blue sky, his eyes prominent in his tanned face. Wrinkles streamed out from their corners, like cracks in an ice floe, above a blinding white smile. In the curls of his black hair, some grey strands twisted over his ears, betraying that he was perhaps older than he looked. He was dressed in a light-blue jacket, and an illegible ID card hung over his chest.

Anna pulled something out of the snow in front of the photograph. It was a grave lantern, its flame extinguished. She screwed off the lid and shone a light down into it. The wick was covered in snow that had found its way in through the ventilation holes in the top. She tipped it upside down, shaking the snow out, then lit the wick with a well-worn Zippo with an engraving of a winged dagger on its side. When Anna was completely sure that it was burning strongly, she dug a hole in the snow all the way down to the ice sheet and placed the burning lantern inside. Now it was sheltered from the wind.

She stayed on her knees looking at the picture. Illuminated by the lantern, a halo of light encircled the man's face, its flickering flame bringing his eyes to life. His name was Yann Renault. He and Anna had been together for almost a year when he was kidnapped by IS in Syria on an assignment for the aid organization Médecins Sans Frontières. It was supposed to have been their final posting. Anna would move to the village of Seillans in the mountains of Provence, where Yann's parents ran a little hotel. The plan was that they would take over the hotel when Yann's parents retired. But if you want to make God laugh, tell him about your plans.

Yann Renault was buried at the cemetery in Seillans while Anna was lying in a coma at the hospital in Germany. To the world, Yann was a hero who had sacrificed his life to spare his fellow hostages. Only a handful of people knew that it was Anna Aune who had saved them. Even fewer still knew what had really happened when Yann was killed.

She pulled back the stiff sleeve of her survival suit to reveal her watch. The hands were ticking over, breaking free from midnight. All Saints' Day was over. The dead had been remembered. The machinery of the world ground on.

When Anna climbed back into *Sabvabaa*'s cabin, Zakariassen was sitting in the driving seat with his hand resting on the wheel. He had an irritated look on his face, but refrained from commenting on the delay. She turned around and glanced out of the hatch at the metal equipment cases on the ice. Forty cases with everything they needed to survive for almost a year. A year without having to think about anything other than work, eat, sleep. Now more than ever, sleep seemed like the greatest of earthly pleasures.

"The ice floe may break apart while we're away," she said.

Zakariassen looked at her.

"If that happens, you'll lose all your equipment," she continued. "Your expedition will end in complete failure."

The old man looked at her for a few moments before his eyes flitted away, fixing themselves on a point on the wall in front of the worktable. Several moments passed before he shook his head firmly, and placed his hand on the throttle.

"We have a duty to help people in distress," said Professor Zakariassen in a firm voice, shoving the throttle forward.

6

In the Inuit language, *sabvabaa* means "flows swiftly over it", but as Anna sat next to Zakariassen she couldn't help thinking that "bumps slowly over it" would be a better description of their progress.

The wind had increased in strength and, in order not to lose control, Zakariassen was driving well under the normal cruising speed of twenty-five knots.

Sabvabaa hovered over the ice on a cushion of air trapped under the hull by its heavy rubber skirting. Although the air cushion meant fewer obstacles, and *Sabvabaa* floated easily over blocks of ice and open fractures, the lack of friction beneath her was also a problem when the wind hit her from the side. Zakariassen constantly had to adjust his course with the steering wheel, which controlled the rudders on the large propeller driving the hovercraft forward. *Sabvabaa* was lurching forward like an inebriated wino, and every time Zakariassen increased or decreased the power, Anna sensed a slight nausea rising in her throat.

She took a deep breath and tried to look straight ahead. Snowflakes whirled into the lights like white moths on a warm summer night. An image as far away from reality as it was possible to be. Her fingers were still ice cold, and a thermometer on the instrument panel told her that the temperature had dropped to minus thirty in the short time since she had seen the flare. She felt the seat shake, heard the rattling of objects in the cabin hitting each other. A faint stench of diesel. Outside, the North Pole was pelting the windscreen with ever more snow. She was trying to focus, trying to imagine what had happened at the Chinese base, and what they would find when they got there, but the monotonous rumbling of the engine kept skewing her concentration.

Back to the picture of Yann still lying on the ice.

Anna remembered precisely where the photograph was taken.

In Syria, at a refugee camp on the outskirts of Ain Issa, two years, six months and twenty-two days ago. Yann had invited her to see how everything was going with the boy who had brought them together. Little Sadi had laughed when Anna leant over the cot he was lying in. Tiny bubbles of gurgling delight slipped out of the corners of his mouth. He was seemingly unconcerned that he had lost one leg below the knee. A brutal reminder that the Syrian civil war didn't care whether its victims were soldiers or children.

"Sadi's going to be fine. Kids get used to prostheses much quicker than adults," said Yann as they ate lunch in an air-conditioned tent afterwards. This first meal together was what Yann would later insist was their first date. Anna always denied it with equal fervour.

"I know I'm not the most romantic person on the planet, but driving two hours across a scorching desert to a miserable refugee camp, eating *something* you called lunch from a plastic plate—all while your colleagues argue in French and stick their elbows in my food—is no date, not in Norway. Not even in Tromsø."

Yann always laughed, kissing her. "You don't know what romance is, Anna. You must be pretty glad you met me otherwise you would never have melted, my Scandinavian ice queen."

Now Yann was dead and she was, seemingly, queen of the ice again. Anna knew that she would never meet anyone who could match up to the self-assured, romantic man from the mountains of Provence again. This knowledge had rushed in, filling every cell of her body the moment she woke from the coma at the hospital in Germany. No matter what her father said, no matter how her colleagues consoled her, or what a succession of psychologists tried to get her to do to move on, she saw no meaning in life any more. The only reason she was still alive was that she couldn't bear the thought of her father finding her dead. Anna had agreed to go to the North Pole, but not that she would come back.

"Are we on the correct heading?"

She was dragged away from her thoughts as a gust of wind blew *Sabvabaa* hard into a sideways lurch. She scarcely managed to grab hold of the computer she had on her lap before it slid onto the floor. The clock on the screen showed it had been almost thirty minutes since they had set out for the Chinese base. The laptop display was a satellite image with three moving dots. She knew that the red one was Ice Dragon's position. The blue one was *Sabvabaa*, and the green one was the GPS transmitter on the equipment they had left behind on the ice. *Sabvabaa* was midway between the red and the green dots. On the satellite image Anna saw dark veins in the ice. The fractures that lay ahead of them.

"Yes, we should see the base soon."

Zakariassen throttled up.

The kitchen cabinets rattled behind them as the vessel lurched onwards. Slush sprayed up, splattering the windows as they passed over a broad channel.

"Fuck!"

Zakariassen flung *Sabvabaa* sideways as a huge pressure ridge appeared in the searchlight's beam. The hovercraft began to slide and Anna watched the shards of the towering wall of ice approaching at high speed. White floes. Black shadows. Razor-sharp contours.

Red lights flashed on the instrument panel and an engine warning screeched hysterically as Zakariassen applied full power.

33

He wrenched the wheel steering the propeller, barely managing to force the boat away from the icy barricade.

"Jesus, Anna, stay focussed!" he barked furiously.

Her heart thudded in her chest and she could hear her pulse pounding in her ears as she saw the jagged edge of the ice wall drift past the windows like the spikes of an enormous hedgehog. Her eyes scanned the instrument panel. Something was wrong.

"It might help if you turned on the radar," she said, pushing the switch that Zakariassen had forgotten in his eagerness to leave.

The professor mumbled something under his breath as he leant forward to get a better view through the window. *Sabvabaa* was gliding smoothly forward now, the tall wall of ice sheltering it from the northerly wind.

Anna swallowed her growing nausea and saw that the blue dot on the satellite map had moved up next to the red.

The position was 89 degrees, 37 minutes, 3 seconds north, 37 degrees, 13 minutes, 10 seconds east. Not far from the pole itself.

"We should be there by now."

She tried peering through the sleet that was settling on the windows faster than the wipers could clear it. In the glare of the powerful searchlight on the roof, the massive pressure ridge cast long shadows across the ice field. After a while, she caught sight of something blinking in the darkness.

"Stop!" she yelled. Zakariassen yanked back the throttle. The hovercraft stopped dead. He peered out.

"I can't see anything."

Her hand groped for the switch to the searchlights, shutting them off. It was a trick her father had taught her when she got her first car, an old Volvo that the mechanic had repaired and repainted. "Turn off the headlights for a second before each corner, then you'll see if there are any cars coming in the other direction," he said, before waving her a worried goodbye as she headed to a concert along the pitch-black, rain-sodden back roads of the Troms valley.

Once her eyes had adjusted to the dark, she spotted them. Sparkling lights on the other side of the pressure ridge wall. They had to be the lights from the Chinese base.

Zakariassen saw them at the same time, and re-engaged the power. The lights from Ice Dragon streamed in through the snowed-up windscreen. They were powerful and floated high above ground, like UFOs. On Anna's display, the green and red dots merged.

An alarm sounded.

The anti-collision warning flashed on the radar screen. The teeth of a beast appeared right ahead of them. Zakariassen swerved abruptly to the left. The hovercraft lunged wildly, avoiding the nearest monster tooth. In the bright light, she saw that they were oil barrels lying in the snow.

Behind the barrels a cabin came into view, painted blue.

Zakariassen steered past the cabin and set the propeller in reverse so that they came to a stop under the UFO lights. Anna didn't notice that she had been holding her breath until black dots began fizzing at the edge of her field of vision.

Her eyes stung as she looked up at the glare above them. Compared to the dark polar night they had just driven through, this was like arriving in a neon heaven.

7

When the engine stopped, *Sabvabaa* became strangely still. Outside, Anna saw the snow swirling in tight swarms through the bright floodlights illuminating the Chinese base. Even though the engine was stopped, the windows still rattled. One of the instruments indicated that the storm that Boris had warned about was on its way. She was looking for an excuse to do nothing, just to sit there in her warm seat, close her eyes, and fade into oblivion. "It's blowing almost fifty kilometres an hour already," she said. "Almost a gale."

"Yes, yes, you think I don't know that already?" Zakariassen looked at her irritably. "We knew what we were getting into." He increased the speed of the wipers to get a better look. Their rubber strips, frozen stiff, screeched offensively at her as they wheeled over the film of ice that had formed on the windscreen.

The deluge of light they were trapped under was pouring down from the top of a tower that thrust up behind a large yellow building. It was at least seven metres tall and around fifty metres wide. More like an industrial warehouse.

Surrounding the yellow building were smaller, red polar cabins in a horseshoe formation. Light came from most windows, but nothing stirred and there were no curious faces to be seen inside. Zakariassen blew onto his glasses, wiping and pushing them back into place on his narrow nose, then looked at the instrument panel. His fingers fumbled for a switch.

Anna jumped at the siren blare from the hovercraft's roof.

The wind and the snow swallowed the blast.

Zakariassen sounded a longer burst. Both he and Anna stared towards the floodlit base. In the red cabins, no doors opened. Nobody came running out of the dark. Apart from the wailing of the wind, the only sound that Anna could hear was a remote, rhythmic pounding. A steady beating.

Zakariassen also noticed the noise. He exhaled slowly through his nose. A worried expression. Anna realized it had just dawned on him that there was no guarantee that this particular rescue mission would end with a simple act of heroism.

"We should let the institute know," he said finally.

The fabric of his survival suit creaked as he picked up the satellite phone receiver that he kept in a holder on the instrument panel.

"Yes, we are at the Chinese base." He spoke loudly when the head of the institute in Bergen replied. "No, we haven't seen anyone yet... What was that? Please repeat... I can't hear... Yes, yes, I'll let you know. We'll take a look. Of course we'll be careful."

He switched the telephone off, stood up and walked over to the worktable, pulling open a drawer and picking up a black object. He turned around, holding it out towards her. Anna saw the holster holding the large Smith & Wesson Magnum revolver that Zakariassen had bought in Longyearbyen.

"I don't use firearms."

Zakariassen had looked at Anna in astonishment when he heard the words. She uttered them in the lobby of the Radisson hotel they were staying at while they were waiting for *Polarstern* to dock in Longyearbyen to collect them, *Sabvabaa* and the rest of the equipment. The hotel was full of Japanese and Americans wandering around in thick socks and oversized down jackets. A sign at the entrance made it clear that boots were not to be worn inside the hotel. Another directed that firearms—revolvers, pistols and rifles—were to be placed in one of the hotel's weapons safes and that the key could be collected from reception.

Zakariassen had been out to buy the Smith & Wesson revolver from a mineworker who was returning home. On Svalbard, all inhabitants are instructed to carry a firearm when venturing outside urban areas. The day before, Anna had seen a mother on a snowmobile dropping her children at a kindergarten right in the city centre, a revolver hanging from her belt.

"You surely don't mean that you don't shoot? You're a soldier, aren't you?" said Zakariassen.

"I *was* a soldier."

"But why?"

"That's my business. I don't use firearms."

"No, no, there's no discussion… We can't be in the North Pole without weapons."

"I have a weapon."

Zakariassen laughed out loud when Anna showed him the Japanese sports bow she had bought in Tokyo years ago.

"You're going to shoot a polar bear with a bow and arrow?"

"I'd rather not. I think I'll manage to scare them off by growling and waving my arms."

In the end, Zakariassen had reluctantly accepted that Anna would use neither his old Mauser rifle nor the revolver—especially after he had seen her use the bow. The targets were empty tin cans she had placed on top of a large block of ice next to *Sabvabaa*. Quickly and effectively, and at a distance of twenty metres, she dispatched every single one of them. As the bowstring launched its arrow, an echo bounced back from the surrounding ice like a sharp whip-crack. When the professor picked up one of the targets, the arrow had penetrated straight through the tin that had contained the *lapskaus* stew they had eaten for dinner the day before.

*

Zakariassen pressed the leather holster holding the revolver into Anna's hand and pointed to the snow whirling past in the bright light outside. "We cannot walk out into a full storm in zero visibility without protecting ourselves against polar bears... You won't be able to shoot a bow and arrow now... You of all damn people understand that, surely."

Anna sensed her own physical disgust as the revolver's metal brushed her hand. She tightened her fist.

"No, I can't."

"You can't shoot a bow in these conditions," he protested.

She got up out of her seat and walked to her bed at the back of the cabin, pulling out the ragged North Face bag that was stored underneath it. She unzipped it and hunted her way through underwear, socks, T-shirts, long johns and books she had never got round to starting. Under an unopened bottle of Lagavulin single malt whisky, she finally found a leather sheath. She opened it up and pulled out the knife it was shielding, a long, matt-black blade terminating in a solid leather handle. A hunting knife she had won in an arm-wrestling contest against an American marine in Bosnia. The soldier hadn't realized that he was facing a three-time Scandinavian youth arm-wrestling champion. Her technique beat his strength with ease; it took two seconds for the loudmouth to cave in once she forced his arm down.

"I *am* armed, see?" Anna opened the side pocket of her survival suit, slipping the knife into it as Zakariassen looked on in frustration. He grunted something and picked up the cartridge clip he always placed on the windowsill after being out on the ice with his old Mauser rifle. It clicked damply as he pushed it in. He ran the moisture out of his hair with his hand and looked back at Anna firmly.

"Now we had better get out there and find out what the Chinese are playing at."

8

As she clambered down from *Sabvabaa*, Anna felt the gale thrusting ice-cold needles into the exposed skin around her eyes. Even though she had a ski mask over her face, the wind was whipping snowflakes at her eyelashes, where her body heat thawed them before they froze into a hard, icy crust.

Anna turned away from the wind and saw Zakariassen climbing down after her with his rifle slung over his shoulder. She pulled her ski goggles over her face and thrust her hand into her pocket to check that her mobile was there. It was connected to *Sabvabaa*'s Wi-Fi and if the Northern Lights and the solar storms relented soon, there was a slight chance that she would be able to call or send an SMS. Zakariassen trudged past her in the snow, his silhouette stretching out behind him like a black yeti as he moved towards the floodlights. Reluctantly, she followed. It was hard work walking in the snow. The wind ripped and tore at her body, trying all the time to force her back. From inside her constricted hood and behind the huge goggles now covering her face, Anna's line of sight was limited. As she walked, she constantly turned her head to get a better perspective. The flickering snowflakes dragged the light from Ice Dragon into the dark like fireflies. Anna realized that she ought to be feeling safer here, on this massive base that could almost be a small town, but her senses screamed otherwise. The darkness and the ice fields beyond the reach of the floodlights definitely felt safer.

She turned her head to the left, her narrow field of vision sweeping past the yellow building to a smaller, grey cabin with a flat roof. A heavy snowdrift had blown up against its wall.

As she was looking the other way, the first two polar cabins in the horseshoe formation came into view. Both of them had wide doors to their fronts, but no windows. Two chimneys stuck up from the roof of the one further away. The drifting flakes performed an extra pirouette as they struck the invisible smoke the chimneys exhaled.

She walked behind Zakariassen, sheltered from the wind along the edge of the large building. The thumping noise grew louder the closer they got to its front. Zakariassen walked around the corner and vanished. For each step that Anna took towards the corner, her legs grew heavier. She had been here before. Old memories sparked into life again. In her brain, these memories became electrical impulses rushing along her nerves to her senses. The snowflakes became dandelion seeds.

The seeds tumbled from the sky and, backlit by the low evening sun, looked like paratroopers in a vast invading army. The atmosphere was relaxed. The soldiers in her troop were talking trash about the previous night's karaoke at the officer's mess at Film City.

Anna was second in line. She was on her first overseas mission with the multinational NATO force in Kosovo. An American soldier walked ahead of her. Sebastian had a good voice. At the karaoke, his version of 'My Way' was one of the better ones. He turned to her just before the corner of a bombed-out shopping centre in downtown Priština.

"You good?" he asked, walking around the corner.

She nodded and looked behind to check on the others.

A boom.

The corner sheltered her from the explosion. Karaoke Sebastian, from a little town in Minnesota, lost his life to shrapnel from a NATO cluster bomb. Blue on blue. Killed by one of his own.

*

Anna stopped just before the corner. In the middle of the space between the large building and the polar cabins, she saw three small heaps of snow several metres apart. Snow was blowing up and over them like a thousand tiny ski jumpers.

Instinct told her that at the very moment she turned the corner, there was no turning back. She would be a soldier again. And just as the magnetic force below the ice pointed every compass in the world in the same direction, Anna Aune clearly attracted misery no matter how far she tried to remove herself from it.

She stepped forward and rounded the corner.

9

The storm wind from the Russian tundra smashed into Anna like an invisible freight train.

Zakariassen was standing a few metres further ahead, in front of a door banging in the wind.

Boom. Boom. Boom.

He was staring at something in the doorway; then he turned slowly towards her. She saw the floodlights above him reflected double in the large ski goggles covering his face and glasses. His pupils were hidden beneath his deep eye sockets and bushy eyebrows.

"Is something wrong?" she yelled.

Her question vanished in the wind. It was freezing cold. Snowflakes carved into the bare skin between her ski mask and mouth.

The open door was flapping in the wind.

Boom.

Boom.

Boom.

Anna forced herself to put one foot in front of the other, struggling through the deep snow towards Zakariassen. Now she saw what he had seen. In the doorway there was a man crouching on all fours. His head was bowed, looking straight down at the floor, as though he were searching for something.

As the door swung towards the man, she thought he would move to avoid trapping his fingers. But when the door blew open again, the man was in exactly the same place.

Boom.

Boom.

The door frame tore a gash in her glove as she grabbed it. Zakariassen was just standing there, staring.

"Hey, what's wrong?"

"I think... he's dead." Zakariassen yelled the words in her face, his spittle freezing on her goggles.

Anna held the door open against the wind with her back while she bent down towards the man. Now she saw that he was covered in white frost. The hair on his head was covered with ice crystals. An icicle hung from his nose.

She touched him on the shoulder. She was wearing heavy gloves, but the sensation sent a chilly shiver up through her arm, a feeling that the motionless body was exuding a cold evil. When she tried to pull the man towards her, he wouldn't move an inch. His hands were rooted to a layer of ice on the floor. He was like one of the dead mountaineers on Mount Everest, those who succumbed so high up that even the helicopters couldn't reach them, only to remain on the mountain for all eternity.

The ice people.

"You're right," she said, turning towards Zakariassen. "The only place this guy is going now is six feet under."

"What?"

"He's stone dead!" she yelled, making sure the old professor heard her.

Zakariassen's eyes blinked madly. "Did he freeze to death?"

"No, but he *was* frozen to death."

Zakariassen gazed at the ice man. "What's the difference?"

"He's crouching on all fours. If he died naturally, he would be lying on the floor, or leaning against the wall. Or he might be the world's most patient suicide, but I have my doubts about that."

Anna pointed towards the white hands planted in the ice.

"Even at twenty below, with that amount of water on the floor it would still take at least two hours before it froze solid. Nobody's going to be able to stay still for that long. Something must have happened to put this guy in the deep freeze so quickly."

"An accident?"

"I sure hope so," she said, turning towards the wind. The circle of red polar cabins around the large building suddenly looked completely different. They might have been a safe harbour from the coming storm. Now they could be harbouring something else entirely.

She felt the hairs on her neck bristle.

Zakariassen peered into the darkened space, and her eyes followed his. She couldn't see anything in there, but suddenly understood that the man in the doorway wasn't the end of this. There was somebody else inside the building.

She let go of the door and backed up two steps.

"Now we have to be really fucking careful," she said.

Anna moved away from the ice man quickly. From Ice Dragon. From this Hades on ice.

Zakariassen said something that disappeared with the wind. "…more…"

He shouted as he pointed into the dark space.

The wind stole her words before they reached him. "No, we need…" She looked down along the wall. There were no other doors in sight. She decided to walk around the building's perimeter to investigate what was on the other side. When she looked back, Zakariassen had vanished. She scanned around before realizing where he must be.

"Daniel!" she yelled. "Come back, it's not safe in there!"

But he either didn't hear her, or didn't want to.

"Damn it. Fuck."

After fumbling to open the pocket where she kept the large Maglite, she walked up to the door, shoving it against the wall and kicking snow under it until it stayed there.

Anna inhaled slowly, focussing on steadying her pulse, then lifted a foot and stepped past the frozen man. Her boots crunched.

A flashlight pulsed in her mind.

An image of a man with three eyes.

She crushed the memory and, holding the torch with an out-stretched arm, tried to focus on the here and now. The gloom closing around her felt physical, a spectre of shadows groping and tearing at her. She was trained to be rational, but each signal in every nerve cell was screaming that this was a fucking terrible idea. The torch beam carved through the darkness and struck something solid. There was a figure ahead of her, and it was not Zakariassen.

10

Without thinking, Anna raised the Maglite, gripping it hard, ready to strike the man standing right in front of her. In one reflexive movement she hunched her tall body down into a smaller target, but the floor was as slick as an ice rink.

Anna slipped.

The Maglite was knocked from her hand as she broke her fall. The torch rolled away over the icy floor, its beam streaking around like that of a lighthouse in fast-forward. The light hit walls, girders, walls, girders… walls… a foot. A face. Another face. The torch stopped and, in its ray, she saw something moving.

"Anna!"

It was Zakariassen, crawling towards her on all fours. The reflective strips of his survival suit gleamed vividly.

"Oh my God! You cannot go off like that, Daniel! You scared the living shit out of me!"

Vapour clouds gushed from his mouth. His eyes were wide open with shock.

"They're all dead!"

Cracks were beginning to appear in his cut-glass accent.

"They're dead, Anna—there are dead bodies everywhere!"

She grappled forward along the ice, picking up the torch. The man she thought was about to attack her was still standing in the same spot. He was covered in a white skin of frost. Tiny icicles hung from his arms. He had been flash-frozen to the floor, just like the man in the doorway. Beneath the frost, Anna could see from his face that he was without a doubt Chinese, or East Asian at least. He was dressed in a thin down jacket, and from what could be seen of his shoes, he seemed to be wearing slippers. The man had not dressed for the deep cold.

Behind him she saw two more figures. Two ice men, frozen stiff at a table, upon which were some frosted shapes that Anna presumed were laptops.

One body was lying next to the table, sunken down into the ice that covered the entire floor. A foot had broken off and lay alone. Anna sensed the nausea rising in her throat as she looked at the breakage. It was cut as sharply as the salami Galina shaved in the kitchen with the electric slicer for her father's guests. There was not a drop of blood to be seen. The man had been frozen solid before he fell. The foot must have broken off when he hit the floor, like an icicle falling from the gutter.

From the roof above the frozen men hung a deluge of water, halted in free fall and turned to ice. Where the frozen flood hit the floor there was another body part sticking out. An arm. There was a head as well, split in two, the brain a pale grey pulp. One half of the skull was cracked into two more pieces, the eye socket ruptured, a little snowball hanging from it by a thin thread. Anna's torchlight flickered in the dark pupil that she glimpsed under the glassy surface.

"You see, they're all dead!"

Zakariassen's voice had risen to a screech. Anna could see his breath floating before his face like a ghostly airship. The lenses of his Oakley goggles were already covered with a thick layer of frost. Now Anna suddenly felt how cold the building was. There was a profound chill emanating from below the ice, dense, unstoppable. It felt as though only the flames of hell could warm this place up. As she tried to lift her foot, the ice clung to pieces of her boot's rubber sole.

Zakariassen mumbled something. He was struggling to open his mouth. Drops of blood burst from his frozen lips as they tore apart in the cold. His words came in a torrent, filling the room.

"What in hell has happened to them all?"

"I don't know."

Anna walked over to the two ice men sitting at the snow-covered table. Now she saw that both their heads were bowed and their hands were covering their faces. They had tried to defend themselves against whatever had killed them. Their laptops were wrapped in snow and ice. She pressed one of the keys on the nearest keyboard. Snow crunched under her fingers. The computer was as dead as its operator. A couple of sheets of paper had blown up against the screen. She tore one of them loose. The paper was stiff and covered with handwritten Chinese characters, nothing that might tell her what they had been working on. She turned, moving the beam of light slowly around the room. The ice men cast long shadows against the walls, but nothing in the room appeared dangerous. Just a few cabinets containing tools, coils of cable, a coffee machine. The jug was split and covered in frost, the coffee frozen like a black reptile as it crawled out of the cracked glass.

She pointed the torch upwards.

The beam hit the frozen waterfall hanging down from the roof. The streams of water had frozen on their journey towards the floor, sprawling into the air like a sculptural still frame of a skyrocket at the point of explosion. It was impossible to see where the liquid was coming from, but there was no doubt that the icy waterfall had something to do with whatever had killed the men below. Anna poked a finger under her face mask, stretching it out a little to let in some air. She couldn't smell anything. The air she was inhaling felt almost viscous.

"Any idea what it could be?" she asked.

Trying to avoid looking at the dead, Zakariassen shone his own torch towards the ice waterfall.

"It might simply be water."

"These people were not killed by water. They froze to death in seconds."

49

The professor looked at the frozen liquid hanging from the roof, thinking.

A sharp crack interrupted his thoughts.

A shot.

From outside.

11

Fucking idiot!

Silent accusations raged inside her mind as the shot rang out. *How can you be so completely stupid, Anna?!*

The road to hell is paved with good intentions. She had ignored her instincts, howling in chorus, warning her not to follow Zakariassen inside. The victims of such gruesome deaths could have been murdered. If so, the murderer would not be far away.

One of the first rules she learnt in the army was never to run towards a wounded comrade without securing the area first, no matter how much they were screaming for help. Forget this basic rule and you risked an enemy sniper seeing to it that you'd be the next one lying there, begging for rescue in no man's land while your life slowly bled away.

She managed to think of all of this before the shot's echo died out in a metallic snarl that rang in the ears. It sounded like whoever had fired was standing by the doorway.

"Down!" she yelled to Zakariassen. With one hand she thrust herself around on the ice. Now she saw a clear movement in the dark. Something white.

Another crack.

She rolled over in case the shooter had seen her in the gloom. Another boom. Again something white moved.

Harshly metallic, it boomed one more time—Anna finally realized what she was looking at.

"There's no… Jesus fucking Christ… it was just the door."

Her nerves had called her bluff. The cold gripped her head like a vice. She couldn't think straight. Without letting go of the

51

torch, she got up on her legs and walked slowly towards the door, trying to keep her balance on the ice. As she was walking past the ice man in the doorway, Anna realized that one of his hands had broken off. Three fingers held tight to the door handle. The rest of the hand lay crushed behind the door frame. She noticed her own footprint in the palm of the broken hand. She must have stepped on it on her way in.

"Go by the book now, Anna—get an overview of the area first," she said aloud to herself. The pit of her stomach told her that a hidden danger was lurking, but now the threat was coming from outside. She nudged the door open with her shoulder. There was nobody in direct sight.

The storm had grown in strength in the few minutes they had been inside. The snow strafed across the yard, making it impossible to see the cabins on the other side. The weather alone made going outside feel like a suicide mission.

"What the hell has happened here, Anna?" Zakariassen was standing right behind her. Feeling the Mauser's barrel press against her thigh, she pushed him back.

"Stay here. Don't go out before I say so," she said, and squeezed out of the door into the snowstorm.

She ran crouching along the wall and around the corner of the yellow building. Once on the other side she was protected from the wind, her back pressed hard against the panelling. There were no cabins here for a killer to hide in. The blue cabin they passed on the way in was so far away that only a sniper rifle would have a chance, but the snow would make it impossible to see her from that distance.

The cold tore at her lungs as she inhaled calm breaths, trying to clear her head. Trying to analyse the situation.

Scenario 1: The men in the building all died in an accident. If that was the case, where was the person who had fired the flare?

52

Scenario 2: The men were murdered. Someone had managed to escape and send up the flare, but then the murderer had probably tracked them down and killed them too. Which would mean the murderer was still out there somewhere.

Her paranoid mind clung to the second explanation because the next move was so damn simple.

They had to leave.

With the torch held high, ready to strike, she walked around the corner and back into the storm wind again. The chill immediately brought tears to her eyes and, as she was blinking them away, she saw a movement in the snow.

Someone was standing in front of the building.

Her body shrank into a tight coil. She threw herself to the ground, feeling a sharp pain as the fall pressed the knife in her side pocket into her hip. A blast of wind carved a passage through the snowdrift. The figure became clear.

It was Zakariassen. He was staring at something above the roof.

"What are you doing?!" She had to yell to be heard over the wind. "I told you not to come out before I said so. I was about to stick my knife in your back."

The professor met the anger in her voice with a helpless waving of the arms.

"I couldn't stay in there, not with those... ice men... I was freezing to death," he stammered. Her eyes darted around. The brief glimpses she caught of the windows in the cabins surrounding them betrayed no sign of movement. There was nobody to be seen, but they were standing in the most exposed position possible. A few metres ahead of them lay three snowdrifts. The floodlights twinkled on something metallic under the surface of one of them.

"That's a tank, up in the tower."

Anna granted herself a brief glimpse upwards. An amateur with more will than talent had painted a large, bright-blue dragon on

53

a tarp fastened to the tower's cross bracing. Green flames hissed from the monster's gaping jaws. Next to it, two Chinese characters painted in red: *ice, dragon.*

The tank Zakariassen was talking about was barely visible behind the tarpaulin. On top, thick layers of ice glittered. "I think whatever killed everyone came out of that," he said. "It must have sprung a leak."

Anna looked towards the yellow building. If his theory was right, there was still a vital piece of the puzzle missing.

"Come on!" she shouted, seizing Zakariassen's hand and dragging him with her away from the surrounding cabins.

Three steps and they were back to the ice man in the doorway. The torchlight found his remaining hand. What she was looking for wasn't there. It wasn't lying next to him on the ground either. The man in the doorway was the only one who might have shot up the flare. But where was the gun? Again she felt the hairs on the back of her neck rise. She had a strong sense that someone was watching her. Anna rotated on her heels, allowing her eyes to sweep over the yard.

A silver glimmer caught her eye. The wind had now blown free whatever was lying under the nearest pile of snow. Something was fluttering. Something she wanted nothing to do with.

Zakariassen followed her gaze. "What is that... that in the snow?"

The fact that he had seen the same as her gave her no choice. If the snow was hiding what she feared it was, it was going to be impossible to leave the Chinese base.

"Get your rifle ready."

He looked at her uncomprehendingly from behind his goggles. Zakariassen still hadn't realized what the rescue mission had led them into.

"Walk with me, but keep your eyes on the cabins and if you see anything... anything at all... let me know." A flash of awakening dawned in his eyes and, crouching down, he loaded the rifle, looking around nervously.

They ran side by side towards the fluttering object. Anna hit the ground just next to it without once taking her eyes off the cabins' windows.

"Watch the windows. Shout out if you see something."

She pushed the snow off the silvery material. She saw now that it was the hood of a down jacket, buried in the snow. A tangle of black hair stuck out from beneath it. Pale skin was visible underneath. The head of a man. At first she saw something she thought was an eye, but the position was wrong. Then Anna got final proof that what had happened at Ice Dragon was no accident.

In the middle of the dead Chinese man's forehead was a thick welt of blood, hardened around a bullet wound. Anna felt the nausea climbing towards her throat. Her field of vision narrowed. The world was swallowed by an explosion of white fireworks.

12

On the ice, the driving snow was settling on the contents of Anna's guts. She barely managed to turn away from the wind and pull up her ski mask before retching. She scraped off the slime that was already freezing around her mouth. The cold stung her face. She stayed doubled over and gasping until she was sure she wasn't going to throw up again. Then she pulled the mask back down over her face and turned around. The professor was staring awkwardly at her. His eyes blinked rapidly. He held the rifle up to his chest.

"Are you OK?"

"Yeah. Yeah."

"What happened?... It was like you disappeared—I couldn't get through to you."

Anna looked over to the yellow building where the ice men were. Her eyes traced the bright floodlight beam up past the fluttering dragon. The glare blinded her eyes.

She turned away from the stark light, and saw that she was lying in a white room, under a white sheet. All around her were people dressed in white. She was trying to speak, but something in her mouth was gagging the words. One of the figures in white came over to her. A man. His hair was hidden inside a white hood, but trickles of red blood were running from the seams and down over his forehead. He removed the mask. It was Yann.

"How's it going, Anna?"

She tried to reply, but the object in her throat stopped her. Her hand fumbled towards her mouth, grabbing an air tube and yanking it out. She could speak at last.

"How can you be alive?"

"I'm doing well, but it's too early for you, Anna. There's much more for you to do yet." Yann kissed her on the forehead. His lips felt cold against her skin. He peeled back the white hood, and black blood ran from a hole in his forehead.

Anna blinked, forcing her eyes away from the floodlights, and met Zakariassen's stare. "I... I just fucking lost it for a moment... Everything's OK now, don't worry."

She felt her heart kicking. The professor looked down at the dead man. His face was already covered by a thin layer of snow. The bullet hole had turned grey.

"He was killed?..." It barely merited a response.

Anna looked around. She still couldn't see any movement in the windows of the red cabins. She spat in the snow in an attempt to get rid of the taste of puke and breathed deeply.

"You have to listen to me now, Daniel... Do *not* panic..."

"What?!"

Mistake. Those were not the right words. Breathe deeply. Take one thing at a time. Anna gestured towards his old Mauser.

"You have to cover me."

Zakariassen held the rifle away from his body as if it had suddenly become a venomous snake. She grabbed hold of him, turning him so that he had full sight of the red cabins.

"If you see anything now, don't yell, just shoot!" she growled into the wind. "I need to search him."

Her numb fingers ran over his lifeless corpse and the snow around him while she avoided looking at his head. There was no weapon.

She walked over to the next snowdrift and kicked off some of the snow. A figure appeared. This dead man was lying face down, and the only thing to hint that he had been shot in the back was a slight tear in his down jacket.

Before walking over to the last drift, she cast a glance at Zakariassen. The old man was leaning into the wind, his rifle pointed straight ahead. An easy target if anyone armed were hiding in one of the cabins, but she couldn't do anything about it right now.

When she had managed to dig away some of the snow covering this latest victim, Anna saw that he was lying on his back, staring straight up. His eyes sat glazed in his pale face. She removed a glove and placed a finger on his exposed throat. There was no sign of a pulse, and when she went to lift her finger, it snagged a little against the skin.

No doubt about it, the man was dead.

His down jacket was ruptured where the shot had hit him in the centre of his chest. His arms were splayed out to the side like an angel in the snow. He had thin jogging bottoms on under the jacket, fur slippers on his feet. He had no weapons of any kind. Anna had hoped that one of the three was the killer—it was not unusual for a mentally disturbed individual to end a mass shooting by killing himself. But none of the bodies suggested suicide. And the murder weapon was gone. There was only one conclusion to draw from what she had seen: The killer was still out there.

She turned and saw her long shadow stretching to the nearest of the red cabins. There was still nothing to see in the windows, but now every part of her trembled. Blood pounded in her ears. She ran back through the snow to Zakariassen.

"Everyone's dead and somebody has killed them, Daniel." She shouted point-blank to be heard above the wind. "We need to get the fuck away from here right now!" She grabbed his hand, leading him back through the snow to *Sabvabaa* like a child.

58

13

The moments it took until the diesel engine warmed up enough to start *Sabvabaa* felt like an eternity. The windscreen wipers were working at full power, but in the snowstorm it was impossible to see far. If the killer were hiding in one of the cabins he must have seen them coming. *He.* Anna didn't know much, but she knew that this was the work of a man. Perhaps more than one. They were holed up there with their weapons. As soon as she turned the key, they would hear her, and the race would be on.

From that instant she only had the time it would take for them to run from one of the possible hiding places. In those few moments she had to turn the hovercraft around and get herself and Zakariassen away from the Chinese base, back to the safety of the ice.

She grabbed the satellite phone without looking down, raising the receiver to eye level and scrolling down to Boris's number, looking from the window to the phone and back again. The speaker emitted a pulsating tone as she dialled. There was no contact with the satellites. The solar storm was blocking the connection.

"The telephone's fucked—you'll have to try the radio," she yelled to Zakariassen, but she got no response. The professor was slumped forward in the seat next to her. After they had fled back to the hovercraft she had tried to get him to sit in the driving seat, but the professor seemed panic-stricken. Daniel had just sat there, clutching his old Mauser and murmuring something about how this wasn't how it was supposed to turn out… This wasn't the plan.

"Forget about your plans, Daniel, all we need to do now is see about getting the fuck out of here," she yelled in an attempt to break through his inertia. But Zakariassen just stared, his eyes glued to the floor. During their short time at Ice Dragon they had both suffered a kind of mental collapse. Anna knew where her post-traumatic stress came from, but what had put him in such a state? She told herself it was a completely natural reaction to all the dead bodies he had seen. A nightmare no one could be prepared for.

At last the diesel light blinked on and she turned the key. The engine rumbled into life at the first attempt. She placed both hands on the little wheel without taking her eyes away from the window. If someone was coming towards the hovercraft now, the snow would obscure them until it was too late. She would see them sooner with the lights on, but that would also give away their position.

Zakariassen had shown her how to manoeuvre the hovercraft in Longyearbyen and during the first few days after the German icebreaker had dropped them off, but he still preferred to be at the wheel, which was fine by Anna. She had never been interested in any vehicles but motorbikes anyway.

The din from the engine was brutally loud. *Sabvabaa* shook as powerful fans sucked the polar air down below the hull and the pressure lifted the hovercraft off the ice. The wind began pushing *Sabvabaa* sideways as soon as she was floating on a cushion of air. Anna manoeuvred her so that she was travelling into the wind, just as Zakariassen had taught her. The propeller bit into the wind and the rudder forced the airstream to the side. The little hovercraft began to rotate.

The building containing the ice men slipped into view through the windscreen.

She held on frantically to the wheel as *Sabvabaa* continued rotating away from Ice Dragon. Steering a hovercraft was completely different to driving a car. The craft leapt into the darkness. The floodlights vanished to the rear, swallowed by the night. Her hand fumbled across the instrument panel until she found the headlight switch. When the lights came on she saw the blue cabin straight ahead.

Anna jerked the wheel to the right but the storm wind forced *Sabvabaa* sideways towards the cabin.

"Daniel, I can't control the boat."

Zakariassen blinked and looked up. It took a few moments for him to realize what had happened. He awoke from his trance.

"Let go of the wheel!"

His hand shot forward.

"Throttle! More throttle!"

She pushed the throttle down as far as it would go.

The blue cabin became two, then three, as the juddering from the engine rattled the windows. Something in the cabin tumbled off a shelf, sounding like marbles smashing into one another. She didn't look back. Everything now was a matter of getting clear of the cabin. From the driving seat Anna could see the blue panelling just beyond the side windows. The hovercraft would be clear in just a few seconds.

A forceful wrench, the screeching of aluminium sheeting shredding as it was ripped free from its rivets. *Sabvabaa* jumped, trembling and pivoting around the edge of the cabin. One of the panels struck the side of the boat. There was a loud bang from the back.

"Stop! You need to stop! The propeller has been hit!"

Zakariassen jerked the throttle back to idle.

Another crash. Glass shattered at the back of the cabin.

The wind pummelled Anna in the neck. She turned around, seeing snow sweeping in through the window above her bed. A bright light flickered outside the broken window.

Flames.

An alarm wailed.

"We're on fire!" screamed Zakariassen. "God, get out!" His spit struck her ear.

"No, stay here. I'll fix this."

She shoved the panicked man out of the way and fumbled under the seat. Her fingers found a plastic handle and pulled a fire extinguisher free.

It took her three strides to reach the hatch. Snowflakes frozen into ice whirled into her face as she pushed it open. Outside, a huge hole gaped in the cabin wall where the collision had torn off the panelling. In the glow of the flames she saw barrels through the gash in the wall. Oil barrels.

Fantastic.

Sabvabaa was ablaze right next to the Chinese fuel depot.

The flames were coming from somewhere under the housing surrounding the propeller. She ran across the hull towards the flames, which the wind was blowing outwards at an angle. The stench of diesel struck her. Black smoke was spiralling out of the flames. The wind sucked the smoke up towards the Northern Lights, corrupting them.

Anna yanked out the fire extinguisher's pull pin and sprayed foam towards the base of the fire beneath the propeller. The blaze hissed and wheezed at her, brandishing its burning claws and refusing to die.

14

Anna had to put the fire out before it reached the insulation in the cabin walls. If that happened, *Sabvabaa* would be ablaze in seconds. Finally the chemical powder managed to drive away enough oxygen to smother the flames. They flickered feistily up into the air before dying out in cinders, doused by the dark.

As she was entering *Sabvabaa* again, she felt a stinging pain under one of her elbows. Twisting her arm, she saw an ember deep inside a hole in her survival suit. With a knife, she picked out the fire's final attempt to burn her to death.

"Is the engine damaged?" Zakariassen was sitting in the driving seat, mercifully out of his funk by now.

"No idea, I can't see a goddamn thing out there. Try starting it."

He twisted the key and a loud, painful whining sound filled the cabin.

"The starter motor's working anyway… but it sounds like the engine's not getting any fuel."

The professor turned off the ignition. Quiet. Anna looked outside. The cabin they had collided with was blocking the view towards the Chinese base. She leant forward, turning off the lights. Darkness consumed the cabin. Behind the cabin she could see the glare from Ice Dragon's floodlights.

"Daniel, I need you to do something for me now… Go out and keep a lookout."

Sabvabaa was equipped with three Iridium satellite phones, a VHF transmitter for air comms, a VHF receiver for talking to ships and a 100-watt radio transmitter. Anna tried them all while Zakariassen kept watch outside.

She only took her eyes away from the window for brief moments as she tried to get through once again on the satellite phone. She couldn't see anything moving in the bright light around the red cabins. The wind was whipping the snow sideways across the floodlights, which drew an almost perfect circle around the base. At a distance, Ice Dragon looked like one of those plastic snow globes with miniature cities inside them that parents buy their kids for Christmas. The ones you shake to make it snow.

If Anna Aune could have shaken Ice Dragon now, blood would have rained down.

The crash from the collision must have let the killer or killers know that the rescue crew in the hovercraft were in trouble. Now they had regained the upper hand. Maybe men were walking out into the murk now, preparing to surround them at any moment. Zakariassen could only watch one side of the hovercraft as Anna tried to sound the alarm.

At last she managed to engage the emergency beacon.

The ARGOS transmitter was a black plastic waterproof box that looked a bit like a coffee canister. It would automatically broadcast an SOS signal with *Sabvabaa*'s exact location up to satellites orbiting above the North Pole—that is, as long as the battery held out.

When that was done, Anna climbed out of the hatch and hunched into the storm. She stood in the shelter of the propeller's fire-damaged housing while Zakariassen had his head inside the engine. The wind clawed at her and she had to fight hard to keep her balance. When he was finished, the skin on her face felt like a rigid, ice-cold mask.

The professor climbed into the cabin with a charred hose in his hand. His survival suit was iced up and filthy, and he stank of diesel. He tossed the burnt plastic remains towards Anna. "The problem is the fuel line. It was torn off in the collision, diesel sprayed right out onto the engine block… It's hot as hell when the engine's running, that's why it caught fire," he said with barely concealed irritation.

"OK, how much time do you need to install a new hose?" Anna didn't take her eyes off the red cabins. Her neck muscles ached with stiffness.

"One… maybe two hours, but we can't drive through this blasted storm." Zakariassen laid the hose on the worktable. He suddenly looked tiny and shrivelled inside his oversized survival suit.

"I've tried the radios but everything is dead. Either it's the weather or something must have happened during the collision," she said. "Is there anything you can do about that?"

"Yes, in the worst case they're broken, but it's probably just a cable. It's easy to change them all at the same time…" His voice died out, his gaze losing focus. "But all the spare parts are still at base. Shit." He looked at her, frustrated. "I'm sorry, I had no idea we were walking into this hell. Have you really tried all the satellite phones?"

"Of course I have! Try yourself if you don't believe me!" She had to breathe in deeply to keep a lid on her anger. "The satellites are being blocked either by the atmospheric conditions or by the storm. I've activated the emergency beacon—the rescue centre must know that we are in trouble."

The professor looked at the black ARGOS box anxiously, and the green light that was blinking. "What if it doesn't work?"

"Why wouldn't it? Emergency beacons are built to go down with sinking ships. It'll work from here without any problem, but it's just going to take time in this weather. The Russians don't have any bases on the ice this year. The nearest helicopter is probably in Greenland, Svalbard… or maybe Novaya Zemlya." As

65

she spoke, her eyes never lost sight of the base outside for more than a few moments at a time.

"This storm can't last for ever." Zakariassen stared down at the floor. Through his grey hair she could see the shiny crown of his head, the liver spots drawing a map of an unfamiliar continent.

"But we can't stay here any longer, Daniel," she said. "I have no idea what happened at the base. Maybe there was an accident in the building, but the Chinese we found in the snow were shot and killed, beyond any shadow of a doubt. That means that there's at least one killer at the base."

"Were," corrected Zakariassen. "Don't murderers usually flee?"

"Where to though? We're at the fucking North Pole. There's nowhere to run to. If you're alone on the ice in this weather, you'll freeze to death." Anna looked out at the snowstorm. Ice Dragon's lights trembled behind the snowflakes as though the electricity were being pumped out of a beating heart. Maybe he committed suicide, she thought. A simple solution to any problem. Then the realist in her took over. The alternative scenarios. How the pieces in this bloody game of chess might be manoeuvred.

"If whoever did this is still here, it must mean they couldn't get away... Which makes us their only hope of escape. *Sabvabaa* is their only route out of here," she said. No matter which step she tried, she kept returning to the same strategy. A move she in no way wanted to make. But there were only a few chess pieces left, and she was the one with power to save them.

The queen.

"If we are going to survive this, we need to get out there again. We're the ones who need to attack, Daniel. We have to catch the killer."

15

"Calling anybody on this frequency! Mayday! Mayday! Mayday!" Zakariassen intoned in a flat voice, like a dispirited priest in an empty church. He was sitting at the radio and turning the frequency shifter. "In the name of God, there must be someone we can get hold of."

Nothing but white noise came back from the loudspeaker. Anna did what she always did when she wasn't sure what to do. She walked over to her bed, pulled out the bag from underneath it, yanked open the zipper to the little pocket at the front and took out a box of snuff. Sitting on the bed, she stuffed a wad of it up under her upper lip. The first of the day. Still for a moment, she felt the nicotine quivering around her nose as a sense of relaxation spread throughout her body.

She looked out.

Except for the snow drifting by, there was no movement to be seen beyond the hovercraft. For a moment she thought, why bother? Wasn't this the opportunity she had been waiting for? Couldn't she just sit here waiting for whatever fate would bring? But the old man's tense look as he sat at the radio brought her to her senses. The steadfast soldier took over. She couldn't desert Daniel Zakariassen now.

"Daniel, how much ammo do you have?"

The professor jumped a little.

"Um, there's a full magazine in the rifle and six rounds in the revolver, and I have a lot more besides that." He stood up, happy to have a simple task with a clear objective: find the boxes of ammunition. Count them. Zakariassen walked over to the little kitchen cabinet hanging on the wall next to her bed, opening the door and shoving tin cans and packs of crackers and spaghetti to one side.

"I left the boxes here somewhere." She heard his heavy breathing. The sleeve of his survival suit creaked as he stretched his arm into the cabinet. He pulled out rice and potatoes from the bottom shelf.

"Strange… They must have fallen down…" He reached in deep under the shelf. A couple of sharp snorts, then he pulled out one red box and a larger grey one. Both lids were open.

"How has that happened? I closed them really well…" The professor was looking down at them, exasperated. Anna leant in. It was no mistake. There were just a few cartridges left inside.

"It's a mystery… The bullets must be here somewhere… I don't understand."

His indignation was overtaken by confusion. Anna pushed the professor aside, shining her torch into the cupboard. She spotted a narrow crack at the back, against the wall, stuck her finger into it and felt the cold wall against her skin, but there were no cartridges.

"You're completely sure that they were in the boxes?"

His eyes blinked fearfully at her. She almost regretted asking. Who could be completely sure of anything any more?

"Yes. *Yes*. Completely sure. Why would I put them anywhere else?"

The cold from the smashed window found a way in down her neck. Her skin quivered. How long had they been outside while Zakariassen was busy with the engine? Ten minutes? Fifteen? She had been standing sheltered from the wind behind the engine housing and now tried to remember the view from that position. She couldn't see much in the snowstorm, being most concerned with trying to spot anyone coming out of the base. Could somebody have gone round the other side? Climbed up onto the hull, crept over to the smashed window and got into *Sabvabaa* that way?

She turned towards the window above her bed. The remains of the shattered glass were still stuck in the seal, which had partly dislodged from the hull. "Well, I guess I can finally change the fucking thing," she thought. She ran a gloved hand over the shards, but it was impossible to figure out if anybody had climbed through.

"What are you doing?" asked the professor. He was still standing at the cabinet, holding the almost empty box of cartridges.

"I just had a crazy idea that the ammunition could have been thrown out of the window when we crashed," she lied. She saw the scepticism in his eyes. "It's worth checking every angle, isn't it?"

"I've counted. We have fourteen cartridges in total," he said, "including what's already in the guns."

She saw that he was looking for an answer that she couldn't provide. Would fourteen cartridges be enough to keep them alive until they were rescued?

"Fram X expedition, this is a distress call, Mayday, Mayday, Mayday," Zakariassen chanted monotonously. There was no response. "Mayday, Mayday, Mayday."

"Daniel, we really have to get out of here now." Anna placed a hand on Zakariassen's narrow shoulders. He sent a final distress call before switching off the radio. When the lights showing the signal strength and the frequency faded, it was as if the rest of the world ceased to exist. Now it was only the two of them, *Sabvabaa* and whatever awaited in the cabins on the ice.

Anna made him check that his Mauser was actually working. She watched Zakariassen go through the motions of loading the weapon, making sure the cartridge ejected from the chamber as it should, and then got him to take out the magazine and push the cartridge back in. She instructed him to stuff the extras into his breast pocket, within easy reach.

"What about you?" Zakariassen held out the revolver in his hand. If she accepted, Anna felt as if its weight would shatter the floor beneath her. She would fall through the ice below *Sabvabaa* and drown.

"I'll manage with my knife. After you."

16

When she heard the hovercraft's hatch bang shut behind her, Anna suddenly wanted nothing more than to turn back, creep into the snug cabin, turn the heaters on full blast and bury herself deep down into her sleeping bag. Fire up the samovar and make some strong tea. Not give a shit about anything, close her eyes and hope for the best, be it rescue or ruin. But her body wouldn't listen. Her bones and muscles ignored her brain's protests, tearing her away from her fragile bubble of civilization.

She ran towards the closest cabin, not daring to breathe until she was in its shadow at the rear. Zakariassen followed, walking swiftly backwards with his Mauser raised to counter any threat emerging from the darkness. When he finally reached the cabin he was snorting like a beached whale.

Behind the professor's slender frame, Anna could just glimpse *Sabvabaa*, propped up against the fuel depot. Their little home looked a picture of misery. The stern was scorched black, the cockpit lights were off, and huge drifts of snow were already settling in front of its windows. Strange how fond one can become of a twelve-by-six-metre aluminium can.

When the professor had caught his breath again, they crept between the cabin and the one next to it. The storm was gusting stronger in the narrow passageway, and wading through this wind tunnel was like walking underwater. The low thrumming of an engine could be heard from the cabin to the right. Straight ahead of her in the middle of the yard the dead Chinese man's hood flapped in the wind. Anna didn't believe in life after death, but right here and now she would have given anything for the man to make contact from the hereafter and tell her where his killers were.

As she stopped at the corner, Zakariassen's rifle barrel prodded at her.

"Watch it, Daniel, I don't want a bullet in the back." She nudged him away as her eyes scanned for movement behind the windows in the other cabin. The door to the cabin on the left was less than a metre away.

"Stay here and keep a lookout," she instructed him. "Count to fifteen, then turn around and check that nobody's coming from behind." Zakariassen turned immediately. Anna wrenched his head abruptly towards her. "Look back for five seconds and then ahead to the yard for fifteen. Fifteen... five... fifteen... five. Got it?"

He nodded and nuzzled the Mauser into his shoulder, pushing himself against the wall and aiming towards the cabins ahead. She stuck her hand in her side pocket and pulled out the hunting knife.

One, two, three...

Anna charged forward with the knife in her hand. She grabbed the handle and tore the door open, diving into the warmth with the blade poised.

The door slammed shut behind Anna and she huddled her body into a ball. The glare of a powerful ceiling lamp stung her eyes. As she blinked, trying to adjust to the light, she caught the smell of foul grease. Rows of shelves lined the walls of the cabin. Somebody could easily be hiding in between them.

"Don't be scared, we're here to help you!" she shouted, listening, but hearing only the sound of the wind outside and water drip-dripping on the floor. The snow on her survival suit was melting in the cabin's warmth, trickling off her.

The cabin was a workshop.

Yellow toolboxes with "DeWalt" printed in large black lettering were stacked neatly on the shelves. Screwdrivers and spanners hung next to axes, nail guns and long ice drills, mounted on the walls.

Anna walked further inside, past the shelving, and saw engine parts and hoses piled up against the back wall, next to a large workbench. There was a net on the wall containing something that looked like a parachute. A big wooden crate plastered with red and yellow labels sat padlocked on the floor. A sled with a harness lay on the floor next to an enormous tyre. One side of the tyre was split and had come loose from the rim.

Someone had honoured the classic garage tradition of hanging up a *Playboy* poster on a cabinet—a Chinese woman posing on some stairs. She was dressed in a tiny purple costume that pushed her breasts up towards her face, and had purple rabbit ears on her head. "China Lee" was printed in extravagant lettering at the poster's corner.

There was nobody in the cabin. Anna turned around and saw a steel cabinet next to the door. A large padlock and a hacksaw lay on the floor in front of it. The lock had been sawn off.

She opened it up and saw empty racks and cleaning rags. A weapons cabinet. But where were the weapons? She counted ten rifle racks, and the shelves at the base of the cabinet were spacious enough to hold a large amount of ammunition.

Seeing a single 9-millimetre cartridge lying under the bottom shelf, she realized that the cabinet had contained revolvers or pistols in addition to the rifles. Having made this less than reassuring discovery, she shoved the hacksaw in her pocket in case the killer had other secrets locked away. She grabbed a handful of cable ties and a roll of gaffer tape from a table used for bending pipes. In war, you'll always find a use for cable ties and gaffer tape.

When she came outside, the front of Zakariassen's suit was covered in a layer of snow, frozen stiff. The storm was growing steadily stronger, the temperature plummeting. If they weren't able to find a safe bolthole soon, the North Pole would kill them.

"What was in the cabin?"

Anna slipped into the passageway and ran to the other end to check that side was clear.

"It's just a workshop."

She decided there was no point in alarming Zakariassen even more by telling him that the killers were now armed with enough weapons and ammo to start a small war. The next cabin caused no such concerns. When she flung open the door, all she saw were three large generators.

To get to the cabins on the north side of the yard they had to walk back through the floodlights, utterly exposed. For a second Anna thought about asking Zakariassen to shoot them out, but she didn't want to waste the scarce ammunition.

She was trying to run, but it was impossible. The storm that Boris had forecast was attacking them with all its might. It was blowing so hard that it was barely possible to breathe without turning away from the wind.

Two metres from the cabin, she saw something.

This time it was real. A movement in the shadows. She saw two eyes glinting in the floodlights, the light glimmering in two irises.

"There's something there."

Out of the corner of her eye, she saw Zakariassen turning around in slow motion.

"Take cover!" she yelled into the wind.

The professor raised his rifle. Whatever had been hiding in the shadows was gone. She saw a grey figure scuttling past the cabin beyond them.

A blast cut through the howl of the storm, and another as the Mauser discharged. Zakariassen fired one, two, three times.

"Stop!" yelled Anna, but it was too late.

17

Zakariassen kept shooting until the magazine was empty. Each time he squeezed the trigger, the rifle barrel recoiled and his slender body shuddered. When the shots subsided, Anna hauled herself up and ran over to him.

"You don't need to shoot! It was just a fox!"

Zakariassen looked at her, confused.

"Sorry, my fault—I got it wrong. I thought I saw someone between the cabins," Anna said.

Behind his goggles his bushy eyebrows drew taut in dissent. "But there aren't any foxes at the North Pole in midwinter."

"I guarantee you I saw an animal. It had a tail and ran behind the other cabin."

"Mountain foxes only come as far as the North Pole in summer," the academic continued defiantly. "I—"

"All right, OK, but we can't stay here. The only people who don't know we're coming now are already dead," Anna interrupted, dragging the professor behind the wall he had just shot a hole in. "Reload."

"It's so damn cold…" His skinny fingers trembled as his took the extra cartridges out of his breast pocket and tried to jam them down into the magazine. One cartridge dropped to the ground. Anna looked down, scooping it up in a handful of snow. She positioned herself against the wind, blocking it out as Zakariassen blew off the ice. He reloaded and pushed the magazine back into the rifle.

The snowfall was so intense that Anna was only able to see the first of the cabins in the row they were standing in. Her fingers and toes were dull, numb. If they were going to spend as much time searching the rest of the base, they would freeze to death long before anyone had the chance to kill them.

In the military, Anna's strategy in this situation would be to find a position that she could defend until reinforcements came to their assistance. But whoever was hopefully coming to their aid now would be sending emergency rescue teams and medics, not soldiers. The attackers would kill everyone except the pilots they needed to fly back to the mainland.

A gust of wind blew into the hood of Anna's survival suit, filling it with snow.

"I… I'm fucking freezing." Zakariassen's teeth chattered and, as he spoke, Anna saw the panic in his eyes. Her own paranoia was crushing her chest with the strength of a sumo wrestler. They couldn't stay out in the storm any longer.

"Let's take the whole row at the same time," she yelled, a false confidence in her voice. "I'll open the door while you cover me." Then she ran around the corner before Zakariassen could protest. Anna ripped open the nearest door and registered two empty sofas and a massive TV, before running on. In the next cabin, two abandoned bowls of rice on a pair of tables told her this was the crew's mess.

When she burst open the door to the last cabin in the row, she recognized the dry stench of scorched dust.

Electronics.

Several radio transmitters stood stacked on top of each other on a shelf. She walked in slowly with the knife poised and ready, high above her. Shadows from the radio cabinets slipped across her face. The outline of something appeared behind the edge of the shelves.

A figure, dressed in orange.

She backed up. There was a flickering in her eyes. Her vision was failing her. Like an amoeba, the figure split into five people in orange jumpsuits against a scorched black wall. Yann was among them.

"Shit shit shit! Fuck fuck fuck!"

Anna shouted the words, shaking her head, drawing in deep for breath. A psychologist had told her that this could happen. Post-traumatic stress triggered by sounds, smells or sensations. Her mind flooded with flashbacks and stopped taking in information from the outside world. The reminders were more real than reality itself. The psychologist called it "super memory". Yann was coming closer and closer. She saw his windblown hair; time ticked by slowly. A gate in the wall opened behind him. A gigantic black-clad figure entered, a man-mountain. He was holding something in his hands. Hellfire.

Anna squeezed her eyes shut so hard it hurt. She sucked air deep into her lungs, letting it circulate as if it were a brand-new sensation to be savoured and assessed. She reopened her eyes. Saw her blue moon boots standing in a puddle of water. The flickering faded. Her vision returned.

She took a step backwards. Something jabbed her in the back. She whipped around and saw that it was one of the posts holding the cabin up. When she looked back into the cabin, the orange figure was still there.

"I am armed!" she yelled, but the figure didn't move.

She walked forward with the knife stretched out before her, seeing an axe in the corner of her eye, lying on the floor behind the shelf holding the transmitters. The orange figure sat slumped, his head resting on the desk in front of three large computer screens, upon which colourful images of the Northern Lights rotated.

With her fingers clasped so hard around the knife handle that it was physically painful, Anna walked slowly forward.

It was a man.

Something that looked like a black ski helmet hung on a stand next to him. Her angle of approach made it look as though the helmet was in fact his head, removed from his body.

The motionless man was wearing an orange down jacket. On the back there were Chinese symbols cleanly embroidered around an illustration of the same dragon that hung from the tower. The man had black hair with a hint of grey, like dirty snow in a coalmine.

When Anna reached his side, she saw that his head was resting on a keyboard. His eyes were closed, as if he were sleeping. A wispy beard covered his chin. She took off a glove and pressed her index finger against his throat. The skin was cold and clammy against her fingers.

Flecks of blood covered the floor under the chair the dead man was sitting on. The drops were dark red at their centre, brown, almost black at their edge. The Chinese man had been dead for several hours. She noticed that there were no bullet holes to be seen in his jacket, then turned and looked back. She now discovered what the axe on the floor had been used for. There were deep gashes in the backs of the radios. Inside the warped metal, pieces of hacked cable hung across smashed circuit boards like severed guts. The man's killer had made the effort to destroy any means of communication with the world beyond.

The killer had not troubled himself with two rows of tall glass cabinets standing against the wall. They were filled with black boxes with blue lights blinking on the front. The low humming of fans could be heard from within. Two black and grey cables hung out of an empty shelf in one of the cabinets.

She walked out, letting the dead man sleep on.

18

Zakariassen was kneeling in the passageway behind the next cabin when Anna came out. The Mauser was resting on his thigh, aimed towards the three dead Chinese men out in the yard, as if he were scared that they would come back to life again and attack.

"There was one more in there," she shouted over the howling wind. Zakariassen nodded stiffly. He clearly wasn't interested in the details.

There were now five cabins left. She breathed deeply and ran on.

Each time she entered a cabin, Anna felt the tension rising. Opening a door was like squeezing the trigger in a game of Russian roulette: sooner or later, there would be a bullet in the chamber.

The first cabin was a sickbay with medicines, bandages and a washing machine. Then there was a cabin with eight neatly made beds standing empty. In the third were satellite images of the ice hanging above a large meeting table, and a bed hidden behind a screen on which there was a painting of steep mountains climbing out of the sea.

No more dead, none living.

Two cabins left. The one further away was a garage with two wide doors. One of them stood open and an oil barrel with a pump on top could be seen inside. Anna signalled to Zakariassen to take that cabin first. She ran hunched past the nearest cabin, then through the open door. There was a small green tractor behind the other door. Anna caught the reek of diesel from the pump in the oil drum. Somebody had been refuelling not too long ago. It creaked as she walked. Wooden planks covered the floor.

"Come on, there's nobody here," she said, waving the professor, who was standing against the outer wall, into the shelter of the closed door. He walked in, but stopped abruptly. "There's been a vehicle here." The professor pointed at a small puddle of oil with the imprint of tyres soaking into the garage's wooden floor. Outside, the snow had long since covered any further trace of it. Anna looked at the tracks on the garage floor. A car or tractor could have driven away over the ice as long as a fracture or pressure ridge didn't get in its way. If so, the killer could have just stopped out on the ice, hidden in the endless darkness. It was one way of surviving the storm.

"Where can it have gone to?" asked Zakariassen.

She stuck her head out of the door and looked around the corner of the garage, hoping to see *Sabvabaa*'s lights, but got just a face full of snow blown out of the black night. She pulled her head in again and wiped her face dry.

"In this fucking shitty weather Godzilla could be standing ten metres away and we wouldn't even know it."

Zakariassen stared down at the oil stain on the floor.

"Do you think he… fled?" he said, hopefully.

"Or they. Killing that many people is a lot of work."

"We need to check the last cabin, too," she said. They both looked over to it. The last room. The gun's final chamber. The only place a killer might now be.

"Why can't we just… stay here?" Zakariassen's voice was trembling. "We'll just pull the door shut. It's warm." He pointed at an oil heater shoved under a bench covered in mechanic's tools. Outside the open garage door the red paint of the final cabin glimmered under the bright floodlights. The windows were dark, the lights were off. Exactly how Anna would have arranged it if she wanted to make sure she could see without being seen.

"No. We have to check the last cabin too."

"Please, I can't take it any more." Daniel began sobbing. "I'm so afraid." He was crying so loudly that for a moment she was paralysed. Then Anna put her arms around him, pulling him close to her.

"It's all right, I'm scared too," she said, looking him in the eye. "But it's good for us, only idiots feel no fear. Fear keeps you sharp." It was true. As a soldier, suppressed fear and controlled paranoia had kept Anna Aune alive through three civil wars on two continents.

When she had managed to calm Zakariassen down, they went back out into the snowstorm again.

They walked along the wall, sheltered from the wind, towards the front of the cabin.

"Wait here." Anna bent down and crawled on her knees around the corner.

She could see some grey stains in front of the door, partly hidden by the snow. Creeping over to a position directly under the window, she reached her arm up and pounded the knife butt hard against the glass. She jumped up immediately. Saw a pale face. Two black hollows for eyes. Her own reflection in the glass. A miserable person in a godforsaken place. In the darkness, nothing moved.

"Come here!" she shouted to Zakariassen. He crept around the corner to her. "Hold the door as I go in. If I get shot, shoot back, but try not to hit me." Zakariassen gripped the Mauser hard in his hands and nodded.

She got up next to the door and waited until the professor took hold of the door handle. One nod and he thrust the door open.

Crouching low, the knife in one hand and the torch in the other, Anna penetrated the darkness. As soon as she was inside she sensed a sweet smell, like freshly carved flesh.

19

First Anna made sure that nobody was behind the door or on the opposite side before swinging the torch beam back and forth across unmade beds. There were people in two of them.

"*I am armed!*" she shouted as loud as she could. "*Stay down!*"

No reply.

She pointed the knife's blade towards the figures in the beds, ready to launch. It felt as though the room's darkness were seeping out of the motionless shapes.

The torch beam found a head in the nearest bed. In its light, she saw a large stain on the floor, and recognized the cloying smell of coagulated blood.

The second individual was staring straight up at the ceiling with eyes wide open. She walked towards him. It was a young man with long hair. He lay in a dark-blue sleeping bag and Anna could see white duck feathers in his black hair. There were two small holes in the sleeping bag, directly over his chest.

"What are you doing?"

Zakariassen was standing in the doorway. The floodlights outside drew him like a black silhouette against the snowstorm. His shadow cut through the open door and lay across the second dead man like a dark curtain.

"There are two more. Both shot."

"Oh God… oh God." His voice sounded harrowed and lost. "Will this never end?"

Anna stuck the knife back in its sheath. "It's over now. We've been everywhere on the base. There are no survivors."

Zakariassen turned and looked towards the garage. The wind had changed direction and was blowing snow in through the open garage door.

"The murderers must have fled," he said.

"Where to though? There's nowhere to hide out there."

"The Arctic is twelve million square kilometres," said the professor. "Disappearing is not so difficult."

"Yeah. Let's hope the motherfucker who did this just disappears."

Anna looked at the two dead men. She rewound through her memory, trying to add up the dead. There had been five or six ice men in the big yellow building. Three lying shot outside. The man with the orange jacket in the cabin with the radio equipment, and then these two poor bastards, killed in their own beds. Probably while they slept.

At least eleven dead.

"I just don't understand, why would anyone want to kill peaceful scientists?" stammered Zakariassen.

"For the same reason that peaceful men kill women. There are a thousand reasons, an argument, jealousy, problems with money."

"Yes, one person I understand, but this… madness…"

"Right," said Anna, heading for the door. "This is the work of a maniac. But… the dark season and the isolation have chewed a hole in the head of many a strong man. It wouldn't be the first time."

Zakariassen slammed the rifle butt against the toe of his boot so hard that Anna feared he was going to fire a shot by mistake.

She got scared for a brief moment that *this* old man would suddenly run amok, or do something crazy. Professor Zakariassen had spent five years preparing his expedition. Everything was laid out in the finest detail. He had brought so many spare parts for *Sabvabaa* to the North Pole that he could build a second hovercraft. The gear was checked, double-checked and triple-checked before they left, but there was one thing Zakariassen couldn't pack, no matter how much he tried. The professor didn't have the magic ingredient that distinguished successful people from the rest.

Luck.

Even a genius of a scientist with his pockets full of Nobel Prizes could not have foreseen that the world's next mass killing would take place at the North Pole.

"What are we going to do?" asked Zakariassen.

The snow was blowing across the ceiling, sprinkling down on his head, his ragged hair buckling like birch saplings in a wintry forest. He hadn't wanted to enter the dead men's room. His eyes avoided looking at them both.

"There's nothing more we can do here. We just have to get back to *Sabvabaa* and set up the trip flares around the boat so no one can sneak up on us. And then you'll have to fix the radio antennas. The solar storm or whatever the fuck it is stopping us from getting any radio contact will die down eventually. We'll just fire up the heaters and hold out until help comes."

Suddenly Zakariassen smiled. A boy's hope that everything would come good in the end. "Yes, good idea, Anna. That's a good plan." He lifted the Mauser onto his back, ready to walk back to the hovercraft, when Anna suddenly heard a noise.

A word.

She turned around and saw a dead man getting up out of bed.

20

The dead man climbed out of Zakariassen's shadow, his face rising into view in the glare of the floodlights streaming into the cabin. He raised a hand as if to shield his eyes against the light and said something incomprehensible in Chinese, before collapsing on the bed again. Anna walked towards him.

For a moment Anna thought that this undead person was a woman. The face was pale. The eyes had fulsome lashes, and long black hair swept over a large, smooth forehead. The nose was narrow, the lips broad and shapely.

"Can you hear me?" Anna asked.

The figure stirred, the sleeping bag slipping halfway off the body. He had a red fleece over his torso and something that looked like a T-shirt was wrapped around his ribcage. It was difficult to see because of all the blood that the fabric had absorbed.

"What happened?" It was a man's voice, surprisingly deep. His English was clear and pronounced.

"You've been shot. Can you remember who did it?"

"No…" He pushed his thin arms in under himself, trying to get up again.

"Don't move. Stay still so we can look at your wound." Anna placed a hand on his chest and pushed him down gently. Dark blood stuck to her fingers once he was down again.

"Is he… Has he been shot too?"

Zakariassen was still standing in the doorway. The floodlights illuminated a halo around his dishevelled hair, making him look like a figurine of Jesus.

"Yes. Get inside and close the door."

Zakariassen didn't move. "What if the killers come back?"

"In that case I would move away from the door. You make a brilliant target standing right there." He took a slow, hesitant step inwards.

"No, as a matter of fact I need bandages. Run back to the sickbay we saw on the way here." She leant over the Chinese man and placed two fingers on his carotid artery.

"There's no way in hell I'm doing that. We have to get out of here now." Zakariassen's voice cracked in fear. "Please Anna, can't we just leave before the killer comes back?" Patience in battle had never been Anna's thing. As she turned towards Zakariassen, he backtracked away from her. The look in her eyes must have been terrifying.

"Why the fuck do you think I'm trying to keep this poor bastard alive, Daniel?" she fired back in Norwegian. "If there is anyone at all who might help us find out who's behind this massacre, it's probably him. But right now he's about to die from blood loss and shock."

She scrutinized the wounded man again, continuing to speak to Zakariassen as she turned her back to him. "Now do exactly as I say. Go outside, get your arse around the back, and run as fast as you can to that cabin. Find four of the biggest compresses and loads of bandages. Four rolls, minimum. And morphine would be amazing." It fell quiet. She could hear him breathing through his nose. A step. The slamming of a door. Zakariassen was obeying orders.

The Chinese man's unusually large eyes stared in fright at Anna.

"Who are you?" he asked.

"My name is Anna Aune. We're the crew from the Norwegian Fram X expedition. Our base is eight kilometres further south. I saw your emergency flare. We're here to help you."

He kept staring. She had no idea if he was taking in what she was saying or whether he was in shock. She spoke slowly and clearly. "Can you help me?… Do you know what happened here?"

The only response she got was a couple of rapid blinks.

"Was it you who set off the flare?"

"No, I've just been lying here." He coughed and writhed in the bed. Anna laid a hand on his shoulder.

"You need to stay still. We're going to find something to help you." Her frostbitten lips formed something hopefully resembling a reassuring smile. "Is there anything you remember… about what happened to you?"

"No… I was sleeping… A noise woke me up… Someone was standing in the doorway, then there was a boom. When I woke up again my chest was burning terribly. When I touched it my hand was covered in blood. I was scared for my life and screamed and screamed for help… but… no one came." The man twisted his head towards the man lying in the bed next to him and stared blindly up at the ceiling.

"Then I saw Guan was… dead." He started to cry. Tears streamed down over his soft cheeks.

"Don't be scared—everything is going to be OK. We're here with you, and you are safe now," Anna lied, forcing out another stiff smile. "But it would help if you could tell me everything you can remember."

The Chinese man barely nodded.

"The man at the door, did you see who he was?"

He blinked quickly. Tears crept into the corners of his eyes. "No, it was dark and I was sleeping, and everything happened so quickly. I think he said something to me, then he raised his arm as if he were pointing at something, then that noise and… I must have blacked out. When I woke up, nobody was here. Just Guan. That's all I know." He began crying again.

"It doesn't matter. Just relax and we'll figure it out. We're here to help you."

Anna put her arm around him and lifted him up a little. With her other hand she felt along the bed under his back. If he were concealing a weapon, it would be somewhere close.

"What's your name?"

"Shen Li… Jackie."

"OK, Jackie, just lie still and my partner will be here soon with a medical kit. We'll see to your wound. Help is on the way. It'll be fine, Jackie." Being a nurse was not so different from being a soldier. The objective justified every lie as long as it kept the spirits up, even when all hope was gone.

Jackie was wheezing heavily as he breathed. He looked across to the dead man in the neighbouring bed. "The others?… What happened to them?…"

Anna tried to keep a blank face, but her eyes betrayed her. Jackie looked back at her in sheer terror.

21

When Zakariassen finally came back, he brought a first-aid kit with him. The medicine was marked with incomprehensible labels, but Jackie seemed to be fading fast, so Anna took the chance that the syringe that looked like morphine was precisely that. The professor helped to hold Jackie still against the bed until she got the needle into his arm. It wasn't long before she noticed Jackie's muscles relaxing.

When the morphine sleep came over the Chinese man, she got Zakariassen to lift him up. Anna saw that the mattress was soaked through with blood from the bullet wound, but was still in one piece. There was no hole from the bullet that had passed through him. Jackie had been elsewhere when he was shot. She remembered the stains in the snow outside the door. They could have been blood.

"Did he tell you who shot him?" asked Zakariassen.

"No, it was pitch-black, he saw nothing." She swung the torch around. The beam glided over the beds, the walls, the sleeping bags. Sporadic glimpses of colour. It suddenly felt as if the dark had a will of its own. That objects moved as soon as the light vanished. The beds almost had her surrounded. The sleeping bags unfolded themselves, slipping over her head, over her body, choking her. Anna sprang up, inhaling deeply. The beds retreated. The sleeping bags lay where they had been. The paranoia dispersed.

"I saw nobody at all outside. The killer must have fled. The only logical thing for him to do would be to take the vehicle from the garage," Zakariassen declared with a hint of newfound determination. "We're safe now."

"Sorry, I hate to disagree with you, but how far do you think anybody is going to get in this weather? Let's say that you're right. Right now the killer is sitting in a warm vehicle. You know the terrain just as well as I do, Daniel, and not even a tank would get past the pressure ridges out there. And he'll be running out of fuel. We have to assume that he's coming back."

Zakariassen turned his torch towards Jackie, still sleeping.

"Then I don't understand why he left in the first place."

"Because he saw us coming. Our lights could be seen from kilometres away. He couldn't have known that it was just us two. But now he does."

Zakariassen looked at her angrily. He hated not being in control. A trembling finger darted up in triumph.

"Then you are presuming that the Chinese have been killed by one of their own. What if it's the Russians behind all this? They would have come with their own transport. Those crooks are doing everything they can to keep the North Pole to themselves. Those bastards are ruthless, you know... You've seen the news: they tried to kill an ex-spy with nerve agent in England in broad daylight, for Christ's sake."

"Yeah. Putin never forgives a traitor, but this defies all sense." Anna couldn't hide her irritation any longer. "If the Russians were the ones orchestrating the accident in the building, why blow their cover by shooting the three Chinese outside?"

Zakariassen grinned victoriously. "Because something went to shit. The Russians panicked, killed the rest and got out of here!"

Anna gave up. She thought about mentioning all the weapons and ammunition that had gone missing, but it wasn't worth the trouble. "Well, let's just hope that whoever did this has vanished for ever."

When the will to argue had faded, they were left standing there, listening.

Outside the wind was howling like a pack of mad coyotes. The cabin walls were vibrating under the pressure. Anna thought that with a bit of luck, even if the killer had ten weapons and a pile of ammunition, they would be useless to him in this murderous storm. But deep inside a sense was rising that the North Pole would have something to say in the matter. That the kingdom of ice would be taking its revenge for the death sentence that humanity had brought upon it.

22

She waited until Jackie was in a deep sleep before she cut open the blood-soaked T-shirt and peeled it off his chest. Dark blood had coagulated in large quivering masses along his shoulders. She found a bottle of antiseptic in the medical kit and sprayed it on a cotton bud to wash away the bloody clots.

The shot had entered under the collarbone and exited directly below his armpit. He had been extremely lucky. A few centimetres further up and it would have hit the bone, shattering it as the projectile changed course inside his body, potentially hitting the heart.

She placed two large compresses on the bullet wound and, while Zakariassen held them both in place, Anna wrapped a bandage as tightly as she could around Jackie's chest. The blood soon began to soak through the fabric.

"He's lost a lot of blood. We need to set up a drip before he goes into shock. Hold this." She picked up an infusion pack from the first-aid kit, tore it open and gave Zakariassen a bag of plasma, quickly inserting the needle that came with it into a vein in Jackie's forearm. The clear liquid began streaming in.

"The world lost a good nurse when it gained you as a soldier."

Anna took the bag from him and hung it on a clothes hanger in the cupboard behind the bed.

"I doubt it. I hate doctors."

"Is he going to make it?"

"Hopefully. But somebody with more experience than me needs to look at the bullet wound before it gets infected."

She took the torch and walked between the other beds. The sheets were all over the place. Those living in the cabin must have been in bed while the rest of the crew were being killed. Were they woken up by the screams of the dying men in the yellow building? The three lying outside in the snow had jumped into their clothes, run out and been shot, but Jackie and Guan had stayed in their beds. Why? She shone the light into Guan's ears. It struck an orange earplug, stuffed deep inside. Rest in peace.

Anna eventually found the hole from Jackie's bullet wound in the bed closest to the wall. The curtain fabric on the front of the wardrobe had been pulled up. On the floor was a yellow nail gun, partly disassembled.

The clothes had been torn off the hangers and lay in a heap on the wardrobe floor. Thermal trousers and one of the red and silver Ice Dragon jackets lay on top. There were bloodstains on the inside of the wardrobe, probably from Jackie trying to band-age himself. The rest of the wardrobe was filled with magazines, books, a toilet bag, a little wooden box, a compact digital camera and an iPhone. She tried gaining access to the phone, but it seemed to be out of battery.

The air crackled electrically above her. The items in the ward-robe drowned in dark shadows as the fluorescent tubes in the ceiling flickered on. Zakariassen had found the switch by the door. When Anna turned around, she saw that her boots had left wet pools of melted snow across a trail of blood. The bloodstains dripped from the bed where the bullet hole was, across to the wardrobe and over towards the door. Had Jackie left the room?

"Can you see any blood outside?"

Zakariassen pushed the door open. White walls of snow drifted past. The storm was raging more than ever.

"No. If there was any blood here it's been long since snowed over. Impossible to see anything now."

Zakariassen shut the door again. The howling of the storm winds abated slightly. He slung the rifle over his shoulder and looked out between the heavy curtains hanging in front of the windows next to the door.

The cabin looked completely different with the lights on. The colourful, sprawling sleeping bags almost made it seem like a hikers' cottage in the Norwegian mountains, apart from the statuette of a golden Buddha with long incense sticks pushed into his hands.

But as soon as Anna looked over to the dead body, the scene changed again. Now she was back in the bleak cabin from *Friday the 13th* that had given her nightmares as a teenager. Was Jason waiting out there in the polar darkness, his hockey mask covering his face?

She grabbed a sleeping bag from another bed and tossed it over Guan's corpse to cover his vacant eyes. Now they had searched the entire base and everybody but Jackie was dead. Anna tried to remember if he had said he had seen just one man. How many were in the vehicle that must have left the base just before they arrived? How big was the crew at Ice Dragon?

She got an idea, and went back to Jackie's wardrobe, taking out the shirt that lay crumpled on top of a pile of clothes. It was bloodstained. She shook it out and saw a label fastened to the collar. Even though there were Chinese characters printed on it, she knew what it was. A laundry tag.

23

After turning off the cabin lights so she wouldn't be seen from outside, Anna pushed the door halfway open, grasping it so the wind wouldn't rip it from her hands as she looked across the open yard. Even if Zakariassen told her he hadn't seen anything, there might still be people hiding somewhere out there. She stood still for a long time, not focussing on anything in particular, just surveying the snowstorm in the hope of catching a movement, something that wasn't there before. Anything.

She had refrained from pulling on the ski mask in order to widen her field of vision, but immediately regretted it. The ice-cold wind paralysed her face, piercing her cheeks as she turned her head. But she concentrated on keeping her eyes wide open behind her ski goggles. Didn't pay attention to anything, simply observed. Just like a French ex-soldier had taught her many years ago. She had been surrounded by buildings then too, but they were occupied. Men, women and children. They were teeming with life.

"Let your subconscious work for you."

On a roof in the middle of Mogadishu, the man was standing with his back to the view. Ferdinand Berger was working as a security consultant for the hotel, which was surrounded by small huts on all sides. From up on the roof they looked like colonies of wild mushrooms. "Don't see what you think you're seeing because you've seen it so many times before. See what is actually in front of you." It was the ninth day of their watch on the same roof and Anna was shit-tired.

Mogadishu was a godforsaken place.

The last representative of law and order, General Sarinle, had been murdered because he tried to save an Italian churchyard from being destroyed by the Islamic militia besieging the city. Anna's mission was to make sure that the hotel the UN mission used as a base was not attacked or bombed before they managed to get out of Somalia. The only bright spot in each watch duty was the daily delivery of fresh bread from the cooks at the Norwegian base out by the airport, a luxury for soldiers otherwise surviving on battle rations.

Ferdinand got her to notice the little shack behind the mosque. The militia had set it up during the night and made the corrugated structure look like it had always been there. When her patrol raided the hideout, they killed five teenagers armed with automatic weapons, Russian mortar guns and recoilless rifles. The boys were hopped up on amphetamines and refused to surrender. Two days later Anna packed up her gear along with the other UN soldiers and the civilian personnel, drove out to the airport guarded by American marines in armoured vehicles, and abandoned Somalia to chaos and death.

The open yard around the large building reminded her of the churchyard in Mogadishu, and she used the same technique as then to assure herself that the storm and the snowdrifts were not hiding anything. The three dead men were lying in exactly the same place. Now the snow had blown up against their bodies again from the opposite direction. The North Pole was burying its dead. The same snow that was settling on the corpses drifted around the corner of the building, past the open door where the ice man still crouched on all fours.

There was no movement, but Anna still had a distinct sense that the danger was far from over. Eventually she had to come to a conclusion based on what her own eyes reported.

"It's clear," she yelled to Zakariassen, and ran out. While she was keeping watch at the door, he had been wrapping Jackie tightly to the bed with gaffer tape.

With the storm wind at her back, Anna moved so quickly that she almost wasn't able to stop when she got to the next cabin. She grabbed hold of the handle, pulled open the door and watched Zakariassen run in ahead of her. The snowstorm made it almost impossible to see anything at all. The only consolation was that if a murderer were hiding somewhere they weren't aware of, he wouldn't see them either.

Hopefully.

As Anna entered, the wind slammed the door closed behind her with such force that a couple of bottles tumbled off a shelf on the adjacent wall. Anna caught a whiff of turpentine.

She found the switch hidden behind a blue apron hanging on a peg by the door, and turned off the cabin's lights. They were able to manage with just the light coming through the window. Now if anyone was watching from the cabin outside, they were at least less visible. The metal shelves filled with medicine and acupuncture equipment glittered in the torchlight. Anna let the beam from hers lead her past a canvas partition hanging down from crossbeams in the roof. Behind it, she found exactly what she had risked her life for.

Above a washing machine and a dryer hung a plastic board with handwritten Chinese characters at the very top. Beneath them hung fridge magnets in different colours. Anna recognized the arrangement from the communal laundry in the basement of the apartment building in Oslo where her first flat had been.

"What are we looking for?" asked Zakariassen.

Each magnet had something written on it, which she guessed was the name of a crew member. The board was divided into seven rows.

"My theory… is that this is something as routine as a laundry list. Even scientists need clean underwear." She pushed one of the coloured magnets. "Each man has his own magnet to reserve a time and day for his laundry."

"Hmm, smart." Zakariassen's lips moved as he counted the magnets.

"Fourteen… fourteen men—how many have we found?"

In her mind, Anna was retracing their steps: the man in the doorway; the one frozen in his slippers inside, plus the two in front of the computer monitors—that made four. The one with the snapped-off foot, five. The man trapped in the frozen waterfall, six. The three who had been shot out in the yard, nine. The man in the orange jacket inside the cabin with the damaged radio transmitters, ten. The man Jackie had said was called Guan, plus Jackie himself.

"I make it eleven dead and Jackie. Twelve people."

In the light from the torch, the deep wrinkles in Zakariassen's forehead furrowed like bottomless ravines. "God, you mean… that we're missing… two?"

Anna felt an endless exhaustion consume her body.

"Yes. Now we don't need to wonder any more. We're looking for not one, but two killers."

24

Anna looked out of the cabin's window, trying to see the garage where one vehicle was missing. The vehicle that two killers had fled in after slaughtering eleven people.

Why?

If there were two killers, the killings were not randomly carried out in a panic. They must have been working together. What had the eleven Chinese scientists done to deserve death? Or was everything that happened on the base really just the work of one madman? An insane murderer who had taken a hostage because he couldn't drive? Because he was wounded?

And where were they headed?

Questions, questions. Walking away from the window and further into the cabin, Anna was struck by a dizzying drowsiness, but when the darkness enveloped her it felt as if she were walking towards a cliff edge in heavy fog.

"Daniel, is it at all possible to drive to the mainland from here?"

The professor looked towards the window. The snow was whipping past, chopping up the floodlights. The light that caught his face flickered like strobes at a nightclub. He walked right over and peered out as though he were hoping to see all the way to Greenland, or Russia.

Zakariassen's face was lit up brightly by the floodlights. His narrow nose cast a shadow against his forehead, splitting his head in two. His eyebrows poked out like the brushwood of wild-grown bushes above his eyes, staring into the storm.

"No. It's just not possible to drive to the mainland," he said finally. "First of all, due to climate change most of the ice cap is now broken up by open fractures. The only way to get over the ice is as we did, with a hovercraft, but there is only one *Sabvabaa*. And the closer you get to the coast of Canada, Russia or Greenland, if that's what those bastards had in mind, the worse the ice gets. When the sea ice meets the mainland, it's forced up. There are bloody huge pressure ridges everywhere. It's barely possible to climb over them on foot."

Anna looked at the laundry board again. The magnets' strong colours jumped out of the dark. She and the professor stared silently at the pen strokes telling an ordinary tale of eleven men who would never live another day. "But…" said Zakariassen, "there's something that doesn't quite add up."

"Yeah." Anna nodded in resignation. "Who fired the flare we saw? We only have Jackie's word that he was shot—what if it was the other way round? What if he killed the entire crew, but some of them managed to shoot back at him and fled afterwards? If that theory is right, there are a couple of poor bastards out on the ice about to freeze to death right now."

Zakariassen corrected her. "They've already frozen to death."

This figment of the imagination exhausted Anna. It felt like she were caught up in the civil war in Somalia again. Just like then, it was impossible to know where the front lines were. Without a front line, even the most skilled soldier couldn't build a defence.

"What… what's the plan now?" Zakariassen asked.

A forceful storm gust shook the cabin. The doors of the drying machines rattled. It smelt of wet wool. Anna gave up trying to understand everything, shuffling through the simplest pieces of the puzzle first.

"First priority is communication. We need to get the radio working," she said. "We shouldn't split up, but this fucking storm is at least giving us one advantage. If the killers are off the base, they can see just as little as we can."

Zakariassen stood still and looked at the light from his torch. His mouth moved, forming a few silent words. Anna had the feeling that he wanted to say something that he was finding difficult to articulate. He gave up too.

"Understood. It's probably best that I go back to *Sabvabaa* and try to find out what has happened with our radio antenna," he said.

"Do you need any help?" Her question arrived without any great conviction. Anna's technical skills with radios were limited to changing frequencies and batteries.

"It's better if you stay here and look after the Chinese guy."

Zakariassen slung the Mauser over his shoulder. The light strobing through the snow sparkled with a blue tinge across the gun's metal. Anna walked towards the door, feeling the cold as she grabbed the handle. She had to fight hard against the air pressure to push the door open. The wind immediately found a way into her ski goggles and mask. The cold sliced a circle around her face. She kept her mouth closed and breathed through her nose.

Outside, there was nothing unusual to see. Anna was already considering the three corpses in the middle of the yard as a permanent feature of the base. The cold would freeze them hard into the ice they were lying on, and the snow would bury them.

"Clear."

She turned and waved Zakariassen out. The barrel of his gun emerged from the dark, followed by his stooped figure, hanging on to the other end. As soon as he took a step outside into the yard, the storm wind dragged the skinny man with it like debris in a flooding river.

"Turn the radar on," she yelled after him. "If they are coming back, then we'll see them." The killers had already become "them". Strangers with familiar faces. The nasty neighbours down the street who you wish would sell up to clean-living Christians.

Zakariassen motioned with one arm to show that he had got the message, before being swallowed by the snow and the dark.

25

Jackie was still sleeping when Anna returned. She stood watching him. In the army, she had always been admired for her ability to read people. In a tense situation, it could mean the difference between life and death. Now she needed to know if this puny man was really capable of killing all the others.

She tried to see under the skin of his pale face, peeling off the mask to reveal his insides, but Jackie wasn't about to give up any secrets. Her eyes glided across his smooth skin like a wet bar of soap, down to the bloodied bandage. What Anna could see was a slightly feminine-looking Chinese man who, right now, was hovering in a strange limbo between life and death.

After double-checking that the plasma was still running into his veins, she pushed a hand down into his pockets. She pulled out a pack of Chinese chewing gum, a lighter and cigarettes in a waterproof bag, a mobile phone, the key to a padlock—nothing that might tell her whether the unconscious man was a killer.

She took the magazines and books out of Jackie's cabinet.

There was a magazine called *Popular Science* with the image of the English film star Simon Pegg posing in a *Star Trek* uniform on the front cover. "The Dark Side of Virtual Reality" was the headline. Three more magazines were different editions of the American technology magazine *Wired*. The last was the finance fortnightly *Forbes*. "Rich List!" screamed the yellow lettering on the cover. One page had its corner folded in as a bookmark. An illustration of a futuristic ship. A yacht floating in a river sur-rounded by dense jungle.

All of Jackie's books were in Chinese and, from the illustrations and pictures, Anna concluded that they were technical manuals about data systems. Only one stood out. On the cover were three Chinese characters. She flipped through and noticed that Jackie had underlined the text in several places.

As she flicked through, a glossy picture slipped out. It was photograph of a woman talking on her mobile as she walked along a seafront. The woman was white, with long blonde hair, and was dressed in tight-fitting jeans with a low-cut blouse beneath a suit jacket. Her eyes and most of her face were hidden behind large sunglasses. Her broad shoulders made Anna think that the woman was or had been either a swimmer or gymnast. Behind her, tall palm trees reached up into a bright-blue sky as a muscular man roller-skated in the opposite direction. Anna guessed that the picture was taken in California, on Venice Beach or somewhere similar. She turned the photo over, but there was nothing on the reverse side. It seemed to have been taken without the woman's knowledge, with a telephoto lens from a long distance. Maybe she was a celebrity Jackie was stalking?

The book and the photograph had to mean something special. She decided to ask Jackie when he woke up, and stuffed them both into her breast pocket.

The sickly smell of blood grew stronger as she walked over to the dead man. She knelt, looking under his bed. The two bullets that had killed him had gone through the base of the bed and into the floor. By pushing a finger down into one of the holes, she discovered that the cabin floor was made of plastic. The bullets were probably buried in the ice underneath. Her gaze panned over to the partly disassembled nail gun that was lying on the floor next to the bed. Why was it here and not in the workshop?

She collapsed by Jackie's bed, exhausted. She looked at her watch. The hand on its green face was ticking towards 7 a.m.

With her head resting on the bedhead, she attempted to connect the threads of the bloody chaos. Above her the trusses supporting the roof vibrated in the storm wind. A pair of long johns, hung up to dry, swayed slowly. The cabin creaked at its joints. In Anna's mind, the threads ended in nothing but impossible knots.

Suddenly she felt something damp beneath her.

Turning over, she saw black water bursting up through the bullet holes under the bed. The water was rushing across the floor towards her. She tried to get up but her body was crippled. The water level was rising, running in through the open zippers on her chest, ice-cold against her neck. She tried to shout, but her throat, too, was paralysed. Seawater streamed over her face. Her vision blurred as the water covered her head. Beyond the window of the swamped cabin, she saw glowing flames reaching up from the deep. A sharp pain arced across her chest. Her lungs were void of oxygen. She opened her mouth and the briny seawater poured in.

"Anna."

She woke up. Seeing a pale, blurry face above her, she kicked out in a panic with both legs, striking the stranger. He groaned, reeling backwards.

"Jesus Christ, take it easy Anna—it's just me."

Her vision cleared to see Zakariassen standing over her. "Sorry, Daniel, I must have dropped off." She peered at the clock groggily. It had only been twenty minutes, but felt like hours.

She stood up. Her eyes tingled. Insects crawled in her stomach. Hunger. If she was going to stay sharp, she would have to eat soon.

"I… I got through on the radio," said Zakariassen as he blew warm air onto his hands.

The words made Anna forget her appetite.

"Fantastic, Daniel!"

In her excitement she slapped him on the back, but he pulled away as though he were in pain.

"The antenna cable had been ripped off, but I was able to splice a temporary connection. The reception was extremely bad, but I got through to the American coastguard. They said when the storm subsides they can send helicopters from Greenland."

"You told them what happened here?"

"Yes, yes… that we found the crew dead, one survivor… that the killers have fled in a vehicle. The Americans were trying to make contact with the Chinese and get confirmation of the size of the Ice Dragon crew."

Zakariassen removed his glasses and began wiping off the snow and condensation. Without them his face had the look of a child's, as if his age and all his knowledge were moulded into the thick lenses.

"Did they tell you to do anything about… him?" They both looked at Jackie, sleeping motionlessly in his bed. The only sign of life was the rise and fall of his chest.

"No, just that we have to try as hard as we can to keep him alive."

Anna looked out through the cabin window. The snow was lashing past as thickly and impenetrably as before.

"Good. We can survive three or four hours with what we have here. The smartest thing to do now is to repair *Sabvabaa* as fast as we fucking can and get back out onto the ice. Much better to defend ourselves out there than sit here waiting for the two missing ones to suddenly show up."

Zakariassen pushed his glasses back onto his nose, looking out of the window. "Unfortunately there's bad news too. I checked. The spare fuel hose is still at the camp." He looked at her, dejected.

"I can't fix *Sabvabaa*. We're stuck here."

106

26

Anna looked at the beds and the sleeping bags in the cabin. Just a few hours ago, fourteen people had been living and working here. Why had almost all of them been killed? What had made rational scientists murder their own colleagues in a place that was impossible to leave? Where any question of guilt would be solved quite simply by counting the bodies against the manifest? What could have made people commit these horrors?

She felt herself becoming limp and powerless. "I can't think straight until I eat," she said to Zakariassen. "I think there was a kitchen in one of the other cabins. Look after Jackie, then I'll go and see if I can find us any food."

Walking the few metres to the other cabin was a struggle. Inside there were two long tables in front of a kitchen. She found several packs of instant noodles in one of the cupboards. She tore the top off two of them and went over to a large plastic drum of water standing on the kitchen bench. Behind it was a stack of plates. As though someone had been interrupted when they were about to set the tables.

Yann was standing with a pile of plates in his hands when Anna and Geir entered the kitchen.

"You're early," he said, shoving the dishes under the kitchen bench.

"No, we're actually half an hour late," she said, a little too harshly.

Yann looked at his watch, surprised. "Sorry, I was in Paris at the weekend, I must have forgotten to set my watch forward again."

"Would anybody like some wine?" An older man in an oversized suit placed a jug on the bench.

"Please Eissa, I would." The man, who Anna would later learn was the owner of the restaurant, poured the wine into a large Coke glass.

"The quality is so-so, but then again the Syrian vintage is below par at the moment," said Yann, raising his glass in a toast.

The wine tasted of blackcurrant, vanilla and pepper with a faint aftertaste of plastic. Yann raised a glass and put his arm around Eissa. The restaurant owner had bits of toilet paper on his chin, nicks from the mandatory beard he had not been permitted to shave off until today. The gruesome years of IS occupation were over. "Cheers to Eissa for letting me borrow his kitchen."

"I would do anything for Yann. He saved my daughter's life," said Eissa.

Yann brushed off the praise and set four bloody hunks of meat in a large iron pan set over a gas burner. The meat sputtered and soon the fragrance of lamb and coriander was wafting through the room. For Anna, who had been living on battle rations for the last week, this was heaven. She forced herself to eat slowly, committing the taste to memory. After a few mouthfuls she noticed that Yann was staring at her in curiosity, a chef awaiting the verdict.

"It tastes absolutely wonderful," she said. "Where in the world did you get hold of such good meat?"

"I know a shepherd a few kilometres outside the city. He gave me a lamb." There and then Anna knew that Yann Renault was someone who could wind up in the most desolate place on the planet and still make friends with hundreds of people in a few days.

When Yann had first invited her to dinner, she said no. He had playing at being offended. "Oh no, you have no choice. You saved my life, the least I can do in this damn place is to make you some decent food." The invitation came after she had stumbled upon the French doctor inside a Free Syrian Army tank, having a heated exchange via a borrowed radio. He was trying to convince his boss that it was safe for Médecins Sans Frontières to operate in Raqqa. Half an hour earlier, from her observation post on the roof of a house, Anna had seen Yann sprinting with a child in his arms. She had also seen the spray of stones flying up behind him, kicked up by bullets from an IS sniper's rifle. If she hadn't returned fire and forced the sniper to take cover, Yann would have been killed.

"Thank you so much, never has a more beautiful angel watched over me," was his response when he realized how close death had come. The flirtatious Frenchman made her blush.

It was Geir, a jovial guy from the sticks and her right-hand man at Special Command, who had talked her into it. He had witnessed Yann's rash, heroic deed too.

"Come on, chill out a little, Anna. What's wrong with eating dinner with a friendly Frenchman?" Yes, what *was* wrong with it, really? She had already fallen for Yann. She had already begun to believe in a future. In another life.

After they had eaten, Yann went over to an old 8-track standing on a rickety sideboard behind the kitchen bench. He wiped his hands carefully on a kitchen towel before threading a new tape reel into the player and pressing play.

"Whoever guesses what this is gets dessert."

The sound of a sorrowful clarinet floated out from the single speaker. After a while, a saxophone joined in. The atmosphere lightened a little, as if the sun were suddenly rising in the depths of a dark night. Geir groaned. "It's music, I know that for sure."

"Leonard Bernstein, the soundtrack to *On the Waterfront*," said Anna.

Yann looked at her, surprised. "Absolutely correct! Fantastic! Are you a musician?"

"No, but my mother was. She loved soundtracks. I grew up with all the classics. *Casablanca, Doctor Zhivago, Lawrence of Arabia*—I've heard them all hundreds of times."

The sound of raucous voices could suddenly be heard from outside the restaurant. The owner went for the door but before he got there it swung open and several women in uniform streamed in. Most of them had Kalashnikovs slung over their backs, and some were holding cans of Heineken. All of them were in high spirits.

As Eissa tried telling the soldiers that they were gatecrashing a private party, Yann shouted, "No, it's OK," and waved the women in. "These are the heroines of the liberation of Ain Issa. They deserve a party."

Yann, of course, knew several of the women in the YPJ, the Women's Protection Unit, a strictly female force that fought in Syria as part of the Syrian Democratic Forces, an alliance of Kurdish, Arab and Syrian militias. He introduced Anna and Geir to the commander, a short woman with large, heavily made-up eyes. If it hadn't been for the uniform and the Kalashnikov, Nuhad could have passed for a teenager. Her company had been at the front line when the jihadis were fought back in Ain Issa; now they would celebrate before the next battle: to liberate Raqqa, where hundreds of people had been publicly beheaded since IS declared the city the capital of the new Islamic State.

Later, Yann put a new reel on. Classical Mexican music, as smooth as liquid honey. "The soundtrack to *The Mask of Zorro*. I love Catherine Zeta-Jones. She's wonderfully beautiful *and* she fences better than most men."

"What does your wife think of your great love for Catherine?"

Anna's eyes met Yann's. She noticed that he had a white spot in his left pupil.

"If I had a wife, she would probably think I was a romantic fool."

"Are you a romantic fool?"

110

"I might just be if the opportunity presents itself."

Out of the corner of her eye, Anna saw Geir glancing at her. She was beginning to feel like a romantic fool herself.

The first sparks of flirtation were interrupted by shouts from outside.

Anna got up and in one movement released the safety on the pistol she was carrying under her jacket. She followed Nuhad out of the kitchen door. A young man was standing in the street outside the restaurant. He was dressed in a Manchester United shirt. He shouted in English, "You have food there? Three days no food." The guards lowered their machine guns. The tension was on the verge of dissipating. As he walked towards the entrance, the man pushed one hand into his pocket.

Two shots cracked as one when Anna reacted, the bullets striking the man in the centre of his chest. The suicide belt under his football shirt detonated, his body disintegrating. The pressure of the blast blew out every window in the restaurant. Anna's face was speckled with something damp. Blood.

She felt a cold fluid running over her hand.

The mug of noodles was full. She pushed it to one side and filled the other one too. She placed both mugs in a stainless steel microwave oven, fumbling around with the unfamiliar buttons before she got it working. She was thinking about Yann. She could still picture his face as clear as day. The unruly curls. The large eyes with laugh lines around them. Would she ever forget him? Would she ever want to?

The microwave beeped.

She slurped up the scorching-hot noodles as she stood at the kitchen bench, feeling the warm food in her belly, sensing her energy return. She heated up two more cups and took them back to Zakariassen. They cooled down on the way there, but he wolfed them down without complaining. He smacked his lips loudly as he sucked up the last of the noodles. "Thanks for that. It's only now I realize how hungry I was." He yawned. Anna felt the wooziness too. In all the tension, they had forgotten to eat, and now came the urge to sleep.

She tried to shake the tiredness out of herself, but the wind's monotonous howling was making her eyes droop.

"We need to get outside."

"What?"

"If they're coming we have to keep a lookout."

Zakariassen groaned loudly, but didn't argue.

Scarcely an hour later, Anna had to admit that even if she and Zakariassen had been two elite soldiers with the best polar equipment that military budgets could afford, they would have lasted half an hour max on watch in the storm. For a retired professor without a gram of fat on him and an ex-soldier who had been out of training for two years, it was simply impossible. The biting cold and the storm wind drained her of her energy and vigilance in just a few short minutes, not to mention the frozen sores that cut into her face.

"This is not fucking working. Once more out there and I'll freeze to death. We need the trip flares," she groaned as the door to Jackie's cabin banged shut behind her. She was shivering uncontrollably after having being on watch for less than fifteen minutes. "If we set them up around the cabin here, we'll get a warning if they come back."

"No, I'm totally finished. I can't bear to be outside a moment longer." Zakariassen's voice was pained and hoarse. Anna felt her teeth chattering.

"Let's solve one problem at a time."

"Then you have to go get the flares. I'll stay here and look after him," said Zakariassen, nodding towards Jackie, who was still sleeping motionlessly in the bed.

112

"It's better if the two of us go together. Jackie's going nowhere."

"Are you not bloody well listening to what I'm telling you?" His voice turned shrill. "I can't walk all the way to the hovercraft again!" She gave in. He was seventy-three, after all.

"All right, but don't make the same mistake I did. For God's sake, stay awake. If I'm not back in half an hour, come and find me." Anna jumped up and down on the floor, beating her arms against her body until the warmth returned. Then she pulled the zipper on the thermal suit all the way up, pulled down the goggles over her eyes, pushed open the door and stepped outside again.

27

In order to make her way to the hovercraft as safely as possible, Anna chose a new route. If the killers had already returned and were lying in wait in the dark, she wasn't about to walk into their ambush.

Hidden in the shadows at the rear of the base, she struggled her way through the wind and the snow while constantly watching the perimeter of the circle of light around the base. Nothing seemed unusual, but she couldn't shake the sense of hidden malice. It was so strong that she wouldn't have been surprised if the dragon up on the tower tore itself free and rained fire upon her. The North Pole was unfamiliar territory. Even the ground beneath her feet might be shielding an enemy.

In the first week at the North Pole, Anna had experienced precisely that. The ice had parted and given birth to a warship.

Woken in the middle of the night by a strange sound, she saw the Milky Way arching across the sky outside the windows like a frosted rainbow. The sight was so spectacular that she switched off all the instrument lights in the hovercraft's cabin to try to get a good picture of it.

Through her powerful telephoto lens, a green and a red light suddenly came into focus. They looked like a ship's navigation lights. After checking on the radar that it wasn't an icebreaker on a collision course with them, she went out onto the ice to take a look. After walking a couple of hundred metres, Anna saw a tall, dark shape rising up above large flakes of shattered ice.

A submarine conning tower.

In the only picture she managed to take before the submarine suddenly dived, men were standing with their binoculars aimed straight at her. The Russian sub must have intercepted the signals of Zakariassen's sonars and burst its way up through the ice to investigate who was producing the sounds.

Anna had no explanation for why the Russians dived so quickly when they saw her. Maybe the seamen were from that superstitious generation of old-timers who believed that a woman brought bad luck upon a ship?

Through the flurries of snow, a red and a green light came into view. No submarine. *Sabvabaa.*

When she eventually got the hatch open and clambered into the hovercraft, her body was trembling violently. Thirty rapid push-ups just about got her back some warmth.

The case for her Japanese hunting bow was lying on the floor. The collision must have knocked it out of the storage under her bed. She opened it up and took out the bow, checking if there was any damage. A stupid thing to worry about now, but it relieved Anna to see that the laminated wood was still intact.

After picking up the crate with the trip flares, she sat down in front of the radio transmitter. She wanted to get hold of Boris to ask him when the storm would pass. Her breath froze to ice on the glass above the device. All of the windows in the cabin were iced shut or covered with a thick layer of snow. She wiped the frost off the piece of tape on which Zakariassen had written *Sabvabaa's* call sign in green ink.

"Whisky… delta… echo… four… four… one… four… This is Fram X calling the meteorologist at the Taymyr base." When she released the transmitter's push-to-talk button, its little speaker emitted a pulsating buzz. "Anna to Boris, are you there? Wake up, man, I badly need some help here." The only reply she got was a scratching, popping white noise.

With a map ruler she scraped a hole in the ice on the window and looked up towards the sky, but the dense snowfall was smothering everything. It was impossible to see the Northern Lights, even if they were still there.

She picked up the satellite phone receiver hanging on the wall next to the radio transmitter and punched in her father's number in Tromsø. The line disconnected with an odd *nee-naw* tone.

She tried calling a woman from her former life. The last time she had seen Victoria Hammer was on a dockside in Tromsø. Anna had gone along with her father to take a look at an old fishing vessel he was thinking of buying and converting into a tourist boat. More and more tourists wanted to go out whale watching, or ski mountaineering on the steep slopes of the Lyngen Alps. Both activities required a boat.

"I just wanted to check in with you, Anna," Victoria had said as she was getting out of the gleaming rental car. Victoria Hammer had taken over command of her secret unit after Ola Kaldager. The group, called E 14 in the press stories revealing its existence, was officially shut down in 2006, but unofficially still lived on, and was in rude health too. Ola Kaldager had been nicknamed "OK", so, on her first day on the job, as she was holding a speech for her carefully selected operatives, Victoria joked that she was "KO". The joke stuck. KO had been Anna's immediate superior in the military, and had called countless times trying to convince her to rejoin. In the end, Anna had simply stopped answering the phone.

They ate lunch at a hipster cafe where young men with well-preened beards served Colombian coffee from convoluted machines.

"Did you get the letter saying that the case against you has been dropped?" asked KO as Anna poked at an omelette. Walnut and honey were not her favourite fillings. "It was the CIA who got the military to change their minds. Did you know that?"

Anna had received a letter from the military lawyer, but it was still sitting unopened at home.

"The CIA want to give you a medal."

She hadn't opened that one either.

"Look after yourself. All you have to do is call," KO had said as she got back into the car to drive to the airport. "Night or day, I'm here for you, Anna."

But now *nee-naw nee-naw* crackled from the receiver again. Anna wouldn't have the opportunity to check whether KO had really meant what she said.

"Fuck!"

She hurled the phone across the cockpit. It bounced between the laptops on the frosted worktable like a pinball. Suddenly she got the sensation that someone was watching her.

She turned around slowly. There was nobody inside the cabin. Beyond the windows the snow was whirling, like interference on an old TV set. There was nobody to be seen there, either.

Instinct drew her eyes towards the floor. The sensation was coming from down there, a feeling that an immense evil had come to life and was watching her from below, that some satanic machinery was grinding into life deep beneath the ice. Machinery that would crush everything in its path.

She squeezed her eyes hard shut again and spoke the words Ferdinand had offered as a parting gift as they said goodbye at a military airbase in England, half a lifetime ago. The words that reset everything. The self-hypnosis worked. The anxiety curled up like flaming paper. Concrete tasks replaced the fear. One: set up the trip flares. Two: sleep.

On the way out, she checked the emergency beacon. The green light was flashing more rapidly than she remembered it had been, but it was still flashing. As long as there was still power in the batteries, the beacon would transmit *Sabvabaa*'s exact location.

Anna was beginning to think about how worried her father would be when he found out about the distress signal. Johannes Aune was the only name she had written as "next of kin" on the form the Nansen Center had made her fill out before she was given permission to leave for the North Pole.

A plastic cover on the side of the emergency beacon's transponder had not been closed properly. The thin plastic lid shielded a small screen with three buttons and a USB socket below it.

When she pressed one of the buttons, a text scrolled across the screen: NEED SPARE PARTS. She pressed again: NEED MEDICAL ASSISTANCE. And again: HAPPY HOLIDAYS, GREETINGS FROM THE NORTH POLE. After having pressed her way through five more messages, she got back to NEED SPARE PARTS. There was only one thing written on the third button: SEND.

The transmitter obviously had preprogrammed messages for polar explorers in case all other forms of communication had ceased to function. She pushed the lid back into place, took two steps across the floor and opened the hatch. The ice-cold storm wind burst into the cabin, swirling up loose papers and filling *Sabvabaa* with flurries of snow. On the way out, Anna realized that she had forgotten the crate with the trip flares and turned back to get it.

If that hadn't happened, she would never have heard the alarm.

A persistent beeping was coming from somewhere right in front of the driving seat. In her eagerness to get there, she slipped and fell on the layer of slush that had settled on the floor. She had just got up again when the sound of the alarm died out.

"Fuck! Fucking hell!"

Anna punched the instrument panel in frustration. Beneath the frost covering the instruments, one screen was illuminated. The radar screen had been activated automatically. She wiped the ice away, the cold biting painfully into her fingertips. An old frostbite wound from a godforsaken Afghan mountainside was making a comeback.

At first, all she could see on the screen was the static of the snowstorm disturbing the radar signal, but then, for a brief moment, a red square flashed at the top of the screen. The square vanished, but on the radar's next sweep, it reappeared.

Closer now.

Out on the ice, the unknown object was heading straight for *Sabvabaa*.

28

"Someone's coming!" Anna burst through the cabin door. She had run the risk of taking the shortest route back.

"Who?" Zakariassen looked at her with a strangely confused expression.

"The killers! The radar intercepted something big out on the ice just now."

Sabvabaa's radar was set up to warn of the approach of any large objects within a range of two kilometres. The only vessel that ventured out into the ice at that time of year was the enormous nuclear-powered icebreaker belonging to the Russians. If she were run over, *Sabvabaa* would barely scratch the hull of such a behemoth. Its propellers would mince Anna and Zakariassen and their flimsy boat into shreds of flesh and splinters of aluminium and plastic that would scarcely raise an eyebrow when the crew docked in Murmansk.

Hope glimmered in the professor's eyes. "Could it be the rescue helicopters?"

"Don't think so. The object isn't travelling faster than five or six knots."

Zakariassen grabbed his Mauser and got up. "Which direction are they coming from?"

"North-west, about two kilometres away. If they maintain that speed they'll be here in half an hour."

Suddenly there was a moan. Anna turned and saw Jackie trying to sit up on the bed. Blood from his wound had soaked into the sleeves of his fleece jacket.

"What... what are you doing?" he stuttered.

"Nothing. Just lie down, you need to rest."

Jackie tried to get up but the gaffer tape binding his wrists held him down.

"Why have you tied me up?"

"So you lie still," she lied. "You've lost a lot of blood."

Zakariassen switched off the cabin lights, pulled the curtains closed and looked out. Anna had obviously managed to teach him something.

"We have to get out of here right now!" he said.

"Shh, not so loud." Anna glanced at Jackie. He had given up trying to tear himself free, and now lay staring up at the ceiling. Even if he couldn't understand Norwegian, he would notice the tension in Zakariassen's voice, but there wasn't much she could do about that.

"We have nowhere to go, Daniel."

"What are you talking about? Two killers are on their way here and you think we should just stick around? It's insanity!"

Zakariassen made no attempt to conceal the panic in his voice. The North Pole had its own way of revealing a person's true character. The cold, the endless surround-sound rupturing of the ice and the feeling that the ground beneath you might give way at any moment pared away the layers of civilization from polar explorers until all that was left was the primitive man.

"We have to try not to panic now. Take a few deep breaths while I think."

Anna pushed open the door to the outside and tried looking out. The snow whipping through the floodlights made it seem as though she were on the ocean floor beneath an endless shoal of white fish. She could only see as far as the next cabin, even though it was only four metres away.

What weapons did the killers have?

Where were they going to attack first?

Anna knew that if she had to save Zakariassen's life, she had to gain a strategic advantage with the meagre support and firepower she had at her disposal. It didn't take long to come to a decision.

"We'll have to lure them into an ambush. I'll be the decoy. You shoot."

29

Anna felt as if she had been sitting behind the tractor in the ice-cold garage for hours. It was enough time to regret the decision to let Zakariassen take up position in the warm sickbay, but if he was going to be able to use his weapon, he couldn't be cold. He had been far from happy when she told him what her plan involved.

"Why should we stay here? We've got good clothes, and if we take the emergency beacon and just walk out onto the ice in the opposite direction, the Americans will find us when they arrive," he argued.

"Then what are we going to do with Jackie? Are we taking him with us? They'll find out that we've been here."

Zakariassen looked at her, irritated.

"Jackie won't know where we've gone."

It had begun to dawn on Anna why Zakariassen had never made a career out of being an expedition leader. In stressful situations, his brain turned to jelly. All the information he needed was in his head, but it was clearly impossible for him to access it when he had to line up his thoughts in a logical sequence.

"The emergency beacon broadcasts a signal to everyone," she said, opening the door. "The killers could locate us just as easily as the Americans. You can see the garage door through the window," she said, walking out.

According to the luminous hands of the Rolex Submariner that Anna inherited from her mother, this conversation had been barely half an hour ago.

It felt like an eternity.

The thick hood of her survival suit was wrapped around her face, but not so tightly that it limited her line of sight. The polar wind slithered like cold rattlesnakes across her cheeks. She was sitting on a toolbox, but the cold from the ice beneath her had long since made its way up through the box to her buttocks.

She picked up the bow that was lying on the floor next to her, tightened the string, loaded an arrow and aimed out of the garage. The strong wind would blow the arrow off course. If she was ever going to hit the target, she would have to wait until whatever was coming was within spitting distance.

"Of the two us, you're the soldier. You need to do it." Zakariassen had held out the Mauser for her as she was laying out the plan to lure the killers into an ambush.

"I can't Daniel. Please understand… I simply can't fire a gun."

The mere thought of holding that old rifle brought a cold sweat to her face.

"What in God's name happened to you, Anna?"

She turned away, unable to look him in the eye.

"We can't waste any more time. We've got twenty minutes before they get here, so you and I need a plan."

Zakariassen's face distorted. An impotent anger filled his eyes.

"Jesus Christ, it's just us against two killers who've taken the lives of eleven men! I'm no soldier. I never even did my military service because I'm flat-footed. The only thing I've ever shot at is a paper target when I took my weapons test. There's a hell of a storm out there. I just won't be able to hit anything."

Anna had to give in. The plan was tweaked. She would attack. Zakariassen would be the backup. Hence the bow.

She could see the sickbay, where Zakariassen was hiding, through a small window in the garage door. His orders were to position himself in the centre of the room with his rifle aimed out of the window, a tactic employed by snipers to avoid being seen from the outside. She hoped he wasn't hiding under a table.

Anna thought she could feel the ice creaking. Something was coming.

First she saw an orange light flickering through the snowfall. A red pickup on gigantic tyres that stood half a metre higher than normal came driving out of the snowstorm at a snail's pace. In comparison to a regular car, the tyres were so wide and its proportions so abnormal that the pickup looked more like an enormous version of the radio-controlled buggies that young boys played with. The sight of a truck at the North Pole made her feel like she was in an absurd dream. Its warning lamps sent beams of light strobing across the row of cabins as it drove towards her hideout in the garage. The truck came to a stop in front of the open garage door.

Anna stood up slowly from the toolbox. The brittle plastic creaked in the cold. Her buttocks tingled as blood rushed back into them. She glimpsed the sickbay through the garage window, hoping that Zakariassen had seen the pickup too.

"Stay inside, Daniel. For God's sake, stay inside," she thought.

She crouched down and crept slowly along the side of the tractor. The pickup's headlights cast intense shadows against the back wall of the garage. She hunched herself into a tight ball so that her own shadow would melt into the silhouette of the tractor.

Anna listened for voices, but heard only music.

Classical music.

Music. First hesitant and careful, then energetic and powerful. Tchaikovsky. *Swan Lake*. As Anna crouched against the open garage door, she made a decision. She would go to a concert with Boris. She hadn't been shopping for clothes for an eternity. She would buy a bright-red dress. It would be perfect with the only proper jewellery she had, inherited from her mother. It would be just as good as the black dress she was wearing the first time she met Yann.

No.

Don't even think about it.

Focus on Boris. As long as the meteorologist didn't look like the abominable snowman, it might become something more, too. The thought cheered her up. A simple, tangible goal.

Outside, a man's voice shouted something in Chinese. When he got no reply, he shouted again, even louder.

His voice was high-pitched and grating.

Anna eased the bow out around the front of the tractor. She tried looking past the dazzling headlights beyond the garage door to catch sight of the man who was shouting. Was he armed now, or were his weapons still in the pickup? Where was the other man?

The creaking of a rusty hinge. The stranger lowered the tailgate at the back of the pickup.

One... two...

She ran towards the light.

30

Anna was out of the garage in two seconds.

With the bow poised in front of her, she aimed towards the headlights. It was impossible to see the man standing behind the pickup, and she was hoping that he couldn't see her caught in their glare. She raised her eyes towards the pickup's cab. There was nobody to be seen inside, but the classical music had to be coming from there. Something was rising up over the steering wheel. Something long with a bulbous tip.

A rocket?

In two steps, Anna was next to the gigantic rear wheels. She saw something bright yellow in front of her. The man was still standing behind the truck. In one swift movement she rounded the corner, fixing the arrowhead against his head in pure terror.

"Don't move!" she screamed so loud that her throat tightened as she sucked the cold air into her lungs. "I'll shoot!"

The man turned around. He was short and stocky, a Buddha of the North Pole. His face was obscured beneath the shadow of his fluorescent hood. Now Anna saw that he was wearing a survival suit. The luminous fabric gave him the appearance of an enormous glow-worm.

He muttered something under his breath.

"Do *not* move!"

She approached him with the bow aimed at his chest. Almost point-blank. Even in the violent wind, she couldn't miss her mark now. He began to raise his arms slowly. He had no weapon in his hands.

"Daniel, are there any more in the truck?"

Anna had no idea if Zakariassen was on his way out of the cabin by now, but it was useful to let the stranger know that she wasn't alone. She crept towards him so as not to expose herself to the other man who could be hiding around the other side of the truck. She caught a glimpse of the man's face through the shadow of his hood. He was completely still; only his broad, narrow eyes moved, tracing the path of the arrow on the bowstring.

After checking that there was nobody on the other side of the truck, Anna grabbed hold of his hood and turned the man around. A forceful kick between the legs crippled him, and he fell face-forward. Her foot shoved him hard into the snow.

"Come out or I'll shoot him!" she growled towards the cab. *Use overwhelming force.* Her military instructor's eternal mantra. Exhibit overwhelming force, whether you have it or not. Never give your opponent time to think or act.

She dropped the bow and arrow into the snow, pulling the hunting knife out of her pocket and jabbing its point against the man's neck. With her back to the pickup, she felt immensely vulnerable. The second killer might be hiding in the truck, but she didn't dare to turn around for fear that the first would take the chance to kick her legs from under her.

"Who else is with you? Where are your weapons?"

She shouted the questions at the back of his head. The Chinese man said something, but the words were muffled by the snow and ice.

Anna saw a movement out of the corner of her eye. It was Zakariassen, running through the snow. In his oversized survival suit he looked like a puppet, the fabric bulging around his limbs. He ran stiffly with the Mauser in one hand and stopped in front of the man lying in the snow. "You… you damn well got him."

"Check the truck, see if there are any more in there."

"Who is he?"

"Listen to me now, for fuck's sake! Make sure there's nobody else in the truck."

At long last Zakariassen got the message. She heard his footsteps walking away. The knife was now poised against the killer's back and she refused to take her eyes off it for a single moment. Her boot rose and fell in rhythm with his breathing. She could almost feel the evil burning up through the sole, as if his wickedness would soon spread into her bones. Instinctively she lifted her foot a little and the man immediately tried to roll around.

"Don't move!" She shoved her foot down again.

Zakariassen yelled from behind. "Anna, look at this!"

"Have you checked the truck?"

"Please... Anna... you need to see this!"

She turned her head without moving her foot, without easing the force against the knife. The edge of her hood blocked her view and she could barely see Zakariassen. He was standing in front of a billowing canvas on the truck bed, the Mauser useless in his hands.

In the bright floodlights, Anna could clearly see a pair of green sneakers poking out from under the tarp.

31

There was a body on the truck bed. Anna could see white legs in the green running shoes protruding from under the flapping tarpaulin. The last man. She dug her foot as hard as she could into the beast in the snow. The killer groaned.

"Who is this?"

The monster mumbled something.

"Gai Zhanhai is…"

"What?"

"His name is Zhanhai… He's dead."

"Why did you kill him?"

"I didn't kill him… I found him."

"I don't believe you!" she roared.

"It is true… I didn't kill him."

"Who are you?"

"Zheng… Marco." His voice was strangely calm, as if it was normal to reply to murder accusations face down in the ice-cold snow in the middle of a snowstorm.

"Is your name Zheng or Marco?"

"Foreigners call me Marco," he said.

Anna was seized by such a burning rage that she pushed the knife's point hard, cutting through the fabric of his survival suit and making him yelp.

"Why did you kill him, Marco?"

"I didn't kill him. He was dead when I found him. A polar bear got him."

For a moment Anna considered telling the man in the snow that she knew everyone on the base had been killed, but the cynic in her decided it was a better idea to see how the killer reacted when he met Jackie. What would he do when he realized that one of his victims was still alive? That was a better plan. But why should this monster be granted the mercy that his victims never were?

She held the knife steady in her hand. Marco wasn't even human. He was the enemy. The puzzle of the laundry schedule had worked out. Two men were missing. Two came back. One alive, one dead. The killer and his final victim. In wartime, this was plenty of proof. Anna saw the look on Zakariassen's face, staring rigidly at her, not Marco, and bracing himself.

The professor would back her up. This was about self-defence. About all the bodies they had found. The evidence that Jackie had been shot.

It was beyond all…

A polar bear got him.

…doubt.

She eased the pressure on the knife. Snow whipped towards her goggles, turning the world grey and dim.

"OK, Marco." Anna spoke in a low voice, the ice-cold air grating against her voice box each time she breathed in, sore from all the yelling.

"This is what's going to happen now. First I'm going to take my foot off your back, and then you'll roll over… If you try anything at all, I'll kill you… Don't think that I won't just because I'm a woman… You understand me, Marco?"

"Yes."

She took her foot off his back and stepped away as Marco rolled over.

"Keep your hands away from your body."

The Chinese man, Zheng and Marco, did as he was told. With his short arms and thick body, he looked like an overgrown child lying on the ground. A well-wrapped, fluorescent toddler making angels in the fresh snow. His face was square, and beneath a small

131

mouth, a goatee beard curled up at its tip. But for the missing horns on his temples, he could have been a devil.

"Daniel, come here!" yelled Anna with the little that was left of her voice. She didn't take her eyes off Marco, but sensed Zakariassen coming up to her.

"Look in his pockets. Check inside the suit too—check everything." The man lay completely still, not even trying to protect himself from the snow that was lashing down.

"Marco, my partner is going to search you... Don't move and don't try anything stupid... You got me, Marco?"

His big head moved slightly inside the hood. Anna took it for a yes, but jabbed the point of the knife against his stomach to be sure he got the message. He lay in the snow, immobile.

"Empty his pockets, Daniel."

Zakariassen was glued to the spot. "He's dangerous," he said.

"I know that—that's why I want you to frisk him."

"He's a mass murderer... We ought to... get rid of him." Precisely what Anna had been thinking a moment ago, but the words of the placid professor sounded ridiculous now.

"No!" she screamed, mostly to silence the voice inside her. "Do as I say! Empty his pockets!"

Zakariassen grunted reluctantly as he bent down and began searching Marco. The Chinese man's suit had two pockets on the outside. The zippers had small red rags hanging from them, making them easier to open with gloves on. In one outer pocket Zakariassen found a waterproof torch and a bag of nuts. In the other, a monkey wrench and a small electric drill.

He put the objects on the ice as he pulled them out. They were soon dusted by the blasting snow.

When Zakariassen pulled down the zipper on the survival suit, there was a red football shirt under it. It was bright red, the number 21 printed in a white circle across his pot belly. The Chinese man looked like a human pool ball.

Zakariassen stuffed his hand into the inner pocket and pulled out a mobile phone. "I've searched everywhere now. There's nothing else."

With some effort, he stood up. Anna saw a red flap on the thigh of Marco's survival suit. Under it, the fabric bulged.

"Check the thigh pocket too."

Zakariassen grunted and bent down tensely again. Taking hold of the red flap, he pulled open the zipper and pushed his hand into the pocket. When he pulled his hand out again, it was grasping the grip of a large revolver.

32

Anna found a Russian assault rifle inside the cab of the pickup, a Kalashnikov placed on a rack behind the driving seat.

The recording of *Swan Lake* that Marco was playing had now reached the mazurka. Its spirited, warbling tones sounded almost comical out in the wintry hell that enveloped them. The wind was so strong that the truck was rocking softly from side to side.

The rocket that Anna had caught a glimpse of the first time she saw the giant pickup turned out to be a plastic model stuck to the dashboard. The streamlined toy had two spherical bulges near its top and bottom and was illuminated from within, glowing alternately blue and violet.

Anna found a flare gun in the passenger seat. It was open and discharged, but there was a smell of propellant in the barrel and congealed blood on one side of the grip. She left the flare gun where she found it, but nudged the Kalashnikov out of its rack, then opened the back door of the cab and booted it out with her foot. Leaping after it, she kicked it away across the ice until it disappeared under the snow. She kicked more snow over the gun as she noted her position in relation to the surrounding cabins. When the Americans came, they would be able to check whether the ammunition in the Kalashnikov was the same type that had killed four of the Chinese men.

Once that was dealt with, she took a deep breath. The worst was yet to come.

Anna had to find out how the man on the truck bed had died. She walked slowly back to the pickup. Marco had loosened the closest edge of the tarpaulin when he opened the tailgate.

The loose end was now flapping like a bat's wing above the truck bed.

Once she made it over to the bed she again noticed the chalky-white skin above the green sneakers. On closer inspection, she saw that the white skin was the fabric of the long johns the dead man was wearing. For a moment she thought about closing the tailgate, fastening the tarp back in place and leaving it all well alone. Everything would be infinitely easier that way. The murderer was Marco. The proof was the eleven dead and the man on the truck bed. If the Americans or the authorities tasked with investigating the crime scene came to a different conclusion, then that was their problem. Not hers.

If.

Anna hated uncertainty with a passion. When an incident was her business, she hated that others knew more about it than she did. Her teachers, who knew far in advance what grade she would get in a maths test. That first boyfriend, who never told her why he broke up with her. Her mother, who knew why she walked into a store on a warm summer day to buy ice cream for Kirsten and herself but never came out again, abandoning her daughters and vanishing without a trace. Marco, who was the only one who knew how the man on the bed of the truck had died.

She leant forward and peered into the dark beneath the tarpaulin. The dead man was wearing a red and black lumberjack shirt and his head was covered by something resembling fur. Anna had to untie the tarp to reach his head. She grabbed hold of the tarp and hauled herself up onto the truck bed. Her fingers grappled with the first strap. As she gradually loosened the tarp, the wind grasped more and more of it. She hadn't even loosened the last strap before a powerful gust ripped it away, sending it swirling up into the air, where it disappeared in the snow and the darkness in an instant.

The same blast of wind also tore off the fur hat that Marco had so considerately pulled down over the dead man's head.

The nausea struck Anna in a flash.

It looked as though the dead man's head had been crushed in a giant vice. Parts of his brain had seeped out of the skull before freezing solid in his dark hair. One ear had been severed and a frozen, black scab ran from the opening of the ear canal and down towards the throat. One eye had been pushed back into the head, where it had burst and frozen, resembling cold porridge. Above the remaining eye, which stared vacantly straight at her, the vice had pierced two holes in the victim's forehead.

33

Anna tasted an acidic tang in her throat. She had thrown up for the second time since arriving at Ice Dragon. Her stomach was now completely empty and as she puked for one last time, the only thing that came up was bile.

She turned her back to the wind, feeling it tearing at her body, and tried to control her breathing. She looked down at her boots in the snow, searching for some normality in the world. She was clutched by a paralysing sense of helplessness, tears brimming at her eyelids.

She didn't want to do anything. She didn't want to be here. She didn't want to be anywhere. She breathed the cold air in so hard it hurt.

"For fuck's sake, Anna! Either go dig up that Kalashnikov, stick the barrel in your face and blow your ugly mug off right now, or fucking start doing something useful!" The storm got the full force of her words. Once they were out, things began feeling a little better. She turned away from the truck and walked into the garage.

Zakariassen was standing there with the Mauser shoved into Marco's back. Anna had forced Marco to sit on his hands on the toolbox, and he was still there. The inside of the garage was sheltered from the wind, but it was still as damn cold as outside.

What does a mass murderer look like?

Anna thought about this as she studied Marco's chubby face. His dark eyes were hidden in the shadow cast by his fluorescent hood, but apart from his pointed beard, he actually looked completely normal.

"Is he dead?" asked Zakariassen, pressing the rifle into the murderer's spine. Nobody could miss at this range.

Marco looked at Anna with what she thought was fear in his eyes.

"What did you do to him?" she asked.

"Nothing. I found Zhanhai like that. I didn't do anything." His black eyes looked straight into hers.

"Did you run him over?"

"No. No… I was out there to fix an instrument… I saw a flare and went to help. Zhanhai was lying on the ice. He was dead when I got there."

Anna glanced at the revolver they had found in Marco's thigh pocket. It was lying on the floor behind him, the same type Zakariassen had purchased in Longyearbyen: a Smith & Wesson .44 Magnum. Marco's had a dragon pattern etched into the metal in gold. Why did a technician need both an assault rifle and a revolver?

"Zhanhai is almost naked. Why did he walk out onto the ice without getting dressed first?"

"I don't know… I just found him like that. It was a terrible sight." Marco thrust out his arms to emphasize his point, a move that only made Zakariassen jam the rifle into his back even harder. He dropped his arms to his side immediately.

"Did you shoot him first?" she went on. "Let him lie there for the bears?"

"No, Zhanhai was dead when I found him. Check my weapons—they haven't been discharged. He was killed by a polar bear."

Against her will, Anna had to accept the truth. She had already come to the same conclusion. The holes in his head were the marks of polar bear teeth. Unfortunately, there was no way the bear could have carried out the other killings too, unless it had somehow learnt to handle knives, dangerous chemicals and firearms. It suddenly dawned on Zakariassen what she was thinking.

"He's lying through his teeth," he said in Norwegian. "That poor bastard on the truck bed was attacked by a polar bear because he was trying to escape. This son of a bitch chased after him, but the bear got him first."

As a rule, the truth is quite simple.

"Yeah. You could be right. That would explain the flare we saw," said Anna. She wished with all her might that the world would go back to being predictable.

Two men. One murderer.

She picked up the hunting knife.

"Check his revolver."

Zakariassen grunted imperceptibly, putting down the Mauser and picking up the revolver. He tilted the cylinder open. All six cartridges were still in their chambers. It smelt of gun oil, but not propellant. Either the revolver had not been discharged, or Marco had cleaned it extremely thoroughly before he came back.

"How are you able to drive on the ice?" she asked.

"I have radar. If there are crevasses, it warns me."

Anna looked out of the garage door towards the pickup with the enormous snow tyres. She saw a black box hanging at the end of a long shaft fixed to the bumper.

"Do you know what has happened to your colleagues?"

"No. What?" Marco's face changed slightly. With a little good-will, it might have been taken as a look of concern. "What do you mean? Has something happened?"

"Come with me. We're going for a walk."

Anna walked behind Marco and Zakariassen through the deep snow towards Jackie's cabin. Zakariassen's Mauser swept through the snowdrift like a paddle, directly in front of her. She stayed two steps behind him in case he tripped and let off a stray round.

As they walked past the pickup, Zakariassen couldn't stop himself from looking up at what was on the truck bed. As he turned away from it and raised the rifle towards Marco's back, Anna saw his face had turned pale. She put a hand on his shoulder and forced the rifle down. He snorted, broke free and bent his body into the storm wind, taking one slow step a time.

When they reached the cabin, Marco stopped in front of the door.

"Go in."

He opened the door and entered, stopping in front of the bed Jackie was tied to. Anna yelled from outside.

"Jackie, do you know this man?" She shouted as loud as her burning throat would let her.

Jackie didn't answer.

"Watch him, Daniel."

She walked through the door and in a wide circle around Marco. The bed was empty.

34

"Jackie's done a runner. Get Marco out of here—stay against the wall outside and wait for me." She pushed the two of them outside, closed the door and, pulling the knife out of her thigh pocket, backed into the nearest corner and dropped to the floor. She absorbed the room around her, trying to compare each detail with how she remembered it had been barely an hour earlier. Her eyes settled on the linen cabinets hanging down from the ceiling. There wasn't enough space behind them for Jackie to be hiding there. She crouched down and looked under the beds. He wasn't lying low in the shadows.

On the bed that Jackie had been tied to, the tube from the bag of plasma lay in a bright coil in the centre of the bloody mattress. The gaffer tape was still fastened to the bed, but the top loop was wrenched and bloody. The blood must have made the tape slippery enough that Jackie was able to twist his way free.

"We're not going to hurt you, Jackie. You don't need to hide from us. We're on your side!" she shouted.

She waited a few moments more before getting up again. Slowly, she walked past the sleeping bag shrouding the dead man and over to Jackie's cabinet. The down jacket and trousers no longer lay on top of the pile of clothes at its base. Jackie wasn't in the cabin, but he couldn't have gone far. Not in this snowstorm. Not with those wounds.

She walked back towards the door, pulling it open. Outside, Marco and Zakariassen were squeezed in tight against the wall. Their sides facing the wind were dusted with a thin layer of snow.

As they walked towards her, frozen flakes scaled off them. Marco stared wide-eyed into the cabin.

"Come back in. No one's here."

Zakariassen jabbed Marco in the back with the rifle.

Once the men were inside, Anna issued her commands. "Don't say a word to him. Just keep him in the cabin. I need to go out and search for Jackie. Switch off the lights and block the door. I'll knock three times, understand? Don't let anyone in. If you hear three knocks, it's me. If not, just shoot!" Zakariassen blinked as he raised the rifle to his chest.

"For God's sake, Anna, be careful."

"Close the door and wait for three knocks."

With head bowed, Anna walked away from the cabin. Soon she saw traces of footprints that were neither hers nor Zakariassen's. They led away from the cabin and across the open yard. She followed them past the four cabins to the northern boundary, coming to a halt at the penultimate cabin. The generator room.

She needed both hands to pull the door open. As she walked her steps reverberated on the floor.

"Jackie!" A dull echo rang back at her from all the metal in the room. "I know you're scared but it's not me you should be afraid of!" She stood still, her back to the door. An escape route if she needed it. The only reply was the steady hum of the generators. Something shimmered on the floor. The reflectors in the ceiling lights shone in pools of water on the floor. Jackie had just been here. He had been in the room.

"Jackie! I'm coming in now and I'm armed. Come out now if you don't want to get hurt." She stood completely still as she counted out the seconds in silence. At one hundred and twenty, she raised the knife and took a tentative step forward. A creak from below. The plastic flooring was covered with metal grating. She felt as though she were walking across a spider's web. It led

142

her to three generators humming in quiet, repetitive drones. The wet patches continued around the back of one of the generators. Her pulse throbbed in her ears and the floor groaned beneath her. She stopped. Listened. An electric murmur, nothing more.

She moved swiftly to where the footsteps disappeared, then swung round to the rear of the generator. Then she saw it.

There was a door at the rear.

Jackie had gone through the cabin and out the other side. A diversionary tactic to slow her down. She rushed to the door, shoving the handle down and pushing it open. Fresh footprints led past the last cabin and into the dark.

Towards *Sabvabaa*.

"Motherfucker!" Anna started sprinting. The storm pounded at her back like a piledriver, and she had to fight to stay upright. When she got past the last cabin, Jackie's footprints took a sharp turn, going back over the yard.

"Jackie!" she yelled into the wind. Red lights blinked to life in the snowstorm.

A sound travelled on the wind.

An engine firing up.

35

Through the storm, she saw the pickup reversing at high speed. Its rear lights painted the whirling snow red. The engine revs increased as the truck spun around. Anna was dazzled by the powerful glare of the headlamps.

She ran out into the middle of the yard and positioned herself squarely in the bright beams approaching her at breakneck speed. She felt the rumbling of the ice in her legs.

"Stop!" Anna yelled even though she knew that the chances of being heard were slim. In an instant she realized that the fugitive had no plans of stopping whatsoever, even though he must have seen her by now. She threw herself to one side, down onto the snow.

One of the enormous tyres bounced a little as the pickup piled through the snow covering one of the dead men. There was a glimmer of red and silver as the rear wheel struck the corpse, sending it tumbling along the ground. When it came to a stop, its frozen arms splayed out to the side.

The pickup lurched close by Anna. The height of the monster tyres meant she couldn't see Jackie inside the cab. The truck spewed diesel fumes before launching further into the snowstorm. Once it was past, she ran after it. Through a gap in the snow she caught a glimpse of Jackie's head in the rear window. In the silhouette of the powerful headlamps, it swung side to side like a pendulum.

The red snow turned pale and grey once the lights had vanished into the squall, but Anna ran on defiantly. The sound of metal smashing metal boomed through the storm. She sprinted even faster towards the noise, soon catching the red lights again. The truck had come to a halt at a strange angle. The headlamps were pointing skywards.

She stopped.

Stood there.

Heard her breath wheezing inside her head. Her chest was rising and falling against the inside of the survival suit. There was a dull ache in her left thigh.

Cautiously, she walked closer.

Through the storm she saw that Jackie had collided with *Sabvabaa*. The collision had pushed the hovercraft several metres away from the fuel storage. The pickup's enormous front tyres had come to a rest along the side of the hovercraft. Part of the roof had caved in. From the back of the truck an arm pointed accusingly straight at her. The collision had thrown the remains of the ruined man right out to the edge of the bed.

Experience told Anna that now was the time to be careful. If you want to survive, you'd better keep a calm head when the shit hits the fan. But she didn't give a fuck. She ran over to the driver's-side door and wrenched it open. She was in luck. Jackie slid out, landing head first in the snow. He stretched his arms out in front of him when he saw her.

"Don't kill me, please," he begged as tears ran down his cheeks, turning to ice. She considered it for a moment. Get rid of the problem. She had crossed her own pain threshold long ago and now all she wanted was for everything to end. At that very moment, all she wanted was to be back in her room in her father's loft, staring vacantly at the wall, fending off the cold in her body and soul with sweet Russian tea.

Avoiding thinking about anything at all.

"Nobody's going to kill you, Jackie," she heard herself say.

36

"I... I ran away because I was scared... I didn't want to die."

The words were barely audible. Jackie was mumbling them as he slumped over the canteen table, where Anna was sitting with Zakariassen and Marco. The light glaring down from the fluorescent tubes in the ceiling cast a huge shadow around Jackie's forlorn head. From where she was sitting, Anna could only see his nose through the long hair hanging down on the tabletop. There was a rustling from the plastic tubing that spiralled down from the drip bag and ended at the hollow needle gaffer-taped to his skin. She had tried to convince him that he would die if his body didn't get enough liquid.

Now he and Marco were shackled to the table.

Anna had found a chain in the workshop, used a bolt cutter to chop it in two, and clasped it to the captives' legs with a padlock she had also come across. She had pinned the table legs to the cabin floor with some sturdy nails.

Now the Chinese men had no chance of slipping away. Her plan was to interrogate them until the Americans arrived. Get the murderers to confess. She refused to give up before she knew what had happened at Ice Dragon.

Marco snapped at Jackie. She took a guess at the meaning of these unintelligible Chinese words: *You wrecked my truck!*

Marco shuffled inside his survival suit and stared at Jackie, his eyebrows scowling in anger. Zakariassen was sitting on the chair next to hers. The old professor had both hands clasped around a glass of water. The folds of his skin stretched tight as his fingers clutched it, the pale hairs between his knuckles trembling in the light.

146

Jackie didn't reply to Marco's accusations, simply staring down at his feet.

Once Zakariassen had inspected the damage to *Sabvabaa*, he got furious too. "Now I can't reach the Americans. The crash completely destroyed the antennas. The fucking thing needs welding." He shot Anna a look as though he were blaming her for it.

"It's not my fucking fault! Give him a smack if it makes you feel any better," she said, pointing at Jackie. Zakariassen just grunted, looking anywhere but at their captives.

"Both of you have to believe me when I say that we have no plans to kill you. But we do have a massive problem," said Anna. "Five of your colleagues are dead… murdered."

Marco and Jackie turned their heads in unison towards her. Both were acting wary, perhaps afraid.

"The rest of the crew on the base are also… unfortunately… dead. There might have been an accident."

Jackie blinked rapidly as though he couldn't understand what he was being told. Then his head dropped towards the table. His body began to shake as he wept in quiet, sombre sobs. Next to him, Anna saw the fear in Marco's eyes. She tried to assess his reaction. Which one was guilty?

"How?" asked Marco. "How did my friends die?"

"They froze to death," said Zakariassen, bluntly. "Or somebody saw to it that they froze to death." He leant over the table, next to Anna. "There's a tank up in the tower above the main building. What's inside it? What are you using it for?"

Marco's lower lip trembled. He was struggling to stay calm. Anna heard him breathing and rubbing his wet clothes as Jackie cried.

Zakariassen picked up the rifle, set it on the table and prodded the barrel into Marco's chest.

"Answer me. What are you using the tank in the tower for? What's inside it?"

147

"It's a secret," said Marco, eventually. "We don't have permission to talk about it. The commander has given us strict orders."

"He's not your commander any more," said Anna. "Everyone here is dead, except you two. Unfortunately that forces me to come to the conclusion that one or both of you had something to do with the deaths." She was amazed at how calm she sounded.

Marco shook his head irritably. Tears crept out. He struck them away quickly with his hand, clearly struggling to control his emotions.

"No," he said. "Everybody was alive when I left the base. I don't know anything about it."

"Why did you leave the base?"

"One of our instruments had stopped working."

"Why wasn't it here on the base?" asked Zakariassen.

A slight wrinkle creased Marco's smooth forehead, as if he didn't quite understand the question.

"This instrument is extremely sensitive... It's positioned away from the base to avoid interference."

"What kind of instrument is it?" asked the professor.

"A magnetometer," replied Marco, reluctantly. "One of Ice Dragon's tasks is to measure variations in the Earth's magnetic field."

"But that's standard equipment. What can interfere with the instrument here?"

He laid his head in his hands. "I'm just a mechanic. I just follow orders."

"So what happened was that you were told that this... magnetometer wasn't working, so you were ordered to drive over there and fix it?" asked Anna.

"We've had problems with the batteries... They're American." It was difficult to hear him through his hands.

"OK. So when you drove off the base, everyone was alive?"

"Yes, the last person I spoke to was Colonel Hong… the commander… He told me to be careful."

"And then you drove out and changed the batteries?"

"Yes… no." Marco lifted his head out of his hands, his eyes glazed with tears. He looked at Jackie collapsed in front of him. His colleague was resting his head on his chest as though he had fallen asleep. "But… I didn't get there before… I saw the flare."

"What did you do when you saw the flare, Marco?" Anna was exhausted by all the questions. She felt like she was in a bad detective show.

"I tried to contact the base here… but nobody responded."

"Didn't you think that was strange?"

"No, I thought it was because of the Northern Lights." Marco motioned up towards the ceiling with his short, stubby fingers. "The lights have interfered with our radios a lot. It seemed like a natural explanation."

"You're all alone on the ice, you have no contact with the base, and then you make the decision to drive towards a flare over the ice when you know it's full of fractures and crevasses. Alone." Zakariassen's tone was drowning in suspicion.

"My truck has radar. If I drive very slowly it's not dangerous." Marco's head jutted up a little. His goatee beard bristled out proudly from his round chin. "Chinese radar is the best."

Anna's eyes focussed on Jackie. He was still sitting hunched over but had stopped crying. "Jackie, can you help us? Can you remember anything now about what happened when you got shot?"

Jackie raised his head, his cheeks streaked with tears, his eyes bloodshot.

"No. Just that I was sleeping… and then a noise woke me up… a bang… Suddenly someone was in my room, but it was so dark I couldn't see anything. There was a boom… then a terrible pain…

149

then I must have lost consciousness because I don't remember anything else." The words came out in fits and starts. He had to stop to catch his breath and it was clear he was in enormous pain. "When I woke up everything was quiet… I was bleeding… I… I screamed for help, but nobody… Guan was next to me… He was dead."

The way Anna saw it there was only one thing she could be sure of. The man who had killed five people, the same man who was possibly behind the gruesome deaths of the ice men, was one of the two sitting in front of her now. Either little Jackie, who insisted some unknown, faceless man had shot him, or Marco, the cool, calm Buddha figure who maintained that the only reason he wasn't at Ice Dragon when all the others were murdered was a faulty battery. But it didn't take a genius to figure this out. There were quite simply no others to choose from.

"Take Marco with you," she said.

Zakariassen looked at her, confused. "With me?…"

"Yeah. Take him with you to one of the other cabins. I want to talk to Jackie alone."

37

Anna stared at Jackie.

She was sitting in the chair directly across from him, separated only by the tabletop. He was looking alternately at her and elsewhere in the room, occasionally raising his hand to brush his hair away from his eyes. His breath was quick, but steady, like a small animal with a racing heartbeat. Her eyes fell to his hands. They were small, with long, slender fingers.

Jackie was the first to break the silence. "What do you want?"

"I want to know who you are."

"My name is Jackie."

"I'm pretty sure you have another name too."

His eyes roamed the room again, landing back on her. Now there was something defiant in them.

"Who are you to be asking all these questions?"

"I've already told you... My name is Anna Aune. I'm Norwegian."

"Are you from the police?"

Anna wondered whether she should lie, and chose a half-truth instead. "No, I'm from the Norwegian Armed Forces... the military."

"You're a soldier?"

"I'm asking the questions here, Jackie."

His mouth narrowed into one thin line. His eyes turned glassy. A tear leaked down one cheek, but Jackie just let it run.

"Are you in pain?"

"I'm thinking about what happened... Why were my friends killed?"

More tears trickled down, but now he was looking her in the eye. She felt like a bitch.

"Jackie, I hate this as much as you do, but you and Marco are the only survivors. If there's an answer to all of this... then the only people who can give it to us are you two."

He blinked, taking his time to wipe away the tears. "You think that I... killed my own friends?"

"I don't think anything. I just want to know your name and what you're doing here on the base."

He looked down at his hands, picking at something invisible on a nail.

"My name is Shen Li. I'm a data technician."

"Saying you work in data these days is like saying you breathe. What kind of data do you work with?"

The words suddenly poured out of him in a clear American accent. "I have a master's in geology with a specialization in remote sensing... so... the collection of geological data via satellite, sonar, telemetry and seismology."

"Wow, very impressive, Jackie. Where in China did you study?"

"I took my master's at UCLA, one of the best universities in the world. Very few Chinese get permission to study there."

"Very few get in no matter where they come from, I would say. I can guarantee you I would never have been accepted." Anna smiled at him. It's vital to establish a relationship of trust with the subject. All those hours of interrogation training were finally paying off.

"Of all the things you could have studied, how did you end up with geology as your thing?"

"My father had a mine... I grew up surrounded by rocks. My father wanted me to become a geologist and take over the business."

"But now you're... at the North Pole?"

His eyes explored the room again.

"My dad died."

The way the words came out got Anna thinking that this was a story she ought to pursue.

"I understand—your mother couldn't keep the mine going then."

His eyes circled back to her. So did the defiance.

"I grew up in Gejiu... It's a city in the Yunnan mountains. In China they call it Tin Town. We've been digging tin out of the mountain there for over a hundred years. But who needs it these days? The day I realized that tin was finished was the day I decided to choose a different path... I studied theoretical mathematics at Beijing University of Technology, against my father's will. But... just before I was due to come home to Gejiu to celebrate New Year... our house burned down. My mother and father died in the fire..." His voice grew weaker as he fought with his emotions. "I think it was God's punishment... because I didn't do as my father wished. So... after that... I applied to study geology at East China University of Science and Technology in Shanghai. I came second in the class and was lucky enough to get a grant to study in the US. After graduating I was offered jobs in a lot of big American companies, but I went home again because that's what my father would have wanted. Then this opportunity came along... so I offered my services at the North Pole because I wanted to honour my father's memory."

Behind the tears, his eyes were blazing.

38

"I was born Zheng He... but that's not me any more. Everyone calls me Marco. Marco Polo was my hero when I was young."

The words reeled out of Marco as soon as Anna had him on his own. He was looking at her as if he were trying to guess what she wanted to know before she had a chance to ask any questions.

"You're Chinese—so why do have an Italian hero?"

"I'm three-quarters Chinese. My grandfather was a monk in Tibet."

"Oh yeah? I thought Buddhist monks weren't allowed to have children."

"China invaded Tibet, but my grandfather was part of the uprising in 1959. He was sent to jail and forbidden to practise as a monk again. So he became a trader and travelled around China until he met my grandmother." He folded his hands and looked at the ceiling. "And Marco Polo wasn't Italian at all, he was Venetian. Venice was an independent republic for a thousand years."

"OK, Marco... so you've revealed how little I know about your hero... and Italy."

He smiled again. "One day I'm going to follow in Marco Polo's tracks."

"Since you're so specific about everything, let me make a small correction... They're called footsteps. You're going to follow in Marco Polo's footsteps."

"No, I'm going to drive my motorbike from China to Venice, in Marco Polo's tracks." He cackled.

"What are you doing here, Marco?"

A tiny wrinkle appeared on his forehead.

"You mean my job… What's my job on Ice Dragon?"

"Exactly."

"I'm a mechanic… I build things… and repair them."

"So you were part of the team that built this base?"

"Part of it… but there were many more of us at the beginning… Everyone came here on *Xue Long*."

"*Xue Long*?"

"China's first icebreaker… *Snow Dragon*."

"So you arrived on *Snow Dragon* and built Ice Dragon?"

"Yes. Most of it was built in advance as modules in Shanghai… but it took several weeks to set up all the buildings and equipment. Ice Dragon is our first base at the North Pole, so it's important that everything is done right."

He smiled at her again.

"Marco, do you know anything about what happened here?"

Anna noticed the wrinkles on his knuckles stretching smooth as he tightened a fist.

"No, everything was normal when I drove out."

"What were people doing then?"

"Some had gone to bed, but the scientists were still working."

"Why were they working so late?"

He shrugged his shoulders.

"There's no difference between early and late here… Sometimes they work late… other times they don't… I don't know why."

"Do you know what the scientists were working on?"

He unfolded his hands, laying them side by side on the table. "They don't tell me much. I'm just a mechanic."

"Then tell me the little that you do know."

His hands found each other again. "Ice Dragon's mission is to investigate the North Pole. We're measuring the ice and the radiation from space."

"Why?"

The wrinkle reappeared on his smooth forehead.

"What do you mean, why?"

"Why is China building a huge base at the North Pole to research things that many other countries have researched before?"

For the first time, a hint of irritation appeared on his face. "Do we not have the right to be here? Everyone on Ice Dragon signed up to serve our country."

"China chased your grandfather out of his own homeland. Why did you come here and not Tibet if you wanted to serve your country?"

Marco knotted his fingers, looking away. "Tibet is China. I am Chinese."

After further questioning had brought her no closer to understanding what had led to the crew of Ice Dragon being killed, she brought Zakariassen and Jackie back into the cabin.

"Did you find anything out?" the professor asked in Norwegian.

"Nothing in particular. Jackie is badly wounded, and seems to be the one most shaken by what happened. I can't figure Marco out. He seems to have a different point of view on most things, but neither of them seems to be mentally unstable. Both volunteered to be here."

Zakariassen's gaze followed Anna's as she looked at the two men. "Neither of them has a good reason to become a mass murderer. But who does?"

"True enough, but if you're asking me to make a guess, it was Marco. Jackie had been shot when we found him," said Zakariassen. "Marco came driving out of nowhere with a body on the back of his truck."

"I agree with you so far. Marco's a mechanic. Maybe he had enough knowledge to sabotage the equipment in the main building."

"So what do we do now?"

Anna looked at Marco and Jackie. It couldn't be any other way. One of the them had to be behind the killings because they were the only two of the entire crew left at Ice Dragon. The rest were dead. She wanted it to be true, but a paranoid thought trickled in: *You're not really sure that there were fourteen people on the base.* She switched back to English. "Your commander—where's his room?"

Marco hesitated a little before answering. "In the cabin up from where me and Jackie sleep."

"Keep watch here, Daniel. I'm just going to check something."

Zakariassen looked at her, confused. "Where are you going?"

"Back in a minute."

Anna was out of the door before he got the chance to ask any more questions.

Outside, the storm grabbed hold of her, but she didn't waste any time pulling her goggles on. The wind wasn't as strong as it had been, and she wasn't going far. As she walked over the yard towards the row of cabins up from the garage, she caught sight of something that she hadn't noticed before. A small heap of snow lay piled against this side of the main building's wall, and up against something protruding from the wall further along. The frame of a small doorway.

There were obviously two entrances.

Inside the commander's cabin was a meeting table against one wall, above which hung a large satellite image of the North Pole. The map was dotted with pen strokes and small Chinese flags that looked as though they were marking the positions between which Ice Dragon had drifted. The course that the lines drew looked like a drunk's journey home after a night on the town. A picture in a thick, black frame hung next to the door. In it, a smiling man stood dressed in a brown uniform with a chest emblazoned with medals. The commander.

The room was divided by a large folding screen decorated with a Chinese landscape painting. Fishermen at sea, standing in skiffs, with sugarloaf peaks in the background. When Anna walked around the screen, she saw a tidily made bed. A leather hat with a red star lay on the sheets. Two cabinets, the same as in Jackie's cabin, hung behind the bed. The commander had been the only one at Ice Dragon with the luxury of a little privacy. On a bedside table there was something that resembled a copper trophy, but Anna recognized it as a distant cousin of her own samovar. The table the tea kettle was sitting on had three drawers, all locked, and seemingly made of mahogany. Two forceful kicks broke the locks, sending a shower of expensive splinters over the neatly made bed.

In the lowest drawer, she found exactly what she was looking for.

39

At first, Marco didn't want to touch what Anna was holding out for him when she came back into the mess.

"Those are Commander Hong's private files," he said nervously. "They are confidential."

"I'm not interested in revealing Chinese state secrets, I just want to know who is who," she said bluntly, pushing the crew manifest she had found inside the bedside table into his hands.

Marco thumbed through the folder with an expression that Anna read as alternating between worry and curiosity. Everyone had their own entry, with a photograph and some typewritten text. The commander had made some notes on the reverse side of each sheet.

On one sheet in the middle of the folder, Marco pointed out his own picture. "Zheng He, Marco—that's me."

An old intelligence briefing tumbled out of a dusty corner of her mind. Anna remembered that Chinese surnames always came first. It was also not unusual for adults to assume a Western nickname, one that foreigners could pronounce more easily.

Zheng He, alias Marco, flipped the sheet of paper over and read his dead commander's comments with particular interest. "The commander is quite... satisfied with me." He smiled boyishly and showed the document to Anna as if it were evidence that he was a good man.

"That's good, because we two have a fucking difficult job to do. I sincerely hope you won't disappoint me either."

*

Before returning, Anna had looked through Marco's cabinet too, trying to find something that might tell her whether he was the killer. She quickly discovered that the man was a football fanatic. Football magazines dominated his reading material. A red pennant and a scarf in the same colours hung on the locker door. The outline of an eagle's head was superimposed on the red, and beneath some Chinese lettering it said: "SIPG FC".

At the bottom of the cabinet were two books. The first was a BMW motorcycle repair manual. Anna recognized the classic R12 design on the first page. The other book was not so easy to understand. Page after page was filled with technical diagrams, and the front cover displayed an image of a skyscraper. There was half a roll of snuff on top of the books. The Chinese had clearly picked up some bad habits from the Scandinavians.

In a plastic box she found something she thought was a games console. When she opened it, a small computer screen with pawns on it appeared. Apparently Marco was a chess player. At the bottom of the container, a bundle of cash lay together with a couple of packs of cards. She counted up the ten-dollar bills. The mechanic had brought almost two thousand dollars with him to the North Pole.

She kept a safe distance from Marco as he dug the snow away from one of the dead men. Her knife pocket was unzipped. If he tried attacking her, she would have the knife in her hand in an instant. The heavy blade would fly through the wind and pierce his chest before he had time to blink.

When Anna was last outside it had seemed as though the storm was dying out, but it was just the North Pole pausing for breath. Now the wind was tearing around the cabins furiously, playing the feeble cubes of plastic and metal like instruments in a hurricane symphony. The clattering din of the orchestra invaded her mind, ripping up her few coherent thoughts into their constituent parts so that they were clear and sharp on their own terms, but impossible to correlate.

Anna had to concentrate just to hear what Marco was saying. He was standing with his back to the wind as he cleared the snow away from the head of the nearest victim out in the yard. The corpse was lying face down and it took some time before Marco could turn him over.

A narrow face came into view. "It's Young Chun Li." Marco dropped the corpse and took a quick step back, as if his death were infectious.

"What did he do?"

"Li was head of security at the base."

This perhaps explained the rigid look of surprise on the dead man's face. Being shot in the back was presumably far down on Chun Li's list of possible ways to die at the North Pole.

Beneath his down jacket, Chun Li was dressed in just a T-shirt, long johns and large, unfastened snow boots dangling off his frozen legs. Something had woken him up, and he had only thrown on a jacket before heading outside. He was unprepared to encounter any threat.

The next pile of snow concealed the man who had been shot in the chest. Marco identified him as Deli Denian, one of the base's cooks. The other cook was the man Jackie had driven over when he tried to flee. The pickup's monster tyres had kicked the body several metres away from the others. When Marco dug him out, he turned away as soon as he caught a glimpse of the battered body.

"That's Jin Fu," he said, in such a meek voice that Anna barely heard him above the wind. She stepped to the side to take a look. Jin Fu's head was a grotesque mash of flesh. His forehead had been crushed by the tyres and his brain had seeped out his ears. The tyre tread was clearly visible in the pulverized grey pulp.

Her stomach heaved but there was nothing left to puke up. She breathed in deeply. Air streamed into her lungs, driving razor-sharp spikes into her chest. Marco was standing with his back to the body. It was impossible to see his face and how he was reacting to this gruesome sight. Would he still react with disgust if he were the killer? He turned towards her.

"Fu's wife was pregnant. He was so happy that he was going to be a dad."

He stayed there, looking at her. Anna caught his dark-eyed stare and didn't know what to say.

"Which cabin were they staying in?" she asked eventually.

"Fu and Denian were in the same cabin as me and Jackie. Chun Li was with the scientists, just up from Commander Hong."

The next stop on this wandering identity parade was the dead man in the cabin with all the computers. Marco didn't need to go all the way in to confirm that it was systems analyst Qiang. His job was running the powerful computers used by the scientists. Qiang had been awake and alone when he was killed, presumably taken by surprise. The others had been asleep in their beds, but something had disturbed them and brought them all outside at the same time.

Anna walked out again. The distance between this cabin and the main building was around twenty metres. When she had seen the distress flare a little over twelve hours ago, the wind hadn't been strong. If the accident had happened before Qiang was killed, he would have noticed it and gone outside. He must have been the first victim.

But what about the others? The men who were sleeping. What had lured them out of their beds?

A yell?

A scream?

No. They had been walking towards the large yellow building without fear.

Without weapons.

Someone had called to them. The murderer. Anna looked at the building. What had happened in there that was so interesting?

40

When Marco pulled open the door to the yellow building, the ice man was still in the same spot, his hands and legs frozen to the floor.

"That's our commander," he said after scrutinizing the dead man for a short eternity. "Colonel Ko Hong."

Anna thought back to the picture of the smiling officer in his own cabin. It was impossible to see the frozen man's face without lying on the floor and crawling underneath him, and she had no plans to do anything of the sort.

"Why does a civilian base have a military commander?"

Marco looked at her again with his impenetrable expression.

"I don't know… I heard that Colonel Hong had been on many expeditions before. He was highly experienced."

"Walk in."

She pointed into the murky interior. Marco bowed awkwardly to his commander before walking gingerly into the dark.

"Careful, it's icy," she yelled, but Marco had noticed the ice on the floor before she said it, and was shuffling forward without lifting his feet. He looked like an overgrown child skating over frozen puddles.

Anna stayed in the doorway with her back to the driving wind and snow. His reflective suit made it impossible for him to hide or vanish in the dark, even if he turned off his torch.

Marco stopped when his torch beam hit the first man, the one frozen in the plunging water like a grotesque propaganda statue celebrating an everyday Chinese hero. Anna stepped carefully as she entered so as not to tread on the commander's hands. Her torchlight glittered in the frost on the man's head.

Mist seeped out of Marco's mouth as she spoke. "What... what happened to him?"

"I was hoping you could tell me that."

Marco looked at her until she grew impatient. She waved her hand brusquely, pushing him onwards.

"I suggest you hurry up if you don't want to freeze to death." She handed him the manifest. "What's his name?"

Marco flipped through the pages. The brittle papers creaked in the cold. He pointed out a face, a handsome man with rather indistinctive features, looking seriously at the camera.

"Yunquing... Xiato. He was an engineer."

"And these two?"

Anna shone her torch towards the two men frozen stiff in their chairs in front of the snow-frosted computers. Marco shuffled forward and walked slowly towards them.

"Kong... and Guang."

"They were engineers too?"

Marco nodded.

"That is... was... Lee Deming," he said, pointing at the man lying halfway sunken in the ice on the floor. "Mr Lee was a software engineer. Before he came here he was working for the Great Leap Forward, a very important space programme. China is going to be the first to send astronauts to Mars." Marco nodded quietly to himself, as if this were an indisputable fact. "Mr Lee was highly intelligent."

"Why would someone go from working on an important space programme to being stuck up here at the North Pole?"

Marco simply looked at her. Anna interpreted this as him not realizing that she couldn't understand what he was talking about. She couldn't be bothered to tell him that what she didn't know about China could fill a bookshelf longer than the Great Wall itself.

"The North Pole is extremely important for China. If the ice melts, our cargo ships will have shorter routes to Europe. That's good for trade, the economy and the growth of China." The words seemed drilled into him by rote.

Anna walked over to the corpse. Engineer Lee's face was half buried in the ice, one eye peeking just above the surface. She couldn't say that he looked particularly smart, but death has that effect on people.

She had seen it herself. One moment you're holding a living being, someone you know, no matter how sick or wounded they are. But then something changes in the eyes—always the eyes—something drains from the pupils. They turn dull, glassy, rigid. If Anna were religious she might have said it was the soul escaping. It's some kind of life force, anyway.

The spark.

That person you knew ceases to exist. In death, the body is a mere sack of flesh stuffed with rotting entrails. In that sense, Mr Lee was a little luckier. The software engineer wouldn't be rotting any time soon.

Marco was unable to tell her who the man with the split head and the frozen-solid eyeballs was. When he saw the cracked skull lying under the arm that stuck out of the suspended waterfall, he turned and scuttled towards the door. Anna let him go. He scarcely got outside before he vomited.

She stayed still to give him a little peace. From the doorway, the vision was a grotesque scene of death. The commander on all fours, and Marco's trembling groans behind him, shrouded in gushes of snowflakes that broke around his body like waves against a rocky headland. He was a wretched figure, in danger at any moment of collapsing and being blown away into the dark oblivion of the ocean, deep beyond the melting pole.

When Marco had nothing left to puke, he got up. Anna saw him staring out towards the open yard, towards the three corpses that lay there. He looked down at the crew manifest that he was still holding in his hand, turning around slowly. The floodlights directly above him cast murky shadows across his face. His eyes narrowed in the darkness.

He shouted to be heard above the howling wind.

"One is missing. There's one crewman who's not here."

41

Fifteen crew members, not fourteen. Anna had been wrong to trust the laundry list.

"It's either Lok Yafeng or Yao Lanpo who is missing."

Anna handed the commander's file to Zakariassen when she got back. She pointed to the pictures of the two unidentified men.

"That means that one of them might be the killer we are looking for."

The old man studied the photographs with an anguished look. "My God, will this never end?"

Lok Yafeng looked like a show-off, a man with a crooked smile under a thin moustache. His hair was brushed back. Yao Lanpo was his complete opposite. A bowl haircut ended just above eyebrows that almost met in the middle. His nose was flat, his chin square and broad. He looked like a professional boxer.

Anna studied the pictures, trying to tear one from the other, crushing them like the head in the hall of death, but it was an impossible puzzle. She looked at Marco, who was now sitting with his stubby fingers clasped around a bottle of Pepsi Anna had found in the fridge. He was pale and quiet after identifying the dead.

"Marco, are you completely sure you don't know who the last victim is?"

He looked down and shook his head.

"What did Yafeng do?"

"He was an engineer... and a pilot."

"And Lanpo?"

Jackie's voice piped softly. "He worked… with me. Lanpo was a data technician."

He was sitting erect. Some colour had returned to his face. Either it was the drip that was working, or the Kit Kat Zakariassen had given him while Anna and Marco were outside. The professor always made sure to fill his pockets with chocolate before going out on the ice. It helped against "the wobbles", as he called it when his blood sugar dropped. For one reason or another, it seemed as though the professor was now better disposed towards the man who had destroyed *Sabvabaa*.

"Would it be normal for Lanpo to be inside the main building?" asked Anna.

"Yes, he was on duty. We alternated." Jackie looked at Marco as if he were looking for confirmation that what he was saying was correct. Marco said nothing.

She looked at the professor. All she got was a look that said, "Where are you going with this, Madam Detective?"

Anna continued her questioning.

"Did anything in particular happen with Lanpo or Yafeng before… this? Were either of them acting strangely in any way?"

Out of the corner of her eye she saw Marco glance at Jackie for a brief second. Jackie was simply looking down at his lap as if the answer to everything might be found there.

"Yes," said Jackie quietly. "Lanpo said that… he wanted to kill the commander."

Zakariassen started slightly.

"He wanted to kill him?" Zakariassen's voice soared to a higher pitch. "Why didn't you tell us before?"

Jackie kept staring at his knees.

"What do you know about this, Marco?" asked Anna. He shrugged his shoulders once more.

"Commander Hong was not pleased with Lanpo… He said

169

that Lanpo was slowing down the research," said Marco after his normal pause for thought.

"Very well. How was he slowing it down?"

"I don't know... I'm just a mechanic."

Their eyes—hers sore and tired, his black—met each other. The light reflecting in their pupils gave them the appearance of tunnels boring through a dark galaxy of infinitely hidden secrets. A man who chose to play Tchaikovsky as he drove his truck over treacherous polar ice was not "just" anything.

"But you heard Lanpo saying he wanted to kill the commander?" she continued.

Marco looked across to Jackie again, as though it were he who was seeking permission to say more.

"Everybody heard it... Lanpo was drunk... It was very embarrassing."

"OK... Lanpo drank too much and threatened to kill the commander because he was complaining about his work?"

"Maybe."

"Maybe?!..." Anna's voice fluttered like Zakariassen's up to a higher pitch. With all their alibis and evasiveness, interrogating these two was liking drawing blood from a stone. "Tell me plain and simple: what happened between Lanpo and the commander?"

"Lanpo was disrespectful," answered Marco.

"Was he disrespectful to you both?"

"No, Lanpo was a very friendly guy... He played jazz for us. Lanpo's father is a renowned jazz pianist in Shanghai. He plays at Fairmont Peace Hotel every weekend, it's right next to the old bridge to the Bund—"

Anna cut short his digression at once.

"I could give a shit about his father. I want to know why Lanpo threatened to kill your commander."

Marco looked at her bitterly. "He was disrespectful to the commander."

"But how? What did Lanpo do that was so disrespectful?"

He looked down at the tips of his shoes under the table.

"He refused to take the commander's... dog for a walk."

Anna realized too late the problem with her laundry-list theory—would a man who didn't walk his own dog wash his own clothes?

42

Each time Anna looked out of the window, it seemed as though the darkness at the floodlights' edge was drawing a little closer. It was concealing a disturbed, crazy man. The blackness pressed in against the base like water around an air bubble. She and Zakariassen were trapped, just the same. If they stayed on the base they would be the most visible targets at the entire North Pole, clear to see for miles around. If they left on foot, the storm would most likely take their lives. A rock or a hard place. A sense of having overlooked something important gnawed away at her, but she couldn't quite grasp what it was.

Anna spoke to Zakariassen in Norwegian.

"OK, so we've now identified eleven dead, and one more whose mother would struggle to recognize him," she said. "That one's going be a challenging jigsaw puzzle even for a skilled pathologist."

Zakariassen flicked through the commander's personnel files without looking at the photos. The old man no doubt didn't want to relate to the dead as real people, with wives and children, hopes and dreams, just like him. Once. But he had lost his wife to cancer, and now Solveig was waiting for her Daniel beneath a polished gravestone in the churchyard.

"So the last man in the main building is either… the engineer… or Lanpo?"

"Yes," he said, closing the folder.

"And Lanpo was about to be sent home?"

"If we are to believe these two gentlemen."

Zakariassen looked across at Jackie and Marco. Jackie had slumped down in his seat while Marco studied his captors intently, as if the Norwegians were a couple of exotic zoo creatures.

It is said that the Chinese don't like to lose face or to acknowledge that something has gone wrong, but Anna finally managed to extract the story about Lanpo from Marco. Since day one, Colonel Ko Hong had clearly made Yao Lanpo a scapegoat for everything that had not gone as it should at Ice Dragon.

Lanpo was a tall, broad, slightly clumsy man. He attracted attention just by being there, and since Lanpo had a junior position as a data technician, it was safer for the commander to give him hell rather than one of the scientists, even if it was they who were behind schedule. The scientists were hand-picked and had spent years preparing for the Ice Dragon expedition. If the commander got on the wrong side of them, he ran the risk of being replaced. There were thousands of colonels to choose from in the Chinese military.

The final humiliation came when Lanpo was ordered to take Colonel Hong's dog for a walk. Sunzi was a Siberian husky, and Colonel Hong's pride and joy. They had crossed the Greenland ice sheet together the year before. In fair weather the commander let Sunzi pull him on a sled for short distances. When the wind was up he entertained himself by fastening a paraglider chute to the sled, being blown across the ice while Sunzi ran barking alongside.

After a week in which Lanpo had had to get up at 5 a.m. every day to take the hound for a walk, and was never allowed to call it a day until he had done at least three long circuits around the base, he had had enough. He stole a bottle of surgical spirit from the sickbay and spent the rest of the night getting shit-faced.

Early the next day the Ice Dragon crew were roused by the loud, piercing wail of a trumpet. As they opened their doors in a daze, they saw Lanpo standing in front of the commander's cabin with his jazz trumpet, but instead of playing one of the jolly Duke Ellington melodies he usually entertained his colleagues with, Lanpo was playing a barely recognizable, flagrantly tuneless version of *March of the Volunteers*, China's national anthem.

When Colonel Hong woke up and opened the door of his cabin, Lanpo tossed the trumpet at his chest and bawled that Hong was a dictator and a tyrant who was ruining his life, and that Lanpo was going to kill him. Then the inebriated man dropped his pants and pissed in the snow right at his commanding officer's feet, all the while whistling the same off-key tune.

Hong exploded, of course. Lanpo was placed under confinement and was to be sent home with the next supply plane.

"That explains everything," said Zakariassen. "Something snapped. It must be Lanpo behind all this if he was about to get sent home in disgrace."

Anna looked at Jackie and Marco. For one fleeting moment she had believed that all there was left to do was to wait for rescue and let the police find out which of them had killed Ice Dragon's crew. But now, all control had been stolen from her. The last hours on the base were going to be a race between the American rescue team and the mass killer.

43

"Have either of you any idea where Lanpo might be headed?" she asked Marco and Jackie. They looked at each other.

"Home?" Marco suggested, finally.

"You think Lanpo's planning to find a way back to China?"

"The commander's dog isn't here. Maybe Lanpo took Sunzi with him? To pull a sled with food and shelter."

Anna remembered the sled she had seen in the workshop. "How many sleds do you have here?"

The Chinese men looked at each other again. "I can't remember," said Jackie. "At least one."

"Only a madman would try to walk from the North Pole to China, dog or no dog," said Zakariassen.

Marco broke into laughter. It rang out of him in short, sniggering jolts, like marbles tumbling out of a tin box. "That's true. If it was Lanpo who killed everyone, then he's really a madman."

His giggling ebbed away when Marco saw the expressions on the faces of Anna and Daniel. He shuffled inside his fluorescent survival suit and looked away.

Anna knew that Lanpo wouldn't try walking across the North Pole. No one could survive alone out on the ice in this weather without serious expedition gear. The killer had fled when he saw them coming. That meant just one thing. Lanpo would be coming back. If he wanted to survive, he had no choice. He was alone, but armed. Armed to the teeth. If just one of his weapons was a rifle with a telescopic sight, their lives would be in danger as soon as the storm eased up. Anna knew all too well how a sniper could take cover in the darkness, hundreds of metres from his marks.

She walked over to the nearest window and peered out. Now she was glad that the storm was showing no signs of abating. The dense snow was raking the yard like machine-gun fire.

"How do we switch off the lights out there?"

Again, she got no reply from the two Chinese men.

"Listen! Do you two not understand that if the floodlights are still on when this storm is over, we'll be sitting targets for this fucking mass murderer?"

It felt absurd trying to convince Marco and Jackie to work with her against a common enemy, when half an hour ago they had both been under suspicion. She pulled out her hunting knife and laid it on the table between her and Marco, its point aimed at his pot belly.

"Marco, you and I are going outside to get those fucking floodlights switched off."

He waddled in front of her towards the main building. Snow filled the air so densely that Anna could scarcely see further than a couple of metres ahead of her. The only sign that she was on the right track was the steadily stronger glow of the floodlights. When she saw the building's wall, she began to dread that they were going to have to navigate the ice-cold chamber of horrors once more, but Marco cut across towards the side, away from the door where the deep-frozen commander kept watch over his dead men.

Anna looked around constantly as she walked. The thought that a mentally disturbed mass killer was somewhere out in the darkness was making every muscle in her body tense. When she looked ahead, Marco was gone. His tracks disappeared around the corner. Was he going to try attacking her? She stepped away from the wall, pulled the knife out of her pocket and walked with

176

it raised past the corner. But Marco wasn't there. She could barely see him, down at the other end of the building.

"Pull yourself together, you paranoid bitch," she mumbled as she trudged through the snowdrift towards him. Marco was waving with one hand while the other reached out towards the wall. He was grabbing the handle of the narrow door she had seen earlier and, as he did so, snow swept down from the door frame. When she saw the light streaming out and striking his face, Anna suddenly realized what she had been overlooking. What she had forgotten.

"*Don't* go in!"

She ran towards Marco. He let go of the door, raising his short arms and backing away from her knife.

"The switch for the floodlights is… inside," he said. Anna saw a yellow sign on the door. It had indistinguishable Chinese characters printed on it, but below was the international symbol for high voltage.

"What's in there?"

Marco looked out at the storm. "Circuit breakers, light switches and… something else…"

Anna cursed herself for missing the obvious. The biggest building on the base might have more than one room.

"Something else?"

The words crackled menacingly in her mind. She motioned with the knife. "Don't try anything stupid now, Marco. Just open the door very, very slowly."

He dutifully obeyed, gripping the handle again and prying the door gently open. She peered inside. The room was brightly lit. Yellow walls and a white floor. In the middle of the room, a coil of thick cables and cords hung down from the roof. They disappeared behind two large metal cases that were stacked one on top of the other. There was a computer sitting on the upper case. Judging by the length of the end wall, Anna guessed that the room was around six metres across. The doorway took up barely a metre, so on either side of the door there were almost three metres of external wall.

Now she knew where Lanpo was.

44

War is a game of chess with people as the pieces. In order to win, in the absence of overwhelming force, sometimes a piece needs to be sacrificed. Anna had two pieces to play with: herself and Marco. Prioritizing was simple.

"Turn around and walk backwards through the doorway," she ordered him. Marco stared into the bright room. She was expecting a protest, but he just shrugged his shoulders as usual, turned around to face her, and began backing up towards the door.

She walked carefully after him, making sure to position herself slightly to the side of the opening. If Lanpo were hiding in the room, he would have to spend some time figuring out where she was. After shooting Marco.

When the shadow of the door frame fell over Marco's face, he looked directly at her. The corners of his mouth crept upwards above his devil's beard. A crooked smile. He shuffled deeper into the room. A terrifying thought raced through her mind. If Marco was the murderer, he knew something that she did not: where he had hidden the missing weapons.

"Stop!"

Anna crouched down. Marco kept walking backwards.

"Stop!"

The blade of the hunting knife was suddenly between her fingers, her arm poised to throw. There were four metres between her and Marco. Would she hit? He clearly thought so, and stopped.

He was now standing a couple of metres inside the room. An excellent target if Lanpo were hiding along the wall. Her eyes tried to focus beyond the whirling snow on where Marco was standing. He looked right back at her.

"Is anyone there?"

He turned calmly, looking towards the cables and shiny metal cases.

"No."

What if Marco and Lanpo are working together? Am I about to walk into a trap?

She felt the arm holding the knife begin to quiver. Marco stood still inside the unfamiliar room, awaiting her next move.

Anna reached into her pocket and pulled out her mobile phone.

"Catch."

She threw it towards Marco. It landed on the white floor, spinning a couple of times until it stopped next to his foot.

"Take a picture of the whole room."

Marco looked down at the phone, then at Anna.

"Why?"

Anna shook the knife in her hand in case he had forgotten who was holding it. "Just do what I say. Take a picture now."

He took off his gloves, bent down and picked up the phone. The flash burst brightly each time he took a picture, and the light clung to Anna's retinas. She looked away, feeling the snow hitting her face and the wind blowing the crystals away again before they had a chance to melt. She could just see the garage, its door standing open. She thought about the tractor parked inside. Would they be able to use it to get out of Ice Dragon? How many could fit inside its little cab?

"Here."

Marco threw the mobile back to her. It vanished quietly in the snow a metre in front of her. She had to remove a glove to push at the screen. The cold gnawed at her fingertips as she swiped through the pictures Marco had taken. There was no armed killer on either side of the door.

The mobile died.

The North Pole had sucked the life out of the battery. As she pulled her gloves back on, her fingers hurt. She walked inside, heat returning to her body the second she was out of the storm. As she pulled the door closed after her, the noise of the wind became just a remote rustling. The insulated walls dampened the sound.

The first thing Anna noticed was that a wall covered with hastily arranged insulating panels separated this room from its larger neighbour, the one with the frozen corpses. The cable and cords she had seen from outside ran down from a dark funnel in the roof and disappeared again through a large hole sawn in the ice behind the metal cases.

She walked past Marco and over to the hole to take a look. She could see nothing but her own shadow on the inky surface. The water was missing the slush that usually formed in just a few minutes as the ice-cold air froze the surface water. Powerful electric heat lamps suspended from the roof were keeping the room temperature well above freezing.

Anna felt something dripping onto her neck and looked up. The drops were coming from the funnel in the roof from where the cables emerged. A few metres further up they disappeared into a grey, shapeless mass that swayed in the dark. It suddenly dawned on Anna that she was looking at the interior of the tower on the outside of which someone had fastened the spray-painted Ice Dragon. As she switched on her torch and shone it up into the hole, she saw that the grey mass was ice that was frozen around the tower's girders. The ice was presumably coming from the same source as the frozen waterfall in the room next door. She blinked as several drops hit her face.

Now she saw that the wall panels were dented and had large stains beneath the roof funnel. The liquid that had killed the people in the room next door had flooded into this room too, but the heat lamps must have melted the ice.

She walked over to the laptop that had been left on top of the metal cases. It resembled the lumpy machines she recognized from the military, built to tolerate wind and weather and being dropped from great heights. There was a lacquered box next to it, which she opened. It was a chessboard. Its colours were faded, as if it had been out in the sun for a long time. The pieces were simple, carved out of cheap wood. Instead of being black and white, Chinese pieces were yellow and red. It was one way to kill those long working hours. The laptop screen was dark, but a pulsing blue light indicated that that the computer was in sleep mode.

"What do you use this for?"

"The engineers use… used it to control our instruments… in the water," said Marco. He was still standing in the same spot, in fear of what Anna might discover, or too scared to disclose what he knew the room was concealing.

She turned towards the back wall. Three large metal cabinets were pushed against it. As she approached them she heard a low buzzing from inside.

Electricity.

"Which switch for the floodlights?"

Marco pointed. "The second cabinet… furthest to the right."

She opened the door and saw a single row of circuit breakers.

"The second from the left is for the floodlights." Anna reached for the switch, sensing the smell of scorched dust in the air. Her hand hung there a moment. She turned towards Marco, who still hadn't moved. Did he know something about the cabinet that she didn't?

"Come and find the right switch. I don't want to make any mistakes here."

He walked across the room, looking neither at the hole in the ice nor at the laptop. Once at the cabinet he stretched out his hand towards one of the large circuit breakers. Pulled it down.

The world fell dark.

45

Pitch-black settled around Anna, as if the room had never existed. The ground disappeared beneath her feet. Fireflies sparkled in her retinas. There was an insistent thumping from her own pulse inside her skull. Her hand darted out, striking Marco in the face, then grabbed his collar.

"Don't move."

A harsh humming sound filled the dark, then a green light flickered into life above the door. The room was born anew. She looked around her. Nothing had changed. Nobody had come in.

"That switch wasn't only for the floodlights?"

As usual, Marco betrayed no emotion.

"Our generators are... a little unreliable. The floodlights take a lot of power. Maybe..." He reached out his hand towards the middle cabinet. He sought permission with his eyes. Anna nodded and took a step back, and Marco opened it up. Several of the breakers had tripped. He pushed them back up, and the ceiling lights fluttered on again.

"We've never switched off all of the floodlights before... I don't think the generators managed to reduce the supply... The voltage got too high and the power surge blew out the other breakers." Marco nodded, apparently pleased with his own explanation. Suddenly the expression on his face changed, and Anna felt a cool breeze against her neck. She turned around and saw Jackie's pale face coming out of the darkness. He stopped dead at the door, but stumbled forward, prodded into the room by Zakariassen, who was walking behind him.

"Anna, what's going on now? There was a power cut in our cabin." He stopped and looked around the new room. "What is this place?"

"Not now, Daniel. We don't have time. Go outside and keep watch while I figure this out."

"But why—"

"Listen! If the killer is close, he's already seen the floodlights being switched off. If I were him I would take the chance to get myself over here. So, leave Jackie here, go outside and keep watch until I come. Please."

It was obvious that the professor hadn't the slightest wish to be standing outside alone, but he pushed Jackie further into the room and walked out. Jackie was left in front of the hole in the ice with a down jacket over his shoulders. He hunched his body together, trying to cover as much of his body as possible with the jacket.

"What the hell is this place?" Anna asked. "What are you doing here?"

Marco looked around, studying the objects in the room as though he had never seen them before.

"We're doing research," he said with an air of grandness. "On important matters."

"What kind of important matters?"

"The North Pole is melting. It's important."

Anna sensed a hot-blooded impatience, but tried to breathe calmly.

"I saw a tank up in the tower above here, so I'm guessing that these cables"—she was pointing at two heavy, frost-encrusted cables coiling among thinner leads and steel wire in the hole in the ice—"have something to do with the tank."

"I'm just a mechanic," said Marco. "This research is secret. The scientists don't tell me much about—"

He yelped as she kicked him to the ground so hard that he spun around on the ice like a hockey puck.

"Tell me what the fuck you're doing here!" she shouted.

"We're looking for minerals on the ocean floor," said Jackie.

Marco raged at Jackie in Chinese, but all Anna needed to do was lift a foot to get him to shut up. Jackie walked over to the coil of cables, lifting his head and looking up at the dark funnel.

"Nitrogen. It's liquid nitrogen... in the tank up there. We use it to cool down our exploration equipment." Anna looked down at the ice hole.

"We're at the North Pole. Isn't it cold enough as it is?"

"The atmosphere is, but not the ocean floor. Down there it's no colder than minus three. We're looking for minerals with a brand-new Chinese invention, an extremely powerful geological radar. It generates a huge amount of heat. Without nitrogen cooling, it would melt."

Jackie walked over to the laptop.

"May I?"

He looked at Anna, and she nodded her assent. When he pressed down one of the keys, waking the screen, it displayed a live stream of a rectangular box lit up from different angles by strong lights. Anna saw a long, slender fish swimming slowly through the beam. The video image was coming from the ocean floor. The thought that there might only be a metre and a half of ice stopping her from tumbling down into a four-kilometre-deep abyss was unsettling.

"That box is our georadar. It was invented to explore meteorites," he went on. "But in space you don't need the cooling system."

"So that explains why the rocket scientist was here."

"Yes, it was invented by engineer Lee."

"The radar is nothing new though, so why do you want to keep it a secret?"

"Denmark, Canada, Russia and the US maintain that only they have the right to profit from the resources here. China

185

has almost a fifth of the world's population. It's not fair to exclude us."

Anna leant in towards the screen and tried to get an idea of how big the box really was. She noticed some trails behind it, like those a tracked vehicle would make.

"OK, but conducting research isn't illegal…" The words were had scarcely left her lips when a shot was fired outside.

46

It was a shot from a high-calibre rifle. A moment later, Anna heard an extended howl.

"Stay here!" she yelled at Jackie and Marco, and ran out. Hopefully the fear of whatever was happening outside would keep them in the room.

Her overexerted brain had already forgotten that the flood-lights were off, and she rushed unthinkingly out into the pitch-dark, totally night-blind, threw herself down into the snow and stayed still, listening. The snow settled on her as her night vision slowly returned.

Zakariassen was nowhere to be seen.

She pushed herself around on the ice with her legs, trying to find him. Around the bright cabin windows all she could see was total darkness. Without the floodlights, she was enveloped by the North Pole. The little corner of civilization that the Chinese had built ceased to exist. Now this freezing world was as it was always meant to be.

Ice. Snow. Cold. Night.

A curvature in the darkness grabbed her attention. It drifted out in front of one of the windows. Now, through the snow, she could see a silhouette. Anna fumbled down along her snow-caked body, managing to open the flap of her side pocket and feeling the handle of her hunting knife. She began creeping over with the knife in her hand. The figure in front of the window was caught by the light. In the darkness, he couldn't see her.

"Anna! Get out here!"

The piercing voice gave the figure an identity. Zakariassen jumped as she stood up just a few metres in front of him.

"Jesus Christ, you scared me."

"Was it you who fired?"

"Yes."

Zakariassen's voice was scarcely audible in the wind. Anna stayed where she was with her back turned as he struggled through the storm towards her.

"What's going on? I told you to keep watch outside the main building."

Zakariassen was breathless. Condensation had frozen to icicles on the ski mask below his mouth.

"I was keeping watch, I was, but then came a… I thought it was a polar bear. I spotted it over there." He was pointing towards a couple of bright windows. "It looked like it was coming straight for me, but it was impossible to see clearly. I feared for my life… I just aimed where I thought it was and fired."

"Was that what howled?"

"Yes. Unbelievable that I hit it, but that wasn't a bear howl…" The icicles under his chin trembled. "It sounded like a dog. That's why I left my position, to check if the poor thing was bleeding to death somewhere over here." He shook his head in resignation. "I didn't find anything. It must have run off."

"There's only one dog I know about here, the husky… the commander's dog."

Zakariassen nodded, then looked down and kicked at the snow. "Yes. That must have been it. Poor wretch, it came looking for food and shelter only to get hit by a bullet. Damn shame."

Anna looked beyond his guilt-ridden face into the dark. They were hidden by the polar night, but so too was the other man, out there somewhere. "The Chinese guys are saying that Lanpo might have taken the dog to pull him all the way to land."

Zakariassen looked at his rifle, wiping snow off the barrel.

"That's total nonsense, but if he has tried something like that, maybe the dog ran off… Maybe the bastard's lying dead out on the ice."

"We can hope." Anna turned around. She couldn't see anything behind the cabins, sensing only the ice, and its cold.

This was no place for humans. Even the Sahara was more hospitable. On holiday once in Morocco, Anna had had two Tuareg as camel guides across the desert. The blue-clad men almost always found water in the most surprising ways. When they didn't, they let the camels sniff their ways to water sources under the sand. But ice is nothing more than ice. She couldn't dig down to the warmth. It could be melted and drunk, but the heat had to be brought from elsewhere, and when that was exhausted, the ice would get the better of you.

She gave up trying to see anything in the dark, trying instead to shake the cold from her limbs.

"Wishful thinking won't get us out of here," she said. "We need to get the trip flares set up now. I'll do it if you keep watch in there… and try to find out what the Chinese are really up to. I get the feeling that it's got something to do with why everyone was killed."

Zakariassen looked up at the tower above the main building. The structure was barely visible through dark and the snow flying through the air. "I don't think they were doing much more than us. They just had so much more money so they could run their experiments on a much bigger scale."

"Well, if I believe what that guy Jackie is saying, it's a lot more than that. He claims that the scientists were looking for minerals. They've dropped some radar thing down to the ocean floor."

"A radar… thing?" Zakariassen leant close in to Anna to hear what she was saying.

"Yeah, but what the fuck do I know about that? Best you speak to him yourself."

Anna was sick of speculation. She had to focus on a few tangible tasks. Priority number one: survive.

47

The mechanic, Marco, proved to be a quick learner.

Anna went into the room in the main building with Zakariassen and brought Marco with her to get the trip flares. She showed him how they worked and how to set them up.

Marco set up the next trip flare without any help at all. It struck her how crazy the situation was. A potential mass murderer laying traps for another potential mass murderer.

Anna and Marco worked their way around the base in the snowstorm until they were both so frozen that they could no longer move their fingers and their toes were numb. They had slogged their way around to the hovercraft, where the crashed pickup was still resting up along the hull. The headlights illuminated *Sabvabaa* like a sombre monument in the dark. Anna decided to kill two birds with one stone. The truck could be useful. It was best not to abandon it until it was out of power.

"Let's warm up in your pickup," she shouted to Marco above the wind. She walked to the passenger side, reached up and opened the door. He climbed up on the footboard, but stopped and stared at the dead man on the truck bed.

"What shall we do with Zhanhai?"

"Nothing right now. It's eight thousand kilometres to the nearest undertaker and he's not going to decompose before help arrives." She regretted the words as soon as she saw the expression on his face. "Sorry, I'm insanely tired. We can move him later."

Anna nudged his foot. Marco clambered in through the open door. He got into the driving seat, and as soon as the door closed, everything fell quiet. The windows were covered in a thick layer of snow that insulated them against the growling of the wind. The cab was lit up by the reflection of the headlights, a cold, grey glow like the X-rays the doctors had shown her at the hospital in Germany.

"Entrance wound on the left clavicle. Projectile found in multiply fractured left hemipelvis. Collarbone and hipbone are partially shattered. Extensive internal injuries in tissue and gut, but lungs are unaffected… The gods were smiling on her." From what she could grasp of what the American doctors were telling her, a bullet tearing through your torso was bad news. The only thing Anna asked for was to be filled with morphine. To forget. To forget what happened to Yann.

She noticed that Marco was staring at her missing earlobe, as if her thoughts were escaping from there. He had pulled his hood down off his head. The snowflakes on his face made it look as though he were wearing the same white makeup as the geisha who had served Anna hot tea and warm sake in the anonymous backstreets of Tokyo many years ago.

"Start the engine, Marco."

He pressed a button next to the steering wheel. The engine came to life with an almost inaudible humming. The wipers started, cutting perfect semicircles in the snow on the windscreen. Anna saw the radio antennas lying like felled trees on the roof of *Sabvabaa*.

"You need to get us down from here," she said. Marco stared dubiously. "The hovercraft—can you reverse the truck off it?"

He pulled the gearstick backwards. The truck rattled as it scraped across the hull until it reached the edge and dropped into the snow. The enormous tyres absorbed most of the shock. Anna felt like she were in her father's little fishing boat when it was slapping between the waves out at sea.

As Marco was backing the truck away from *Sabvabaa*, she noticed that the hovercraft had come out of the collision surprisingly well. There was a large dent in the roof above the smashed window, but the boat looked otherwise undamaged. She made a mental note to ask Zakariassen to check if there were a spare fuel hose in the workshop that might fit the engine. *Sabvabaa* was still their only way out of there. The boat could travel for at least a couple of days on full tanks. That ought to take them quite close to the coast of Greenland.

She looked at her watch. Close to three o'clock, but was it morning or afternoon? In any case, the American rescue helicopters should have reached them hours ago. She looked up at the sky, but it was impossible to see anything through the dense snowfall. Even with the best navigation instruments in the world and night-vision goggles that turned darkness into day, the storm was probably impossible to overcome. She put her fingers against the ventilator, enjoying the painful pleasure of the blood beginning to circulate in her fingertips again.

Marco put the truck in neutral, put his hands in his lap and stared at the model rocket glued to the dashboard. The lights in the round spheres at the top and bottom of the fuselage alternated between blue and violet like miniature Northern Lights.

"Isn't it incredibly distracting to have that thing in the windscreen when you're driving?" Anna had no real desire to start a conversation, but was worried about falling asleep in the warmth.

"It was a gift from my father. The Oriental Pearl brings good luck."

"So your father is interested in space travel?"

"My father is a lift attendant. He works in the Oriental Pearl."

She looked carefully at the rocket. Now she saw two small holes in the fuselage. Windows.

"Is it a model of a building?"

"Yes, of course. You don't know what the Oriental Pearl is?" Marco looked at her with an offended expression. "It's the third-highest building in Shanghai. My father erected the bamboo scaffolding for the men who built it. When it opened, he got the job as lift attendant because he's not afraid of heights."

It still wasn't clear to Anna what good it did a lift attendant not to be scared of heights, but she didn't have the will to ask.

"That's why I signed up," Marco went on. He pointed towards the Ice Dragon tower. "Now I've built an even taller tower than my father."

"Eh? Your tower is only, what… twenty metres high?"

"Twenty-two point five five." A proud smile broke across his face. "But Ice Dragon is standing at the top of the world. Above us there's only sky, so my tower is the tallest of them all." He laughed his strange, hacking laughter. Two dimples appeared in his round cheeks. Anna felt the laughter spreading and joined in. It felt good.

"I'm sorry," she said, "for earlier, when I kicked you. I'm not usually like that."

Marco's survival suit lifted around his head as he shrugged his shoulders. In the warm air, a sense of friendship drifted out into the cab. This used to take up a big part of Anna's life before, this sitting around in vehicles, killing time by shooting the shit about everything and nothing. War isn't like in the movies: 99 per cent of it is waiting around, but for a soldier that's often the worst part. It's then that you can start to lose it. Talking shit kept the mind off what was coming.

She heard music. *Swan Lake* was still playing at a low volume. "You like Tchaikovsky?"

"What?"

"The music you're playing… *Swan Lake*."

Marco was smiling. "My girlfriend likes this kind of thing. She thinks I ought to educate myself."

Anna moved and felt something hard in her front pocket, the book from Jackie's cabinet.

"Do you know what this is?"

She pulled out the worn-out paperback. He glanced at the cover for a brief moment. "That's mine. Jackie borrowed it from me."

"OK, but what kind of book is it?"

"*The Art of War*. It's well known in China. It was written thousands of years ago."

Anna closed her eyes, mustering the words from memory. "Hence that general is skilful in attack whose opponent does not know what to defend; and he is skilful in defence whose opponent does not know what to attack."

Marco's dark eyes betrayed a hint of amazement.

"Sun Tzu was required reading at the military academy," she said. "Sun led the army of a powerful emperor, but these days it's mainly guerrilla armies that follow his strategies."

"Yes, Master Sun was far ahead of his time," said Marco. "You know, most of the modern world was invented in China."

"Big words, but what about space rockets and computers?"

"We invented fireworks and the abacus. Same-same, but different."

Anna felt dry laughter sneaking out of her sore throat again.

"You can keep it. I'm no longer a fan of war." Marco handed back the book. She took out the glossy photo that was stuck between the pages.

"Do you know who this is?"

Marco studied the woman. "No."

"Did Jackie ever mention a girlfriend?"

He shook his head. Anna pushed the book and the picture back into her pocket, feeling the exhaustion in her eyes. She bit her tongue to sharpen herself up.

"What do you know about Jackie?"

Marco's eyes looked distant. "Not much… He's a quiet guy. Doesn't say much. He came to us from Mongolia. I think he had a really boring job there in an awful factory. He was very keen to use his training from the US."

"What did he study there?"

"Something to do with geology… 3D data, the kind of thing geologists use to find oil under the seabed." The answer sounded close enough to what Jackie himself had told her. Anna updated her file of mental notes on Jackie. Interested in the art of war. One of few Chinese to study at an American university. An ambitious man.

Then she opened Marco's.

"And what about you? What did you do before you became a mechanic?"

"Am I being interrogated again?"

"Yep."

He twisted in his seat, looking away. "I was born in a shitty little village ten hours by bus from Shanghai. When I was finished with school I moved in with my father in Shanghai. He got me a job with a friend, at a motorbike workshop, so… I became a mechanic."

"You didn't want to study any more?"

Marco laughed.

"No, the only thing I wanted was to get out of that shitty village. It was so incredibly boring there that people would pay to watch paint dry."

"I found a pile of money in your cabinet. Have you been saving up for a rainy day?"

Marco's seat creaked as he turned towards her. "Have you been poking around in my stuff?"

"Of course."

His pot belly pressed against the survival suit as he breathed in. "Fu and me liked to play poker. Sometimes the others joined in too. The deal was that whoever won the most would treat the others to a big party when we got back to China. I'm in the lead."

He grunted a wheezing sound out of his throat. "I was in the lead."

"Well, that's one explanation."

He looked her in the eyes.

"I'm no murderer. I haven't killed anyone."

The red lights of the dashboard lit up one side of his face. One half glowed devilishly red; the other was obscured by the dark.

48

Anna and Marco carried Gai Zhanhai's frozen body back to the garage. She was trying not to think about what she was doing, staring rigidly ahead towards the building the whole way. They laid him down with his battered face towards the floor, pushing his corpse as far under the workbench as it would go. Then Marco fetched one of the sleeping bags from his cabin and placed it over him. With his eyes closed, he remained standing next to the corpse for a few moments. He walked out in silence. Anna pulled the door shut behind him.

When she came back into the room inside the main building, she was exhausted. Doing physical work in a raging storm was like running underwater—everything went ten times slower and took ten times as much strength, and the cold sucked the energy from the body like a black hole in space. It was a small miracle that she and Marco had managed to set up the trip flares around the base without activating any of them.

The room was like a sauna when she came in, and the Zakariassen she found there was now hyped up with purposeful energy. He was bending over the Chinese laptop while Jackie sat motionlessly against the wall on an offcut of insulation. The only thing he moved were his eyes, back and forth between the people in the room.

Zakariassen motioned at Anna to come over to him. "You need to see this. Now I know what the Chinese are up to here."

"Yes, Jackie said they were looking for minerals."

A condescending smile appeared on his face. In normal circumstances, Anna would have found it offensively patronizing, but she was too tired now to care. He leant over confidentially and switched to Norwegian.

"These wise guys are stealing minerals from the Russians," he chuckled. He obviously considered cheating the Russians a noble exploit.

"Stealing?" Anna sensed Marco's eyes on the back of her neck. He couldn't understand them, but he probably understood that they were talking about something important.

"Wait a minute."

"No, come and look at this!" Zakariassen's voice was irritatingly loud and shrill.

She felt tired and dizzy all of a sudden and had to support herself against the wall.

"Give me a moment... please, Daniel." Now it was she who was speaking too loudly, almost as if she were on the verge of losing control.

A memory flickered past: a dark room, and sun streaking through gaps in the blinds. The shafts of light hitting Yann's shoulder as he squeezed through the door with a breakfast tray in his hands. The sunshine meeting his smiling face. Somewhere beyond the blinds, a brass band playing. The taste of sweet coffee as he kissed her. But then she woke up in a dark room. Yann was gone. She could hear the sound of people entering. They were talking to each other in low voices. She tried to ask them if everything was OK with Yann. A desperate hope that someone would reassure her that it had all been a dream. But her mouth wouldn't obey the thought. Something was being swabbed across her skin. It stopped for a moment, then a sharp prick. Sleep liberated her from knowing anything at all.

"Let me do something first."

Anna was attempting to make her voice sound as calm as possible as she tried to rein in Zakariassen's enthusiasm. "I don't want these two looking over my shoulder."

She picked up some zip ties and cuffed Marco and Jackie's wrists behind their backs, then to solid stanchions in the wall. She checked Jackie's pulse—a little on the weak side, but regular—and gave Marco a look that said, "Sorry, but that's how it goes," before walking back to Zakariassen. The video images of the radar equipment on the laptop screen had been replaced by an out-of-focus close-up of a sea cucumber hanging off the side of a rock on the seabed.

"What did you want to show me?"

"Take a look at this…" Zakariassen's slender forefinger pushed a green joystick in the centre of the keyboard. The sea cucumber disappeared in a dark cloud coming from somewhere behind the camera. For a few seconds, everything turned black… then the camera began to float up above the cloud. A dark mountainside slipped by.

"The image is coming from an underwater vessel, a bloody mini-sub three thousand metres below the surface," Zakariassen said with triumph in his voice, as if he had discovered an unknown form of life. He was operating the green joystick with his finger. "I can control it remotely from here."

The submarine climbed upwards. Something glittered in the light. Bubbles from the ocean floor. The air bubbles drifted straight up in tight formations, like smoke from a chimney on a still winter's day.

"You see?"

"Yes…" She looked impatiently at Zakariassen. He smiled back. "Just wait. I'm going to show you…"

He pushed on the controller. The submarine turned. Now Zakariassen was the self-assured captain that she recognized from *Sabvabaa* once more, in his element as the king of servile mechanics. Shrimp and minute plankton drifted past as the underwater vessel turned, then its light beams struck the seabed.

At first Anna couldn't understand what her eyes were seeing. The sight was so far from what even her wildest imagination would have thought possible in this icy-cold region of the world.

She was looking directly into hell: black smoke roiling up from volcanoes.

49

The volcanoes loomed up like sharp spearheads. The clouds of smoke coming from them were so numerous, and the smoke so pitch-black, that Anna felt like she was hovering above an endless array of polluting factories.

If her fate was to drown right here, it would be a swift burial as her body sank down into one of the volcanoes and was cremated in a cloud of ash. She heard Zakariassen make a smacking sound. His mouth was hanging open, his eyes blinking rapidly, engrossed by what he was seeing.

A large object glided in towards the volcanoes. It was painted red with short arms sticking out at the front. Another mini-sub.

"Now watch this," said Zakariassen with amazement in his voice. "This is just utterly fantastic. That sub is steering itself. The Chinese have programmed it to look for minerals."

The sub's whirling propellers made a column of smoke teeter on its voyage towards the surface. A mechanical arm reached forward. Metal claws broke a black stone loose from the side of a volcano and dropped it into a basket hanging beneath the sub. The propellers spun again, sending the cloud of smoke into a spiral as it turned. The underwater vessel drove away from the volcano and Zakariassen manoeuvred his own sub after it.

The lights of the red sub hit something that looked at first like yet another volcano, but when it came closer, Anna saw that the mountain was a tall, tubular machine. A red strobe flashed at the top, and the machine was standing on metal legs stuck into the seabed. The tube looked like a lunar module, just much taller and with a wide funnel around its upper section.

The mini-sub slowed until it was hanging motionlessly above the mouth of the funnel. The basket tipped downwards and a load of volcanic rocks dropped into the funnel.

In the room, everything was quiet. Even though Jackie and Marco were sitting tied to the wall, they could still see the images on the screen. Jackie betrayed no emotion, but Marco was wearing an irritated expression.

"You see that? It's absolutely incredible… unbelievable, just fantastic," Zakariassen said, slapping a hand against the metal crate. "Do you see what it is?" He didn't wait for an answer. "It's a mine!"

Behind the lenses of his glasses, his eyes shone excitedly.

"It's sensational… Do you see? The Chinese have managed something that no one else has done before. They're running a bloody mine at the North Pole. At a depth of three thousand metres!"

Anna saw the reflection of her own pale face in the computer screen as she was studying the mining machine. A black cloud was spat out of a pipe on the side. It hung weightlessly in the water as a powerful light came to life at the top of the machine, sweeping around. Fish could be seen in its beam as it glided across cables and cases on the seabed. The light vanished after a few rotations. A hatch opened. A basket was pushed out to a hook that was suspended at the side of the machine. The hook opened its jaws, taking hold of the basket.

Anna heard a whirring sound. A wire rope was being pulled up out of the hole. A fine rain of crystals fell from the mass of ice up in the tower as the cable was wound up into it. There was a smell of sulphur and dust. On the screen, she saw the basket vanishing out of shot.

"What are you doing?"

Zakariassen was grinning like a kid in a sweetshop. "The mine is completely automatic. Jackie showed me how to start it."

Down in the hole in the ice, the metal threads vibrated as the cable pulled the basket up. An air bubble clung to the wire rope. Anna watched it. As the rope approached the heat lamps in the roof, the bubble burst.

She was trying to get Zakariassen's attention. "Let's leave this stuff alone. We have no idea how to operate it," she said, but he continued staring down the hole.

"Daniel... have you forgotten that there's a mass murderer on the loose out there somewhere?"

He looked at her. His bushy eyebrows frowned in irritation. "But you've set up the trip flares—they'll warn us if anyone is coming."

"Yes, in theory, but this Lanpo guy has killed eleven, perhaps twelve people. He must be pretty sharp."

Zakariassen's throat gurgled as he breathed in. "What if he killed them because of the mine? If this is the reason for all this hellishness... wouldn't it be wise to find out what's down there?"

The steel cable continued to coil up out of the sea, bringing bubbles of air with it.

"Nothing down there is so valuable that it's worth killing twelve men for," argued Anna. "Leave this stuff alone now."

"Rare minerals are worth an awful lot..."

"OK, fine, I'm sure you're right about that," she said. "But I don't understand what Lanpo's plan is. Let's assume that he's found something so fucking valuable that he believes, in his twisted mind, that it's totally logical to commit mass murder so he can get his hands on it. How's he going to get it out of here?"

"He might have an accomplice who can come and get him." Zakariassen was never the type to give up if he had found a train of thought that seemed rational to him.

"Yes, but for fuck's sake, Daniel, we're at the North Pole! If *anyone* is coming to pick him up, it has to be by helicopter. The only people who have access to that kind of equipment are the Russians, the Americans and us."

"Russia is corrupt as hell. Everything has its price."

Down in the large hole, the sea was bubbling forcefully around the wire, bursting at the surface. There was no smell, but Anna walked several steps back all the same.

"Is it gas?"

Zakariassen bent down. His shadow on the water was shattered each time the bubbles burst.

"No, it's just warm water. The volcanoes you saw are called hydrothermal vents. They form when the seawater seeps down into fissures in the ocean floor and then hits lava oozing up from the Earth's core. The water starts boiling, rises back up and pulls minerals up with it… understand?"

Anna nodded reluctantly.

"When the water cools, the minerals sink back down again. That's how hydrothermal vents are formed. They've been boiling down there for millions of years."

His words floated around in Anna's head without really sticking. "Did Jackie tell you all that?"

"No," he said with a haughty grunt. "When I saw the Chinese set-up here I understood immediately that this was no regular search for minerals." Zakariassen swept his hand around the room. "This is an industrial operation."

He laid a finger against the wire cable. Drops of water teemed off and trickled across his hand.

"My theory is that the Chinese have made a massive discovery of the rarest minerals. That's why they have this huge data room. The researchers can… could… analyse the seismic data continuously. If they found something interesting they could take a sample immediately. Everything they have on the seabed can be controlled remotely and moved. Even half a ton would make an enormous difference in the global market for extremely rare minerals."

"But why are they taking the risk? When this comes out won't China most likely be expelled from the Arctic?" asked Anna.

"Who's going to expel them? Nobody owns the Arctic yet. There's no law here. Look at us: Norway has kept on hunting whales long after the rest of the world banned it. We say it's for scientific research, but whale steak is on sale for all to see in Tromsø. We even export it. Everything is still up for grabs at the North Pole, which is why the Fram expedition is so important."

Zakariassen let go of the wet cable and studied his fingertips. A dark-red streak of rust was clearly visible against his pale skin.

"Norway needs to take ownership of the territory here and defend our rights before everyone else arrives," he went on. "There are no troublesome natives demanding independence. If we're not careful, China and Russia and the rest are going to snatch everything that's here from under our noses, and then the heroism of Amundsen and Nansen would all be for nothing. We were here first!" The burning look in his eye got Anna thinking that Zakariassen was one of those old-fashioned explorers after all, convinced of his unassailable right to declare a newfound territory his own.

The conversation was abruptly interrupted by an alarm. A light on the wall began flashing orange.

The bubbling in the hole grew more intense. The hook at the end of the cable came spilling up, pulling the basket after it. The cable came to a sudden stop and the basket hung suspended, swaying above the opening in the ice. It was larger than Anna had imagined, about a metre wide.

It was filled with black grit and some shiny lumps of another material. The lumps were stuck together like the cells of a beehive. Between the grit and the lumps were flakes of something that looked like dirty ice.

Muddy water drizzled off the grit and splashed onto the snow. A nauseating smell of rotten eggs spread through the room. Anna heard a loud ticking noise, like an egg timer in a hurry.

Either Jackie or Marco said something just as Zakariassen grabbed hold of the basket, pulled it towards him and stuck his hand into the contents. He broke off one of the shining lumps.

It popped.

Anna saw a bright glimmer of light at the bottom of the basket. Zakariassen screamed and pulled back his hand, but it was chased by a flickering green monster.

50

A clenched fist of searing heat punched her in the face. The basket from the icy depths had transformed into a reactor of incandescent flames.

Zakariassen screamed again. Green flames snaked wildly around him. The grit in the basket was burning as if it had been impregnated with high-octane fuel. Anna backed off, but the flames pursued her. She threw herself to the floor and forced her face into the ice, clasping her hands around the back of her head as she caught the stench of scorched hair.

When she realized her hair hadn't caught fire, she looked up again. Zakariassen was turning around, encased in dancing whirls of flames, which were casting pulses of green, orange and blue light towards the walls. Marco and Jackie lowered their heads to shield themselves from the blaze.

Anna breathed in through her nose. The smell of scorched hair and skin was overwhelming. Zakariassen was still on fire as he fell, writhing around on the floor. She got to her feet, and tripped rather than ran towards him, kicking snow free from the ice. Raking it together in her hands, she threw it at his head.

Zakariassen tore off his glasses and thrust his hands against his face. She kicked more snow and ice loose, throwing the frozen water over him and brushing back the flames from the survival suit, where the fabric had started bubbling up in the heat.

"You need to cool your face down!"

She was screaming to make sure that Zakariassen heard her as she pressed more snow against him. The smell of incinerated hair was intense. He splashed the ice outwards across his face. Between flakes of snow, his skin was a furious red.

"We have to get you into the water!" She grabbed the hood of his survival suit and slung him like a rag doll over to the hole. Burning pieces of ice were still falling from the basket, but the flames licking the air had died out.

Zakariassen let out a short wail just before she shoved his head under the water. His hands grasped Anna's, trying to force her to loosen her grip, but she kept pushing his head down. He glared at her in fury from under the surface as clouds of bubbles raged out of his mouth. Silently she counted: *One thousand and ten... one thousand and eleven, one thousand and twelve...* At twenty, she wrenched his head out of the water.

Zakariassen inhaled in sharp, gasping breaths, his hot skin steaming. His face was contorted in anger.

"You're fucking drowning me!" he managed to scream before she forced him back under the water. By the third time, he had lost the will to protest, his hands lying limp on the ice as she held him down. After another twenty seconds submerged, she lifted him back up. He wheezed as he sucked air into his lungs.

"How does your face feel?"

"It's burning, and I'm fu-fucking cold." His teeth chattered as his fingers fumbled around his face. The skin was red, his eyebrows had been singed off and his grey hair was streaked with black, but he seemed otherwise unhurt.

"Does it hurt to breathe?" she asked.

He breathed in, but was consumed by a coughing fit. He waved her off with one arm. "I'm all right... I just swallowed something."

"Great, so you didn't get any smoke into your lungs. You have to let me know if you run out of breath."

Carbon dioxide is a creeping death. The gas can infiltrate the body, forcing oxygen from the lungs, numbing and choking you

209

just when you think the danger has passed. Anna looked at the basket. Steam was rising as filthy water dripped through its bars like dark blood. Below it she saw Marco and Jackie staring back at her in shock.

Anger took hold of her. She walked around the basket towards them.

"What the fuck is this stuff? Are you trying to kill us?" Trying to escape Anna's fury, Marco and Jackie pushed themselves in towards the wall as though trying to force their bodies through it, but the zip ties kept them bound to the spot. She felt her blood pulsing hard and fast against her temples.

"Anna! It wasn't their fault!" Zakariassen yelled after her. "Listen, it wasn't their fault!"

She saw that Marco looked genuinely shaken. It was difficult to see what Jackie was feeling. His head was still bent down and his long fringe shielded his eyes.

"Listen to me. It wasn't their fault," Zakariassen repeated. "It was burning ice. I should have known that."

She used her furious energy to twist her feet around on the ice. Her tired joints popped as the rest of her body followed.

Zakariassen was kneeling, one arm hanging down along his body. Water was running off his survival suit, taking soot with it and colouring the snow and ice around him grey. He was standing at the centre of his own dark halo, a black hole in white space. He was holding a lump of steaming substance towards her. It was melting as she looked at it, running into black rivulets trickling between his fingers.

"It started burning because there's methane in the ice... methane hydrate." A pale finger pointed towards the heat lamps in the roof. "When the ice came up, it began to melt and then the methane escaped. The lamps must have ignited the gas."

She looked at the lump of ice he was holding. "How the hell can ice burn?"

"The Arctic was once dry land. Dinosaurs lived here. Animals that drown, or fall into the swamps, every living being that dies and decomposes without being exposed to air, turns into methane, just as the oil in the North Sea was formed from dead algae."

She walked over to the hole in the ice. The water was calm now. Snow and pieces of ice bobbed like islands in the sea.

"Don't the Chinese know this?"

"Yes, I assume they do, but they probably have routines for that kind of thing. Switch off the heat lamps, air out the room…"

Anna looked around. Her eyes rested on the metal cases. She lifted the laptop off and opened the lid of the one on top. It was full of olive-green gas masks. She picked one of them up, waving it in front of Jackie and Marco's faces.

"Thanks very much for the warning!"

"I tried… to stop you," Jackie mumbled.

He had said something or other when the basket came up, she suddenly remembered, but she buried the thought just as quickly. Her rage needed a whipping boy.

51

"Where the fuck are the helicopters?"

Anna was standing in the doorway to the main building, staring aggressively into the snowstorm. She wanted nothing more than to get away from the two men chained to the wall in the room. Away from the twelve dead and the murder mystery that was a Pandora's box of ever more gruesome riddles.

The light streaming out of the doorway struck the dense falling snow and turned into a rectangle of light, pulsating in the air. In the pitch-darkness, the rectangle looked like a magic portal. A few short steps through the snow and into the gate of light would lead her to another world.

A world with a village, situated beautifully at the top of a valley squeezed between two mountains.

On bright, cloudless days, days without heat haze, the Mediterranean could be seen from the park above the village, where pensioners gathered to play boules in the evenings. From the viewing point it was only a short stroll down to the square, where a gigantic tree stretched out its branches to shade every table. There were three restaurants, but they looked like one when the residents fought for space with the weekenders. And then, with a full belly and a head suitably muzzy from the local rosé, all you had to do was walk a few hundred metres through the narrow streets to the hotel. That was how Yann had described it.

She never saw the village between the mountains. She was never served a Pernod by Yann's father, who had taught his son to mix drinks at a perfectly illegal young age. She never got to eat at the square in front of the hotel, where Yann had served the guests and learnt four languages in tips.

This lost world streamed out of the shimmering portal, bleeding her dry. Her legs began to tremble. Her head buzzed. She struggled not to think about everything that never was. She took a sudden step backwards and bumped into something. A distant voice filtered through the buzz.

"Anna, can you hear me?…"

She turned around. Zakariassen was standing right behind her.

"Sorry, the wind's so noisy… What did you say?"

He was staring at her, cocking his head like a nervous sparrow.

"I said… I can't imagine anyone being able to land here in this rough weather. We'll just have to wait. We're safe here for now."

"Good that you're calmer now."

His sparrow's head tilted even further down.

"The people I spoke to said they would be putting all their resources into reaching us. We have no other choice than to trust them, I guess."

Anna reluctantly had to admit that Zakariassen was right. Only a pilot with a death wish would try to fly into a snowstorm at low altitude across a landscape covered in pressure ridges. She kicked the ground hard and watched pieces of ice spraying into the darkness as she mumbled into the wind.

"This fucking ice. It's getting on my nerves."

Zakariassen looked at her, confused. "Sorry?"

Yeah. What did she mean?

The ice.

It was everywhere.

The whole world was ice.

There was so much of it that the different types had their own names. Pack ice. Pressure ridges. Blue ice. Congelation ice. Old ice. But in contrast to every other landscape Anna had been in,

213

here there were no bushes, no flowers, no streams, no forests, not so much as a scree. The ice was a gigantic body stretched over the entire Arctic, and she felt like a microscopic flea crawling across it. A pest that might be exterminated at any moment—but in contrast to the flea, she was well aware of it.

"Nothing," she replied. "It was nothing."

She took one last look at her shadow dancing in the portal of light, and closed the door to shut out her imaginary world. The room they were in was the safest on Ice Dragon. There was only one way in, and the walls seemed to have been built with sturdier materials than the other cabins. But even if the temperature in the room was well above freezing, Anna could feel the cold seeping in from the ice men next door.

Jackie and Marco were quiet. They weren't speaking to each other and seemed to be lost in their own, private bubbles. Anna studied their faces. Jackie's was pale, his long hair hanging down over narrow eyes and long lashes. His thin nose and plump lips were in sharp contrast to Marco's broad face and little mouth, which always seemed to be breaking into a feeble smile above his goatee beard. She assessed them both. They and Lanpo, if he were still alive, were the only survivors of a crew of fifteen.

Zakariassen noticed her gaze. "Do you believe that story about Lanpo?"

"All I know is that these two gentlemen agree that the guy was mentally disturbed in one way or another… and if the story is right, Lanpo had good reason to hate the commander," she replied. "And Lanpo is the only one we haven't found." She saw that the name Lanpo piqued Marco's attention. He was probably wondering what they were talking about. "But the fact that Lanpo is missing is really fucking convenient for both of them."

Her eyes met Marco's. He looked down and recoiled into his bubble again. "Right now it feels like we all agree that the enemy is out there on the ice. All eyes need to be looking outwards, not in."

Zakariassen looked at the Chinese men. He cleared his throat, walked over to the ice hole, and spat into the snow. "We've got control of these two bastards now anyway… The best thing to do is wait here until the storm blows over."

Even though there was nothing she wanted more, Anna couldn't relax as much as him. It was amazing how calm Zakariassen had become after making contact with the rescue services. Even though the Americans had promised to move heaven and earth to help, here and now nothing had changed. They were shut inside a little room with two potential killers, with a third suspect out there in the dark somewhere, probably heavily armed and mentally unstable. Anna smelt the stale stench of sweat. She brushed her hand through her hair to wipe it away from her face. The strands were sticky and tangled in her fingers. The inside of her head felt at least as bad.

"Fuck!"

Zakariassen startled. "What's wrong?"

"Sorry, but I just can't calm down. I'm going crazy not knowing what happened here."

He looked at her. His eyes blinked behind his glasses. "Maybe this is how it starts… a new war."

"Why would anyone want to wage war at the North Pole?"

Zakariassen lifted a boot. "Right under our feet are the greatest undiscovered resources in the world. It's like the Wild West in the age of the pioneers. Nobody ever thought about the North Pole as a place worth owning, only as a place to be conquered by explorers."

He suddenly chuckled and smiled at her.

"Have you ever heard the story about when a journalist asked the mountaineer George Mallory why he wanted to climb Mount Everest, come hell or high water, even though he had failed twice before? Because it's *there*, said the stubborn old fool. Because Everest is the highest mountain in the world, because nobody has been there before… because that's what people do when they are looking for the meaning of life. That's what he said…"

He pushed a lump of ice over the edge of the hole. It bobbed up and down in the seawater among the bubbles forming and bursting on the surface.

"We can pretend that it's not true as much as we like, but humans are like worms gnawing their way deeper and deeper into the Earth. Living just to eat and shit. If there had been gold on Everest, I doubt there would be any mountain left to climb today."

The water bubbled strongly and the lump of ice was pushed towards the hole's edge. The pressure of the bursting bubbles forced the lump up, rolling it over.

Anna abruptly walked over to the laptop.

"Show me that image again… the one with the volcanoes."

"Why?"

"Just do it, please."

Zakariassen came over to the laptop, pushed his glasses up onto his forehead and leant towards the screen. The glasses were blackened along the rims from the fire and the metal arms glimmered in psychedelic rainbow patterns.

He began manoeuvring the mini-sub away from the mining plant. The camera captured one of the volcanoes belching smoke up from the Earth's core. The bubbles streaming from the ocean floor glittered like stray stars in the light.

"The bubbles, are they methane?" asked Anna.

"Yes, the methane's trapped inside the ice, which the heat from the lava is melting."

Her eyes followed a large cluster of bubbles. They climbed right up and disappeared out of sight in a couple of seconds.

"What happens to the gas?"

"It climbs up out of the sea and evaporates in the atmosphere." The lecturer in Zakariassen came to life. "The methane emissions have increased a hundredfold in the Arctic region in the last twenty years due to global warming. It takes twelve years for methane to break down in the atmosphere, which is not as terrible as CO_2, but it contributes to climate change, no doubt about it…"

Anna looked down at her feet. At the rigid crust of water keeping them all floating across the deep ocean. The 9 per cent density that separated ice from water. She envisaged billions of gas bubbles on their way towards her.

"What happens when the methane meets the ice?" She really didn't need anything else to worry about, but couldn't stop herself asking.

Zakariassen looked down at the ice too. His scorched eyebrows looked like the legs of a contracted centipede.

"The gas gathers beneath the ice, then gets released when the ice melts."

A groan escaped from Anna's sore throat.

"Oh well… so what I was thinking was the only safe place in this shithole… is in fact just one fucking huge gas bomb?"

52

"There goes paradise," thought Anna as the storm wind slammed the door to the room shut behind her. When a windowless room with an ice floor but not so much as a chair to sit on seemed like heaven, she knew the ice had succeeded in making her feel as insignificant as a flea.

She was trying to see the cabin that she knew was only tens of metres further ahead, but the snow drifting by was whipping the faint lights from the windows into a restless fuzzy haze. She prayed silently that her sense of direction would keep them on the right track and not lead them all out into icy oblivion. Anna fought her way forward as she tried to keep Jackie and Marco in her torchlight. Beyond its beam there was pure darkness.

Anna couldn't see him, but she hoped that Zakariassen was still walking with his rifle aimed at both men. She seriously doubted that Jackie and Marco would try to run off. They had been at the North Pole longer than her and ought to have known better than anyone that setting out onto the ice alone was suicide. And now, hopefully, they realized that she and Zakariassen were actually trying to save them, not kill them. Anna took an extra turn around the cabin before she followed the others inside the mess.

Zakariassen's newfound optimism met her in the doorway.

"We're safer here," he said as Anna stamped the snow from her boots.

Exhausted and drained, she wasn't able to hold back the irritation grating the inside of her head like sandpaper.

"Safe?… Even if the gas isn't seeping up here right now, this base is floating on top of a bomb. We have zero contact with the outside world and we're stuck here with two potential mass murderers!"

Her fierce voice made Jackie and Marco look up from the bowls of noodles they were already eating. Zakariassen must have let them help themselves from the kitchen. "And as if that wasn't messed up enough, we have a disturbed lunatic who might come roaring in at any minute! I've felt much fucking safer in Taliban villages in Afghanistan."

This eruption forced Zakariassen back.

"Are you worried about something?" Jackie was looking at Anna.

"Yeah, I'm worried as hell, but that's not your problem. Just eat." His face glistened green as an imp's under the fluorescent tubes. Was he getting sicker, or was it just a reaction to the chilli in the soup?

"I know how you can find Lanpo." Jackie's voice was clear and distinct, but Marco waved him off dismissively.

"No, let's not talk about that," he said, his hand in front of Jackie.

Jackie pushed his hand away. "They're are trying to help us. We have to help them."

In three swift steps, Anna was standing in front of him. "What are you talking about, Jackie? Do you know where Lanpo is?"

"No. But I know how to find him."

Jackie was holding out his left hand towards Anna, pointing at an area of skin just behind the thumb.

"I have a GPS chip inserted here," he said. "Everybody got one before we arrived here."

Anna looked at his hand. Squinting a little, she could nearly see an almost invisible scar.

"Is this right?" she asked Marco.

Marco glowered at Jackie again as if they were about to reveal state secrets.

"Commander Hong said it was for our own safety," Jackie went on, not seeming to care about Marco's accusing glare. "If we got lost or had an accident, then somebody would always be able to find us."

It took a couple of seconds for Anna to realize what this meant. "Where's the software that tracks the chips?"

"On Colonel Hong's laptop, but only he had the password," Jackie answered. "The software was only to be used in emergencies."

Anna felt the fatigue filling her head like cotton wool. "But you said we could find Lanpo!"

Jackie pointed at Marco.

"*He'll* find him."

Marco was still scowling at Jackie. He uttered some angry words in Chinese and Jackie countered with a furious tirade. Anna let them argue while she was thinking about what she had just found out. She banged her fist down on the table. The empty noodle bowls jumped and clattered, and the squabbling stopped at once.

"Marco, it was no coincidence that you found the guy who fired the flare, was it?"

Marco's eyes slipped away, searching for something on the wall.

"I saw the flare."

"Yes, so did we—we came to Ice Dragon because we knew its exact position… but flares hang from parachutes—they fly with the wind. But you managed to get to him anyway—you drove right up to where he shot the flare from." She walked over to Marco, placed a hand on his head and twisted it towards her.

"What Jackie's saying is true, isn't it? That you're the only one who knows exactly where Lanpo is… right now."

53

The engine of Marco's pickup hummed quietly.

Inside the truck, Anna felt a comfortable, but utterly false sense of normality. The snow whipping against the windows could have been coming over the Tromsø mountains, and the truck could have been on its way to the little cabin her grandfather had built just after the war, carrying the materials up the mountain himself.

Could have.

But on the other side of the rear window she was leaning her head against, there was a dead man whose head had been crushed in a polar bear's jaws. And the man next to her was, at best, a reluctant ally. She and Zakariassen had taken Marco out to the pickup, leaving Jackie in the canteen, chained to a chair.

"Does your truck have its own GPS receiver?" was the simple question she had put to Marco.

She'd had to squeeze a reluctant yes out of him. This guy would be a real find for any employer big on discretion and secrecy.

"That was why you found… Gai Zhanhai so fast." She only remembered the name because she still had the commander's personnel files in her hand. "You knew exactly where he was."

Again there came a low grunt that could, perhaps, be interpreted as a yes.

Now Marco was pushing his stout fingers against a large display in the middle of the dashboard. A digital map blinked to life. Pulsing red dots filled the whole screen.

"That's them?" asked Anna.

"Yes, those are everyone's positions."

He pointed at two dots that were overlapping each other. "That's me… and that's Gai Zhanhai."

Zakariassen leant across her to get a look at the screen. She smelt the rank stench of a male body that hadn't been washed in a long time, blended with the smell of soot, burnt hair and camphor.

"How are you getting any satellite signal, what with the snowstorm and the Northern Lights?" she asked sceptically.

"Chinese satellites are very reliable," replied Marco, with a tone that Anna took for pride. "They can cope with any conditions." He took off his gloves and placed two fingers on the screen and the map zoomed out. Twelve dead. Two living. The red dots marking the positions of everyone at Ice Dragon floated together into one large, glowing mass, like a clump of bacteria.

An infection on the surface of the ice.

Marco pushed his fingers outwards again. The bacteria shrank to one red dot in the middle of a vast white nothingness. He used his fingers to manipulate the map on the display. Anna was trying to understand what scale the map was, but all the menus were in Chinese. How far had Lanpo actually got?

Something red suddenly cut in from the edge of the screen. Another red point in the whiteness.

"That's Lanpo's GPS chip," said Marco.

"How far away is he?" asked Zakariassen.

"Around… two kilometres."

"Can you tell which direction he's moving in?" asked Anna.

Marco tapped a finger against the red dot and a bubble of Chinese characters appeared. It wasn't necessary to know Chinese to understand that the wavering line leading to Lanpo's position was the route he had taken since leaving Ice Dragon.

"In the last hour… Lanpo has moved about twelve hundred metres… towards us," said Marco.

Anna felt a cold shiver shoot down her neck.

Lanpo was alive.

The killer was really alive.

Zakariassen switched back to Norwegian. "Oh God, the evil bastard's coming for us... What do we do now?" The scorched centipedes above his eyes were crawling up his forehead. "We've just got to get out of here now... Marco can drive, right?"

She heard herself answering, and it was the old version of Anna, the one who was always calm when everyone else was panicking. "No, we have no way to warn the rescue team. If the helicopter lands while we're away and Lanpo's here, they'll think he's one of the survivors. He's armed and could force them to fly him wherever he wants."

"OK, but for Christ's sake, he's alone," said Zakariassen, punching the door panel hard. "There are two of us, and now we know exactly where he is. It has to be possible to stop him!"

The dot marking the mass murderer's position shone bright red. If the GPS signal was correct, Lanpo was only two thousand metres away.

"There's something I haven't told you, Daniel." Anna's voice was still calm. "Lanpo is heavily armed. I found a weapons cabinet in the workshop. It had been broken into... and he'd taken everything."

A deep furrow formed under Zakariassen's mouth as his lips squeezed together.

"Why didn't you say anything until now?"

"Because I couldn't do anything about it. But if we're going out there to... find him, it's only fair that you know the risk we're taking."

"God..." Zakariassen collapsed in his seat. "So we have no choice. We'd be sitting ducks out there. We have to stay here, then... and pray to God that help arrives before he does."

Anna looked out of the side window, which the force of the wind was keeping free of snow. She could see a faint light from the window of the nearest cabin. It was no more than five or six metres away, but the snow was lashing away most of the light.

"At the moment the storm is on our side. Lanpo won't be able to see more than ten metres out there, and if we leave the base he won't have any idea where we are." She put a finger on the screen. "And as you say… now we know precisely where he is."

She heard Zakariassen's breath gurgling in his chest as he stared at the red dot on the screen. "But we can only see where he is while we're sitting in this truck… And you don't think he'd hear us coming in this thing? We won't be able to take him by surprise."

"Probably not." Anna pointed at the display. "Marco… I just need this. Can you take the screen out and make it work by itself?"

"I can't damage the truck, it belongs to China…" He got no further. His face made a smacking sound, like a suction cup being fixed to glass, as Anna forced his head against the rear window. "Don't you understand that I'm trying to keep us alive? Or are you happy to sit here waiting to be killed?"

Marco tried to wrest his head free from her grip. "I'm not a soldier… I'm a mechanic—"

"And I'm not asking you to kill anyone. I want you to do a mechanic's job." She wrenched him away from the window, twisting his head towards the screen. "Your task now is to get that thing out even if you have to take apart the whole truck. When you've done that, you're going to connect it to a battery so I can carry the whole lot with me. Got it?…"

A bang and a glimmer of light cut her off. Outside the truck, a bright flash cut through the snowstorm and the darkness.

54

"Watch him, Daniel!" she screamed.

In one movement she switched off the engine, leapt over Zakariassen, pulled open the door handle and dropped out of the truck. Her fall was broken by the soft snow, and Anna was up and running in an instant. She had taken several steps before she noticed that something was very different. The storm was losing strength and the snow was falling diagonally to the ground. It wasn't blowing in her face any more. Now it wouldn't be long before the Americans could land. Thoughts raced through her head, but her eyes focussed on just one thing.

The steadily fading light of the flare that had been set off.

As she ran, Anna fumbled to find her hunting knife. The last sparks died out and she was surrounded by the dark. She kept running blindly on. A green light came into view. *Sabvabaa*'s right navigation lamp. She knew she must be near where the tripwire had been set. A distant rumbling sound could be heard, as if someone were beating a drum. She felt her hopes soar. *The helicopters are coming!*

Anna had been to war against all kinds of enemies. The professional soldier, the mad, the brainwashed, the born-again, the desperate. Of all these, the professionals are the easiest: they all think more or less alike, no matter which country, politics or ideology they are fighting for. The winner is decided by three things: the strength of your forces, your tactics and a pinch of luck.

The worst opponents are the desperate. People who have nothing left to lose are totally unpredictable. Even brainwashed religious fanatics are the puppets of intelligent men behind the scenes. After a few shocking defeats, you know what's coming and can be prepared.

The ice she was running across was all of these enemies in one. The North Pole couldn't win the war against humanity. Now, the kingdom of ice merely wanted to take revenge, and, in this battle, there were no rules. The ice opened up beneath her feet. She fell, consumed by the darkness.

Out of the dark, the sun emerged.

The silhouettes of refugees, sitting sheltered from the sun in the opening of a silver tent. They stared listlessly at Anna as her car drove past.

She saw Yann standing in front of a Red Cross tent.

"Welcome to Ain Issa."

Air conditioning chilled the inside of the tent. It took a few moments before her eyes got used to the half-light. Just visible was a row of small beds in which children were sleeping under white sheets. A nurse got up from her chair when she saw Yann. They exchanged some words in French.

"He's over here."

Anna followed Yann to one of the beds. A little boy was asleep there, a pacifier in his mouth, his black hair curling around his head.

"He needed a name, so now he's called Sadi," said Yann. "In Arabic it means *the lucky one who will live for a hundred years*. We thought it would be good for him to have a little luck on his side after his rough start in life."

The French doctor lifted up the lower edge of the bed sheets. Sadi was dressed in blue pyjamas, but the leg below his left knee was gone. The pyjama leg was neatly folded and fastened with a safety pin. The boy grunted, spat out the pacifier and opened his eyes. They were amazingly blue.

"Hi, Sadi, do you want to say hello to the woman who saved us?" Sadi grunted again. Yann took it for a yes and picked him up.

"Do you want to hold him?"

Anna took him in her arms, feeling the stump of his leg against her chest. His little body was soft and warm, and smelt of soap and vanilla. His blue eyes stared at her and he smiled, all gums.

"It looks like Sadi rather likes you, Anna."

Gurgling laughter spluttered from Sadi's mouth, followed by drool. Warm spittle struck her face.

Anna was roused by the cold water running down her neck. She was lying on her back and could see the dark sky above her. In her mind it was even darker, a timeless void. She tried to restart her brain. Where was she? Why was it so cold?

A gentle rocking and the dank cold told her senses that she was lying in water. She saw her feet bobbing between the ice crusts in front of her. She reached out her arms until they found something solid. It was the edge of the open fracture she was lying in. Everything came rushing back to her at once.

Ice.

Death.

She felt a leaden tiredness. The sea splashed against her face. How easy would it be to let go of everything? Lean back, let the water fill the survival suit, transforming it from a lifesaver to a coffin, then wait until she was beneath the surface, suck the icy water into her lungs and hope that the shock would stop her heart.

The end.

But her defiant instinct fought back, taking control of one arm and using it like a paddle to push her body to the edge of the ice. Her primal instinct rolled her over, carefully, so the water wouldn't run into her open hood. Her other arm grabbed hold of the edge and stubborn muscles pulled her up out of the water.

She sat on the snow and saw the split that had consumed her cutting further out into the ice, its sharp edges like the teeth of an endless saw. The low, rumbling helicopter sound was the noise of the ice being ripped to pieces.

An object was floating in the water. A thin wooden pole, whatever was left of the flare. The North Pole had torn the ice apart, forcing the floes away from each other and snapping the line stretched between two trip flares. It had lured Anna in. Running in the pitch-dark, she hadn't seen the fracture until it was too late. It was scarcely half a metre wide, but she must have stepped right into it. She took hold of her torch, switched it on and shone it towards the far edge of the fracture. There were blood spots on the ice. She touched her forehead and saw her hand smeared with blood. As she fell she must have hit her head on the edge, knocking herself unconscious. Without her survival suit she would have drowned.

She was overcome with an icy shiver, her body trembling as she threw her arms backwards and forwards, thumping herself on the back to get her circulation working again.

The sound of an engine emerged from the dark and she was caught in a powerful beam of light. She turned and saw the pickup driving out of the storm.

"Stop!" she roared, waving her arms. The truck stopped abruptly, a door opened and Zakariassen crawled out. He balanced on top of one of the enormous tyres and jumped down onto the snow.

"What's happened, Anna?…" He walked towards her with eyes wide open. "You're bleeding." He looked around. "Have you been shot?"

"No, it's just a graze. A fracture opened up here and like an idiot I ran straight into it." She felt the fabric in Zakariassen's gloves rustling as he put a hand against her cold forehead. "This wound doesn't look good. It needs bandaging."

"It's just grazed. A plaster will do."

He walked up to the split in the ice and saw the wooden stick floating in the water. "Nobody was here?"

"No, false alarm. The flare was activated when the fracture opened up."

Above the monster tyres another door opened and Marco emerged. He stood still, looking down at Anna like an emperor on his raised throne. She tried to read his blank face. Was Marco happy or irritated that she was still alive? Her shaken brain was sending her warning signals. Zakariassen was standing next to her.

Marco was free. And he was alone.

55

What's the best thing to do after suffering a powerful blow to the head, and a probable concussion?

Anna was thinking about this as she walked through the snow back to the main building. She remembered a football match she had seen with her father. He was a Liverpool fan and, after fifteen years lost in the wilderness, his team was ready to meet Real Madrid in the Champions League final. It ended in disaster. First, the Liverpool goalkeeper Loris Karius managed to throw the ball straight at the legs of a Real Madrid striker to concede the opening goal. Then Karius let a long-range shot he should have hung on to slip through his hands for another. Liverpool lost 3–1. It later emerged that Karius had suffered a concussion early in the match that was making him dizzy and impairing his vision. Liverpool lost their biggest match in fifteen years because the keeper literally couldn't keep his eye on the ball. If Anna were being completely honest, she had rarely felt worse, so why was she about to climb up the tower at Ice Dragon?

Because she had no other choice.

Lanpo was alive. The killer was on his way back across the ice, but she wasn't ready for the encounter yet. She had to get to the top of the tower to keep lookout.

Zakariassen had received strict instructions to watch Marco. He hadn't tried to escape in the truck when he had the chance. Now the mechanic was disassembling the GPS receiver.

"You don't need to tie me up, I'm not going to run away... I realize that you are good people," said Jackie as Anna checked that the zip ties were still keeping him in his chair.

"Nice that you finally see that." She felt that the ties weren't so tight as to be cutting into his wrists. "But it's best that you sit here for the time being." To her own surprise, she felt a smile spread across her face. Jackie smiled back.

"Thanks for doing so much to help us."

After checking that his bandages weren't soaked through with blood and that the drip bag was still streaming into his veins, she went outside, leaving Jackie looking small and lonely behind her.

"Keep an eye on them both," she said to Zakariassen, who was standing next to the truck with the Mauser in his hands. He nodded, as Marco jumped down from the truck holding the GPS tracker. "Come out and shout for me when Marco's finished. I'll be up in the tower keeping a lookout."

"How are you going to do that? It's pitch-dark!"

Anna brandished the device she had taken from *Sabvabaa* when she was setting up the trip flares. "I took your thermal imaging camera... If Lanpo tries sneaking in I'll see his body heat."

"For God's sake, be careful."

"I'll try."

"I meant... with the camera... It cost tens of thousands of dollars." Zakariassen gave her a sheepish smile.

Anna felt a painful aching at the back of her head as she walked along the rear of the main building. Then something suddenly dawned on her. She could no longer hear the wind. For a moment she thought that her hearing had been damaged, but then she realized that the storm had died down and the sky had cleared, as if God himself had sucked the clouds up into space, where a billion stars pierced holes in the eternal night.

She stepped through the deep snowdrifts that had blown up against the footings of the tower. The light from her torch found what she had been hoping to see: a ladder, fixed to the outside of the tower. The ice covering the rungs glistened softly in the light.

She grabbed hold of one of the steps.

Starting to climb.

Four steps higher, she noticed how cold it had become.

Her nostrils drew tighter and her lips grew harder with every breath. Together with the storm clouds, space had sucked up what little warmth was left at ground level. The cold in the steel rungs began forcing its way through her gloves.

As if it weren't already cold enough, halfway up the tower that Marco claimed was the world's highest, the ladder disappeared into a cloud of grey ice. The frozen ice hung from the tank on the inside of the tower, covering several steps. It must have frozen solid in a fraction of a second. It looked like an explosion that had been paused at the moment of detonation. Snow had settled on the tips of the frozen fingers of fire.

Anna broke off one of the tips and held it up to her nose. It smelt of nothing. She placed it against her lips, where it caught slightly. It was just water. She dropped the piece of ice and it whirled through the air, landing in the snow in silence. It took a while before her cold brain found a route around the ice mass. She had to twist around, climbing up along the edge of the ladder.

She climbed laboriously, one careful step at a time, up to the lower edge of the tank in the tower. Now she realized that, rather than one, there were two tanks, mounted one above the other. Only the higher one was visible through the cloud of ice. It was marked with Chinese characters, but also with a chemical formula that she recognized. H_2O. Water.

The tank below, the one that Jackie had said contained liquid nitrogen, was completely packed in ice. Anna saw a cable running from the water tank and into the ice cloud. This was where it had happened. The accident, or the sabotage that froze space engineer Lee and the other scientists in the main building to death. She tried to see where the damage had occurred, but what she could see of the tank looked untouched.

One hand slipped on the icy rungs. Her breath hung frozen as she stopped dead. She gathered herself, grabbed hold once more, feeling the solid grip of her glove. She climbed onwards.

Slowly. Slowly.

Upwards. Upwards.

Colder. Colder.

Eventually her steadily weaker torch beam revealed that the ladder disappeared through the floor of a large box that had been built around the top of the tower. With his usual reluctance, Marco had told her that it was possible for a person to climb in to change the floodlight bulbs.

When Anna stuck her head through the hole, the light was reflected from glistening cables that vanished into circular covers fixed to the wall. There was just enough space for her between the cables and the covers. Before she climbed in, she had to remove the bow she had slung over her back. She threw it and the quiver of arrows into the room and hauled herself in.

Back in the mess she had wolfed down a box of instant noodles. The pork it contained now gave her enough energy to rip off one of the covers and remove one lamp from each wall. Two of them were stuck there, but the other two slipped out easily as though someone had taken them out not too long ago. The holes in which the lamps had been mounted gave her a view in all directions and had just enough space to stick the thermal cameras through. On the screen, blue tones bled into each other like watercolours. Just blue. There were no warm-blooded beings hiding in the dark beyond the base.

Anna put down the camera and swapped it for the bow. In the narrow space, she had to hold it horizontally to tighten it. Without the camera, there was not much to see. The only ice she could see were those areas brightened by the cabin lights. Other than the fact that it consisted of dark-grey shapes illuminated by the starry sky, the landscape could only be guessed at. If she were to have a chance of hitting Lanpo, he would have to walk through the lights from one of the cabins, and even then her chances were slim—Anna had bought the bow on impulse, but had never practised to any serious degree. The distance from the tower down to the cabins was almost a hundred metres.

But the bow was all she had.

Before she walked to the tower, Anna had tried picking up the rifle. Its steel had burnt against her skin. She had felt sick and sweat had beaded on her forehead.

She was filled with a sense of powerlessness.

"You can't run away from post-traumatic stress." That was what the drab psychologist in his beige office had said. "You have to learn to accept the pain, and it's only then that you can start to put it behind you." He made a rectangle with his hands. "This is an exercise that might help. Imagine that you have a DVD recorder that you can replay the painful memories on."

"Ordinary DVD, or Blu-ray?" she asked.

"Blu-ray is best—that way you get more details and better stills." The psychologist wasn't going to let himself be tripped up by a little attempt at irony. "Imagine that you are recording the whole incident, preferably starting a little while before the painful part. After you have recorded it on your mental DVD… imagine a TV screen where you can play back… the event, just like you would do with a normal movie at home."

"I don't have a TV at home." That was the first time she saw a trace of irritation in the psychologist's gentle face.

Now she was looking out into the dark, forcing herself to remember.

It had been just like this then, too.

When it all began.

Up high.

The butt of a sniper rifle jammed into her shoulder.

234

She and the weapon were one back then. She could tear down and reassemble the Barrett MRAD in the pitch-dark. She knew how to adjust the sight to compensate for wind, air pressure and the Coriolis effect, the Earth's own rotation.

But all the training in the world couldn't prepare her to see a child abandoned in a cardboard box under the burning sun, to hear its painful cries. Through the sight, she had seen that the baby couldn't be more than two or three months old. Its only protection against the sun was a dirty blue football shirt. It got Anna thinking that the baby was a boy. She didn't know which despicable human had abandoned this helpless child; the only thing she did know was that this little boy was going to die.

"We can't let the kid die."

She remembered the exact words.

"You know it's a trap."

The reply came from Geir, who was lying next to her with so much gear strapped to his compact body that he looked more like a pack mule than a soldier. A radio transmitter on his back, pockets of extra ammo on his chest, as well as hand grenades and emergency supplies. It was his job to be Anna's spotter. He would be keeping a lookout for "threats". Anything that might be the enemy.

In this Syrian city, the enemy was IS.

The jihadi soldiers had overrun it and declared Raqqa the capital city of the Caliphate, their extreme version of an Islamic state.

"It's fucked up, but that boy is a trap, I guarantee you." Geir brushed grey dust off his face as he looked at her. It had fallen on their heads as they scrambled up the ruined steps to get onto the roof. "The box is the perfect place to hide a bomb. The boy is a honey trap. If we try to get him out of there we'll been blown sky-high."

Anna and Geir were the advance guard for a company from the Syrian Democratic Forces that was positioned down on the street with their boss, Lieutenant Eilertsen. The three Norwegians had been sent to Syria by their government as "advisors" to help the liberation forces. Anna left the difference between "advisor" and "soldier" to the generals; for her, everything was about the here and now. The company couldn't push forward if the square in front of her wasn't secured. If there was a bomb in the cardboard box, it could possibly be triggered with a well-placed shot. But she wasn't about to kill the baby.

Checkmate.

Then there was a movement above the boy. When she raised the rifle, Anna saw a dog emerging from the remains of the walls of a grocery store on the other side of the square. Through her sight, she could clearly see its ribs beneath its grey-flecked fur. The devastated city swarmed with stray dogs that roamed the streets hunting for food. By the time Anna realized what was about to happen, it was too late. The dog ran over to the box, poked its head into it, clasped its teeth around one foot and dragged the boy out. He let out a heart-rending scream and floundered helplessly with his arms as the dog pulled him across the ground. Anna squeezed down on the trigger and tried to get the dog centred in the crosshairs, but it was already partly obscured behind a damaged climbing frame. If she shot now, she risked hitting the boy.

Geir looked through his range-finding binoculars and yelled out instructions. "Two hundred and... forty metres. Westerly breeze."

She turned a dial to adjust the scope for wind and distance, concentrating on breathing calmly. Her pulse was a distant echo in her ears. As a sniper, she was trained to pull the trigger between heartbeats. Something moved at the edge of her field of vision. She ignored it. The only thing that mattered now was saving the boy's life. Her forefinger pulled in the final hair's breadth of slack on the trigger. She would shoot the moment the dog came out from behind the climbing frame.

"Civilian!" yelled Geir.

Feet appeared in the scope. A man was running towards the dog. He was wearing a white sleeveless vest over an olive-green jersey. In the middle of his chest was a red symbol that Anna recognized as the sign of the French relief organization Médecins Sans Frontières.

That was her first encounter with Yann Renault.

Through a gun scope.

His dark, curly hair bounced around his head as Yann chased after the dog. The sun glinted on something he was holding in his hand. He threw his arm forward, and a metal can whirled towards the animal and hit it in the ribs. The dog dropped the boy. It barked at Yann, but he wasn't scared off. He picked up a stone and threw it. The dog growled again, and for a moment Anna thought it was going to attack him, but then the dog turned abruptly and ran off.

Yann picked the boy up. She saw blood running from the boy's foot where the dog had bitten into him. The doctor turned and ran back with the boy pressed against his chest. The boy's fearful eyes peeked over Yann's shoulder. Then something appeared between her and him. Gravel and grit sprayed up behind the running man. A moment later, the sound of a shot reached her.

"Sniper! Second floor. Up! Up!"

She followed Geir's instructions automatically. A gaping hole in the wall of a bombed-out apartment block filled her scope; then there was a bright glimmer from behind the shadows. A sniper was shooting at the doctor. Before the sound of the next shot reached her, Anna shot back. In one smooth motion she pulled back the bolt, cleared the spent cartridge, loaded a new one into the chamber and shot again. She never blinked. She was watching for movement in the darkness.

There was none.

There were no fresh shots.

She never knew if she hit the IS sniper.

When she dared to look above the scope, Yann was gone.

A couple of weeks later, the French doctor invited her to the refugee camp to visit the boy she had saved. When Yann placed little Sadi in her arms, she felt a happy sensation in her belly. When her eyes met Yann's, her cheeks flushed.

That was how it all began.

The joy.

The pain.

Anna stopped her mental DVD player.

She was breathing way too fast, so got up on one knee. The tower rocked slightly as she moved. It felt as though she had a lump stuck in her throat, making it hard to breathe. Her vision was muddled. She concentrated on taking control of her panic attack. She knew that it was all just in her mind but was trying to get her body to understand the same. Eventually her breathing calmed down.

She leant her head against the hole in the wall and looked out of the tower. There was nothing to see, not even with the thermal camera. In the weak starlight, she tried to see if the fracture had widened. As she and Zakariassen had done when *Sabvabaa* was first lowered onto the ice, the Chinese had found an ice floe that was at least a metre and a half thick, a guarantee that it would hold for many more months, but she no longer trusted anything about the ice.

Anna stretched an arm outside to help her blood circulation. Her hand rested on a hinge that stuck out from the roof above her head. Her fingers fiddled with it as she tried to focus on the landscape beyond, but a sharp pain cut into her back as something hit her. She twisted around and saw a black box lying on the floor, below a swinging trapdoor. It had fallen down from a void in the roof. She shone her torch on it and was able to see a mass of cables inside the small space before the weak light faded. Connections for the floodlights. Someone had hidden the box in there.

The killer.

But why?

She picked it up. It was surprisingly light. In the light of the stars she saw three holes at its rear. Above them, incomprehensible Chinese characters were written, but she had seen these kinds of holes before.

Anna knew what the box was for.

56

Anna climbed slowly and painstakingly down the ice-cold, slippery rungs, away from the memories of Yann.

Almost as soon as she had got both feet back on the ground, snow blew up from the drifts again. The wind was picking up. It was as if God, or the North Pole itself, had tamed the storm for a moment just to trick her into believing that everything would work out. Clouds, blacker than the night sky, rolled in from the horizon, blanketing the stars. The short period of calm had been the eye of the storm.

The wind lashed her across the ice to the cabin where the man in the orange jacket lay dead between the racks of servers. She walked over to a cabinet where two black and grey cables hung out from an empty shelf, opened the glass door and held the black box up. It looked like it would fit. The box was what she thought it was: a computer or hard drive.

Anna checked that the dead man's jacket was still in one piece, without bullet holes in his back, then coaxed her hand in under the table and felt her way down the front of the jacket. Her fingers found something hard. A knife handle. It looked like a normal kitchen knife. She crept under the table and saw several deep gashes the knife had sliced into the jacket. This killing seemed to have been a panicked and impulsive act, in contrast to the other murders at Ice Dragon, where the crew had been either frozen to death or shot in cold blood.

She crawled back out from under the table and stood up. Her eyes moved from the dead body to the three screens, which were now showing hyperrealistic pictures of the Northern Lights looming over the ice. Everything in the room had been created by humans, artificial and cold. The laminated plastic table the dead man rested his head on. The retouched images of nature on the screens. The digital tech behind the glass doors. The only product of the natural world was the corpse. Alive, he had got in the way of something. So he was killed.

Anna's intuition, her only tool in the absence of hard facts, told her that it was here, in front of the blinking computers, that everything had begun.

When she returned to the mess, Zakariassen was sitting at a table with Jackie. They were speaking in low voices. Zakariassen was probably trying to find out more about the subsea mine. He stood up abruptly when Anna came in.

"Have you seen him? Lanpo, on the ice?"

She turned around. There was nobody else in the cabin.

"Where's Marco?"

"He's still in the workshop, trying to find a battery that'll power the GPS."

"You mustn't leave him alone."

"I've blocked the door. He can't get out." Zakariassen pointed at the drip bag hanging from the lamp above Jackie. "The bag was empty, so I changed it."

She saw the empty bag lying on the table.

"You need to go back and watch Marco. I need to speak to Jackie now."

"Oh… What do you need to talk about?"

"There's something I'm wondering about… that only he can help me with."

Zakariassen looked at Jackie, and switched to Norwegian.

"I saw you going into the… cabin with the computers. Was there something you were looking for there?"

"Maybe. I found a hard drive up in the tower. Somebody had made the effort to climb all the way up there and hide it."

Zakariassen's eyelashes fluttered behind his thick lenses. "Did you find anything on it?"

"That's what I need Jackie's help for."

He cast a glance at Jackie again.

"I know quite a bit about data. Would it be better if I had a go at it?"

"Thanks for the offer, but we can't spend any time on that now. The hard drive's not critical. What is important is that you make sure Marco sorts out the GPS. We have to stop Lanpo if he really is on his way back here."

Zakariassen clamped his mouth shut and sighed through his nose. A few long nasal hairs blew in the breeze. "What if Lanpo's dead?"

"But you saw what I saw. His signal's moving. Lanpo's alive."

"It might be that a polar bear got him too. The signal could be coming from the bear's guts."

Anna felt her impatience boiling up in her chest. "Might… could… That's too much guesswork for my taste. Let's do what I'm saying now. You look after Marco, I'll take Jackie with me. OK?"

Zakariassen breathed in heavily. Anna noticed that his eyes seemed watery, grey and resigned. He likely realized that no matter what happened, the expedition he had worked so hard towards was over. He was seventy-three. There weren't going to be any more polar expeditions. The only thing that mattered now was trying to survive until help came. Then he could travel back to Norway and try to find meaning in the few years that he had left. She felt a sudden warm fondness for the old man, and put her hand on his shoulder.

"Are you OK, Daniel?"

He smiled quickly, blinking away the moisture from his eyes.

"Yes, yes… I'm all right. We'll do what you say, you probably know best."

57

The wind thrashed grains of ice into the faces of Anna and Jackie as they walked across the yard. Inside the cabin with the servers, they laid the body on the floor and covered it with a tarpaulin from the workshop. She took Jackie's wrists and fastened them to the back of the dead man's chair with zip ties. Then she picked up the hard drive from the table.

"Do you know what this is?"

Jackie looked at the box, then at her. "A hard drive…"

"I know that much already, but do you know what's on it?"

"No."

Anna was determined to find out why so many of the crew at Ice Dragon had been killed, and she was gambling that Lanpo wasn't about to show up right away. Since someone had risked life and limb to hide the hard drive up the tower instead of anywhere else on the base, it had to be extremely important. She plugged it in and connected it to the network. It made a quiet whirring noise and a blue light on its front blinked into life.

"Jackie… you said you were working with data here. Can you tell me why this hard drive was removed?"

His narrow face turned towards her. The glare of the computer monitor bled across the smooth, pale skin of his forehead. Blue lights danced above his long eyelashes. Jackie shook a lock of hair away from his eyes. "I don't know… All the data from the ocean floor is stored here. But to be on the safe side, the data is spread across several hard drives, in case any of them get damaged. Maybe the one you have is damaged?"

"Right. And you usually store defective hard drives up in the tower out there because... that's the simplest solution?"

He looked at her, surprised.

"Who put it up there?"

His reaction and the question seemed genuine.

"Maybe Marco. What do you know about him?"

"He's a decent guy, seems to be a skilled mechanic, maybe likes gambling a bit too much."

"Did Marco owe anyone money?"

"No, but I think Fu and the others... owed him money."

She looked at the tarpaulin covering the dead man.

"The guy who was working here... was he one of the ones who owed Marco?"

Jackie's shoulders rose as he took a deep breath.

"Maybe..."

The hard drive suddenly emitted a grating sound. It was as if the processors had come across something especially interesting. Anna noticed a glimmer of light flickering in the corner of her eye. It was coming from the black slalom helmet hanging on a stand behind the dead man. From inside the helmet. It suddenly struck her that the North Pole was no place for slalom skiing. She walked around the table and took it off the stand. A cable was hanging down on the floor, from where it snaked behind the server cabinets. Where the visor ought to have been, hovering images flickered in the helmet's dark interior.

"What's this?"

"Virtual reality... 3D," replied Jackie. "We use it to study the geological data."

Anna twisted the bow off her body to give herself more room, then pulled the helmet over her head.

The cabin walls fell away.

The world became vast.

She was standing on a plain between serrated mountaintops, which were painted in surreal colours: bright orange at the peaks, yellow and dark green further down. Blinking letters hovered right in front of her: *Missing or corrupt information in this dataset. Restore data from latest backup? Yes? No?*

She place a finger on the virtual *Yes*. The letters became bigger.

Somewhere beyond the helmet a hard drive spun at high speed. Anna was pulled towards and past the mountains so quickly that she almost lost her balance, even though she knew that she wasn't really moving. A dark-blue hole appeared behind the mountains. It grew larger, opening up wide and devouring her. Deep down in a chasm, orange and red lights glowed. An object lay on a ledge at the side of the chasm and above it hung Chinese characters. A yellow triangle was blinking. The object was cylindrical, but broken in three places. Anna realized that she was in a crack or fissure in the ocean floor. The three-dimensional world she was floating in had to have been created by the radar on the seabed. She took a couple of unsteady steps to get closer to the broken cylinder.

The ground shook beneath her feet.

A distant sound forced its way into the helmet. Then a violent rumbling.

From outside.

From the real world.

58

Anna tore off the helmet. Before her, Jackie's face was surrounded by a glowing halo, as if the sun had risen outside the window. She ran out into the snow.

Night really had become day. *Sabvabaa* was surrounded by flames. Enormous columns of fire towered above the hovercraft, sprouting from the blue cabin it had collided with and swaying in the wind like giant trees. The snow rushing past stole light from the fire and pulled it into the dark like strobe flashes. Anna headed towards the inferno but felt as if she were standing still as the firestorm blazed past.

The silhouette of a man was visible on *Sabvabaa*'s hull, the trees of flame scattering burning fir cones onto his red and yellow survival suit. Zakariassen was climbing into the vessel.

A moment later, she saw the hovercraft door opening up again. Zakariassen emerged carrying a fire extinguisher. He ran across the hull towards the side of the boat that was facing the fire.

"Daniel! Get the hell away! The fuel's going to explode!" Anna roared, but the storm snatched her warning and tossed it away over the ice. Zakariassen disappeared around the back of the boat, only his upper torso visible against the flames as he was briefly shrouded in a cloud of foam from the fire extinguisher.

Anna ran in a crouching zigzag towards the fire. The snowdrifts that covered the dead Chinese men cast stark shadows in her direction. The firelight slithered across the icy crust that had formed on the surface of the open fracture, catching its sharp edges. There was no time to run around it. Anna leapt over the half-metre gap and landed crookedly on the other side, falling and rolling, but used the energy to find her feet again.

Zakariassen saw her and jumped down from the hull, running over to meet her halfway.

"Get down!"

She shoved him down with brute force into the snow and threw herself down next to him, her head facing the opposite direction. She stared out towards the darkness between the flames and the main building.

"What are you doing? We have to save *Sabvabaa*!" he yelled.

"We have to save ourselves first!"

Zakariassen followed Anna's eyes in the dark.

"Do you think that… it was him who did it?"

"Fires don't usually start by themselves at twenty below. Did you hear any shots?"

"No, nothing."

She wiped away the snow that had been smeared on her snow goggles. The light from the flames ruined her night vision, and it was impossible to see anything in the darkness beyond the base. A quick glance at *Sabvabaa* revealed what Zakariassen had risked his life for. The side of the boat facing the flames was covered with foam from the fire extinguisher.

"This is a diversion. Lanpo's trying to lure us out. If I were him I would have gone around to the other side by now." The killer could run unseen in the dark surrounding the base, approaching them shielded by the shadows of the cabins. The description Marco and Jackie had given of this stocky, awkward man no longer sounded right. This attack was not the work of a mentally unstable person.

"We can't stay here… We'll make brilliant targets in this light. I'll have to get out there and take him. Daniel, cover me."

She stayed there until Zakariassen had raised the rifle out of the snow, then began crawling towards *Sabvabaa*. The heat of

247

the fire scorched the bare skin between her goggles and the ski mask. Freeze to death, burn to death—the list of ways to die at the North Pole was never-ending.

Once at the hovercraft, she got up and sprinted around to the other side to take shelter behind the hull. She looked towards the open yard. There was nothing to be seen, so she jumped up onto *Sabvabaa* and ducked through the hatch that Zakariassen had left open as he was bringing out the extinguisher. The fire was heating up the cabin, but the windows facing the fuel depot were covered with foam. Hopefully, *Sabvabaa* wouldn't catch fire.

Inside, she crawled on her knees so as not to be seen from outside. The bed beneath the smashed window was heaped with snow that had blown in. In the heat of the fire, small streams of water trickled off it.

She crept through the puddles and reached a hand under the bed. Her fingers fumbled around and snatched at a rucksack. Inside was a small spade, bottles of energy drinks, some combat rations and a sleeping bag with space for one. Her last resort if *Sabvabaa* were totally destroyed and all other emergency gear went to hell.

She grabbed one of the satellite phones from the table the radio transmitter was sitting on. She found the on button and tried calling Boris again, but, as before, the only answer was white noise from outer space.

On the way out, Anna saw a red light blinking on the emergency transponder. When she got the cover open, there was a message on the display: *Rescue team will arrive at your position 7.30 p.m., local time.* Her watch showed that that was almost exactly an hour away. One hour to survive. One hour to make sure Lanpo didn't.

59

"The Americans will be here in an hour."

Zakariassen's eyes grew wide behind his glasses and goggles. In the light of the fire, Anna saw pearls of sweat hanging over his scorched eyebrows. "Are you sure?"

"Yes, they sent a message to the emergency beacon."

The wind had turned again and increased in strength. The North Pole had returned to its original strategy. Snow showers whipped over their heads, lit up like fiery comets by the sea of flames. The fire at the fuel depot also illuminated the ice between the cabins. There was no one there.

"So, we just find somewhere safe to wait then?" the professor asked.

Anna shook her head.

"We can't. Lanpo has a rifle. He can see us from the darkness but we can't see him. He could sneak up and pick us off one by one."

"So what then?"

"I have to go to him. Come on!"

She got up. Zakariassen ran after her, parallel to the fracture. The light of the huge flames cast long shadows across the ice.

Anna stationed Zakariassen in the alley behind the workshop.

"If you see anything on the ice except for a rescue helicopter, shoot. Got it?"

He moved his head in a way that she interpreted as a yes. She ran around the corner and over to the workshop door, pulled back the iron pipe that Zakariassen had barred it with, and walked in. Marco was nowhere to be seen. Anna roared at the top of her lungs.

"It's me! Come out, Marco, or I swear to God I'll burn this cabin down to the ground too!" There was a rustling behind one of the shelves. The mechanic emerged with a terrified expression on his face. He was brandishing a large spanner.

"I didn't know who it was." He hung the spanner back in its marked position on the tool wall. "I heard an explosion. What happened?"

"Lanpo blew up the fuel depot. Now I really need your GPS to find him!"

Marco turned his stout frame towards the tool bench and picked up the screen. He had fastened two large batteries to the rear with gaffer tape. His fingers had black lines under the nails from the work, which left behind a smudge each time he touched the screen. "It works… but I have no idea how long the batteries will last." The satellite map appeared. Anna saw the red bacterial dots marking those dead and alive.

"Where's Lanpo now?"

A grimy fingertip pushed the map upwards until a solitary dot came into view. The skin around Marco's eyes wrinkled. "Lanpo's going… towards the south-west…" The dot marking the killer's position had left behind a digital trace. When Lanpo's dot met a line of latitude, it jumped backwards and forwards, as if the man out on the ice were actually having difficulties overcoming the obstacle.

"How far away is he?"

"Right now… about nine hundred and sixty… four metres."

How far could a man run in ten minutes in this weather? Anna looked at the empty weapons cabinet.

"Do your weapons have infrared laser sights?"

"Yes of course," Marco replied. "How else would we hit anything in the dark?"

That explained how Lanpo had been able to hit the fuel depot from such a distance in the snowstorm. The infrared had picked up the warmth of the cabins, turning night into day.

"Find something I can carry the GPS in," she said.

Marco walked over to a shelf stacked with several black carry-cases. He opened one up and took out an instrument, then laid the improvised GPS finder into it and carried it back to her. She slung the strap over her neck. Now it would be enough to cast a quick glance at the screen to follow Lanpo's position.

"As I said, I don't know how long the batteries will hold out." Marco looked at his contraption with unease.

"I'll take the risk. Come here." She took his hand and led him over to a steel workbench. She bound his wrists around a table leg with zip ties. Worried wrinkles spread across his forehead.

"What if Lanpo... kills you?" he asked.

"Well, then you two aren't my problem any more."

Anna saw a ski pole standing next to the damaged monster tyre, took it with her and walked out. It was as though the fluorescent fabric in Marco's survival suit glowed extra brightly as she left him behind.

"I'm going for Lanpo now!"

She shouted at Zakariassen as she entered the snowstorm. "The bastard's only a kilometre away." She pointed towards the cabin with the computers. "Keep watch over Jackie in there, but make sure to take a look out of the door every other minute."

Zakariassen looked down at the carry-case she had around her neck. The dot marking Lanpo's position glowed in the darkness.

"For God's sake, be careful, Anna," he said. "Don't take any risks."

In his oversized survival suit, he looked smaller and slighter than ever before. The old man had a scared look in his eyes. She realized that it was the fear of what would happen if she didn't return. But she had no choice. He had to stay at Ice Dragon.

251

"I know exactly where Lanpo is," she said, holding up her hunting knife with exaggerated self-confidence. "The pig won't know what hit him."

Zakariassen broke out into a coughing fit. His thin body bent double and the Mauser swung from side to side as he struggled to get his breath back. When he looked at Anna, he had tears in his eyes.

"Anna… I want you to know I'm sorry I dragged you into this." His voice was weak. "All I wanted to do was help."

"Don't worry about that now. I was obviously born to get into trouble." She reached out her arms to hug him. "Take care of yourself, Daniel. I'll be back before you know it."

Anna let go of him and walked quickly into the storm before Zakariassen got even more sentimental.

60

In forty-seven minutes, it would all be over.

The luminous hands of her watch were telling her this was all the time she had before the Americans came. Forty-seven minutes to find Lanpo and neutralize him. Under these extreme circumstances, that could only mean killing him. In the glow of the fire she was walking after her own shadow, but suddenly the light faded. When she turned around, she was just able to see the remains of the fuel depot collapsing into the ice. Some flames struggled free from the sinking cabin, rose up and were ripped to shreds by the wind. Darkness returned.

With her back to the storm, she dropped down on one knee to wait for her night vision to return. The snow was settling around her like a body bag. In just a short while she would be transformed into a snow sculpture. With her head deep inside her hood, she was in her own little universe, far removed from everything. The darkness seeped in and exhausted her. She wanted nothing more than to sleep.

A soft voice entered her mind.

"Are you OK, Anna?"

"No, I'm not fucking OK."

"I believe in you. You can do this."

"Bloody easy for you to say, Yann, you're dead."

He didn't argue back.

Willpower took over. It ordered a hand down into the snow, lifted her goggles away from her face, and rubbed the snow into her eyes. The cold quickly brought her to her senses as the storm wind tore the snow off her back and forced Anna Aune back out onto the ice. She switched on a headlamp she had taken from the workshop.

In front of her, she could only just make out the vague outlines of blocks of ice. Her determination forced her to set one foot in front of the other. With the wind at her back, the challenge suddenly became to keep her pace down. There could be numerous fractures concealed under the fresh snow.

The ski pole from the workshop functioned like the white cane used by the blind. She thrust the tip into the snow to check if the ice would hold. When she reached the towering wall of pressure ridges *Sabvabaa* had almost collided with, she found some shelter behind an ice block and took a closer look at Marco's improvised GPS receiver.

Lanpo's red dot was now scarcely four hundred metres away. It was still moving westwards. Anna pulled out her secret weapon, the heat-seeking camera. Holding it in one hand, she clambered up the craggy ice blocks. Fresh snow had settled high up on their peaks, and her feet constantly lost grip on the slick surface. While she climbed, her feet kicked away loose lumps of ice, the howling wind drowning out the sounds that might have forewarned Lanpo. She switched the headlamp off, grabbed hold of the tallest block and hauled herself up, high above a deep fissure in the pressure ridge.

The storm wind snatched at her hands as she balanced the camera over the edge of the ridge. In order to see anything, she had to push her goggles up. The snow hacked away at her eyes and, on the screen of the heat camera, the only thing to be seen were shades of dark blue. By twisting herself around on the ice block, she got the camera aimed towards the south. Rippling across the screen like an amoeba in a constant state of flux, a yellow speck appeared: the heat from a living creature.

The killer was on the other side of the wall of ice.

The vision opened up her skin's every pore. Through the warm suit, her body absorbed the icy cold like a sponge. Anna felt like a brittle glass sculpture. If she fell now, she would be smashed against the ground like the ice men in the big yellow building.

She swiftly ducked down so as not to be seen, but was too reckless. She lost her footing, starting to slip downwards into the breach. She dropped the heat camera and grasped at a protrusion in the ice. Her body twisted and she came to a stop, hanging halfway into the deep crack. She kicked her legs until her boots gripped the ice again. On the way down, she tried to memorize Lanpo's precise position on the other side of the pressure ridge.

Once she was down, she walked slowly towards the end of the ice barricade with the knife in her hand. She counted her steps as she walked. The wind increased in strength where the wall of ice ended. When Anna stopped, her hood flapped violently. If Lanpo had seen her at the top, he would know which way she was coming.

"Come on Anna, you can do this."

"Shut the hell up."

She flung herself away from the pressure ridge, met the headwind and struggled her way back along the other side of the wall of ice. She counted her steps, stopping at one hundred and fifty. Now she was back where the heat camera had captured Lanpo's body heat. The wind carried flood waves of snow over the pressure ridge, but there was nothing sheltering by the wall.

The endless howling of the storm wind suddenly grew in strength, as if a new set of string players were beginning to play in a symphony orchestra. But this was not the sound of violins. It was the darker sound of violas. The wailing stopped suddenly, then returned. It wasn't the wind making the sound.

It was something else.

It was coming from a large block of ice that Anna could barely see in the dark, just a few metres away. A hideout for Lanpo. She ran towards it, the hunting knife up and ready. Her shoulder took the force of the blow as the storm wind flung her the last few metres. She stood panting, her back pressed against the ice.

Right or left?

Never take the first route you think of.

Always be unpredictable.

Anna went to the left with her back pressed up against the ice block. She let the wind guide her round. When she got to the other side there was nothing in front of the raised blade, just a huge snowdrift that had blown up against the ice.

She switched the headlamp back on, its beam of light illuminating the snowdrift. She could see dark spots. Traces of blood passing over the drift.

Anna turned off the headlamp again and ran to the side of the snowdrift. If Lanpo had seen the light, she wanted to be in another position when he arrived to investigate. The howling was replaced by barking. He had to have the dog with him.

She stooped as she walked along the edge of the snowdrift, letting one hand hang down into it in order to have something to guide her in the dark. The barking dog was directly in front of her. Now she could hear something else, too. Rougher, deeper. A snorting, wheezing sound.

She raised her hand to the headlamp, held the knife above her head, and switched on the light.

The bright light captured another snowdrift. But this one was moving across the ice. It twisted in the wind towards her. Then she saw three black circles in the white.

The nose and eyes of a polar bear.

61

Anna realized her mistake in a split second and cursed herself once more. The pursuit of Lanpo had given her tunnel vision. Humans aren't the only ones that give off heat at the North Pole.

The polar bear pushed its ears back and dropped its head. It was ready to attack. Anna yelled at the top of her lungs as she wriggled out of her backpack. The bear swung its broad head from side to side. Something behind it stirred. She tore the spade out of the backpack, continuing to roar as she brandished the spade and her knife.

The dog barked again, and the bear turned around. Anna took a step forward. When the bear turned back to her, she lashed out with the spade, hitting its snout, before she retreated again. The bear snorted, lifting a paw to its nose. Anna raised the knife. If she attacked the bear now, she had just one chance. The knife had to strike at its throat beneath the jaws.

A grey form rushed out of the darkness. The dog snapped at the bear's rear before pulling back into the darkness again. The bear whipped around again. Anna saw a black stripe across its fur, travelling across its protruding ribcage. The dog launched forward once more. The predator swiped violently at the dog, which shimmied backwards, barked and leapt forward again. The bear tried again, but again the dog danced elegantly away, growling and snarling at its foe.

The bear let out a frustrated roar. It shook its head from side to side, then turned away, hobbling into the darkness and vanishing with the dog on its tail. Anna dropped to her knees and stared out at the darkness towards where the polar bear had faded from view, trying to hear it over the whistling of the wind. She was breathing so fast that stars came to her eyes and keeping hold of the knife was difficult.

The dog came running back. It looked like a wolf, its ears standing erect above the head, its snout long and pointed. Its coat was grey, almost white, its eyes bright sparkles in the darkness. A husky. It had to be the Chinese commander's dog.

"Sunzi! Sunzi! Good girl, Sunzi!" Anna shouted.

Her cries coaxed the dog towards her. Sunzi began to lick Anna's face, her wet tongue leaving trails of slobber on her ski goggles. Anna threw her arms around her, pulling Sunzi into her and feeling the warmth of her breath against her face. The dog whimpered and whined. She saw red on her wagging tail, a mixture of fresh blood and congealed lumps. It must have been the bullet wound from Zakariassen's Mauser.

"Did the polar bear try to get you, hmm?… Did it smell your blood?" She tried to touch the tail, but the dog whined and pulled away. "Relax, I won't do you any harm."

Sunzi was standing a few metres away, whining softly and occasionally turning her head towards the dark. She barked towards the vanishing polar bear.

Anna crawled backwards and found the backpack that she had slung into the snow. Digging down into it, she pulled out one of the food rations, tore it open and held the fatty mass of meat out for Sunzi. The smell lured the dog towards her. She sniffed sceptically at first, before guzzling the food down greedily.

Anna picked up the GPS. The screen was covered in snow after the fall and the batteries would soon be dead, but the red dot marking Lanpo's position was almost in the centre of the image. He couldn't be far away.

To find her bearings, she turned all the way around with her eyes fixed to the dot on the screen. Lanpo was still to her west.

She didn't have time to check the distance before the screen blinked black, but now she had a mental map. The pressure ridge stretched westwards. Lanpo couldn't be more than a hundred metres further along.

"Come on girl, I'm trying to find someone—are you going to help me?" The husky ran around her eagerly, tongue dangling from her maw. When Anna started walking, Sunzi followed.

Her near-death experience stuck with her. Every sense was on high alert. The surroundings revealed themselves in high definition. Every snowflake that darted through the air was a potential danger. Anna could hear her boots breaking through the ice, each crunch a warning of the fractures that might tear open.

She counted each step.

At eighty-three, Sunzi barked.

Something cracked in the dark.

She stopped dead.

Listened. Tried to distinguish a threat in the cacophony of the howling wind, the creaking of the pressure ridge and the rustling of her survival suit around her ears. Finally, she heard it again. Several sharp snaps in quick succession, like a flag flapping in the breeze. Sunzi barked again. Anna tried hushing her, but she ran towards the noise and vanished in the dark.

She ran after the dog, looping in an arc to avoid being hit if Lanpo heard Sunzi and started shooting. As she ran into the hard headwind, the ice-cold air felt as thick as jelly. Sunzi was barking fearsomely somewhere away to the right. She dropped down on one knee, peering towards the sound. Something was lying in the snow ahead of her.

A pile of snow disappeared, only to appear again. For a moment she feared that Sunzi had led her back to the polar bear, but then she heard it again, and it triggered a memory.

*

In her mind, the wind's howl became a staccato thrum.

Helicopter rotors.

A hand struck her on the back, the coarse voice of a man ordering her to jump. The moments before her first ever skydive.

The snap as the parachute opened up. Pivoting around, she glimpsed the helicopter's fuselage shrinking away in the sky above.

The shock when her feet hit the ground. The jerking of the wind filling the chute as it billowed up. The pain from the cords digging into her arms as she tugged out the wind.

Anna walked slowly over to the fluttering parachute.

It had collapsed across an ice block and, as the wind blew at its edges, it made a cracking sound. Sunzi growled and sniffed at an object partly buried in the snow in front of the chute.

A sled.

The cords were tied to it, jumping like white serpents each time the parachute thrashed upwards. For once, Anna ignored her curiosity and did the right thing. She ran in the opposite direction and lay in the shelter of the wall of ice, staring towards the sled. If Lanpo heard Sunzi's barking now, he would surface. His hatred for the commander's dog would be too tempting to ignore.

The snow blowing over the pressure ridge hit the back of her head, pushing the hood over her face. Her view was so poor that she could scarcely see Sunzi. The dog kept running backwards and forwards between the sled and the parachute, her snarling blending with the roar of the storm.

After ten minutes of motionlessness, she got up again.

She walked over to the sled through the deep snow.

Sunzi leapt towards her, pushing her warm muzzle into her hands and whimpering softly.

Anna bent over with her back to the wind to see what was in the sled. The load was covered with a tarpaulin and the rope holding it down was frozen stiff, the knots impossible to untie. She stuck the tip of her knife under the rope, barely registering any resistance as the blade cut it in two.

The snow on the tarp lay in a thick crust, and it stayed there even with the ropes cut. Sunzi was standing so close to her that her breath fogged up the edges of Anna's goggles. She pulled the frozen tarp free, revealing splayed claws. A muted scream rose from her throat as she reeled backwards. Her knife-wielding hand reared up in a defensive reflex.

In the torchlight she realized that the claws were, in fact, the fingers of a hand.

62

No film had shaken Anna more than *Seven*. David Fincher's masterpiece was one of many VHS tapes Welfare Services sent along once a month on the Hercules aircraft to the war-torn airport in Priština. *Seven* was shown in the mess at Film City the week before the American soldier got blown to pieces by a NATO cluster bomb.

What shocked her most of all wasn't the grotesque killings, but the moment the demonic serial killer, played by Kevin Spacey, walked into the police station and handed himself in to Brad Pitt and Morgan Freeman. There and then, Anna knew that this director loved to fuck with his audience. There were no happy endings in this movie.

Without even realizing what she was doing, she had yelled along with Freeman when he shouted his useless warning to Brad Pitt: "Don't open the box!" The others in the audience weren't very pleased with her.

Now it was too late for her as well.

The box was open.

The splayed fingers reached up from a figure encrusted in frost. On the sled, a person was lying folded like a jackknife. The eyes were closed beneath thick eyebrows, the mouth a narrow line above a broad jaw.

When Lanpo's frozen body was revealed to her, all the blood rushed from Anna's head. The North Pole swayed beneath her feet; gravity betrayed her. Down was up. She needed to sit down. There was no question about how the man in the sleigh had died. The hole above his bushy eyebrows left no doubt. Lanpo had been shot. The T-shirt and the long johns he was wearing made clear where it had happened. In his bed. As he slept.

"Fuck fuck fucking hell!"

"Calm down, love," Yann's voice whispered through her mind.

"How? I've been fooled! I've been fooled like a stupid little girl!"

"Panicking won't help. Think about all the angles."

One by one she went through the events that had lead her here. Loose threads weaved together into an obvious pattern, and ragged fractures cut through a white landscape of coincidences, but even a cynic such as her could not bear to follow the clues all the way to their logical conclusion. It was too hideous. These ideas couldn't be right. There had to be something her beaten up, frozen brain had overlooked.

But no matter how she imagined Lanpo might have ended up on a sled, being dragged across the ice by a parachute, the answer came back the same. This was done to lure her away from Ice Dragon.

She finally got up and walked crouching into the wind and the snow flurries to find shelter by the pressure ridge. She pulled out the satellite phone from her rucksack and switched it on. Now the symbol showing that it had contact with the satellites suddenly lit up. Ignoring the cold, she tore off her gloves and scrolled down to Boris's number. The phone's plastic casing was ice cold as she pressed it against her ear.

There was a quivering tone: she actually had a connection.

Boris answered almost instantly.

"Hi Anna. I was almost starting to worry about you." As usual, the Russian sounded tipsy. The familiar voice ought to have given her hope, but instead it felt more like her guts were tumbling into an abyss.

His words confused her.

"Don't mess me about now, Boris. Just tell me that there are people on their way to Ice Dragon."

"Sorry, Anna, I'm not understanding you. Who should be on the way? The only ones I know are on the ice are you two. Have you found the Chinese?"

"You didn't get the message?"

The meteorologist's voice assumed a serious tone. "I know nothing more than what you already told me, that you saw a distress signal coming from the Ice Dragon base. Why, what's happened?"

"Boris, it's a scene from hell here. Everybody is dead. The entire crew. You need to send people here now."

"Dead? How... has there been an accident?"

"No, they've been murdered... everybody. You need to send soldiers, armed." Anna was shouting to be sure that Boris understood the words correctly above the wind.

"The killer is still alive, and he's at Ice Dragon... *now*."

63

The American coastguard picked up even faster than Boris.

"Yes, ma'am." A man with a thick southern accent confirmed that Zakariassen's emergency call had been received.

"Why haven't you notified the Russians? Isn't their base closer?" Anna was trying to shield the receiver from the wind, but it was difficult to hear what the American was saying.

"Don't worry, ma'am... Our team got held up a little, but they will be with you within the hour. How are weather conditions in the area?"

There was no need to check. The telephone was already covered with a thick layer of wet snow. "Stormy with visibility below ten metres."

"Is Professor Zakariassen with you? Can I speak to him?"

"Not right here. Did he tell you that everyone is dead, the Chinese crew has been killed?" Something about the American's steady tone irritated her immensely. It was as if he hadn't heard what she was telling him.

"Yes, the professor told me that you have detained a suspect." The words arrived without the slightest hesitation or surprise. As if such things were a daily occurrence for the US Coastguard. Something just didn't feel right.

Anna screamed out in frustration before switching off the phone. "Well the team had better get here ASAP or someone's arse is gonna get kicked!"

She found the last of the rations in her bag, and with numb, frozen fingers, tore off the plastic, sharing the sausage meat with Sunzi. It tasted rank but, in her state of mind, Anna could have been eating a three-Michelin-star meal without even knowing the difference. She dug some snow loose and sucked it from her hand, the cold flakes of ice dissolving in her mouth. It became a part of her, and she became a part of it, both of them in danger of being wiped from the face of the earth, both of them a source of unwanted friction and defiance in the mechanisms of the world.

With her back to the wind and Sunzi by her side, Anna set off towards Ice Dragon. When she reached the wall of ice, she took shelter there for a moment, trying to imagine what scenarios might be awaiting her. When she got back to the base, the killer would know that she knew what he had done: killed Lanpo, put his corpse on the sled, fastened a parachute to it and sent it out onto the ice to create a diversion before she and Zakariassen arrived. He had made sure that suspicion fell on an outside enemy. The killer had planned every move of his gory game. He had foreseen every countermove. If it weren't for the fact that thirteen people were dead, Anna could almost have admired her opponent's genius.

Her body began to shudder. At first she thought it was her legs shivering.

She clutched her thighs, but the shaking was coming from below. It was the ice that was trembling. Cracking. A light ripped through the dark. A trip flare had been triggered. A juddering bass rumble filled the atmosphere. As Anna jumped to her feet, she was met by the wind shooting keen and cold across the ice. The trip flare sizzled in the darkness, its sparks drifting in the wind. Then another crack. In the dull light, a black snake slithered towards her.

64

Anna ran as fast as her legs would carry her along the fracture that was rupturing the floe, towards Ice Dragon.

The new fissure was already a metre wide. The noise of the tearing ice was drowned out by the storm and her own gasping for breath, but Anna could feel the floe shaking under her feet. Sunzi ran alongside her in silence as if she understood that the killer was near. The base ahead was in darkness apart from the weak light shining from the buildings' windows. The fracture ended at a black hole in the ice, the hole the fuel depot had left behind as it burned through the floe. The sea below had already begun to freeze over. When Anna saw *Sabvabaa*'s red and green navigation lights appear out of the night, she came to a stop. Incredibly, the hovercraft looked almost undamaged. Anna ran over to it and hauled herself up on the hull.

The foam that Zakariassen had sprayed on its side had frozen into a sticky pulp that slipped away beneath her hands. Sunzi stayed on the ice, sniffing at the rubber skirting before cocking a leg and pissing in the wind.

Anna crept through the cockpit until she had a clear view of the closest cabin. Marco's pickup had been moved there. A dark shape was lying in the snow in front of the truck, but in the flickering light from the cabin windows, it was hard to make it out clearly. She crept over to her bed, and dug out her binoculars from the North Face bag. Through the image-intensifier, she could see what it was.

A person.

In the weak light it was impossible to tell who, but whoever it was, they weren't moving.

Anna raised the binoculars slightly. The truck filled her field of vision. It looked empty. She swept back down to the motionless figure. The legs were pointing towards her and she could see the double reflective strips above the knees. It was Zakariassen. One foot moved slightly.

Daniel was alive.

She crept back out and slipped down from the hull. A crunching sound splintered the whistling of the wind. As Anna turned, she saw a new fracture opening up along the front of the base. Thin rifts were darting away from the ice like gnarled fingers. The ice floe on which the Chinese base was built was splintering before her eyes. Sunzi pushed her snout into Anna's face and whimpered quietly, sensing too that the ice was about to die.

She turned around and looked across *Sabvabaa*'s deck. Through the snowstorm, she couldn't see the garage behind the main building. Neither Jackie nor Marco was in sight. A glance at the watch told her that the Americans should have arrived ten minutes ago. She looked up at the dark sky. A sudden gust of wind rushed across her face as if an invisible whale had swum by at close quarters, the snow following in its wake like devoted suckerfish. There was no light in the sky, no sound of any helicopter.

The wind pressure was making the hovercraft's hull judder. The bass rumbling from the disintegration of the ice was closing in on her, but if she were going to rescue Zakariassen, she had to block out any thought of the ground crumbling beneath her feet. As long as the ice held out, so would she.

She picked up the satellite phone and called Boris's number again. A crackling sound cut into her ears. The connection was lost once more. Out in the dark a bright comet was born, another flare hissing up into the snowstorm. Anna forced herself not to look up at the light. She couldn't risk losing her night vision now.

Yann's voice whispered above everything else. "Come on, my love. You're smart. You can do this."

The smartest thing would be to stay put. *Sabvabaa* provided cover and a view over the terrain. It was a position that could be defended. If the whole ice floe broke into pieces, the hovercraft would float in the water. Pure logic dictated that she wait for rescue exactly where she was.

"Go on. You can do anything you set your mind to."

"Yann, you're really fucking annoying, you know that?"

She launched herself into the wind and ran out into the open yard, springing over the fracture to reach the corner of the main building, from where she peered out. From that angle, the truck was masking Zakariassen.

"Daniel?" Her voice battled through the wind.

Several seconds passed before the wind carried Zakariassen's voice back, thin and frail in the storm. "Anna, for God's sake... help me."

She could hear the husky growling behind her. Sunzi recognized the man who had shot her.

She was squeezing the hunting knife so hard that she could feel the pattern of the handle through her gloves. She looked around. Her eyes followed the jagged, black vein in the ice towards the hovercraft, then skittered between the cabin windows she could see through the snow flurries. Empty. Empty. Empty.

"Where are the others?" she shouted.

"I think he's... in the garage."

He.

The monster.

The murderer.

"Please, Anna—please help me."

She looked towards the garage. It was a grey and indistinct behind the blankets of snow flurrying past. The door was still open, but it was impossible to see if the killer were hiding in

269

there. She held up the binoculars and the grey mass became more defined. She could see the oil barrel with its pump and the edge of the tractor behind the other door. Black stains outside the closed door, bleeding outwards, covering the garage. A man dressed in orange standing in front.

Headless.

No, not that, his head was hidden inside a black hood, barely visible against the scorched wall behind him.

Then Yann pulled the hood off, and smiled at her.

"You've got this, girl."

Anna tore her eyes away from the cold binoculars. The garage was just the garage again. She ran from the main building towards Zakariassen.

The cabins danced in a blur before her eyes, her feet sliding in the deep snow, but she found her balance again and grabbed hold of the truck. Zakariassen was lying on his back with his arms stretched out to the side. He wasn't moving. The snow whirled over the roof of the pickup, and some stray crystals of ice darted in through an open window. The cab was empty.

She walked towards Zakariassen with her eyes glued to the cabins on the other side of the truck. One was slanting a little— the ice beneath it had given way. When her foot struck an arm, she looked down. Zakariassen's face was buried deep inside his hood. His eyes blinked in the shadows.

"Daniel, what happened? Are you hurt?"

"No, but… I'm sorry, I've really screwed up this time."

Time froze. There weren't any marks of violence on his survival suit. No bullet holes. No knife slashes. Sunzi stopped barking. It turned eerily quiet.

Something hard prodded the back of her head.

65

The voice accompanying it was just as hard. Familiar, but at the same time foreign.

"Drop the knife!"

Zakariassen's face was frozen in a grimace.

"D... do as he says," he stuttered.

"What are you doing, Daniel?"

"Please, drop the knife or he will kill you."

The hard object shoved her head forward. Daniel had been the decoy as the killer lay in wait on the floor of the truck. Now he was standing at the open window brandishing a rifle or a pistol, its muzzle pushed against her head.

She let go. The snow caught the knife like it was nothing.

"Pick it up," the voice ordered.

Zakariassen sat up in the snow, leaning forward on his knees, and crept over to the hollow the knife had made. He dug it out. His hands enlarged the hole so that it looked like an eye. The black ice stared up at Anna. *Gotcha.*

Zakariassen rose to his feet and stood there with the knife in his hands.

Anna was trying to catch his gaze. "What the fuck is this, Daniel? Don't you realize that you're helping a murderer?"

"No, you're wrong. It wasn't him who killed these people."

"Don't you believe that, Daniel. I found Lanpo. He's dead... He was shot and thrown on a sled to lure us away... To lure me away."

The final piece of the puzzle fell into place.

Her mind fished an image out of her memory: a padlocked wooden box with red and yellow labels. It was in the workshop.

Then she remembered a fountain of ice shooting towards the black sky on the last day of their first week in this frozen world. Zakariassen had laughed like a kid as the ice exploded. The blast sent a shockwave down to the seabed. When the sound waves from the explosion bounced back, they were tracked by the instruments. A cost-effective way of drawing a good map of the ocean floor. Zakariassen had called it a flying start to the expedition.

"You blew up the fuel depot, didn't you, Daniel."

Zakariassen just stood there with his mouth gaping, as if he couldn't get enough oxygen.

"You don't understand… There is something else here, Anna, something much more important."

"What's more important than all the people who were killed? Listen to yourself. You're talking like a madman."

Zakariassen shook his head insistently. "No… No, no, this isn't madness. It's politics."

"Politics? Oh my God, is that how you got your money, Daniel? That huge chunk you were lacking. You were getting paid to spy on the Chinese."

Zakariassen walked in an arc around her with the knife in his hand. He was holding it away from his body, as if he feared infection. "No, it wasn't like that at all. I was just asked to observe them, nothing else. That's God's honest truth. This… What happened here was never the intention… I had no idea."

Frozen hinges creaked as the truck door opened behind Anna. It slammed hard into her back and forced her forward.

She turned around.

She saw the killer. He was different now.

His face was still pale, his nose still narrow, his lips thick and oddly fleshy. His hair hung stubbornly over his eyes, but beneath his long eyelashes freakish pupils stared back at her, trembling with a manic energy. He had shed his mask. The veins in the hand holding the revolver bulged and coiled visibly like tapeworms. Anna saw a dark bloodstain on his trigger finger.

Above the revolver sight, her eyes met Jackie's.

66

Jackie sat down in the open doorway of the pickup, both hands around the revolver. He leant slightly to one side with his injured shoulder hanging limp.

"Tie her up," he said to Zakariassen.

"I don't have any rope," he replied.

Jackie's face flushed with irritation and the blood vessels in his temples throbbed. His bloodstained finger played with the gun's trigger.

"You don't need to tie me up."

His dark eyes studied her without flinching. "What should I do with you, then?"

"Nothing… If you put the revolver down, nothing's going to happen. Nothing worse than what has already happened."

"Everything is Qiang's fault."

Anna tried desperately to remember who Qiang was.

"He attacked me. It was just self-defence… It was an accident," Jackie murmured, as though he were speaking to himself.

"I know. Everybody's going to understand that. Accidents happen." Anna was placating Jackie while noting Zakariassen's position out of the corner of her eye. He was standing just far enough away that it was impossible to reach him easily.

"Can I ask you one thing, Jackie? What are you all really looking for here?"

"Scandium, yttrium, lanthanum, cerium, praseodymium, neodymium, samarium, europium, gadolinium, terbium, dysprosium, holmium, erbium, thulium, ytterbium, lutetium, promethium," he said. Then he repeated the words, rapidly and rhythmically, like a well-learnt rhyme. "That's what we're looking for."

Anna was moving her arms slowly towards her chest. "Means nothing to me. What the hell are they?"

"The names of seventeen elements. The rare earth elements. There are deposits worth billions here."

One hand slid down to the strap holding the GPS receiver against her chest.

"And why are *you* really here?" Jackie asked. "Are you spying for Norway?"

"No."

"But you're a soldier."

"Was."

"You've treated me like shit."

"That was never my intention, Jackie."

He turned the revolver over in his hand, shut one eye and aimed it at her.

"I've done nothing wrong… Everything is Qiang's fault."

Now she remembered who Qiang was: the man in the orange jacket in the data room. She had been right. It had all started there.

"What did Qiang do to you?"

Jackie was staring back at her but it was impossible to tell if he was hearing what she was saying. "You're no good. You came here and took me captive. I was wounded, but you tied me to the bed like a dirty criminal."

Anna squeezed on the clip of the strap holding the carry-case.

"And I'm really sorry about that, Jackie, but you have to understand the position I was in too. I was trying to make the best of a difficult situation. We just wanted to help."

"I don't know what I'm going to do with you… You're a pain in the ass."

"You don't need to do anything."

"Scandium, yttrium, lanthanum, cerium, praseodymium, neodymium, samarium, europium, gadolinium, terbium, dysprosium, holmium, erbium, thulium, ytterbium, lutetium, promethium." He said the rhyme slower this time, the barrel of the revolver rising and falling in time with the syllables.

She switched to Norwegian.

"What did the Americans say to you, Daniel, when they told you you had to help this wacko?"

Zakariassen's head jerked towards her as though it were being pulled on an invisible chain. "They said… that there's something here that could destroy the world. That Jackie had found it and so he had to be protected at all costs. Why should I doubt them?"

"Stop talking!" Jackie yelled. The veins in his temple bulged even more.

The muzzle of the revolver swung in an arc towards Zakariassen. Anna released the clip from the strap, grabbed it hard and slung the GPS receiver around like a hammer at Jackie's head.

67

The bag struck Jackie on the shoulder and the revolver recoiled in his hand as he pulled the trigger. Daniel yelped and staggered backwards. Anna was already making her escape.

She ran into the darkness, each step in a new direction.

Right.

Left.

Run. Run!

The revolver thundered behind her. Just by her legs, shards of ice sprayed up and blew away in the wind. Then another burst. She didn't know where Jackie's shot hit; all she knew was that her legs were twice as long as his, and he was suffering from his presumably self-inflicted wound. With every metre that she put between them, the revolver became less deadly, and the darkness protected her better. She had no idea where she was heading. She just ran.

Out towards the ice.

Towards the void.

The last cabin emerged from the darkness.

There was a bulging in the ice. A dark vein broke open right in front of her. She jumped and cleared it just as the staccato cracks of machine-gun fire burst behind her.

She dropped to the snow and rolled.

The bullets zipped over her.

She got up again and continued towards the cabin, pulling open the door and running inside to be met with the stench of rancid grease. Marco was still chained to the tool bench, staring at her in terror.

Anna swivelled and saw the weapons cabinet next to the door. She grabbed one side and leant backwards, dragging it out so it stood parallel to the door, then shoved it at the top with both hands so that it toppled and went over. There was a bang from outside just as the cabinet began to fall. Jackie's next shot was drowned out by the noise of the cabinet slamming to its side on the floor in front of the door.

"Down!" she yelled at Marco. He hunkered under the work bench despite his hand still being zip-tied to the table leg.

Anna lay behind the steel cabinet facing Marco as she listened for the footsteps she knew were approaching the cabin from outside. The shadow of the bench obscured Marco's face, making him look like a headless torso.

"Don't give up, Anna."

She clenched her eyes shut and pressed her head against the cabinet.

Bam!

The metal shook as the bullet sliced through the door and hit the back of the cabinet.

Bam!

Splinters sprayed and a screwdriver tumbled from the tool wall above Marco. His head reappeared as he staggered up, struggling desperately to wriggle free from the zip tie.

Bam!

The metal dented right in front of Anna's face. She heard sounds in the snow outside. Jackie was tugging at the door handle.

Bam!

The shot flew over the cabinet. The *Playboy* model China Lee got a bullet in the breast, her violet rabbit ears quivering as the poster was perforated. Anna pushed herself into the floor, trying to make herself as small as possible. She stayed there, counting every second. It lasted and lasted. Then she heard a distant sound approaching. The grunt of an engine.

She huddled tighter.

A crash. The whole building shook as it was rammed across the ice. Tools showered down from the walls like snowflakes of iron and steel. Marco yelped as a hammer struck him on the head. Then came the creaking of metal. She twisted her head and looked up.

Just in time to see the weapons cabinet falling towards her.

Blackout.

68

It's strange how obvious everything seems once you have the answers.

Zakariassen's strange eagerness to come to the aid of the Chinese. His constant switching from fearlessness to fright. Anna's father telling her that his childhood friend was struggling to find the last of the cash to finance the expedition. There were plenty of people who wanted to conduct research at the North Pole and the competition to coax money from sponsors' hands was tough. Then, as if by magic, the money had suddenly appeared.

These thoughts coursed through Anna's mind with brilliant clarity, even though now it really did feel as if her head were clamped in the jaws of a polar bear. She tried to move, but the immense weight of the weapons cabinet was holding her against the floor.

"Marco, can you help me?" Her voice was shaky. She tried twisting her head to see him, but the cabinet had her pinned down.

"I can't get free either," he shouted back.

Of course. All thanks to you, Anna, she thought to herself, but tried to focus on her breathing. She twisted her legs and wriggled her toes. Her back wasn't broken. At least that was something. She could hear nothing from outside but the howling of the wind and a weak hissing sound. Why had Jackie given up?

Something cold squirmed under her stomach. Water.

Now she realized what the hissing sound was. It was the sea spouting up from somewhere inside the workshop.

Another sound forced its way through the walls. A low rumbling. The building trembled, then began to tumble to the side. As the cabinet shifted, its shelves cut into Anna's spine. Greased by the seawater seeping in, gravity pulled the cabinet downwards. Her fingers found a protrusion on the wall to grasp on to as the cabinet slid over her.

A sound of metal scraping against plastic.

The weight on her spine vanished.

Marco screamed.

She got up on her knees on the tilting floor and saw the Chinese man crushed behind the weapons cabinet, which had slid down to the lower end of the cabin. The water running in through a split in the floor was already sloshing far up the side of the cabinet.

Anna let go of the protrusion and slid down towards Marco, slipping into the seawater. Now the only thing keeping them afloat was the plastic floor.

"I can't get free." Marco was pulling frantically at the zip tie binding him to the tool bench. Anna waded around the cabinet, grabbed the end of it and pushed. It budged a little, but as soon as she let go it slid back towards Marco again.

The workshop listed downwards even further, and seawater cascaded in.

A long row of shelves tore itself free and crashed into the end of the weapons cabinet, pivoting it around, away from Marco and into Anna, pinning her against the wall. She tried to struggle free, but the shelves wouldn't shift. Was this how she was going to die? Drowning in a filthy plastic shack? She looked around her. All the tools had dropped into the water. She needed a knife or saw. Her panic was climbing at the same rate as the water.

She closed her eyes and repeated her mantra over and over until a sense of control returned. *See what's really there, Anna.* Her memory rewound to the first time she entered the workshop, when she had seen yellow boxes, screwdrivers, monkey wrenches, axes, nail guns and ice drills hanging on the walls. Engine parts and hoses. The parachute in the netting. Two spare windows. A sled for Sunzi. A spare tyre. The weapons cabinet bust open. She fast-forwarded to what had been lying on the floor in front of the cabinet. A sawn-off padlock.

"I've got a hacksaw!"

Marco stared at her, his eyes wide open. "Where?"

"In one of my pockets, you can cut through the zip tie with it."

He leant forward and stretched out an arm, feeling his way down in the narrow gap between the shelves and her body. He found her hip pocket and forced his hand in. Sparks rained down from the roof. The lights cut out. Marco groaned in the darkness and she felt his fingers fumbling around her thigh.

"Got it."

He pulled out a solid object. She heard the fabric of Marco's survival suit as he moved, then the sound of metal against plastic. He began sawing.

Outside, Sunzi was barking madly and battering against the workshop door. The darkness was consumed by the ear-splitting crunch of the ice tearing itself apart. Anna sensed the shelves pressing harder into her belly as the building began to flip. Seawater climbed along her spine, ran into her survival suit and soaked her face.

"No! Fuck this!"

She barely had time to curse fate before seawater rushed up over her head. The inky darkness forced its way into her eyes and drove water up her nostrils. *The ice sends its regards. We've been waiting for you.*

The pressure against her stomach suddenly vanished. Fingers closed around her hands, pulling her towards them, up out of the sea. Marco's breath was warm on her face. He pulled her with him towards the end of the cabin and forced himself against the door.

"I can't do it… I can't get the door open," he groaned.

She grabbed hold of him and threw herself against the door too, but an invisible force held it shut. Anna looked Marco in the eyes as she gathered the last of her strength. "Come on! Now!" They launched themselves at the door again. It caved.

Shards of ice struck Anna in the face as the Arctic Ocean flooded into the cabin. The sea wrenched at her, its freezing fingers clutching at her body under the survival suit. She floundered as she struggled against the flow. Beyond the open door, she glimpsed the light from a cabin shining from the ice. The sea quickly raced up towards the roof. The cabin sank. The ice beneath the surface opened its saw-edged teeth, smirked and swallowed.

So there you are.

69

Anna was sinking.

The sea had filled her survival suit, its coldness like razor blades against her skin. It pressed painfully against her eardrums. She reflexively pinched her nose and blew out to balance the pressure.

Her legs struck something solid. She coiled up and pushed off it, the kick sending her body through the water towards the door. Then, a sharp pain in her elbow. Marco was hauling her out. Her lungs throbbed as the last of the air forced its way out of her mouth. She saw a trickle of air bubbles rising through the water, then her vision began to dim. Her arms were useless, paralysed by the cold.

Why are you so scared?

Yeah, why? She had been heading down this road for so long. She saw a vision of the grave lantern, miles away, burning on the ice until the snow smothered the flame. The snow would form a little mound over it, then the wind would sweep across it, grinding it down again. Over and over until the lantern was swallowed by the ice. The memory of Yann would stay with it as the ocean currents drove the floe towards the North Pole and away again. The ice would reach open water. Its warm currents would find a crack in the ice's defences, forcing its way in, breaking the floe into ever smaller pieces. The lantern would drift out into the open seas, gnawing away at the ice's insides. Even the old ice, a survivor of season after season, would eventually melt away. Its hold on the grave lantern would loosen, and then it would drop to the ocean depths.

"I'll wait for you there, Yann."

She let her arms hang limply away from her body, opening her mouth and tasting the salt water. One gulp and it would fill her lungs. She would be with Yann. But then she was grasped by the arms of another. She began to rise through the water, faster and faster. Her head broke the surface.

She sucked in the air in one long gasp. Her arms splashed in the water. She tried to shout but her mouth wouldn't obey. Marco was already up on the ice, but her waterlogged suit was dragging her down again.

Marco grabbed hold of her hood. She tried to pull herself up, but her arms had turned to jelly. Another head appeared before her. Sunzi's teeth clasped tight around the hood and, together, she and Marco dragged Anna out of the water.

Unwillingly, the sea released its prey.

Prone on the edge of the channel, Anna tried to breathe, but the cold just made her cough uncontrollably. Snow clung to her face. Her teeth rattled, sounding like a piano with its guts ripped out. Her vision was a blur.

A twisted arm bent down towards her and she scarcely noticed that Marco was taking hold of something on her chest. The freezing cold released her. She felt snow scraping against her naked skin as he dragged her out of the drenched suit and across the ice.

Marco laid Anna down. Snowflakes drifted over her as she lay in her wet underwear. Sunzi was barking and licking her face, and the dog's rough tongue spread a moment's warmth before the cold bit back. Chill after chill convulsed her muscles. When the cramps eased up, Anna was in no condition to move. The ice was creeping into her body, from above and below, from inside and out.

Gotcha now.

She barely noticed that Marco had come back with an object in his hand. He walked right past her. She tried to turn her head to look after him, but her muscles refused. A pungent stench spread, but her senses were so scrambled she didn't recognize it. Then she heard an explosion. A warm breeze rushed over her head.

Marco shouted something indecipherable into her still-frozen ears. She felt him grabbing her and pulling her up, turning her body around on the ice. In the darkness, Anna saw light. Flames were breaking out of the windows of one of the cabins.

The heat hit her face, melting her frozen body and soul. Wonderful. She wanted to sleep.

"Anna… can you hear me? Look at me!" She could see Marco straight in front of her, his hands gripping her by the face. "You need to get out of these wet clothes or you're going to freeze to death!"

She tried to do as she was told, but it was impossible. Marco took hold of her, stripping her undershirt off over her head. All she could do was lift her legs enough so that he could peel off her wet long johns.

Anna stayed there, naked and huddled before the burning cabin, with Sunzi's body squeezed close into her. Marco ran to his cabin and came back with underwear, trousers and jackets. As the fire warmed her through, he dressed her as though she were a young child. The flames were licking out of the cabin walls and the glowing in the windows made it look like an enormous pumpkin at Halloween. The blaze lit up the base. Marco's pickup was now gone. Zakariassen had vanished.

The cabin collapsed like a smouldering accordion shrouded in black and white smoke.

When the last of the flames died out and the cabin was nothing more than a black pit in the ice, Anna struggled to her feet. Her head was thundering. Deep wounds with bloody scabs encircled her wrists, but her body felt warmer than it had done in years.

"Tha… thank you, Marco."

The Chinese man smiled crookedly and shrugged his shoulders. His small frame towered over the ice.

"You saved my life, so now I guess we're even," he said.

She tried to say something but was overtaken by a coughing fit. Coils of barbed wire snaked through her chest. She finally got the words out. "How did you start the fire?"

"Your boat. There was a spare diesel tank there."

Anna turned around. The wind had died down and the storm was finally weakening. Snowflakes pirouetted aimlessly around *Sabvabaa*'s hull. A wide fracture had sawed its way just past the hovercraft, ending in the hole where the workshop had stood. The sled and some plastic pipes bobbed in the sea, and the adjacent cabin was leaning towards the hole. Smaller cracks stretched out from the rift towards the main building. The droning of the ice floe tearing itself apart could still be heard, but further away now.

Marco was looking around too.

"What... what are we going to do now?" he asked.

Anna turned and looked out from Ice Dragon into the darkness beyond. Jackie had taken the truck to drive out to a rendezvous point, to the helicopter that was on its way, but Zakariassen would never have abandoned her. Jackie must have forced him to go along.

She and Marco were safe on Ice Dragon. If the ice broke so much that it swallowed the whole base, the hovercraft would still float. Boris had been notified. The Russian helicopters would arrive as soon as the conditions were good enough. Sheltered from the wind and with dry clothes, they would manage until help came. Anna inhaled the cold air deep into her belly and curled her toes inside her boots, feeling the snug warmth. She turned back to Marco.

"What we're going to do now... is find Jackie."

70

Anna didn't need a GPS to find Jackie and Zakariassen. The tyre tracks were still clear in the snow.

Marco collected two sleeping bags, a few shovels, some boxes of noodles and three flasks of hot chocolate heated up in the microwave. Anna added a few more trip flares. A kilometre and a half might not seem far to travel, but at the North Pole the weather can turn so quickly that you can freeze to death fifty metres from rescue.

While Marco was packing, she went to the room beneath the tower. She disconnected the cable that led to the mine on the ocean floor, turned the laptop off and looked around the room. There was one thing she was sure of: it had all been about this. The room with the ice men next door had not been the most important room. The scientists had gathered there late at night, even those who were off shift, all crowding round the computers to get a look at something important.

But it was happening here.

Beneath the hole in the ice.

Something bigger than volcanoes and mines.

She looked at the laptop. The ceiling lamp was reflected in the shock-absorbent plastic. What was she supposed to do about it?

When she came out again the wind had dropped to a light breeze, but it was snowing more heavily. Marco was waiting for her, holding Sunzi back even though it was clear that the only thing she wanted was to haul the sled out of there. They let her lead them onto the ice.

The last that Anna saw of Ice Dragon was the painting of the beast on the tower. The pale, anaemic monster glared after her, forlorn.

"Jackie painted the dragon," said Marco. "He was always saying that he was the Dragon Man."

"Dragon Man… What's that about?" asked Anna.

"I thought it was just one of his jokes. He also said he was going to get a dragon tattoo when the expedition was over, in memory of his father. I never really understood why."

The snow and ice crunched under their feet. Anna tucked her glove under the string of the bow, which was slung over her back. She pulled it up a little and heard the hollow sound of the bow hitting the quiver of arrows.

"I was wondering if you knew what Jackie was doing before he came here."

"I'm sure I've told you before. He came from Inner Mongolia. He was working at a factory in Baotou… extracting minerals. The job and the city, he hated them both." Marco let out a short cackle. "I can understand why. Baotou is hell on earth."

"Oh. I thought Mongolia was just camels and pretty mountains."

"It might be in some places… I've never been there, but I've seen pictures of Baotou. The factories there dig up the earth and spray tons of dangerous chemicals into it to draw out rare minerals. Afterwards the factories flush the chemicals out into a lake in the middle of the city. All the animals have left and there is nothing but dead plants for miles around."

"Sounds awful. How can people stand to live there?"

"Money. Money is the only thing that grows in Baotou."

"Right… Do you think what Jackie said is true?… Are there minerals here worth a fortune?"

"Maybe… I don't really know." Marco shrugged his shoulders. "Like I said—I was never told very much about what the scientists were up to. They just told me what I was supposed to assemble, or take apart."

He stopped abruptly.

"I applied for this job at Ice Dragon because I wanted to do something exciting. What an idiot I was. I could be sitting in my workshop in Shanghai right now talking shit with my friends and eating some good noodles. Or going to the movies with my girlfriend."

He clasped his head in his hands, sobbing. His voice trembled as he spoke.

"This is terrible… What am I going to tell Fu's wife? He's expecting a son in two months. The poor kid is never going to meet his father." Marco began crying. She reached out her arm and placed a hand on his shoulder, trying in vain to think of something wise to say.

Sunzi whimpered and pulled on the sled. Marco raised his head and yelled out a few sharp words in Chinese. The husky fell quiet.

Marco stood still while he gathered himself, then tugged on the bridle. Sunzi dug in and pulled the sled forward. The ice crackled as if the sled had turned it electric. They walked quietly on into the darkness. The tyre tracks in the snow became clearer. The truck was not far away. Sunzi increased the tempo, but just a few minutes later she smelt salt water. A fracture in the ice, so fresh that the water hadn't yet frozen over again, was blocking the way forward. They were forced to abandon the tracks and walk along the channel until it narrowed enough that they could hop over. As soon as they were back on the trail of the tyre tracks on the other side, Anna stopped. In the light of her headlamp she noticed that there was only a thin layer of snow over the imprint of the tyres. They weren't far away now.

She slipped the bow off her back, pulled back the string and released it, feeling the bow vibrate in her hand. There were ten steel-tipped arrows in the quiver. Marco gave Sunzi a box of noodles and murmured into her shaggy ear. She whimpered a couple of times before wolfing the noodles down in two gulps, turning quiet.

Anna pulled the tarpaulin off the sled and pointed at the flare gun, the only weapon Jackie had left behind. She had tried to find the Kalashnikov from Marco's pickup, but it must have slipped through a crack in the ice.

"If you have to shoot, don't do it before you're at close range." Marco looked anxiously at the gun.

"Jackie has tons of weapons, so why are we chasing him?"

"Because I don't want the little bastard to get away with everything he has done. If Jackie manages to convince whoever he's working for that you were behind the killings, Marco, they're going to kill you right here, right now. Or hand you over to China, who are going to treat you just about the same. I doubt you can afford the kind of defence lawyer who can get you off the hook when all the evidence is sitting four thousand metres under the sea."

"Makes sense. I'm no rich man," said Marco curtly before picking up the flare gun and checking that the single remaining cartridge was still in the chamber.

"But we have a slight advantage. Jackie thinks we drowned in the workshop. I think that's why he left so quickly. He must have to get to a certain position before a certain time in order to be picked up."

Anna tied Sunzi's harness around a block of ice. The husky whimpered unhappily, but she couldn't risk taking Sunzi any further. She ran her hands through the dog's fur, leaning into her broad head and whispering a few words in her ear. "You have to wait here, but we'll come back and get you, Sunzi." The dog licked her all over her face before Anna left, walking after Marco into the snow towards the truck's position.

Heavy snow dropped straight down around them, muffling all sound. Exhaustion tore through Anna's beaten-up body as she tried to focus her thoughts. On Zakariassen. She hadn't found any traces of blood where Jackie had shot at him. So the idiot had still to be alive. She tried to psych herself up by getting angry with him, but it didn't work. The old professor had been tricked. He was just trying to do his best. Her thoughts turned back to the only real argument she'd had with him.

It was when Zakariassen told her that the Norwegian state oil company, Equinor, was one of the Fram X expedition's biggest sponsors.

"I thought we were supposed to be saving the North Pole, not destroying it," Anna said, fired up by the shot of aquavit Zakariassen had poured to celebrate their first Saturday on the ice.

"Yes. But what difference does it really make if someone starts drilling for oil here?" he said in irritation. "If we don't find oil here, someone else will. The Russians or Canadians, or the Danish for that matter. Now they can get back at us for stealing the oil in Kattegat from them."

"You're a scientist—shouldn't you be protecting nature?" she said, her hackles rising. Anna was in the mood for an argument, something to tear her out of her stupor and make her feel alive.

"Fram X's goal is to research changes at the North Pole. We can't stop the ice melting. Nobody can." Zakariassen's face turned sullen. "There are seven billion people on the planet, all of them in need of energy. We scientists must play our part. As adults, it has to be possible for us to hold two opposing ideas at the same time." He looked out at the pitch-black ice beyond the window and nodded slowly, as if in agreement with his own reasoning. "If the North Pole melts it will of course be very unfortunate, but it will also open up many opportunities. A cargo ship from

Asia could spend a third of the time sailing to European ports compared to going through the Suez Canal, or around the Horn of Africa, as they do now. Shipping vessels pollute much more than cars, you know."

"Do you think the polar bears are OK with that?" she threw back at him. "Holding two thoughts at the same time? My cubs are starving to death, but at least it's good for the rest of the world?"

"Many people are starving to death too, considerably more people than there are polar bears in the world. And there's nothing I can do about that either."

Blunt words bounced back and forth between them until, eventually, Zakariassen sat down demonstratively at his computer to signal that the discussion was over. But the anger that fizzed inside Anna did her good for a while, until she could no longer fight sleep. Until the nightmare returned.

She halted without first knowing why. Then she realized that Marco was standing rigid a few metres ahead of her with one arm raised.

"There," he whispered.

A red light blazed through the falling snow.

71

With an arrow on the bowstring, she walked towards the red lights.

A sudden gust of wind whirled the falling snow to one side, revealing the truck. The red pickup was slanting down into the ice, the bed pointing up. The glow from the brake lights rippled strangely. Anna motioned for Marco to stop, then ran to the truck's side with the bow ready to let fly.

The pickup had driven into a channel. Seawater and ice floes lapped across the hood, lit up from below by the headlamps.

Anna turned around, releasing the tension in the bow. She peered through the dark falling snow, but neither Jackie nor Zakariassen was anywhere to be seen.

A scraping sound. Metal slipping across the snow and ice. The pickup was sliding down into the water. The sea glowed a bluish green from the headlamps shining towards the underwater ice. She saw a head through the front window. A pointed nose. Grey hair. Zakariassen was sitting in the driving seat.

She waved towards Marco, pointing him towards the other side of the cab. He raised the flare gun aloft and walked forward. She moved towards the car, glancing down at the ice before her feet. The fresh snow could be hiding new fractures. She stopped a metre from the vehicle.

"Can you see anything?" she shouted to Marco, who was now standing on the other side. He pressed the flare gun against the window and leant his head on the glass.

"No, just him."

Zakariassen was slumped over the wheel. Seawater sploshed lazily around his knees.

"Daniel, can you hear me?" He didn't respond. Anna stretched out towards him, but she could only reach the rear door from the channel's edge. "Keep a lookout, Marco. I have to get him out of there."

Anna tossed the bow off into the snow and pulled at the door. It was locked.

"Daniel… Daniel! Can you hear me? You need to wake up!" She slammed her hand hard against the window. She saw two holes in the front window. Two bullet holes, so close together that they looked like one. Someone had fired from inside the truck.

She saw Zakariassen suddenly moving his head.

"Daniel, it's me… Anna! I'm going to get you out!" She continued hitting the glass as she screamed in the hope of getting his attention. Even though Zakariassen was wearing a survival suit, it could still fill with water. Then the temperature drop, the hypothermia, would deaden his senses. "I'm going to get you out, Daniel, but you need to help me… You need to climb over into the back seat so I can reach you." While she was trying to get Zakariassen's attention, her eyes wandered back out to the dark landscape. If this was another of Jackie's traps, he would be here soon.

Daniel twisted his torso until he saw her. He had lost his glasses so his eyes blinked in confusion. His skin was pale, almost as white as the snow. He coughed. "Is that really you… Is that you, Anna?"

"Yes, it's me, Daniel, but now you need to help me. Come here and unlock the door so I can get you out. Do you understand? Can you do it?"

"Anna, I'm so sorry… I've made a complete mess of everything… but I tried to stop Jackie. I tried to turn the truck around to come back and save you, Anna… I really tried. I couldn't get the gun off him." He showed no sign of moving. Anna noticed a dark stain on the belly of his survival suit.

"Are you injured, Daniel?" Anna was shouting to make sure that he heard her.

"Tell your father… tell Johannes that I never intended to do any wrong." Zakariassen's voice was distant and muted by the window. "I just wanted to help."

"You can say that to him yourself. Daniel, you have to come this way now." There was a crunching sound as the truck shook and slid forward. Anna had to let go of the door she was standing next to and step back so as not to be dragged with it. The pickup stopped when the huge back tyres hit the edge of the channel. Now the entire cab was in the water and it was impossible to reach the doors from the ice.

Without thinking, Anna stepped up onto the tyre, grabbed hold with one arm across the bed, and pulled herself up. Once on the bed, she punched at the rear window.

Zakariassen was still sitting behind the steering wheel. The sea was pouring through the broken windscreen and the water had climbed up to his chest. Her fist slammed against the rear window again, but it wouldn't give. She lifted a foot and kicked at the glass. Nothing happened. She kicked again. The truck rocked beneath her, but the window held fast.

"Fuck!"

She readied herself, then jumped up with both legs stretched in front of her. She felt the glass give way when her boots hit, before she fell back down on the truck bed. She rolled quickly over and got up again. The window was smashed, but held together by laminating glue.

"Daniel, I'm coming!"

She kicked desperately against the glass. Her boots made deep depressions with each strike. The packing holding the window in place gave way, the rubber peeling away, and the entire window came loose and fell into the cab.

Anna brushed away the glass pieces stuck around the edge

and reached her arms through the opening towards Zakariassen. The sharp smell of seawater tore through her nostrils.

"Daniel, can you hear me? Turn around and crawl over the seats towards me." As she leant further in, the truck lurched forward. Finally, Zakariassen reacted. He turned around slowly as the sea lapped around his survival suit as if it were about to freeze.

"Can I ask you for a favour, Anna?" he said in a barely audible voice.

"Whatever you want, Daniel, but please just give me your hand."

"The truth is that I didn't come to the North Pole to research ice melt or to discover oil or other minerals. Millions of years ago a meteorite landed here—that's what I wanted to find… That's why it's so easy to find minerals right here. When the meteorite struck, the geological layers were turned upside down. If I had found it I could have named the rock after Solveig. She would have liked that."

The old man coughed painfully.

"A stupid idea. That's the end of that."

"Not at all, Daniel, this is not the end of it. We'll find your meteorite… Just grab my hand so I can get you out of here." Anna leant even further through the window opening, but Zakariassen stayed in the front seat. She could hear the trickling of seawater running into the truck.

He coughed again and raised his voice. "Solveig's sister lives in London, in Hampstead… There's a beautiful park there that we used to go for walks in. The English have a fine tradition of buying a bench for a park and having your name engraved on it. Could you do that for me, Anna? Set up a park bench in memory of me and Solveig?"

"You're more than capable of doing that yourself—just take my hand now and I'll have you out of here in a second!" Anna reached her torso even further in, but noticed that the change in weight was making the pickup slide even further into the channel. She had to lean back to stop the movement, but lost her footing on the slippery truck bed and fell.

The bed shook. The back wheels lost their hold and the pickup began to slide beyond the channel's edge. Anna stood up on the rocking truck bed.

"Daniel! For God's sake, please grab my hand!"

The cab was swamped. The water had climbed up to Zakariassen's head. He didn't move. His eyes were closed, as if he were sleeping.

"Daniel, wake up!"

His grey locks of hair vanished under the seawater spraying through the windscreen. Anna felt the bed tilting on its edge. She lost her balance, throwing herself blindly over the side of the truck and hitting the ice. The truck slipped down into the channel like a metal seal and disappeared beneath the surface, spraying seawater over Anna. She watched the truck reappear on the surface, coming to rest as it bobbed in the disturbed water. For a brief second she saw Zakariassen's head before it fell forward below the water.

The back end of the pickup raised itself out of the sea. A light from inside the cab was suddenly turned on. The truck sank like *Titanic*, illuminated from within. The water around the body began to boil, a cascade of bubbles released from within; the back end tipped on its edge, and the bodywork glided silently into the black sea.

"Daniel!" She screamed and screamed, but he was lost. The only thing Anna could see now was a lonely, green trainer floating quietly between the bubbles.

72

Anna stayed sitting on the ice, staring at the water, until the last bubble burst on the surface. Marco stood quietly nearby. When the sea settled bright and still, she stood up slowly and looked around.

The deep tyre tracks went through the snow to the edge of the channel. A few flecks of oil were left on the ice where the underside of the truck had scraped past. She picked up her bow, turned on her headlamp and began to walk through the snow in gradually larger circles around the tyre tracks. Marco waited as Anna walked with her head down. Finally she found what she was looking for.

Boot prints. Without another word, she began to follow the tracks. Marco hesitated, but then ran after her. The prints led to an area where the ocean current had driven the ice floes into each other, twisting up craggy ice blocks as it did so. Jackie's tracks were clearer now. It had not been long since he had walked this way.

The pursuit led them between two large ice blocks leaning towards each other. Anna stopped just before this natural tunnel, listening until she was completely sure that Jackie wasn't hiding in there. She turned off the headlamp and walked in. The sound of her footsteps was amplified by the ice's echo. The corridor narrowed gradually, and Marco had to walk behind Anna to get enough room. Ahead of them the dark, icy landscape glimmered. Suddenly something brought her to a stop.

A sound.

Hissing, as if from a detuned radio. She set an arrow on her bowstring and checked that Marco had the flare gun in his hand before walking on towards the sound.

Through the snow she saw a light moving in the dark. It lit up Jackie's face. He was standing out on the surface behind the ice blocks. The light was coming from what he had in his hands. It looked like a radio. A short, thick antenna pointed up into the sky. He was wearing one of the Ice Dragon jackets. Staring down at his hands, the killer would have looked like a lost tourist if it weren't for the Kalashnikov lying in the snow next to him.

Anna raised the bow slowly. She pulled back the string, breathed carefully, and aimed directly below his illuminated face. Towards his chest. Jackie was twenty metres away and the dense snowfall was obscuring her view. A sudden, rumbling sound, like a drummer beating his brushes against gigantic cymbals at a great tempo, made Jackie turn towards Anna just as her fingertips released the string. The arrow streaked past his face and vanished into the dark. Jackie dropped the radio and threw himself at his firearm.

Anna launched herself backwards towards Marco, and both of them fell to the ground. Without the light from the radio she could barely see him through the darkness. The sound of the cymbals grew in volume. A helicopter was on its way.

Then the staccato pounding from the Kalashnikov drowned out the rumbling of the helicopter for the few moments it took Jackie to empty the magazine. She felt a hail of ice strike her face as the shots pulverized the ice above her. The blistering light of the muzzle flash stayed burnt on her retinas.

She was back on her feet as soon as the sound died away, pulling a fresh arrow out of the quiver as she leapt up and placing it on the bowstring. She ran towards Jackie with the bow raised.

The helicopter's growl climbed to a crescendo.

Just above the trembling arrowhead, she could see Jackie crawling backwards along the ground. She had him now. Anna pulled back the bowstring as far as it would go, ready to release.

Then everything turned white. A bright light from the sky blinded her. The arrow dropped from the string. Snow was blown into her face as the helicopter descended towards the ice. It was impossible to see where Jackie was in the intense backlight. Anna turned and ran back towards Marco, who was still lying in front of the ice block.

"We have to get out of here!"

She grabbed him, dragged him to his feet and pulled him with her between the ice blocks. Behind her she could hear voices. Someone was shouting for them.

Anna shoved Marco into the ice tunnel. They were almost all the way through when the ice outside was bathed in light. Marco stumbled and fell, and she had to jump over him. She tried to stop, but slipped along the ice until she was outside the ice blocks at the same moment as another helicopter landed. In the glare of the landing lights she saw white figures leaping from an open side door as soon as the aircraft touched down. Red laser beams swung over the ice.

Anna backed up beneath the ice blocks, but the beams came after her. Like luminous beetles, the bright lights climbed up past her feet, not stopping until they reached her chest.

73

"Do not move!" a low voice yelled. "Raise your arms above your head!"

Four soldiers in white camouflage suits ran out of the glare of the helicopters towards her. The one at the front, a large muscular man with a face hidden behind snow goggles and a white mask, approached with a rifle raised, pointed straight at her.

She raised her arms, standing still, as she heard Marco's wheezing, frightening breathing coming from behind her.

"Get on the ground!" shouted the soldier.

She got down and felt hands searching her entire body. Pain surged through Anna's wrists as the soldier poked his gloved fingers up under the seams of her jacket. She felt another hand slapping against her thigh, opening the pocket and pulling out her knife.

"Get up!"

Anna clambered up again and saw her own face reflected in the soldier's huge goggles as he stood right in front of her. The three other soldiers stood in a semicircle behind him. All with automatic weapons, all aimed at her.

"Where are you from?" When the soldier who was speaking turned his head, she saw dark skin behind the glass of the goggles.

"From Ice Dragon base… Who are you?"

He didn't answer, only looking over Anna's shoulder towards Marco.

"The man you came to pick up is a dangerous killer," she said.

He ignored her, simply turning towards the other soldiers and pointing towards the helicopter. "Get them in."

The three soldiers approached her.

"Who are these people?" Marco's voice was trembling.

"Just stay calm. Don't try to resist," said Anna.

"Can you tell us who you are and where you are taking us?" She was trying to suppress the anger in her voice as she spoke.

"Ma'am, please do as I say. Get into the helicopter."

His broad, southern accent left no doubt as to which country the soldiers were from. She felt a hand pushing against her back, and began to walk. The helicopter rotors were still turning, blasting her face with an ice-cold wind.

The aircraft was painted black and entirely without markings. The fuselage was smooth and aerodynamic, like a stealth fighter. A long spear protruded from under the cockpit windows, a boom for mid-air refuelling. When she got closer she saw the US Army roundel and stripe painted on the black fuselage. She stopped in front of the side door and turned to the soldier immediately behind her.

"Where are you taking us?"

He pointed towards the cabin.

"Get in."

She turned back, placed a hand on the helicopter floor, set one knee on the edge and hauled herself in. The soldier pushed her towards a row of seats at the back and followed her there, waiting for her to sit down, then fastened a seatbelt around her before sitting in a seat across from her.

Marco looked at her in fear. "What's going to happen to us?"

She tried to answer in an optimistic tone. "I don't know, but at least we're getting away from this fucking ice."

"What about Jackie?"

"He's someone else's problem now."

She turned away from Marco, not having the energy to answer questions she didn't know the answer to. Behind the head of the soldier in front of her, she saw the pilots studying the landscape outside through night-vision goggles fixed to their helmets.

The last man, the southern soldier, hopped up into the cabin, pulling the door after him. The pilots took hold of the cyclic stick. The rpm increased. The helicopter shook, struggling free from the ice.

The ice was flooded by the spotlights for a few moments. The ice blocks cast long shadows in all directions. The shadows moved like living beings as the helicopter began flying forward. Then the lights were turned off. Outside the windows, everything went dark.

In the weak green instrument lights from the cockpit, Anna noticed that the Americans' uniforms didn't carry the usual name tags or American flags. The lack of identification told her who they were. She had trained several times in the Florida swamps with other soldiers from the same unit. The US Navy SEALs were elite soldiers, specially trained to operate in small groups in rivers, at sea, in swamps or along enemy coastline. Just like her own division of the Armed Forces Special Command.

It suddenly struck her that Sunzi was still down on the ice. She turned towards the soldier to her side and shouted loud to be heard above the noise of the engine.

"We had a dog with us—we can't just leave it there."

The soldier gave no sign of either hearing her or understanding what she said. He simply raised his gun up to his chest.

After trying to yell the same to the soldiers opposite her, she gave up and leant her head against the cabin wall. She thought about the husky left alone in the darkness. The cold wouldn't kill her, but if a polar bear turned up she hoped Sunzi would be able to tear herself loose from the ice block Anna had fastened her to. An overwhelming sense of depressing powerlessness came over her. No matter how far she tried to flee from it, death always followed. She closed her eyes to shut out reality, and the vibrations from the engine made her face itch.

She leant forward again and looked out of the side window. White and red navigation lights blinked out in the dark. The helicopter was flying in tight formation with the other aircraft. The helicopter carrying Jackie. Why were heavily armed US Navy SEALs being flown all the way to the North Pole to pick up a solitary spy? The only danger on the ice was Jackie himself. She tried to remember Daniel's words. He had said that Jackie had discovered something, a secret that was obviously more important to the United States than all the people he had killed. She wasn't able to think more than that. She was trying to let go of her fury over her own powerlessness. Now she couldn't do anything about it anyway. The world's mightiest military power had taken control. One single soldier meant nothing.

Daniel was dead. Jackie was alive.

The world was a bloody, unfair place.

Anna folded her arms across her chest to prepare herself to do what soldiers do when they are on their way to an unknown objective. Sleep.

But her attempt was abruptly interrupted when the helicopter made a sudden turn. She felt her backside lift out of its seat as the aircraft dropped through the darkness. Outside, she saw lights on the ground. The trip had only lasted a few minutes.

The ice wasn't finished with her yet.

74

As soon as the helicopter touched down again, the southern soldier pulled open the door and jumped out, followed by a second man. The door was quickly closed again, but Anna managed to see the light from several windows in the dark. She was back at Ice Dragon.

The helicopter had landed on the ice just beyond the boundary of the base. She could just glimpse figures walking past the illuminated cabin windows. The soldiers were on the way to secure the area.

The helicopter engines were still idling, pumping warm air into the cabin. The pilots were not saving fuel—they must have had full tanks when they arrived. There was probably a tanker aircraft circling above the North Pole right now. Maybe more than one. The United States had endless resources to draw from once they set their minds on something.

The two soldiers guarding her and Marco had stationed themselves at each door. For a second, Anna evaluated whether she could turn what the SEAL instructors in Florida had taught her about close combat in tight spaces against them. But one glance at the one nearest her and she gave it up as a lost cause. The young soldier was watching what she was doing very carefully with both hands on his weapon, a Heckler & Koch rifle with a powerful telescopic sight and bipod fixed under the barrel. A sniper at the North Pole.

Anna looked over at Marco. He was sitting with his head leaning on his chest. Unbelievably, he had managed to fall asleep. She sensed her own exhaustion and leant back against the padding of the cabin's wall, shutting her eyes, trying to let the steady thrum of the engines drive every thought away.

From where she was sitting, hidden away at the back of the bar, she saw Yann Renault before he saw her.

The French doctor entered dressed in a white shirt with the entrance pass to the conference he was participating in hanging from his neck. Several men and women watched him as he walked past the bar counter. When Yann spotted her, his face lit up with a big smile. He came over and gave her a kiss on each cheek. When he sat down next to her, Anna felt strangely proud.

"You look beautiful," he said.

"Thank you."

On her way into the bar, Anna had almost not recognized the woman reflected back at her in the glass door. She was wearing a red dress she had bought that afternoon.

Her hair curled around her shoulders after energetic use of the hotel's hairdryer and styling mousse. A rarely used family heirloom, four Russian coins from the era of the tsars that had been fastened to a silver chain, dangled around her neck. She had even bought foundation to try to even out the tan lines from her uniform on her bare arms. She couldn't remember the last time she had spent so long getting dressed up.

"How are things with Sadi?" she asked, unsure of how to kick things off.

"Brilliant—he asked me to say hi, actually, and was wondering if you could buy some new dummies for him next time you visit. He somehow manages to lose those he has in the most mysterious places."

"Shouldn't he stop using them soon?"

The wrinkles around Yann's eyes tensed as he smiled. "You'd better take that up with him yourself. I wouldn't dare. Sadi is an extremely strong-willed young man." His eyes moved to the crystal glass in front of Anna. A spotlight directly above them shone through the drink, making it glow golden-brown.

"What are you drinking?"

"The most popular drink in the world, according to the bartender."

She raised the glass towards him.

Yann picked out the cocktail stick swimming in the brown liquid and smelt the lemon peel twisted around a crimson berry. "Sugar, bourbon, a dash of Angostura... Is it a real old-fashioned?"

"Is there anything Yann Renault doesn't know?"

His laughter turned several women's heads. "I did tell you that I grew up in a hotel, right? Every day after school I did my homework in the bar while my dad was mixing drinks for the guests."

"It's a wonder you didn't turn into an alcoholic, then."

"Ah, who says I'm not? We Frenchmen never stop drinking long enough to find out." Yann laughed again and pointed at the cocktail glass for the female bartender, who was already standing in front of him. She ignored a couple of men who were trying to order and began mixing right away. Anna spotted her reflection behind the bottles on the shelf above the bartender.

Her dress had become a field uniform.

She was lying behind a rifle. She saw her own eye in the scope, unnaturally big, divided in four by the crosshairs. The rifle barrel moved. Aimed at Yann.

Anna lurched awake with a feeling of being in free fall. The two soldiers raised their weapons as she tried to struggle free of the seat. The sudden commotion woke Marco. He looked at her, terrified.

"What is it?"

"Sorry, I... was dreaming."

308

He looked up. "We've stopped."

At first she didn't know what Marco meant, but then she realized that the droning of the engines had disappeared. They had been turned off. The southern soldier briefly pulled open the cabin door.

"You two are coming with me now."

"Why?"

She felt a rifle butt press hard against her shoulder. A short, forthright voice came from the soldier behind her.

"It wasn't a question."

Anna got up and stepped towards the open cabin door. The short half-hour of sleep had made her stiff and sore.

"Where are we going?"

She jumped down onto the ice and walked ahead through the light snow towards the cabins. Behind her she heard the snow and ice crunching under Marco's feet and the soldiers following him. She walked past the hole into which the workshop had sunk. There was a thin layer of ice on the surface already. On the other side of the yard she glimpsed a hole made by the cabin Marco had set on fire to stop her freezing to death.

The lights from the windows in the remaining cabins were too weak to illuminate more than a few metres of ice. In the dark, the big building was almost invisible. She looked at the piles of snow covering the dead Chinese men. The soldier led her past the door where the deep-frozen commander was. Either the wind or someone had pushed the door closed in front of him.

She rounded the corner.

Two soldiers were standing guard in front of the main building's other door. As she walked towards them, she looked towards the garage. One door was open. The soldiers had been in there. When she reached the door, one of the soldiers opened it for her. She went in, squinting from the bright light.

Four people were standing inside the room.

She heard a woman speaking Chinese in an irritated tone of voice. A man was answering tersely. Jackie. One soldier stood watch right behind him.

When Jackie saw Anna, he suddenly stopped talking. Her eyes darkened. Voices roared in her head. She began to run towards him. The other two people turned. The woman Jackie was standing next to ducked down into a defensive position, clenching her fists and raising them in front of her face. A blonde ponytail twisted around the shoulders of her padded jacket. The soldier took hold of Jackie and hauled him backwards.

The man next to the blonde woman shouted something and stretched out an arm, but Anna was looking at nobody but Jackie, who was backing away across the room.

"Stop!" shouted the woman.

Anna took a long stride, but when her foot hit the ground it snagged on the man's outstretched leg. She tripped, fell and tumbled over on the ice. The woman launched herself at Anna, grabbing hold of one arm and twisting it behind her back as far as she could. Anna felt a knee in her back.

"Stay down!"

The head of the man who had tripped her up appeared in her field of vision.

"Anna," said a voice she recognized from a previous life. The grey eyes of Senior Operations Officer John Odegard were peering at her through a grey fringe. "How're you doing?"

75

"It's possible we've found Yann Renault."

The American intelligence officer's words ignited a desperate hope in Anna. She was meeting the CIA agent at a cafe at an intersection in central Kilis, a Turkish border city. It was a glorious chaos, with military vehicles, cars of Syrians fleeing the civil war in their homeland, and people on their way to the Sunday market. Donkeys and children competed to see who could make the most noise.

She had got to know the seasoned agent at a joint intelligence briefing for countries involved in the war in Syria. Anna and John bonded over his Norwegian ancestry. His father had fled from the Sognefjord during the war and never gone home again. John had gone into detail about his plans to visit Norway in his retirement.

Now the American intelligence officer was her only hope.

"We have a possible sighting in a town far to the east of Syria… Al-Suwar. One of our satellites got a fluke picture." The grey-haired CIA agent was squinting in the bright sunshine. The creases around his eyes made him look like a kindly grandfather. He took a folded sheet of paper out of his jacket pocket and set it on the coffee table. When Anna unfolded it, she saw five orange dots in an open space at the centre of a building surrounded by palm trees. The picture had been magnified many times over and was highly distorted.

"This is our report about the kidnapping of your boyfriend," said John, pushing a file across the table. "You didn't get it from me." Anna forced herself to read what it contained.

The short text beneath the CIA letterhead was a witness statement from a water vendor. He had seen two minibuses from Médecins Sans Frontières stop at a crossroads in a village some distance south of the Turkish border. Three pickups had appeared at high speed out of a side street, cutting the buses off. The IS fighters had jumped down from the truck beds and surrounded the vehicles.

The drivers got out with their hands in the air. They waved dollar bills at the attackers just as they had been trained to, but the IS soldiers were not after money. They forced the drivers to lie down in the middle of the road, pointed pistols at the backs of their heads, and executed them.

The soldiers then took the two minibuses, abducting a German nurse, an English physiotherapist and a French doctor, Yann Renault.

John pointed at the satellite photo.

"This is the police station in Al-Suwar. The building was damaged when IS took the city, but we think that the jihadis are holding the hostages in cells in the basement." The CIA agent glanced around the room. The anonymous Japanese 4x4 he had arrived in was parked on the other side of the street. Two young men in baseball caps, sunglasses and long beards were sitting at the table behind them, their muscles bulging beneath sun-bleached T-shirts. His bodyguards. "And for Christ's sake, this is not information you got from me, just so that's said." John smiled, taking a sip of his Turkish coffee.

Anna held up the satellite picture to the sunlight, trying to peer through the blurred pixels from space, interpreting the orange dots. Could one of them really be Yann?

The ceiling lamp was burning into Anna's eyes. John reached out a hand, but she crawled away.

"What the fuck are you doing here, John?"

"Please, Anna… Can we speak like civilized human beings?"

"Not for as long as your goddamn man is here… Haven't you seen what he did?"

"Yes, we've seen the bodies… It's terrible."

Anna got to her feet without any help. She pointed indignantly at Jackie, who was at the back of the room.

"Your agent has killed fourteen people!"

"Yes, we were told that there were many dead here, but for us the situation isn't so clear-cut," said John. "And we—"

"Clear-cut?" Anna broke in. "An hour ago this monster killed my colleague, the one you tricked into coming to this hellhole."

John Odegard looked at her, worried. "Is Professor Zakariassen dead, too?"

"Yes. He's sitting in a truck at the bottom of the ocean. Jackie shot him and left him for dead when they crashed into a channel."

John looked at the blonde woman. "What do we know about this, Lara?"

"Jackie confirms that the vehicle he was in drove into a channel. He tried to rescue Zakariassen, but was not able to." The blonde had a strong jaw and narrow nose. Eyes: bright green. There was something familiar about her, but Anna couldn't put her finger on it.

Beneath a large down jacket, the woman was dressed in a green fleece. A Palestinian scarf was tied loosely around her throat. Her trousers were khaki-coloured with broad side pockets, the informal uniform of CIA agents on mission.

"That's a lie. Jackie shot him and left him for dead!" Anna looked at Jackie. His eyes were cold, dark hollows in his face. "I was there and tried to save him—just ask him!" Anna turned to look at Marco in the doorway. He was looking at the people in the room in fear.

"We'll look into this, Anna. When we're back we'll go over what happened here in detail. I assure you." The CIA agent looked

313

over at Jackie, who was still being held by the soldier guarding him. "If it really was our agent who committed the killings, he will be punished." Jackie said nothing. His eyes were narrowed into thin lines.

"We don't have time for this, John," said Lara. "The AWACS is reporting a lot of helicopter activity around Murmansk. The Russians could turn up at any moment."

"Anna, we really need your help now." John pointed at the stack of metal cases next to the hole in the ice.

"There was a laptop here. Do you know where it is?"

She sensed a twinge of delight.

"No idea. Your agent has probably stolen that too."

Lara's eyes darkened.

Her broad shoulders heaved under her jacket. Now all of a sudden Anna realized where she had seen the American woman before. On the photograph that Jackie had hidden in his book on the art of war. Lara must have been his handler. The agent probably didn't know that her spy had taken a picture of her on the sly.

"Jackie says that the laptop was here when he left the base. There was nobody else here except the Norwegian woman and the other Chinese guy."

Rage blazed through Anna again. "Yes! And do you know why he didn't take it with him?" She spat the words out at John. "Because he thought we were going to drown. He blocked us in the workshop and rammed it into a channel."

"Anna… this is not solving anything."

"Great, because I've got no interest in solving any of your problems."

Lara stuffed her hand down into the side pocket of her khaki pants and pulled out a Glock pistol. She pushed John to one side, stood in front of Anna and aimed it at her head.

"Get the laptop now!"

"No!"

314

Anna closed her eyes, leaning forward until she felt the pistol's muzzle against her forehead.

"I mean it," she heard Lara say. "Give us the laptop."

Anna didn't respond, just pressed her head even harder against the weapon.

"I have a spare laptop." It was Marco's voice.

The pressure against her head was suddenly gone. Anna opened her eyes and saw Lara walking towards Marco with the pistol in her raised hand.

John's face was pale and tired. "Sorry. She wasn't going to shoot, OK?"

"Why are you here John?"

He looked at her in resignation. "You know I can't answer that."

"Are you here because I'm here?"

He brushed a hand through his grey hair. "Everything is connected, yes."

"The laptop you're looking for is up there." She pointed to the hole in the roof through which the cables ran down. He looked at her in surprise.

"You're sure?"

"Yes."

"Lara, the laptop is up here," he shouted to Lara, who was on her way out of the door with Marco. She quickly came back, jumped up on the metal cases to reach the funnel in the roof, pushing a hand inside. She fumbled a little before she found what Anna had hidden inside the roof cavity, then pulled it out. She jumped down and said something in Chinese to Jackie.

The soldier let go of him and Jackie began connecting the machine to the cable controlling the mine on the seabed.

"What are you going to use it for?" asked Anna, fighting to sound calm.

Lara looked at her with hostility. "If you don't get that bitch out of here, John, then I will."

John put a hand on Anna's shoulder and tried to force a smile. "Come on, let's find a place where we can sit down and talk awhile."

He led her out of the room. Outside, he stopped and looked around in the dark.

"You probably know this place better than I do… There must be some kind of canteen here, right?"

She pointed towards the right cabin. As they walked, he spoke in a friendly tone.

"I paid you a visit at the hospital in Germany… Did you know that? You were in a coma with so many tubes sticking out of your body that… God knows, really…" A snort, a kind of mixture of a chuckle and a cough, snuck out of his broad nose. "I would have stayed there until you woke, but the job… you know… the damn war in Syria never stops."

"Have you seen what's inside there?" Anna pointed towards the door hiding the man, frozen stiff.

"Yes."

John walked in silence up to the mess and pulled open the door. "Let's get out of the cold."

Anna went in. An older man was sitting with a soldier at one of the tables. He was dressed in an oversized Canada Goose jacket with a baseball cap on his head, golden lettering embroidered across the brim. The soldier got up quickly when he saw Anna, his weapon swinging towards her, but John waved him away dismissively.

"It's OK, Robert, she's with me."

He led her to another table on which there stood a bowl of rice. A pair of chopsticks had been stuck into the rice, which had been stirred through with a red sauce. The abandoned meal suddenly brought up a memory of the creamed rice her father always served as dessert on Christmas Eve, and the tradition of hiding a single almond in it that he kept up long after Anna and Kirsten had moved out.

She tore herself away from the memories and looked John straight in the eyes.

"You gave Daniel the money for the expedition. It's your fault he's dead."

John shook his head. "No, nobody knew that this was going to happen, and I had nothing to do with the money that the professor received. This is Lara's operation."

"Charming woman."

"Well, these are not really ideal circumstances to get to know one another. We are under huge pressure. To be honest I had hoped to sort all of this out quietly... pick up Jackie and fly straight back to Greenland."

"Was it you who asked Daniel to bring me along on the expedition?" she continued.

John raised a suntanned hand.

"Listen... trust me. Honestly, I had no idea that you were here... until I saw your name on a report from Lara. I totally lost track of you after you were discharged from the hospital in Germany. I sent an email to... what's your HQ called... Camp Rena? All I got back was a message that you were in recovery. *Unspecified leave of absence* I think were the words they used. When Lara told me that you were going to join the expedition to the North Pole, I thought it wouldn't hurt to have a skilled soldier trained to survive in extreme conditions on our team."

"Why did you recruit Zakariassen and ask him to go to the North Pole?"

"No, no—you think the Central Intelligence Agency is interested in what a retired professor is fooling around with in Tromsø? He'd sent an open application for sponsorship funds to an American research website. After we learnt that the Chinese were going to build a base on the ice, we first tried to get them to tell us what they were planning through official channels. The answers we received were vague and didn't quite match up to the size of the base, so Lara flew to Tromsø to meet the professor. When she realized that he was fairly serious, she made him an offer for us to fund the expedition to the tune of three million kroner. All we asked in return was for him to keep an eye on the Chinese. No more than that."

Anna noticed that the old man was following the conversation carefully.

"Jackie was 'HUMINT'… A completely normal intelligence source," John went on. "We spy on China, they spy on us. Keep your friends close and your enemies closer." He opened out his arms as if their surroundings could explain everything. Anna knew that the CIA agent was pulling a trick. Conjuring up a white dove while doing the real magic behind his back.

"When the bosses found out that I knew you from Syria, they asked me to help Lara out if anything should happen," he continued when she said nothing. "I was out playing golf when I got the call."

"The CIA doesn't send one of its best analysts all the way to the North Pole on the basis of old friendships, though, does it?"

His fingers stroked the edge of the rice bowl.

"You took advantage of me, John," she said. "And a naive man who thought he was doing a good turn for global politics."

"Now you're being unfair, I think… You know perfectly well the rules of the game."

He flicked a finger against the chopsticks before pushing the bowl away suddenly.

"Every country spies on all the others. Right now even Norway, the nation of peace, has a spy sitting in a Russian jail, if I remember correctly. The North Pole is going to be the site of the next gold rush, and everyone wants a piece of it. And the Russians… they obviously want to be king of the hill. Putin has reopened Alakurtti, the old polar base from the Cold War. There are ten thousand soldiers there alone. They're planning on building a brand-new city on Kotelny Island to lay claim to the ocean floor beneath the pole. Thousands of people living protected from the cold under one roof. If the Russians get their way, they'll own the North Pole. Then into this mess jump the Chinese."

"I know full well what a spy is… Your agent is something else entirely. He has murdered people. You owe it to me to tell me the truth. What are you really up to here, John? What are you looking for?"

She saw the old man turning away when he heard the words. He coughed and took a handkerchief out of his jacket to blow his nose.

The CIA agent leant across the table and lowered his voice. "Have you heard about something called the seventeen rare earth elements?"

Anna realized that John was going to avoid telling the truth for as long as possible. She played along. "Should I have?"

"Yes. If you ask me, the rare earth elements should be on the syllabus at elementary school. The world as we know it would come to a stop pretty damn fast without this stuff. There are minerals among the rare earth elements that are critically important to the production of cell phones, computers, electric vehicles, wind turbines… Everything that we take for granted. The trouble is that China extracts 90 per cent of the world supply, and the US imports 70 per cent. So we are fairly dependent, you might say… In 2010 China tried to exploit their position by cutting their exports by 40 per cent overnight. The price went through the roof. Tech companies had a knife at their throats and no one else to buy from. China was hoping that the producers would move their factories there. It took a year of negotiations and threats to boycott China before exports got back to normal."

He pushed back his sleeve and quickly checked the time.

"A waste of time when you see what our dear president is up to nowadays. But after the export squeeze we've been very interested in where China gets its raw material from. They've already bought up huge mineral deposits in Africa. They're moving into South America, and now they've started looking for rare minerals here too. Jackie grew up in a mining town that extracted the rare earth elements. We thought he could be useful to us... There is probably an enormous amount of minerals here on the seabed. Maybe enough that the US doesn't need to import from China any more. We want our piece of the North Pole."

"You wanna know something, John..."

He looked back at her carefully.

"That's complete bullshit... The CIA doesn't fly Navy SEALs to the North Pole at the worst time of year just because China has discovered minerals there. That's not why you're here."

John smiled stiffly.

"You don't give up... I like that."

"I thought I liked you."

His nostrils hissed as he exhaled through his broad nose. "The only thing I can say is that the mission has nothing to do with you... We'll be done shortly. Then we're going back to Greenland. You can take a flight to Denmark from there."

"Actually, I prefer to wait for the Russians."

John shrugged his shoulders.

"As you wish."

He ran his fingers over a solid wedding band.

"You won't believe me when I tell you this, but I've really been thinking about you a lot, Anna. When I dropped you off at the Kurdish military camp... what actually happened? There have been a lot of rumours... speculation."

He looked straight at her.

"What happened when you entered Syria to rescue Yann?"

"Go to hell."

A genuinely hurt look cut through John's eyes. He fumbled for something to say, but was interrupted by the southern soldier opening the door.

"Lara Kowalsky wants to see you."

John sighed and stood up.

"Stay here and look after her."

He walked out while the soldier stationed himself at the door. Anna felt her throat knotting up.

76

John's question set memories of everything she had tried to hold back streaming through her mind. Her chest tightened up. A lump in her throat made it hard to breathe. Her pulse thundered in her ears. The room shrank. She looked up at the ceiling and sucked air into her lungs.

"Hey… Are you OK?" the old man asked.

She rubbed her knuckles hard against her ribs, feeling real pain. Gasped in more air, taking her time to really feel that it was OK to breathe. Inhaled once more, as calmly as possible.

"Yes, I'm just very tired."

"You're completely nuts, Anna."

She remembered the words just as he had said them. Remembered that John Odegard had not tightened his tie all the way to the neck. That there was a chip in the handle of the coffee cup she was drinking from. That three sparrows were hopping around in the shade under the table, bickering over breadcrumbs. A little boy was sitting on the sidewalk with his hand in his mouth. He had a dirty smear on his cheek and snot running from his nose. His mother was talking loudly to a woman selling bananas while she tapped something into her mobile phone.

Everything.

Everything.

She remembered far too much.

"You're completely nuts, Anna."

That was what John blurted out when she told him what she was planning. She was meeting him again at another cafe, another intersection. The car he came in was different, a black Land Rover. Three bodyguards this time. He agreed to help her. The CIA agent had a problem that couldn't be solved through the regular channels.

"We believe IS is holding an American hostage with your boyfriend."

His golden ring glinted as he pushed a photo across the dusty coffee table. He had confided in her that he took off his wedding band when he was in the field, and always put it back on again when he returned. It was his way of getting back to daily life.

She picked up the picture. A middle-aged man with unkempt hair and thick glasses was smiling at the camera. A clerical collar peeked from under his throat.

"His name is Robert O'Leary. The guy's a Catholic priest from Boston. He was in Turkey on assignment for the Catholic aid organization Caritas. O'Leary was kidnapped in the streets of Aleppo six months ago. His church in Boston has raised three million dollars to get him released…" John shook his head and took a sip from a glass of Diet Coke. "But I think, unfortunately, that IS is going to use him for propaganda. Fucking savages."

When they had agreed the plan and how the operation would play out, Odegard drove Anna into Jandaris, one of the Kurdish-controlled areas of northern Syria.

"Here, but no further," said John as he dropped her off at the gate of the Kurdish guerrilla camp. "If it all goes to shit, then I have never met you… OK?" He laughed, gave her a hug and a kiss on the cheek. "Take care of yourself."

At first the sentries didn't want to let an unfamiliar woman in, but when Anna showed them her military ID card and a picture of herself taken on exercises, the guards eventually agreed to take her to the camp commander.

They escorted her past the endless rows of grey tents that the Kurdish warriors were living in. Formerly regarded as terrorists, the Kurdish guerrillas were now being brought in from the cold in the war against IS. It was a fragile alliance. The guerrillas hated the Islamist fighters for the torture, rape and slaughter of Kurds in the towns and cities they conquered, but the Kurds' final goal didn't dovetail with that of Western forces or the Turkish military. The Kurds had been fighting more or less constantly since the Second World War against the governments of Iraq, Syria and Turkey in order to establish an independent state. What would happen on the day IS was thrown out of Syria, nobody knew.

Eventually Anna found the woman she had met in the restaurant kitchen in Ain Issa. Nuhad hesitated for a second when Anna, the woman who had saved her from a suicide bomber, told her what she needed help with.

"I'm sorry that no more from my company can come with us, but Daesh will be suspicious if there are more women than men in the vehicle," said Nuhad. "Daesh"—"those who sow discord"—was the name given to IS by normal people in Syria and Iraq. Nuhad took Anna over to a rusty Hyundai van with two bullet holes in the side. She opened the back door and handed Anna a burka.

Nuhad laughed when Anna stood in front of her like a black shadow in the bright sun. "Pretty ironic that the chauvinist jihadis have given us the perfect disguise." Ready to go, Nuhad and Anna sat in the back of the van while two Kurdish men, who introduced themselves as Joro and Samal, climbed into the front.

They arrived in Al-Suwar early the next day. They were stopped at two checkpoints, but the young men with long beards let them through after studying Joro and Samal's fake Syrian IDs carefully. Joro steered the van through the partly destroyed town and slowly through the neighbourhoods surrounding the police station until Anna found the best hideout, an abandoned factory building out in an open field on the opposite side of the main road leading to the prison.

As night fell, the van was reversed into the factory. Then Anna and the Kurds took their weapons, water bottles and boxes of military rations and arranged themselves on the roof. They took turns sleeping and keeping watch through the night.

Anna had been studying the police station through her binoculars.

The building was in the centre of Al-Suwar and partly concealed by tall palm trees. Behind it a slender minaret rose into the sky. The police station's facade was blackened by fire, and most of the windows were damaged. Next to her on the roof were Joro and Samal, both dressed in civilian clothes. Joro, the elder of the two, dropped the binoculars with which he was studying the police building. Deep lines cut across his face like cracks in a dried-out lakebed. "What are we waiting for?" he asked.

"The captives," said Anna without taking her eyes away from the binoculars. Without Geir by her side she would have to calculate the distance to the police station and wind speed herself. Luminous numbers in the rangefinder told her that the scorched wall was precisely eight hundred and thirty-eight metres away.

Three hours after midday, Anna felt like her head was going to explode. Nuhad came up to the roof with a Thermos and a cup, into which she poured hot tea.

"Tea is better in the heat," she said, passing her the cup. "It'll make you sweat so the body cools down."

Anna was a coffee drinker and would really have preferred water, but drank the tea Nuhad had offered her politely.

"This guy must be really special," said Nuhad. Beneath her black hair, her eyes were studying Anna urgently. "You're taking a big risk by coming here."

"So are you. You didn't have to help me."

"No, this is our war. I'm fighting for a free Kurdistan."

"Aren't you scared? There are only four of us and there must be fifty IS fighters in the prison over there."

Nuhad simply grinned and picked up her American M16 rifle. She pointed towards a row of yellow smiley-face stickers along the butt. "I've sent eleven IS fighters to hell. They believe they won't get into paradise if they get killed by a woman."

She unwrapped the Palestinian scarf from her hair. Soiled and crumpled, it fell onto her shoulders.

"All I need to do is show them my hair and they all run away," she said, and laughed.

"There's someone coming."

Samal pointed towards the square in front of the police station. People were streaming in from the narrow streets surrounding it. Through the binoculars, Anna could see men with long swords in their belts and automatic weapons walking behind them. The residents were being forced out of their houses.

A screaming metallic noise.

Anna pivoted the binoculars towards the sound. A gate was opening at one end of the police station. Eight IS soldiers emerged, followed by five people dressed in orange jumpsuits. The hostages had black hoods pulled over their heads and behind them walked three black-clad men. The executioners.

"Start the car," said Anna.

Nuhad got up and ran crouched across the roof towards the stairs.

"I'll take the men in black, you two take the rest," she whispered to Joro and Samal.

She unfolded the bipod on the camouflaged Winchester Magnum rifle Nuhad had lent her, whipping open the cover of the telescopic sight.

"The range is too long," protested Joro as he rested his Kalashnikov against the edge of the roof. Next to him, Samal pushed the Oakley sunglasses he was so proud of up over his Palestinian scarf and propped an old gun that looked like something straight out of the First World War next to his Kalashnikov.

Through the sight, Anna could see every single bullet hole in the wall of the police station. She nudged the rifle down so that the head of an IS fighter settled in the crosshairs. He looked very young, probably not more than eighteen. She eased the rifle towards the left and noticed the hood of a hostage. It was a big, strong man. The crosshairs passed over to the next hostage. This one was thin, quite short. The third was tall, with a little hair sticking out from under the hood. Anna watched as dark-brown curls wafted in the wind. His broad chest pressed against the fabric of the jumpsuit.

It was Yann.

77

Anna's memory was interrupted when the two soldiers keeping watch in the mess received a message on the radio. Robert, as John had called him, stood up.

"They need me in the room."

"Go ahead, I'm in control here," said the southern soldier.

"Shall I join you?" asked the old man, standing up. His voice was hoarse and scratchy.

"No, wait here until you're called."

The soldier left, while the old man dropped back into his chair again. The other soldier positioned himself to block the doorway. His index finger settled directly beneath the trigger guard.

The only easy day was yesterday. That was what they used to say, the SEALs Anna had trained with. The motto was intended to motivate them to train ever harder. She wondered how much the soldier knew about the mission to the North Pole. Or had he just been told to be a bodyguard for the two CIA agents?

She looked at the old man. He must have been well over eighty. His eyes were almost hidden beneath deep folds of skin. A thin moustache hung under his nose, which was patterned with dark blood vessels. She now noticed that the gold lettering on his cap spelled out USS *Skate*. Had he been in the navy? And why, in that case, had he been brought along to the North Pole? She quickly gave up trying to find any meaning in it. Her gaze slipped across to the bowl of half-eaten rice. The man's head was split in two by the chopsticks.

The target is in sight at my position.

That was the message she had sent to John Odegard when she saw the hostages in orange jumpsuits being led out of the police station. When she saw that Yann was among them.

Anna knew that the CIA could determine her position precisely via satellite telephone. She had no idea what the Americans would be able to do in the short time before the hostages were killed, but now John knew that the hostages had been found. She had kept her side of the deal. She put the phone down and concentrated on what she could see through the sight. An IS fighter was setting up a tripod and camera right in front of Yann. IS always uploaded videos of executions onto its own website. She felt her pulse rising and forced herself to breathe steadily. At such a long range, the slightest movement could lead to her missing the target by several metres.

A second IS fighter walked over to the hostage standing furthest to the right. Anna could clearly see his eyes through the scarf he had wrapped around his head. He pulled the hostage's hood off. A man.

His hair was grey, and he was thinner than the photograph John had shown her, but the thick-rimmed glasses were the same. Robert O'Leary, the Catholic priest from Boston. Sweat was running down his face as he blinked, confused, into the bright sunlight. Anna saw his lips moving through her sight. He understood what was about to happen. He was praying to God. The IS fighter said something and grabbed the priest's shoulders. He turned O'Leary so he was standing right in front of the camera. Anna jogged the rifle to the left and saw another soldier standing right behind Yann. His face was uncovered. She clearly saw the young man's wispy beard as he placed his hands on Yann's shoulders and turned him towards the camera, then pulled off the hood.

Yann's face filled the sight.

He was looking directly at Anna. Dark rings hung under his eyes, which had lost all their brightness and passion. Yann was pale-faced after weeks as a hostage. His hair had been matted against his head by the hood he had been forced to wear. She had to hold back the urge to shout out to him.

The IS fighters pulled the hoods off the other hostages and began moving away from them. At the same time, another man dressed in black emerged from the gate to the police station.

He was enormous, a mountain of a man, almost seven feet tall. The other IS soldiers moved out of his way out of respect, or fear. A shorter man walked behind the man-mountain like a scavenger fish following a shark. Anna noticed that the man-mountain was carrying something in his hands, a long pipe connected to a hose that coiled under his arms and behind his back.

The black giant stopped in front of the hostages. His body cast a dark shadow on the ground, the entrance to hell. The shorter man switched on something at the giant's back and, at the end of the pipe he was holding, a flame ignited.

The man-mountain turned towards the scorched wall, pointing the pipe towards it. An orange-yellow surge shot out of the flamethrower's pipe, billowing red hot through the air and hitting the wall like a storm wave hitting a breakwater. The flames floated beyond the walls. Black smoke swirled upwards.

Anna could hear the hostages screaming.

Through the sight she saw the fuel tank for the flamethrower the executioner was carrying on his back. She cocked the rifle.

"Now!" she yelled and squeezed in the final millimetre on the trigger. A low crack could be heard as the magnum cartridge left the Winchester's silencer. It took a second. The projectile struck. The fuel exploded.

The little scavenger and the three IS executioners vanished in a flash of light. The man-mountain flailed, enveloped by the flames consuming his arms and burning them to blackened stumps. The executioner collapsed, devoured by his own inferno.

People were screaming. The residents who had been forced out to witness the executions fled from the square.

"Drive!" Anna yelled via the walkie-talkie to Nuhad, who was sitting in the van with the motor running down on the factory floor.

She turned her weapon towards the hostages. Through the sight she could see that they were standing paralysed before the burning executioners. All except two of the IS fighters were running towards the gate of the police station. She saw the young IS soldier grab Yann, forcing his head back. He was shouting as he held a long knife against Yann's throat.

Anna's eyes sought out the target. The crosshairs settled on the soldier's chest. She let instinct decide when the finger would squeeze in the trigger's final millimetre.

The rifle cracked.

Yann's face was covered in blood.

A gust of wind had driven the bullet a few centimetres off course, and instead of hitting the IS fighter in his upper chest, it had struck him in the throat. Yann jumped to one side as the man fell to the ground with a flood of red gushing from his neck. Anna saw the other IS fighter's automatic rifle juddering in his hands as he fired. The bullets tore bloody holes in a hostage's jumpsuit. She adjusted a dial to compensate for the wind and fired again. The bullet struck the fighter in the chest and launched his body backwards.

As soon as the immediate threat to Yann was over, Anna looked up from her sight to get an overview of the battleground. Joro and Samal's Kalashnikovs crackled in short bursts next to her. The Kurds didn't waste ammunition. She heard a car horn from below as the rusting van drove out onto the road towards the police station.

Anna hoped Yann and the three other hostages would realize that the van Nuhad was driving was their rescue. Nuhad sounded the horn again, and Anna saw Yann turning towards the van. He tapped O'Leary on the shoulder and began to run. The other two followed. The hostages had their hands tied behind their backs and had to run upright so as not to lose their balance.

Alongside the burning executioners, two IS fighters were lying lifeless on the ground in front of the prison walls. The smoke climbed up vertically from the deserted square, cutting a dark scar into the pale-blue sky. The rest of the jihadis had fled back into the police station. Sporadic shots rang out from inside the building, but Joro and Samal's efficient bursts of fire made sure that the IS soldiers were pinned down.

Now Nuhad was almost there. Anna could clearly see Yann through the sight. He was running towards the van. Freedom was only fifty metres away.

78

Anna tore herself away from the memories and opened her eyes. Breathing was still difficult. She tried thinking of nothing at all. *It's all in your head. There is nothing physically wrong with you.* That was what a young doctor on the emergency ward had told her. After a passing French tourist had asked her for the way to the Arctic Cathedral in Tromsø, she collapsed in the street and was taken away in an ambulance. *You experienced a panic attack. Have you had similar attacks before?*

An hour later the doctor came back frustrated and asking why he wasn't able to access her patient records. She mumbled something about not having a clue, then asked him to call a taxi. For the rest of her time in Tromsø, she never went any further than the postbox outside her father's house.

The door slammed as Robert came back into the mess. "There are problems with the cables in there. You know more about that than I do."

The southern soldier looked back at him in irritation. "You do not discuss the operation in the presence of civilians."

Robert fell quiet.

The old man stood up again. "Is there anything I can help with?"

"No, just wait until they are ready for you. Robert will get a call," said the soldier and walked out. Robert took his place at the door. Anna noticed that he was studying her with a curious look.

"Where are you from?" she asked.

"I do not have permission to speak to you." Robert averted his eyes.

She looked at the old man. "And you... who are you?"

"I'm certainly not permitted to speak to you either," he said. He looked quickly at Robert. "But my name's Dan Morton. Who are you?"

"I'm Anna Aune. From Norway..."

Robert's eyes ricocheted between the two of them. "Quit talking!" Anna looked straight back at the young soldier until his eyes evaded hers. Then she crossed her arms over her chest and closed her eyes, focussing on breathing calmly.

The warm Syrian sun blazed through the darkness.

Anna didn't hear the sniper's shot before the bullet hit.

The sound of the IS shooter's rifle reached her at the same time as the van's passenger window exploded. The vehicle began swerving from side to side. For a moment she feared that Nuhad was hit, but then the van straightened up and turned towards the hostages again. Anna pointed her rifle towards the police building. The sniper could be using any one of countless blown-out window openings.

"There's a sniper in the police station," she yelled at Joro and Samal. "Look out for the muzzle flash!"

The sniper's next shot hit the hostage running next to O'Leary. The man fell over and stayed on the ground.

"The tower! He's in the tower!" shouted Samal, pointing up at the slender minaret.

Anna took aim at one of the openings between the columns at the top of the tower. She couldn't see anyone, but took a shot anyway. The supersonic explosion from the bullet would let the sniper know that they had found him. She would force him to take cover.

Down on the road, the van skidded as it screeched to a halt in front of Yann and the two hostages. In a few moments they would be inside. Nuhad rattled off a volley of shots from the shattered

334

passenger window towards the police station, keeping the IS fighters at bay while the hostages clambered in.

Anna saw the muzzle flash sparkling from the mosque tower at the same moment as the bullet hit the edge of the roof, sending a stream of debris up into her face. The sniper had found her. She fired back at the tower without aiming, then reloaded, pulled the gun against her and rolled across the roof to a ventilator shaft further back.

Joro and Samal leapt for cover next to her. She got the rifle into position and saw Nuhad's van beginning to turn back. The ground surrounding it was hidden by clouds of dust as the IS fighters in the police station fired, but a long salvo from Joro and Samal's Kalashnikovs forced them to take cover again.

"Come on, come on," murmured Anna as she followed the van through her sight. Four hundred metres was all that separated it from the safety of the factory.

Suddenly the van halted. The passenger door flew open and a man in orange jumped out. Yann started running back towards the hostage lying on the ground where the sniper's shot had felled him. Anna sensed a numbness spreading through her body. Yann's hands were free now, the zip ties cut. When he reached the lifeless man, Yann grabbed hold and began dragging him back towards the van.

Anna saw some figures running from the police station, but they were still far away. She fired five shots towards the tower as quickly as she was able to reload.

Yann was almost at the van now and O'Leary was reaching his arms out from the back. The priest grabbed hold of the injured man and pulled him inside. Suddenly the ground in front of Yann exploded with dust. Anna heard the staccato thudding of a high-calibre machine gun. An armoured vehicle was driving out from behind the police station, an automatic weapon on its roof spitting out showers of bullets. She aimed towards the upper torso of the fighter behind the weapon. She shot and watched him fall down into the open hatch. The machine gun was silenced, rocking forward.

Joro and Samal were also shooting back at it, but their bullets hit the side without causing any damage. The van shook violently and jumped over rocks and potholes as Nuhad drove at breakneck speed back towards the factory.

Yann wasn't with her.

In the van's dusty wake, Anna saw three IS fighters carrying him between themselves as they ran back to the police station. She knew that there were only two shots left in the magazine. The sight found the torso of the first man, the gun fired, and the fighter fell. It took a quarter of a second to load the last cartridge into the chamber. The two remaining fighters had dropped Yann and dived for cover when they saw their fellow fighter fall, but the last bullet hit one of them before he had even reached the ground.

"Get Nuhad to turn around!" Anna screamed at Joro as her hand fumbled for a new magazine in her side pocket. Now she missed Geir more than ever. Her spotter would have had a new one ready for her before the last shot was fired. She pushed the magazine in and reloaded.

Through the sight she saw the last fighter lying with Yann pulled over him like a shield. His orange jumpsuit was soaked blood red from the waist down. She could see Yann's face clearly. His eyelids opened, his pupils glimmering in the sunshine.

He was alive.

The IS fighter began pulling Yann backwards with him. He had realized that the French doctor was his only hope of getting back to the police station. But the movements the fighter made as he crawled made his torso rise up. Anna could read the nametag on his sweat-soaked uniform. The nickname was written in English: "Baldy". The jihadist's head was no longer totally covered by Yann.

She adjusted the rifle a few millimetres until the crosshairs were centred on Baldy's forehead.

Her breath seeped slowly out of her half-open lips and she could hear the thudding of her heart in her ears. Her finger gave a tiny little extra pressure on the trigger and pulled in the slack as the centre of the crosshairs settled clearly on the fighter's forehead. The words her instructors at the firing range had imprinted on her thousands of times came back to her. "Let your subconscious tell you when the moment is right. Don't force out the shot." She sensed a heartbeat roaring in her ears, then fade away.

She pulled the trigger.

79

Anna shoved the canteen table away from her, toppling it with a crash. The rice bowl spun across the floor and the chopsticks rolled away.

Robert raised his gun, pressing the butt into his shoulder as he took two steps from the door.

"You need to stay in your chair."

She got up, trying to breathe, but it was impossible. Her chest was crippled by cramps. Tunnel walls restricted her vision. Her thighs trembled, her legs weakened, and she fell to her knees. From a distance she heard Dan shouting.

"So help her man!"

The tunnel she was peering through grew steadily narrower. She shut her eyes. *It's just a movie. Memories can't kill.* She held her head in her hands.

"Can you breathe?"

She opened her eyes and saw Robert standing above her. She sucked in the air in gasps, feeling her head clear. A blast of rage chased her anxiety away.

"What did you say?" she asked.

He leant closer.

"Can you breathe?"

She reached a hand behind her.

"I can't hear what you're saying," she whispered.

Robert leant in even closer.

"I'm calling for medical aid—"

He cried out as she stuck a chopstick up under his throat.

"If you move I'll drive this straight through your neck!"

She grabbed hold of his weapon and tore it free from the clip holding it to his chest.

"You can't…" Robert yelled again as she forced the stick into his skin until blood trickled out, forcing his head forward with her other hand.

"Yes I can… if you don't do exactly what I say."

Robert wrenched his head backwards, just as Anna knew he would.

She struck him hard with a clenched fist right at the nerve below his ear. He collapsed, fell backwards and lay unconscious on the floor. Crawling over to him, she pulled out the pistol in a holster on his thigh and kicked it across the floor along with his Heckler & Koch rifle. Then she frisked him quickly and took out a short-blade knife from a sheath fastened to his belt around his waist.

She stood up and walked towards Dan. He was still standing behind the table.

"Please, don't hurt me," he said.

"I'm not going to hurt you if you tell me what's going on here," she said.

"What… what do you mean?"

"Why are you here? What are you helping the CIA with?"

"I can't… I'll end up in jail if I tell you."

As she walked towards him, Dan backed away until he bumped into the oven in the kitchen.

"I don't know how much the CIA has told you… but fourteen people have been murdered here in the last twenty-four hours."

Dan blinked, his eyes under his heavy folds of skin were damp and glazed. "I… I didn't know that."

"One of them was my colleague, Daniel Zakariassen. He came here to help… and got killed because of what's going on here."

"That's not my fault… I didn't know anything about it. I swear, I was only supposed to identify the submarine."

"What submarine?"

He hesitated for a second. "The one the CIA have found… the Russian sub."

Anna thought back to what she had seen inside the 3D helmet. The digital display of the strange cylinder lying broken into three pieces down in the fissure on the ocean floor. A destroyed submarine. Jackie must have discovered the submarine when he was surveying the data from the Chinese radar scanning the seabed. When the spy sent the data to his employer—the CIA—someone in the agency must have given the spy orders to hide the discovery, delete the data… That was what Jackie was up to when Qiang had surprised him. That was where it all began. The killing that unleashed a bloodbath.

"How do you know about that submarine?"

Dan looked at her in fear. "I can't say any more… I haven't spoken to anyone about this for fifty-six years. I had to sign a declaration of confidentiality. Even my wife went to her grave without me ever telling her about it."

Anna came so close to Dan that she could see every pore in his skin, the deep lines and bags under his eyes revealing the body's years of worry and angst. She took the cap off his head and put a hand on his smooth scalp. It was warm and clammy. She looked at the cap, at the gold lettering spelling out USS *Skate*.

"You know what I think, Dan?"

"No…"

"You were a submarine officer."

"Yes."

"And you've been here before… at the North Pole."

He nodded in silence.

"So, what happened fifty-six years ago?"

"I can't speak about it."

"It'll be a big relief for you to tell me everything you know about this submarine, Dan. Get the weight off your shoulders."

She let her hand slide down Dan's head to his neck. Left it there as she squeezed gently. Dan blinked, his bottom lip quivering.

He looked at the soldier lying on the floor. "Please, don't hurt me."

"Just tell me what you know."

Tears began to fall. "As I said to John, I didn't mean to kill them." His voice cracked. "It's the God's honest truth. Those poor Russians, I didn't mean to kill them."

80

"I was junior commander of a submarine in '62," said Dan. "We were sent up to Murmansk in the middle of the Cuba crisis to observe the harbour. Everyone was under a hell of a lot of pressure. When we set off from the base at Kings Bay, the Cuban missile crisis was in full flow... The island was surrounded."

"I know perfectly well what the Cuban missile crisis was. Get to the point."

Dan coughed and sniffed. Anna heard a call on the unconscious soldier's radio. Orders to the helicopters to warm up their engines.

"After a week submerged outside Murmansk... we heard something on the sonars. A Soviet sub with a propeller signature we hadn't heard before. A brand-new type of submarine. COMSUBLANT gave orders to shadow it. After a few days of cat and mouse, the Russians set course under the North Pole. A day later, the Russians suddenly killed their speed, taking the sub in circles. I was junior commander on duty then. I thought we had blown our cover, that the Russians had spotted us."

He breathed in deeply as he spoke.

"And that was when we heard it, the most terrifying, hellish sound you can hear as the crew of a submarine... the Russians opening their torpedo hatches. Then the sonar operators heard a torpedo being fired through the water. Straight at us. I gave orders for hard a-port and to fire a double salvo of torpedoes. I didn't even have time to warn the captain. I had to make the decision there and then. We thought we were all dead men.

"Thirty seconds later we heard an explosion in the ice above us. Nobody knew what it meant until it was too late... The Russians were only trying to shoot their way out of the ice." His voice died away for a few moments.

"Our torpedoes hit the Russians one minute and eleven seconds after we heard the explosion. One of them was a dud, but the second hit, and it was enough... I'll never forget the goddamn sound... when the Russians' hull broke up and sank. It was almost three thousand metres deep. Those poor souls never had a chance."

Tears were running from his eyes.

"What you're telling me is that an American sub sank a Soviet sub by mistake back in 1962?"

"Yes."

"And it's been kept secret until now?"

"Yes... When we got back to base, military intelligence and the CIA were waiting for us on the dock. Nobody was allowed to leave the vessel. Intelligence had intercepted a radio message from the Soviet sub a few days earlier. The captain had sent word to Moscow about problems with the cooling of one of the nuclear reactors. They probably suffered a crisis beneath the ice. The Russians had no idea we were following them, they weren't firing towards us... they were doing it to blast a hole in the ice, to get to the surface. They were just trying to save themselves."

He started to cry, the tears rolling down his wrinkled cheeks. "But how could I have known? I thought that the Russians had fired a torpedo at us... I just did what I thought was right... defending us like I had been trained to."

"So this was never discovered because the Soviets thought an accident had occurred on board the submarine?"

"Yes... and the navy made me swear not to tell anyone. The whole crew had to sign a declaration of secrecy before they were allowed off the sub. We were told that any breach of the declaration would land us in prison for the rest of our lives... in solitary.

If the Russians found out what had happened, it could lead to a nuclear war."

"And now you're here to help the CIA identify the Russian submarine?"

"Yes, I got a call in the middle of the night. A car arrived to pick me up ten minutes later. I didn't even have time to pack."

Suddenly there was a sound from outside.

Someone was heading towards the mess.

81

"Stay there and don't say a word!"

Anna ran towards the door. She got there just in time to press herself against the wall before the door opened. The southern soldier entered. Just as he had registered Dan's tear-streaked face and Robert lying unconscious on the floor, Anna stepped up behind him and held the knife to his throat.

"Drop your weapons."

His low voice grated in her ears. "You're insane. How do you think you're getting out of here?"

She pressed the edge of the blade against his neck.

"Get rid of your weapons. Now."

The soldier threw his automatic and a pistol towards the floor. "We're at the North Pole. There's nowhere to run to."

"I wasn't thinking of running away." She forced him out of the door and walked him towards the main building.

The two soldiers were still standing outside the door of the room where John and Jackie were, on the other side of the yard. At first they didn't react to the sight of Anna walking towards them with the guard, but then one of them pointed.

"She's got a knife!"

Both of them raised their weapons.

"Stop! Let him go!"

Anna pressed herself into the southern soldier's back, shoving him forward towards the two men.

"Stop, or we'll shoot!"

"Watch to CIA commander, we have a hostage situation out here." One of them was speaking into his radio while aiming at Anna. "The Norwegian woman has escaped."

She pushed the soldier towards them.

"Drop your weapons."

The soldiers kept aiming at her.

"Stop! We will shoot."

She kept walking towards them. The man she was hiding behind was breathing heavily. She caught the reek of sweat.

Behind the soldiers, the door flew open.

John Odegard came out.

"What the hell are you doing, Anna?"

"I want Jackie."

The CIA agent gesticulated wildly. "Did you not hear what I said? If Jackie has killed everyone here, he'll be punished. This is so foolish. Put down the knife and we'll forget all about it. I understand that you've been through hell, but in an hour we'll all be out of here. You can even come visit me, Anna. Give your body some summer sun."

"I know why you're here… Dan told me everything."

His eyes scanned the yard. "If you really do know, then you'll understand why the mission has been so extremely important."

"I want both the Chinese guys out here," she yelled. "Marco and Jackie."

"You know that's not going to happen, Anna."

He signalled to the two soldiers, who then moved closer to the door. He then pushed a hand under his jacket, pulled out a pistol and cocked it, raising it slightly. The lights flickered in the steel around the muzzle.

"Can you just give it up already, Anna? Let's get this finished, pack up and go home. There's nothing for you here. Just go back to Tromsø, spend some time with your family."

"I cannot let Jackie get away."

"He's not going to. We've got him."

"Is he going to be punished?"

John took a quick glance at the door behind him, checking that it was closed.

"Yes. If it turns out that he's guilty."

"I don't believe you."

The CIA agent tilted his head slightly, as though Anna were an unfamiliar creature that needed studying from all angles. "Well I'm fucking sorry about that, but it's not my problem."

"John, have you seen the people in that building over there? Have you seen how they died? They were killed by the man you're protecting."

John's face hardened. "I don't answer to you. I represent the US government. Your choice is simple. Release our soldier and drop the knife. This is your final warning."

In the corner of her eye Anna saw the two soldiers raising their guns. At a range of three metres, they couldn't miss. The barrels of their weapons jutted out from the shadows cast by their bodies like sharp spearheads. She could hear the heavy breathing of the soldier she was clinging to, his heart pounding rapidly under his uniform jacket. She couldn't kill him. She was at the end of the road.

Her rage had hit an impassable wall. The ice would get her after all. There were no more options.

Yann was dead.

Daniel was dead.

And she was so endlessly tired, all the way to her bones. The knife slid away from the soldier's throat. She dropped it and pushed him away from her.

John lowered his pistol.

"Thank you," he said.

The soldiers approached her and took firm hold of her arms.

"It's OK, boys," John said. "Anna won't give us any more trouble, right?" He pushed the pistol back in his jacket and walked towards her. "Let her go." The soldiers let go of her arms and dutifully backed off a few steps.

"I've never told you this, but I had a daughter who would have been your age today." He spoke quietly. "Ellie was a wonderful human being, but I was too goddamn busy saving the world to be home. My wife called me one night in Seoul… Ellie had been run over by a dumpster truck a hundred yards from our house… while I was busy catching North Korean arms smugglers."

He placed a hand on her shoulder.

"When I lost Ellie I thought I would never find sense in anything again. But we have two more boys, and they needed us too, so we somehow worked through it… in the end."

She caught a silver glimmer in his grey eyes as he squeezed her shoulder lightly and let go.

"Look after yourself Anna."

The sound of a howling siren cut abruptly through the air.

82

The wailing of the siren was coming from inside. A screeching, throbbing sound. The soldiers turned and looked towards the main building nervously.

John walked over and opened the door.

"Get that noise turned off, Lara," he yelled inside.

Inside the room, Anna saw Jackie standing at the laptop. A soldier was kneeling on the floor in front of a green case with its lid open. Cables were running out of it down into the sea.

Lara shouted something in Chinese to Jackie, who pointed at a box next to the fuse panel. She walked over, opened it up and pulled a breaker down. The siren stopped suddenly. Tense breathing flooded the brief silence.

"What was that?" asked John.

"Jackie says it was a methane warning. We need to ventilate the room," Lara replied. Jackie said something else and gestured towards the laptop. She walked over and leant towards the screen.

"John, you ought to see this."

John went back into the room while the two SEALs stood on either side of Anna, far enough that a kick or a punch from her wouldn't reach them. The southern soldier rubbed his neck and glowered at her in anger. Inside the room she could see Marco standing up on a ladder next to the cable running up to the tower, a can of oil in his hand. He alternated between looking back at her and at what was happening on the laptop screen.

The light from the screen lit up John's face blue. "I need Dan here now."

The soldier started running back to the mess.

John motioned to Anna. "Come in."

"No, she is not coming in here," protested Lara.

He ignored her. "She knows why we're here. Let her in."

The soldiers followed Anna into the room. When she approached the laptop screen, Jackie backed off until he was leaning against the soldiers standing behind him. The screen was displaying an image from the ocean floor: a round shape, halfway submerged in the sludge, casting a black shadow towards a rock face. The other soldier got up from the green case and pointed at a protrusion in the middle of the grey form.

"This here is the submarine hull, and that sticking up out of it is what's left of the conning tower."

The plates in the hull had been bent and twisted by the pressure as the sub foundered after the torpedo strike. A control fin protruded from the mud, the ribs in its construction clearly visible as the metal skin was pressed inwards by the water pressure. Behind the screen, she saw Jackie. He was standing completely still. She could see him staring at Lara, who had her back to him. Whether it was with hate or lust, it was impossible to tell.

Anna heard a creaking in the snow. Dan arrived, walking slowly with the southern soldier. He looked nervously at the people gathered around the hole in the ice.

John walked over to him, placed a hand gently on his back and led him across to the laptop. "We've found a wreck. Is this the submarine you sank?"

Dan studied the crushed wreck in silence.

"It's… it's not so easy to tell," he said at last.

"I can get in closer." The soldier pushed a button on the keyboard. The mini-sub that was filming the wreck glided forward towards the submarine's tower. Its grey form filled the screen. Anna saw letters and numbers beneath a layer of mud: KS 2.

"Yes, now I see it… It's K 2… The S usually means that it's an experimental prototype. It was one of the very first

350

nuclear-powered November-class submarines," Dan said. He sniffed, stroking his cheek.

"Here's the position of the other object," said Lara, pointing at a part of the screen showing where the submarine wreck was located on the ocean floor. The Navy SEAL manoeuvred the mini-sub away. Anna watched a long, wriggling fish swim out of the crushed hull and thought about the dead Russian seamen. Were they still inside? Would there be anything left of a human after such a long time? Anything the family could be given to bury?

The lights of the mini-sub swept along the rock face. Anna looked at John, who was watching the screen carefully.

"There!" Lara tapped a finger against the screen. "That's the torpedo."

She pulled Dan towards her to bring the old submarine captain closer to the screen. "Is that right? Is that your torpedo?"

He squinted at the screen. Anna saw a long cylinder lying almost buried in the sludge on the ocean floor. "Yes, that's a Mark 37 torpedo," said Dan. "We launched two of that type that day. One missed."

Anna tried to read between the lines of what Dan was saying. Above her Marco was staring at the screen from the ladder he was standing on. She looked at the spanner and oilcan he was holding. What had he been repairing? She looked over to the hole above the ice. The metal basket that had brought up the explosive material was gone. In the corner of her eye she saw the soldier pick up a remote control that was connected to the green case via a cable. The mini-sub's robotic arm came into view at the edge of the screen image. A black box was hanging from its metallic claws.

"The charge is armed and ready."

He pressed a button.

The claws approached the torpedo and placed the box on its dented body.

"Extracting torpedo now."

The claws opened wider, folded their metallic fingers around the cylinder. Then clouds of grey mud rose from the seabed as they started to lift.

"Torpedo is free from the seabed," the soldier said.

She heard Lara's voice. "Bring it to the basket. And get it up. We need to get out of here soon."

"What are you going to do with the torpedo, John?" asked Anna.

"Get rid of it, of course," he replied without moving his eyes from the screen. "The Russians are going to find the wreck sooner or later. Without an American torpedo at the scene, the accident is still an accident."

He inhaled deeply and turned towards the soldier stationed at the green case.

"You got radio contact?" The man looked down at the case.

"Yes, signal is strong and clear."

"Good. Get the mini-sub back to the mine."

"It's best if your man does the operation," the soldier said to Lara. She said something in Chinese to Jackie. At first he didn't answer. Lara repeated the question. He mumbled something and approached the laptop, closely followed by the soldier guarding him.

Anna walked behind John. "How are you going to get rid of it?"

"We don't have much choice with this little time. We have to get it as far away from the submarine wreck as possible, and then detonate it."

83

Anna felt her skin prickle. "You can't blow the torpedo up here! Don't you know there's methane seeping up from the ocean floor?"

"Our mission is to remove the torpedo. If we can't do that then everything else has been for nothing. If the Russians find out that we sank one of their submarines with a torpedo, all hell will break loose."

"You don't understand... We had a fire here before you arrived. Zakariassen was trying to take a sample of the minerals from the seabed... It self-combusted in this room."

John looked hesitantly at Jackie, who was controlling the mini-sub.

"Is that correct, Jackie? Is there a risk?"

He simply shrugged his shoulders.

"I need an answer from him, Lara." Lara uttered some curt words in Chinese. Jackie's reply was brief.

"He says he doesn't know... They never had any problems with the gas before the Norwegian woman showed up."

"Drew, are there any alternatives to blowing up the torpedo?" asked John. The marines' explosives expert ran a hand over his cropped hair.

"The torpedo would have to be moved to a safe location. But it's been down there for fifty-six years... It's impossible to say how that will have affected the stability of the explosives."

"Give me the short version," said John impatiently. "You're saying it's possible?"

"Yes, but we'll need to bring in a specialized submersible that can dive to three thousand metres... remote-controlled from a nuclear submarine. It's going to take a least a week to get an operation like that underway."

"My God," said John, rubbing his head.

Lara looked at him, irritated. "We don't have a week, we have minutes. Our orders are clear. We have to blow up the torpedo and evacuate ASAP. With the torpedo gone, nobody can prove that we sank the sub."

"OK, let's raise it as far up as you think is safe, then blow it up," John said. "We need the debris scattered over a large area."

"Don't worry, there won't be much left." Drew placed his hand on a key, ready to arm the explosives. "Take it up," he said to Jackie.

John pulled a satellite phone out of his jacket with a look of resignation. "I need to speak to Langley."

"John! This is my operation and I'm saying we have to do it now," said Lara.

Something in him snapped. His voice was full of frustration. "Yes, this is your fucking disaster of an operation to tidy up, you can be sure about that. You're handling an agent who has to answer for fourteen murders! But until anyone says differently, right here and now I'm the highest-ranking officer... I'm going out to call Langley... Nobody do anything until I'm back."

John turned at once and left. The room fell quiet. The only sound to be heard was that of Jackie's fingers tapping on the keyboard and the whir of the winch pulling the wire up out of the water. Anna looked down at the hole, where the sea was completely still. A few bubbles burst on the surface. The ladder creaked as Marco climbed down. He put down the oilcan and his tools and walked towards Anna.

"No, stay here," said Lara, walking between Jackie and him to block his path.

"I don't want to be here," said Marco.

She shoved him back. "You're staying here until I say you can go." The silence returned, broken only by Dan's sniffling as he wiped his nose with a handkerchief.

The door thumped open and everyone turned around as John came back in, still grasping the satellite phone. His face was grey, as though the ice were getting under his skin too.

"We're doing it," he said. "But don't blow the torpedo till it's reached two hundred metres or so. That'll spread the debris out nicely."

"Copy that," said Drew. He looked at Jackie. "Tell me when…"

"A thousand metres now."

Anna saw the wire rising up out of the water. The winch hummed. The wire rose faster. Jackie punched at the keyboard. The torpedo came into view on the computer screen. It was much too long to fit inside the basket. Its grey nose was sticking over the edge. Jackie must have placed it with a lot of precision: a fraction to one side and it would have fallen off.

Jackie bent his head towards the computer screen, as if he wanted to see every detail of the torpedo. Anna could make out something written on its tip. A message from the torpedo crew: *"You started this Russki!!!"*

"Two hundred metres," Jackie called out.

The winch stopped. The wire swayed slightly back and forth in the water.

"Arming," Drew turned the key, then looked at John.

The CIA agent nodded.

Anna steeled herself, staring at the torpedo. Jackie was staring too, still leaning forward unnaturally close, his arm covering part of the screen. Something wasn't right.

"What are you doing?" Anna grabbed his hand, pulled it away and saw what was written on the screen underneath: *50 M.*

"No—"

Even muffled by the sea, the noise of the explosion drowned out her warning.

"What the fuck," she heard Drew say. Then the ice started to shake under her feet, and a fountain of water and green flames leapt into the air.

84

The flames unfurled from the ice, splitting the room in two.

Anna heard a scream coming from inside the fire as a rumbling noise filled the air.

Dan reared back from the fire but slipped on the smooth ice.

"Grab my hand." Anna took hold of him, pulled him to his feet and pushed him over towards the door. Marco was standing motionless, as though entranced by the fire. She grabbed him and dragged him over towards the exit too.

Outside it seemed for a moment as though the floodlights had been switched on again, but the light was coming from the flames whirling up from the cracks in the ice. In its glow she could see the helicopters behind the cabins, their rotors turning at full throttle, the pilots ready to depart.

Flames erupted through the ice by the mess, the force of the blast throwing the cabin forward. The door flew open and Robert tumbled out. The shock wave had shaken him awake.

Anna heard John screaming behind her: "Lara, where are you?"

Odegard was still standing just inside the door. The room was dark now, lit only by the flames raging around the cables hanging down from the tower and around the fuse panel on the wall. Lara came running out from behind the cables, towards the door. Her ponytail had caught fire and she was swatting at the flames in sheer panic as she ran. John tore off his jacket and wrapped it around her head.

Another man followed. On his back Drew was carrying the soldier who had been guarding Jackie. Smoke drifted from the unconscious soldier's scorched uniform. The explosives expert's face was blackened with soot, his eyes white hollows. Outside at a safe distance, John pulled his jacket off Lara's head. Her blonde hair was still smoking.

"Are you OK?"

Lara touched her neck. Her ponytail was just a charred stump. "I'll survive."

When more flames erupted through the darkness to send a huge burst of light across the base, Anna saw John's face lit up brightly.

"What happened?" he shouted.

"Jackie fooled you is what happened. You blew up your torpedo right under a pocket of methane gas trapped under the ice."

"Fuck me," he said.

The southern soldier approached at a sprint. "Everyone to the helicopters!"

John nodded and pointed at Dan, who was looking around in a daze. "I'm coming. Take him with you."

The soldier took Dan's hand. "Come with me, sir."

The old submarine captain and the young soldier started walking across the ice. Suddenly Dan resisted, stopping for a moment to turn to Anna. "I never meant to kill a soul..." he said before the soldier pulled him firmly into the dark.

She looked back into the burning room. The flames from the cables were spreading up and across the ceiling like a weightless river.

"Where's that fucking Jackie?" John's eyes were black points of fury.

The explosives expert Drew looked back. "He was in the middle of the flames when the water exploded sir. He must have burnt to death." Drew gasped for air and grabbed the arm and leg of the unconscious soldier across his shoulders. "The medics need to examine him here."

Drew hauled the soldier further up his back and walked towards the helicopters.

John was staring into the darkness. "This fire can probably be seen from space. If the Russians didn't know we were here already, they certainly do now." He pulled his singed jacket back on.

"Let's go."

Anna stood still and studied the flames.

"Go with him," she said to Marco. "Get away from here."

He looked at her in confusion. "Aren't you coming?" She inhaled deeply, pulled her hood up around her face again, and ran into the burning room.

She was struck by a wall of heat. Half the roof was already on fire, while the back wall was a raging inferno. She dropped to her knees and tried to see in. The laptop and cases were ablaze and sparks rained down from the ceiling. She tried to look for a body, but it was impossible. From outside, a cold wind suddenly tore past her face. The fire was sucking oxygen in. At the very back of the room the flames had burnt a hole in the wall. She attempted to crawl closer towards it, but it was impossible to penetrate the heat.

In this flaming hell Anna was seeking the Devil, but Jackie was gone. The mass murderer had been consumed by the green firestorm he had started. High up under the roof somewhere there was another explosion. The flames burst back at her as the wall to the main building collapsed inwards.

85

When Anna got out of the burning room, the cold air stung her face. The light from the flames was painting Marco's and John's faces red. She gasped for air and bent over. An intense burning smell filled her nostrils.

John looked at her in fright. "My God, Anna, I thought you were finished."

"I just had to…" She straightened up and pulled off her hood. The fabric was warm to the touch. "I just had to know if he was really dead."

"Was he?"

"I don't know—it was impossible to see anything at all."

An explosion erupted from the main building's roof. Anna spun around and looked up at the tower. It had begun to list to one side. The painting of the Ice Dragon billowed in the heat, as though the monster were about to come to life.

Engines roared and one of the helicopters climbed slowly above the cabins. A loud voice called through the dark. The southern soldier was waving from the other side of the yard.

"Let's go," said John. "Are you coming?"

Anna's eyes followed the flying war machine until it disappeared into the darkness. "No, I'm staying here to wait for the Russian rescue crews."

"It's not safe. This base is going to burn through the ice."

"I've got the hovercraft. I'll manage."

"Anna, be goddamn reasonable now. Come with us. I'll make sure we fly you home from Greenland." John reached for her but she pushed him away forcefully.

"Fuck that. I'm not coming!"

She turned and walked away from the burning building.

"You cannot tell a living soul what happened here, got it?" she heard John shout. "If you say anything it's out of my hands. The CIA will make sure that Norwegian intelligence arrests you."

She didn't reply. Just gave him the finger and kept going.

John unleashed the frustrated roar of a powerless man before turning and running back across the yard. Anna walked, her head bowed, along the length of the main building. She could feel the ice shaking violently beneath her feet. Below her, the North Pole was screaming. A spider's web of cracks was spreading across the ice.

The fire was devouring the ice from below. She saw one of the cabins collapsing, consumed by a burning rift in the ice. A cloud of sparks flew skywards.

Flames snarled up from the hole left by the sinking workshop. The light from the fire spread beneath the surface as gas pocket after gas pocket was ignited. The fire dragon from the ocean's depths grew, whipping an enormous fiery tail towards the main building, consuming it.

Anna rounded the corner and ran towards the door at the front, throwing it open. The deep-frozen man was still crouching on all fours, but inside the building was lit up by flames burning through the wall from the other room. The scorching wind rushed over the icy corpses. The fiery shadows seemed almost to bring the men back to life.

The warm glow of light streamed over the frozen bodies. Their eyes glittered from behind a layer of ice that was quickly beginning to melt. Anna sensed that any moment they would come back to life, struggle free from the ice and continue their work researching the ocean floor. She stayed there until a burning beam crashed down from the roof, striking one of the bodies and sending it shattering into a burst of ice. If Jackie had been hiding somewhere inside, he would have fled by now.

Anna closed the door in front of the frozen commander carefully. As she was leaving the building, the last helicopter was taking off. It circled above her, illuminated by the fire like an enormous orange and black hornet. Somewhere inside, John was looking down at her. Anna didn't look up as she walked stubbornly away from the base towards *Sabvabaa*. The helicopter climbed to join the other, then both shrank to nothing but twinkling lights in the dark.

The glow from the fire lit Anna's way towards *Sabvabaa*. The hovercraft's hull was dented and blackened, but still in one piece. Seeing a figure appear before her, she halted suddenly.

Marco was smiling hesitantly at her.

"I thought you needed some company."

She looked back at him in resignation and his attempt at a smile withered. "Or I can just as well find somewhere else…"

"You know where to find a spare room at the North Pole?"

He stood there saying nothing. Then a sound made him glance back towards the fire. Anna turned around. Sunzi was running backwards and forwards between the burning cabins as she barked.

"Sunzi! I'm here!"

Anna waved. The husky saw her and changed direction, barking loudly and sprinting into Anna's outstretched arms with such force that she fell backwards into the ice and rolled around in the snow. She took hold of the dog's collar, pulled her up onto the hull and over to the hatch. Once there, she turned around. The flames were thrusting green tentacles out from the main building's door. Beneath the ice there glimmered a kind of underwater Northern Lights. Marco was still standing down on the ice. "Jesus Christ. Get on board then!" she yelled. He smiled happily and clambered up on the hull.

She pushed him through the hatch and went in after him. After closing it tight, she went across to Marco, who was sitting by a window with Sunzi. The glow from the fire streamed over his face. The black shadows of the windowsills split the light into warped triangles. A face Picasso could have painted.

There was a rumbling that made the windows rattle.

She tried imagining what was happening in the water beneath them. Jackie had made sure the torpedo exploded much too close to the surface. The explosion had ignited enormous bubbles of trapped methane, which had rushed up until they reached the large pockets of gas trapped under Ice Dragon. Then, fresh explosions and new flames, hunting after oxygen, which they found through the cracks in the ice.

This was the North Pole's final trick once its entire arsenal of weather, ice, cold and predators had been exhausted.

A wall on one side of the main building was blown off. The metal cladding was tossed away across the ice like crumpled tissue paper. Blazing gas cylinders rolled out of the building, spinning around and driven on by white-hot flames. The dragon tower began to sway and, as several struts collapsed, the whole structure plunged down through the burning roof. The painting of the Ice Dragon was ripped free and the beast fluttered upwards in flames, lifted upon the blistering air being spat out by the inferno. Both tanks in the tower plummeted, the dragon's eggs tumbling into the fiery waters.

The main building's other door blew open. For a brief moment Anna saw the frozen commander in the doorway before the fire devoured him. Aluminium plates were shredded as the rest of the walls imploded into its own glowing guts. A galaxy of whirling sparks lit up the black sky.

Anna stayed by the window until the final flame died out and everything else was consumed once again by the darkness.

86

A white light sliced the dark in two.

The signal flare climbed up behind the windblown trees on the prairie. Anna felt her heart thumping in her chest. The hunt was on. She grasped her rifle hard and began walking ahead, her galloping heart forcing blood out into her body and putting her on full alert. She could see and hear everything. The trailer passing on the highway behind the horizon. The cattle in the meadows by the road. Dry tufts of grass crackling underfoot. In the woods, the screeching of a crow. The darkness shifting around her. The men in the hunting party were walking in a line across the fields with her, their feet at an unsteady tempo.

Dogs began to bark; an animal replied, or defended itself with a grating whine. From a walkie-talkie a man's voice could be heard.

"The hounds have got the hogs!"

Anna stopped and loaded the rifle, legs apart, just as her uncle had taught her. She could hear the sound of small feet approaching at speed and raised the rifle, pressing the butt into her shoulder, looking through the telescopic sight. The grey dusk turned to red day. The hunting dogs filled her view, a team of pigs before them. The animals were charging out from between the ragged trees. Escapees from the pig farm. The pigs' smooth skin was now overgrown with short hair. Tame pigs had become wild boars.

She took aim at the beast up front, a huge male, and felt a shudder of fear. Her first trophy. Tomorrow she would be fifteen. An adult hunter. Her finger squeezed the trigger. The shot jammed. Calmly, she reloaded just as she had been taught, trying to fire.

Nothing happened.

Her heart kicked hard. Panic ignited in her brain. She pulled out the magazine, its metal cold against her clammy palms. Instead of shiny cartridges, it was filled with something white. She pushed a finger in.

Snow.

A furious howl.

She looked up. The massive male pig was headed straight for her, but its head was strange. Human features behind its flat face. Long hair hanging down over its black eyes.

Jackie was sneering at her.

Long teeth jutted up from the corners of his mouth. Anna tried to run away, but her legs were stuck to the ground. She screamed, but no sound left her lungs. The huge pig reared up before her.

Jackie's jaws opened and a fire-red tongue reached out.

Wet. Anna was woken by the sensation of a rough tongue lapping against her cheek.

It was Sunzi, panting and rubbing her nose against her face. She ran a hand through the dog's thick fur before sitting up, disoriented. A large blue larva lay by her side. Marco was snoring lightly from deep within Zakariassen's sleeping bag. She felt something cold sticking into her neck, turned over and realized that she was lying up against the hatch handle. Now Anna remembered that she had lain against it to keep guard. Against her chest was a knife that she had found in the kitchen drawer. It was ten past eleven. She had been asleep for two hours. She looked out. The window was enveloped by darkness. The Ice Dragon base had been swallowed by fire and sea. She and Marco were all that was left.

Sunzi whimpered again.

"You're probably hungry, aren't you?" Anna whispered. She wriggled out of the sleeping bag, feeling the cold floor against her hands. Without heating, the air inside *Sabvabaa* was almost as cold as outside. But without the biting wind tearing the energy from the body, it felt almost snug. She walked to the back through the pile of snow that had blown in through the smashed window.

She found a can of the Norwegian speciality: Joika meatballs. Daniel's favourite. He had bought five cartons of the reindeer meatballs for the expedition when the local store in Tromsø had them on special offer. Anna peeled off a glove, pushed one finger through the ring pull and tore the lid off. The contents were frozen. She used a knife to cut out some chunks and dropped them onto the floor for Sunzi.

"Here... I hope you like meatballs."

They crunched as the dog gulped them down. When they were all gone, she licked the sauce from the snow.

Anna thought that she ought to eat something too but wasn't hungry. She heard the wind blowing quietly past *Sabvabaa*'s hull. The storm was over. The Russian helicopters would soon arrive. The building containing the ice men, and most of the cabins, had burnt down and sunk with their dead. John Odegard and Lara Kowalsky were on their way back to the United States. Their mission had been a catastrophe, but they had achieved their objective. The American torpedo was gone.

A thousand questions would be asked, but everything could be denied. Everything could be explained. Jackie was dead: a madman had run amok, killing his colleagues. The only unique thing about it was that this time the tragedy had struck Chinese researchers at the North Pole, rather than American schoolkids.

Anna felt empty. Had no idea what she was going to do next. The only thing that had kept her together for the last twenty-four hours had been her rage and an urge to avenge Daniel's death. Now Jackie was dead.

She shook Marco. He twitched in the sleeping bag. She shook him again. His eyes peered through the laced-up opening.

"What is it?…" he asked, sleepily.

"We're leaving."

A little later, Boris called. His voice was no longer slurred by alcohol, just full of anxiety. "Anna, you can't leave Ice Dragon!"

She could hear the worry in Boris's voice through the static in the satellite connection. "Our rescue crews are delayed because we got the same storm that you had right on the nose, but the helicopters can take off in an hour."

"There's nothing left here, Boris. Ice Dragon doesn't exist any more."

"But where are you going to go?"

"Neither Marco nor I has been to the exact North Pole before. According to the chart it's not so far. You can pick us up there."

"Anna, you can't go to the North Pole alone," the meteorologist protested.

"We are alone!"

Her gaze slipped out of the hovercraft window. There was nothing to see but darkness. The Ice Dragon base was long gone. "Whether we stay or go, it's the same difference."

Boris sighed deeply. "In that case, is there anything at all I can help you with in the meantime, Anna?"

"Now you mention it, have you got a good recording of *Swan Lake* lying about?"

She and Marco huddled closely listening to the receiver as Boris found a piece of music that he said was a new recording of Tchaikovsky's masterpiece, played by the Montreal Symphony Orchestra.

The weatherman from St Petersburg chose the Russian Dance.

The wounded tones of the solo violin streamed out into *Sabvabaa*'s gloomy cabin. The music floated above Daniel Zakariassen's narrow bed, past the scientific magazines he loved to read, dancing a pirouette around the hovercraft's dead

367

instruments. The melodies slipped along the walls, above the radio equipment, past the samovar, which was covered in a glittering layer of frost, before swirling past the snowed-in bed and out of the smashed window.

Then the rest of the strings entered as light as a feather. The music conjured up images of ballet dancers in white, whirling above the icy windows like swans. Marco started to cry. As he sobbed, his body trembled. Anna put her arms around him, pulling him close to her, feeling his pot belly against her body. The whole orchestra joined in and the music grew in volume.

Something inside her fell apart.

She couldn't hold it together. Tears filled her eyes. She bit her lip, but a profound, body-shaking tremor rose from her stomach and exploded out of her head. She saw the dead.

Yann.

Zakariassen.

The ice men and their frozen eyes.

She saw young men, almost children, lying in a tin shack, the sun playing on their bloodied bodies through bullet holes in the walls. Dandelion seeds descending slowly towards human remains in a destroyed city. Anna clung to Marco and cried with him.

Boris listened on in silence.

Anna breathed in deeply as the music faded away, feeling the cold air circulating throughout her body. It no longer felt like an enemy out to kill her. Just cold, fresh air.

Anna felt an emotion that, just two short days ago, she thought she would never experience again. She felt happy to be alive. Gratitude that she and Marco could stand on their own feet and breathe in the crisp air, feeling the ice beneath their feet.

The ice felt different.

Friendlier.

As though having purged the venom, it had finally found peace. The ice had burnt down man's arrogant edifices and chased away the black helicopters. The ice didn't care about these two remaining specks.

Anna pulled out a packet of cigarettes from a carton in her bag. She had sometimes treated herself to one on the sly, far away from Zakariassen's keen nose. She and Marco smoked in silence before they started packing the sled.

87

They abandoned *Sabvabaa*.

Anna stopped at the hovercraft's door and looked out at the ruins of the base. In just a few short decades, the last of the icebergs would disintegrate in the ocean waves, then be smashed against the bow of an approaching ship, whirled in the foam along the iron hull down to the propeller, which would crush the final lumps of ice to a slush fading into the sea. The final remains of the ice would be wiped out in the wake of a container ship fully loaded with new computers and smartphones, made from minerals sourced from its seabed.

She pulled off a glove and ran her hand along the dented metal on the outside of the hovercraft. She felt the cold screws that had worked their way through the paint, carefully placed there many years ago by British engineers. Marco was waiting down on the ice with Sunzi, in a harness and eager to go. They had found the commander's sled in one of the fractures. They packed the bare essentials. Cans. Dry food. A tent. Extra clothing. A satellite phone. Ice pick. Rope and first-aid equipment. Anna took *Sabvabaa*'s flare gun too.

She asked Marco to go over to the half-sunken canteen cabin and pick up the Heckler & Koch sniper rifle left behind by Robert. They couldn't set out onto the ice without protection. Marco had to hack the butt out of the frozen water to get it free. He placed the gun on top of the sled's load before fastening the tarpaulin.

Anna took a last look inside *Sabvabaa*. The emergency locator beacon was lying smashed on the floor. It was how Daniel Zakariassen had communicated with the CIA. The ready-programmed messages were almost certainly codes: NEED SPARE PARTS: *The Chinese are gathering minerals from the seabed.* NEED MEDICAL ASSISTANCE: *Send soldiers!* Something inside it was humming.

Destroying the beacon had been childish, but liberating. She hated the fact that she liked the guy. Hated that John had helped her find Yann. Hated that it was the CIA's millions that had brought her to the ice.

You're lying. You hate nobody but yourself.

The thought crackled. It hurt her head.

She turned around, stepped out of the hatch, closed it behind her and jumped down onto the ice next to Marco. In her hand she was holding the only personal item she didn't want to leave behind. The samovar.

She stuffed the tea kettle down into the sled. Sunzi tugged at the harness and the sled started to move. The snow crunched under her boots with every step she took, but otherwise it was completely quiet.

Not a ripple of wind.

No cracking from the ice floes being pushed together.

No rumbling birth pangs as the North Pole lifted ice blocks to the surface.

Not a soul to be heard.

And no engines. The generator cabin had toppled over and was lying half-sunken in the partly frozen channel that had swallowed the workshop and them, almost. Far away, an errant bird squawked. A rigid crust had formed over the hole in the ice where the large building had been. Only a few twisted, scorched iron beams bore witness to the tower that Marco had built. The garage was still standing in one piece.

A few hundred metres from the base, they found a burnt piece of the Ice Dragon painting. A blue eye painted on canvas glanced rigidly out into all eternity. One corner of the green flame was singed by the fire. Marco carefully folded up the canvas and pushed it into his pocket. A lasting reminder.

Anna turned around. The light from her headlamp only just reached *Sabvabaa*, a metallic beetle in the frozen desert. The housing around the rotor: encrusted wings, ready to strike. The slack rubber skirting: legs. Would this hollow metal body ever be filled with people and life again? Would *Sabvabaa* live up to the name she had been given by the Inuit, and *flow swiftly over the ice* one more time?

The last she saw of it was the green navigation light glowing feebly in the polar night.

Neither she nor Marco spotted the figure emerging from the generator cabin and running silently across the yard to the garage.

88

And so it was just the two of them.

And the ice.

Anna Aune and Marco Zheng He walking towards the North Pole.

Sunzi pulled the commander's sled fully loaded with supplies. Their headlamps shone brightly across the icy landscape. When Anna turned around, she could no longer see the base. The world had shrunk to the circle of light before them. Marco was wearing one of Zakariassen's extra survival suits, his belly pressing up against the fabric.

It had been two days since Anna saw the emergency flare. It felt like a lifetime. Fourteen people were dead. Daniel Zakariassen and thirteen men she had never even met before. *Swan Lake* was still playing in her mind as she walked on over the ice.

In the sky, the stars were shining bright and clear, the North Star shining brightest of all. It was cold, but without the wind to battle against it felt like walking on a mild summer's day. Her legs took care of themselves. Anna didn't have to think about anything at all, and so she and Marco walked on in peace.

Half an hour later they reached an area of frozen storm waves: a pressure ridge.

Instead of trying to climb over it, they walked along its edge. In another half an hour they were back on the ice flats again. Anna felt a rumbling in her stomach and stopped at the last block of ice, opened up the sled and pulled out a bar of cooking chocolate.

She shared it with Marco, sitting on the ice block as they ate. The brittle chocolate snapped against their teeth before melting in the mouth, its sweet energy trickling down to the stomach. Anna took a box of snuff out of her jacket, stuffed a wad under her lip and felt the nicotine take effect. She offered the box to Marco, who took two and pushed them into place as if he'd been doing it all his life.

In the light of the headlamp, she saw their tracks in the snow.

"Are you married?" His question arrived out of the blue.

"No."

"Do you have a partner?"

"I had one, but he died."

"Oh. Sorry… My condolences. I'll pray for your happiness."

She smiled. "Thanks. Things are getting easier these days, but I won't say no to kind thoughts." As she said the words, Anna sensed a weightlessness in her chest. *Things are getting easier these days.* It felt true. She hoped it was true. Marco stared down at the snow as he flicked the snuff around under his lip with his tongue.

"I'm saving up for a wife."

"You're saving up for a… wife?"

"Yes. In China a fiancé has to pay the bride's parents in order to get their permission to get engaged. Getting married can cost a fortune."

"Oh right. What if the poor guy doesn't have enough money then?"

Marco spat into the ice. "Then he'll die alone and childless. There are more than thirty million more men in China than women. If I get too old, there'll be nobody who will want me. There's a girl in Shanghai who I like very much. She's called Mo Chou, and I think she likes me… too. But she's asking for a lot. A house and car and a man with a great job."

Anna couldn't stop herself from laughing. "Building a tower at the North Pole isn't a great job?"

Marco spat on the ice again.

"Her father's an accountant. He wants a fortune in dowry."

"My sister's an accountant too," said Anna. "It's a good job, if you like numbers and hard work."

"I'm pretty lazy and don't like numbers," Marco replied, "but I've thought about becoming an elevator installer. It's very simple. You just start with a shaft made by someone else, and then you fill it with an elevator. I've studied a few books about it while I've been here. My father would be happy if I could build elevators he can operate."

Anna laughed again.

"It sounds like a great plan, Marco. Your girlfriend has probably inherited her father's head for numbers. She can do your accounts. Keep count of the floors."

Marco smiled. "Exactly what I was thinking."

A star drifted suddenly across the sky. Its path stretched in an arc above the horizon before it vanished behind the Earth.

"That was a shooting star. Make a wish," said Marco.

"No, I'm sure it was just a satellite."

"Is there any difference?" He laughed his strange, cackling laughter. "I know a good bar in Shanghai for karaoke… Do you like it?" He looked across at Anna from inside the hood of his survival suit. His goatee beard jutted out like a crayfish claw inside a snail shell.

"That's a good wish. Let's go to a bar, Marco. If there's anyone in China who's a worse singer than me, I'll buy the drinks."

After checking their course towards the North Pole, they went on their way. A new row of ice blocks appeared in the light from the headlamps. Anna saw that there was a tight passage between two of the blocks and walked over to it. She passed through and caught the smell of salt. On the other side, the light hit a sea of black. A huge area of ice had broken up. The ice floes had been crushed when they collided, lifting the ice up.

Marco followed her.

"Where shall we go?"

Anna stared through the ice as far as the light would allow. "I don't know if we'll get around here." The husky looked up, her nostrils expanding as they sucked in air. She growled deeply. Anna walked over to the dog.

"What is it, Sunzi?"

Behind a large block on the ice was a polar bear. It must have heard the dog but didn't seem to care too much. Anna could see a long scorch mark running across its ribcage. The animal looked starved.

She turned towards Marco and motioned that he was to stay still. It was fascinating to watch the bear as it sat waiting for a seal to emerge. Anna knew that seals can dive deeper than five hundred metres and can carry enough air in their lungs to stay underwater for over forty minutes. But seals can't steal their air from the sea like a submarine; eventually seals have to surface or drown.

The best defence a seal has is its hearing. Each time the polar bear put its huge paws down, they crushed ice crystals, sending vibrations down through the water. Since the ice floated on the ocean, those vibrations were amplified, like the membrane of a gigantic loudspeaker. The vibrations turned to sound waves in the sea that the seal could hear for kilometres around.

The bear was still sitting quietly and patiently near the fracture in the ice.

Moving her head down above the opening, having certainly heard something on its way up. Its jaws opened wide, ready to sink their teeth into the seal's head the instant it broke through the surface.

It was then that Anna heard the sound.

Vibrations ascending from the ice. Steady and rhythmic, a sound made by no animal. A helicopter.

The bear turned her head. Just then the seal broke through the watery crust. The bear lunged, but it was too late. Its prey

376

had time to take a breath of fresh air and dive. The bear's jaws snapped together hard around nothing but air. Sunzi began barking loudly. The polar bear gave up, turning its famished body and darting across the ice to the nearest channel.

89

The sound of the helicopter was growing louder.

Then a blinking light emerged from the darkness. They were approaching rapidly.

"The Russians are coming—get the flare gun!" Marco almost tripped as he ran towards the sled. He fumbled a little as he untied the tarpaulin, then pulled out the gun, aimed for the sky and fired.

There was a bang and a red glow climbed skywards.

The helicopter dropped its speed and began to circle. Powerful lights were switched on. Anna saw that the fuselage was a bright orange with a blue stripe down the middle. Russian lettering was painted on the door. The helicopter orbited a few more times, flew a little further away to solid ice, and began its descent.

She and Marco started walking towards it. Sunzi barked fiercely as she tugged at the sled's harness. Halfway down the rotors began to blow up snow, sending it drifting into their faces. Anna turned away, the light from her headlamp swiping across the ice. A splash of colour appeared in the dark and disappeared again. She turned her head back towards it.

The beam of light captured a green object.

It took her a few seconds to realize what it was.

The tractor from the garage.

Something struck her on the back.

A sharp pain.

She grasped backwards at it. Her fingers found an object protruding from the fabric of her survival suit.

It felt like a nail.

Anna clasped a hand around it and pulled, feeling it leave her skin directly under her left shoulder blade. In her hand she was holding a nail with blood at its very tip.

She screamed at Marco.

"Jackie's here!"

Marco turned towards Anna from inside the snowy whirlwind. The helicopter had landed and a man was emerging from the side door. Light from the cabin streamed out.

Anna lifted her hand to switch off her headlamp. She heard a quiet thud from somewhere in the dark. A sharp pain seized hold of her. There was a nail in her chest.

"Fuck!"

She got hold of the nail's head, shut her eyes, prepared herself for the pain and the blood, and pulled. The nail came out astonishingly easily. She felt something hard where the nail had hit, and tore open her chest pocket. The Chinese general's book on the art of war had saved her life.

Another nail hit her thigh, forcing its way so deep that its head disappeared into her survival suit.

She ran lamely towards the helicopter as she shoved a hand into her side pocket, but her hunting knife was gone. Another nail hit her, piercing her palm. She screamed out loud and tore it out, setting blood streaming across her hand.

Marco looked at her in confusion. He couldn't understand what was happening. Behind him, the man from the helicopter was approaching.

A fierce anger blazed through Anna. She sprinted over to where she thought Jackie must be. The light of her headlamp dancing over the ice. Every muscle in her body was taut and she knew she was going to get hit again, but didn't give a damn. She found his footprints, but Jackie was gone.

She stopped and turned all the way around, shining the light across the ice, all the way back to Marco. A figure was sprinting towards him from behind.

"Watch out!"

Marco turned, but didn't have enough time to raise his hands before Jackie struck him with the nail gun. Marco cried out and fell. Jackie held the gun against his throat.

Anna tried to walk towards him, but one leg gave way. All she could do was stand helplessly as Jackie dragged Marco up again. She forced herself to walk one step forward.

Jackie was shielding himself behind Marco, forcing the nail gun against Marco's neck.

"Stop or I'll shoot!" His voice was hoarse and rasping.

"I swear, Jackie, you're a dead man."

Anna took another step towards them. There was a bang from the nail gun. Marco yelped and grabbed Jackie's arm. Jackie shoved the mouth of the gun at Marco's temple.

She begged him. "Can't you just let him go?"

Jackie didn't reply, instead hauling Marco backwards towards the man from the helicopter, who was looking at them in confusion.

"Give it up, Jackie, there's nowhere left to run."

"Get back or I'll kill him!"

Marco looked across at her, terrified. "Please, Anna, I don't want to die!"

"What kind of monster are you?!" yelled Anna.

Jackie looked at her for a brief moment with a triumphant expression.

"I am… Zhao Wu the Avenger."

He raised the nail gun towards her.

Anna threw herself to the ground as he shot. Jackie dragged Marco with him, brandishing the gun at the man from the helicopter, who was backing away into the onrush of snow. Anna realized what was going to happen. Jackie was going to escape from the ice after all.

Marco screamed something at her.

She ignored him, turned around and began crawling in the opposite direction. A few metres further away she got to her feet and limped towards Sunzi, who was barking hysterically by the sled. Each time she put her foot down, a hammer blow of pure pain punched through the foot that the nail was stuck into.

She reached the sled, dropped down on her knees, tore off the tarpaulin and saw the Heckler & Koch rifle lying on top. She closed her eyes and repeated the words Ferdinand had told her. Placing one hand on the rifle butt, she grasped hard around it, feeling the nausea bubbling in her throat. Opening her eyes and inhaling, she knocked open the bipod beneath the barrel. Behind her she heard the helicopter engine open its throttle. She settled in, set the bipod on the ice and looked through the sight. Her face began to itch.

The night-vision sight transformed the darkness into a shimmering green day. The helicopter's engines glowed white from the heat captured through the sight. As it ascended, the side door came into view. One of the crew was about to pull the doors closed again, and behind him she could see Marco and Jackie, their eyes mere dots on green faces. The helicopter was climbing, and the door was almost closed.

The rifle butt grew warm in her hands.

Pearls of sweat sprang from her forehead.

The world distorted.

Night became day.

Ice became sun.

90

She's lying on a roof in a city that nobody knows exists, other than those who live there.

Yann's face fills her telescopic sight.

The IS fighter dragging him back has risen up a little.

The torso of the man, who somebody has nicknamed Baldy, enters the crosshairs.

Her finger increases the pressure on the trigger.

Her heart beats once.

She squeezes a little more.

A bang.

She feels the butt recoil into her shoulder.

The bullet shoots out of the barrel at a speed of twelve hundred metres a second.

The projectile takes barely half a second to get there.

At the very same instant, Yann pulls free from Baldy's grip.

He raises his head.

The bullet hits Yann.

Penetrates his brain.

Explodes out the back of his head and into Baldy's chest.

The two men collapse on top of each other on the ground.

She hears herself screaming.

In the crosshairs, Yann's hair blows in the breeze.

Beneath him, Baldy is bleeding to death.

The brown sand soaks up the blood.

Anna doesn't see the flash of light sparkling from one of the openings between the columns high up in the mosque's minaret. The sniper's shot hits her telescopic sight, smashing the Swiss lenses. The bullet is deflected just enough so that the projectile misses her eye, but streaks along the side of her forehead, slicing off her earlobe before entering her shoulder and forcing its way through her body. Her right arm goes limp. Guerrilla Joro leans over her. A lava stream of pain blazes through her into her eyes and burns the vision of him away.

She opens her eyes.

People dressed in white surround her. A tube snakes into her mouth. From her arm hang cables linked to devices, where flashes of shooting stars streak across computer screens. Beyond the window: a grey sky presses down on a gloomy forest. One of the people in white removes his face mask. Yann is smiling at her.

"I believe in you, woman. You can do this."

He leans over to kiss her.

Hot.

Cold.

Sun.

Night.

Anna gasped cold air into her, feeling a sour slime in her mouth. When she took her eye away from the sight, the city was gone. Yann was gone.

The helicopter tilted to one side and was ready to bank. She nudged the gun around and looked into the sight.

The side door was almost closed. She could see Jackie placing his hand at the door's edge and thrusting Marco in front of him, who shoved a hand against the door casing, trying to avoid being forced out of the helicopter.

Anna focussed on breathing calmly. She was trying to sense the direction of wind in her face, trying to assess the helicopter's range. The crosshairs settled over Jackie's face. She dialled the sight a few millimetres away from Marco's head, down towards

Jackie's shoulder. The helicopter increased its forward speed and she let the sight follow it.

She felt the trigger under her finger.

The metal was burning.

Something acidic was climbing rapidly up through her throat.

She felt a hammer blow inside her head.

91

Jackie forced himself up against Marco's back. He saw the ice dashing past beneath the helicopter. In his hand he was holding the gun he had taken from the crew member, who was now staring back at him in terror. The other man was struggling to slide the door closed.

He wanted Marco out of there. Nobody would be coming with him away from the ice. He could force the helicopter pilots to fly him to a deserted place. When they landed he would no longer have any use for them. He would manage it, just as he had managed to get away from his poor mining town in the mountains, get into university and on to California.

He refused to let that idiot Qiang destroy everything.

Why did Qiang, who had never bothered to work late before, have to show up that evening as he was trying to delete the data, just as Lara had asked him to? The stabbing had been the action of a desperate man. As Qiang slumped lifelessly in front of the computer monitors, Jackie knew he no longer had a choice. He could try to convince others that he and Qiang had got into an argument, that the stabbing was an accident, but the result would be the same: a death sentence in China. Everything he had fought for his entire life would come to an end at the barrel of a gun, or an injection filling his veins with poison.

Jackie knew that all of the scientists were working overtime on an important mining operation in the main building. After climbing up to the tanks in the tower, he aimed his revolver at the pipes carrying liquid nitrogen and water down to the radar at the depth of the ocean. The shot rang out louder than he thought it would. He almost fell as the nitrogen and water surged down into the building below.

A few brief screams were all he heard. As he ran around to the front of the building, frost-mist was drifting out of the door, from where the commander had almost managed to escape.

Chun Li and the two cooks emerged running in their under-clothes. "What's happening?" was all that Chun Li had time to say before Jackie shot him. The cooks tried to flee, but got only a few steps. Then he noticed Zhanhai standing in the cabin doorway. Zhanhai ran out into the darkness before Jackie had time to shoot. Guan and Lanpo were still sleeping when he killed them.

Jackie knew than Zhanhai would have to return if he didn't want to freeze to death. He picked up a firearm and climbed back up into the tower, hiding the hard drive and the stolen data there as he waited out in the cold. But rather than Zhanhai, there came a flare; and instead of the CIA, the Norwegian woman showed up.

But all of this was meaningless now. She was lying shot on the ice and would freeze to death before anyone found her. Jackie would transform himself again. And one day he would find Lara Kowalsky and John Odegard. They would discover the price of their betrayal. After all, wasn't his real name Zhao Wu?

The Avenger.

The helicopter tilted even further to one side. Now he would force Marco out.

He leant over him, grasping hold of the hands with which Marco was clinging to the door frame. But then he felt something striking his shoulder with a violent force. He tumbled over Marco.

He was flying.

He saw a dark pattern spinning below him.

He shut his eyes and tensed just before he hit the water. The cold tore through his body as he sank. When he opened his eyes, the lights from the helicopter were looping above him. The light was shot through with a red mist, blood drifting in the water before his face.

He kicked out with his legs, trying to pull through the water with his arms. An intense pain burned through one shoulder. The same arm refused to obey his brain. He floated upwards anyway through the red fog.

Jackie felt his lungs aching. He hadn't had time to breathe in before he fell in the sea, but now it wasn't much further to the surface. He thought about the words in the book he had read so many times, written by a general more than two thousand years ago, but still just as true:

In the midst of chaos, there is also opportunity.

So had it been his entire life.

Opportunities from chaos.

Jackie struck out with his arms, feeling his strength fading, but now the surface was only a metre away. He pushed his arms through the water, floating up to the top.

Something grasped his foot.

Pain darted through his body and exploded in his mind. He screamed, seawater gushing into his mouth. He lurched around. Something enormous loomed before him. Bubbles of air clung to the fur of a white dragon.

The dragon's powerful teeth pierced his thigh. Jackie stretched forward and punched the dragon's snout, but its jaws wouldn't let go. He felt his leg splintering, but the icy water numbed the pain. The dragon was dragging him downwards, away from the channel's edge. The sea pressed against his eardrums and squeezed his skull against his brain. He saw stars before his eyes, tasted blood oozing from his mouth. The white dragon pulled him deeper still. The seawater in his mouth was about to flood his throat as his skull was crushed by a chilling vice of pain.

Jackie screamed the last of his air as the polar bear sank its teeth even deeper into his thigh. The bear swam away, its prey clamped in its jaws, into the dark beneath the ice.

Anna saw Jackie falling from the helicopter.

His arms flailed as his body turned a half-circle in the air. She followed his fall in the sight until Jackie hit an open fracture and disappeared.

She felt something warm on her trigger hand. Slime, scraps of food. She pushed a bloody fist down into the snow to wipe off the vomit and lay there on her back, feeling the cold beneath her. It was soothing, dulling the pain. Warmth spread through her body. She began pulling on the zipper, all the way down.

The cold from the ice ran in towards her chest. She coughed. The lights of the helicopter passed above her. The rumbling increased in strength. A sudden gust of air to the face. The sun blazed in the black sky and drifted down towards her.

92

Anna Aune was hovering in a dark oblivion.

She could hear sounds, but understood nothing. Something moved in the darkness, but she couldn't see what it was. Something was touching her body, but she didn't know where.

A voice got through to her.

"Can you hear me, Anna?" the voice repeated in a staccato rhythm.

She opened her eyes again. A young woman was smiling at her. She had a white hood over her head and a white overcoat with light-blue stripes along the sleeves. The nurse lifted up a cup. Anna felt the cup against her lips and a sweet, lukewarm fluid flowed down her throat. Then she felt a sharp pain. The woman in the white uniform leant over her, pressing a button on the wall.

Blackness swallowed everything again. She opened her eyes.

Her pupils stung when the bright white light hit. Where was she? The light was coming from a lamp directly above her. She turned her head away and saw a curtain hanging down from the roof. It hurt to move her head. A small sink and a mirror were hanging on the wall next to the curtain. She saw her reflection.

She had a large plaster across her forehead, and black scabs on her face from grazes. Under her chin she saw two large, dark-blue bruises. Anna tried to sit higher up, but felt a sharp stabbing pain in her abdomen. She pulled back the heavy bed sheets and saw a plastic tube sticking out from oversized underwear somebody must have put on her when she was unconscious. The tube ran to a bag filling with dark liquid. Urine. Where was she, and how long had she been lying here? Below the hospital underwear, her left leg was wrapped in a bandage. She felt entirely drained. Couldn't focus on a single thing. Her thoughts were like grains of sand in her hand. The more she pushed to remember, the more they trickled through her fingers.

She gave up, let go of the sheets and rested her head on the soft pillow. A movement in the corner of her eye made her look the other way. A man was leaning back in a low chair next to the curtains. He was taller than most, well over six foot, his hair tumbling in chalky white waves from a receding hairline. Sunglasses concealed his eyes. On his red Hawaiian shirt, tropical palm trees flashed impossibly green. His trousers were as white as his hair.

The man stirred, his head bumping the wall, and turned. His eyes blinked behind his dark sunglasses.

"You're awake," he said. There was something familiar in his voice, but Anna couldn't think what it was. The man twisted his tall body out of the chair and came towards her.

"We've been really worried about you, Anna… Is there anything you need?"

She felt the grating pain in her throat as she spoke.

"Where am I?"

"You're in a… hospital. You can relax, you're completely safe now." The man walked over to the sink, taking a glass from the cabinet and filling it with water. "The doctor said that you were extremely dehydrated when you arrived… Try to drink a little."

Anna felt the cold water wash around her mouth. It stuck in her throat as she swallowed. The white-haired man smiled as she drank. When she was finished, he carefully took the glass back.

"I always wanted to meet you, Anna, but perhaps under different circumstances."

She finally recognized his deep baritone.

"You're Boris?"

"Yes, of course. Who else would I be?" She sensed a hint of disappointment in the eyes behind the sunglasses.

"Sorry, Boris, my head is a total mess."

He smiled. "You don't have to apologize for anything at all. The doctors removed a nail from your thigh and you had a serious compression wound on your throat. It's a wonder you're alive."

The memories began to flood the emptiness. The ice. Zakariassen. A red light in the sky. Ice Dragon. Jackie. The submarine. John Odegard. The flames. The hovercraft. She sat up suddenly.

"Marco, where is he?"

"You mean the Chinese guy? He's fine, he's in the next room."

"What about Sunzi? We had a dog with us."

"Yes, the husky is in my backyard for the time being. She's having fun with my dogs until you're well again..." The door opened and a stocky nurse with a head as round as a ball entered. She said a few curt words to Boris.

"I'm getting kicked out now. We'll speak later." Boris stroked Anna's hand and left. The nurse filled the glass with water and handed her three pills on a tray.

"For you. Swallow."

She swallowed the tablets, sensing their bitter taste in her mouth, rinsed down the bitterness with more water, and settled her head on the pillow again.

And slept.

93

"Zhao Wu the Avenger—what's that all about?"

Cigarette smoke curled out of her nose as Anna asked the question. Marco was sitting on a rusty oil barrel next to her and smoking, too. They were sheltering from the biting wind. The street lights atop crooked lamp posts illuminated a scatter of wooden houses.

The nurse with the round head was called Yana, and had informed Anna that she was at the infirmary of the E. K. Fyodorov Hydrometeorological Observatory, a Russian weather station on the Taymyr Peninsula. After a little persuasion, Yana had let them out of their sickbeds to take a cigarette.

"Zhao Wu?..." The smoke oozed out of Marco's nose. "Yeah, that's an old play I've heard about, *The Orphan of Zhao*." He lit another cigarette and his face was bathed in a warm glow. "It's about a boy who's raised by a general without knowing that the general killed his parents and the rest of his family. When the boy finds out the truth, he takes his revenge... killing the general... I think. Why do you ask?"

"It was something Jackie said... that he was Zhao Wu... the Avenger."

"Jackie was nuts."

Anna's throat stung as she laughed.

"Yeah, Marco, you're probably right about that."

He smiled. "Thank you so much for saving my life."

"Thanks to you too. It looks like the two of us have nine lives."

It suddenly struck her that she hadn't dreamt about Yann and hadn't heard his voice in her head since she had shot Jackie.

Maybe he had found peace in the hereafter. Or was it Yann who had given her peace?

A rectangle of light cracked open across the frozen ground. A circle emerged in the rectangle. Yana poked her head out of the door. "There's a call for you, Marco, a woman who says she's calling from Shanghai… in China?…"

Marco jumped up. "It must be Mo Chou." He ran up the stairs, but stopped at the door and turned back towards Anna. "Do you think I should propose to her now?"

"No, Marco. Do it properly. Buy a ring and some flowers when you get home. Women love that kind of thing." He looked at her for a few moments, deep in thought, before walking back into the hospital. The rectangle of light shrank to nothing.

Anna lit another cigarette and looked out over the dark landscape. It was difficult to imagine another world beyond this one.

In Tromsø, life was probably going along as usual.

Kirsten multitasking her way through the days.

In his workshop, her father likely had his head stuck inside a tricky boat engine.

He had gone from shock to shock when Anna called and told him what had happened. Anna skipped the part about Daniel Zakariassen spying for the CIA. He could keep that secret with him at the bottom of the ocean. Her father wanted to fly to Siberia. "I want you home in a proper hospital."

"No, Dad… I'm fine here. It's so peaceful." He only calmed down when she promised to call twice a day to tell him about her progress. "And if any newspapers call… you know nothing about it, Dad. I'm on holiday somewhere."

The sky was rumbling. A helicopter emerged out of the dark and passed low over the hospital roof. Powerful searchlights swept across the ground as the aircraft came in to land behind a few houses some distance away.

The sight got Anna thinking about the story Nuhad had told her when, out of the blue, she had called her in Tromsø a few weeks after being discharged from Sunnaas.

"The Americans are claiming that it was their helicopter that rescued you, but that's bullshit. It was Joro and Samal and me," Nuhad yelled into the telephone, as though she were worried her voice wouldn't carry all the way from Turkey.

She eagerly and dramatically recounted how the Kurdish soldiers had stemmed the bleeding from the IS sniper's shot before carrying Anna down into the destroyed factory, where Nuhad was waiting in the van. Anna was laid in between O'Leary and the other two hostages. Nuhad floored it out of there just before the IS armoured vehicle arrived.

"When the war is over I think I'm gonna be a rally driver!" Nuhad laughed down the crackling phone line. "You should have seen me dodging those bullets!"

After slipping away from IS, Nuhad had pressed forward over the potholed roads on the way out of Al-Suwar. Twenty minutes later, she abruptly swerved off the road as John Odegard's helicopter touched down.

The American medics took Anna and the injured hostage Yann had rescued. She was airlifted unconscious to a British field hospital outside Kilis, where three surgeons were standing by in the operating theatre.

"You died at the hospital, Anna," Nuhad told her. "Your heart stopped twice, but God was looking out for you. The doctors got your heart pumping again."

Six hours and another cardiac arrest later, the surgeons had stabilized her enough that she could be flown further on to the Turkish airbase of İncirlik on the Mediterranean coast, before a transport plane flew her out to Germany.

The hostage whose life Yann had saved turned out to be a

Chinese geologist who had been kidnapped as he was helping the Kurdish government look for oil in Kirkuk. The sniper's bullet had paralysed him, but six months later, through an intricate web of diplomatic back channels, Anna received a personal letter of gratitude from the Chinese president.

When Yann Renault was buried, the head of the Catholic Church in France, the Archbishop of Lyons, and the Chinese ambassador came to the funeral. Yann was hailed in the media for his bravery and his heroic efforts to rescue the hostages.

"I've become a bit of a celebrity, too," said Nuhad. The image of the Kurdish guerrilla posing on the roof of the bullet-ridden van went round the world. In certain places it was mentioned that the Kurds had had a "military specialist" with them, without going into further detail. "It's not right. It was you who saved the hostages, Anna. You're the biggest hero of them all."

"Thanks, but this hero thing is not for me."

"Are you OK now?" Nuhad asked.

Anna lied and said everything was fine, before hanging up.

As she lit yet another cigarette, Anna made a decision. When she got home, she would buy a ticket to Nice. Rent a motorbike. Ride along the Riviera and up the winding mountain roads of Provence, to the village at the top of the valley beneath the two mountains. There she would find Yann's grave. And maybe, if she was ready, pay a visit to his parents. Sit in the hotel bar and drink an old-fashioned.

A forceful rattling and the sound of an angry engine ripped her away from her thoughts.

A strange vehicle appeared from around the corner. A rusty old belt-driven motorbike. Boris hunkered his tall body over the handlebars dressed in a white down jacket and trousers. On a trailer behind him, Sunzi was barking like crazy. The husky sprang off before the weatherman had a chance to stop. Anna was pinned against the wall as the dog reared up on her hind legs with her front paws on Anna's chest, licking her excitedly on the face.

Boris climbed off the motorbike and managed to pull the dog off her.

"Sorry, but Sunzi was missing you so much. I simply had to bring her along… How's it going, my friend?"

"Good enough that they're letting me try to kill myself with nicotine." She held out a pack of smokes. The meteorologist took one. He pushed his biking goggles up onto his head, took his sunglasses out of his breast pocket and put them on before letting Anna light his cigarette.

He took a deep drag, let the smoke seep out of his nose and pointed towards a beach that was barely visible in the glow of the crooked street lights. "Have you seen our musk oxen yet?"

Anna saw some indistinct figures moving down by the sea.

"Nope. I've been laid up in bed, you know."

"The musk ox is the pride of the Taymyr Peninsula… Quite an aggressive creature, I must admit, but they keep the polar bears away, if nothing else."

"Well, that's something."

Anna and Boris smoked for a while in silence. The street lights painted the man in white a pale yellow. She realized that she was curious as to why he was so utterly different from how she had imagined him: as a small, stocky man confined to a tight space. In this gloomy winter landscape, he screamed quite the opposite: "Here I am!" And the sunglasses. She figured it had nothing to do with blending into the background. He noticed her looking, and she glanced away, tracing the grey shapes of the musk oxen wandering along the beach. Sunzi pushed her nose into her lap, wanting all her affection.

Her throat grated as a coughing fit forced its way up and out of Anna's chest. Boris looked back at her anxiously.

"Shall I get the nurse?"

"No, it's OK… One more smoke and it'll be fine. My lungs have been spoilt by far too much fresh air in the last few days."

Boris chuckled. He pointed towards one of the grey wooden houses, where a gathering of men was standing under a street lamp. "I actually came to warn you that the helicopter that just landed is full of police from Murmansk. They are probably going to ask you a mountain of questions about what happened at Ice Dragon."

"Thanks for the warning."

He raised an arm, pushed his sunglasses up and looked down at his watch. "I have to get back to the office now. The weather waits for no man, you know… There's just one thing I wanted to ask you before I go." Boris took out a fold of paper from the inner pocket of his jacket. He opened it up. Anna saw an image of four ballet dancers dressed in white, standing on one foot while the other stretched up at an impossible angle. At the top she read: *Russian Broadway in St Petersburg*.

"These are box seats for *Swan Lake* on New Year's Eve, followed by a five-course dinner and the finest wine," he said. "I had to sell my snow scooter to afford it, so I sincerely hope you haven't made any other plans that evening."

Anna felt a smile spread so broadly across her face that her cheeks hurt.